Bonded by Light

The Bloodline Cure

Sarah Mc White

SARAH Mc WHITE

3

This book is dedicated to my daughter, my shero, Airman Sierrah.

SARAH Mc WHITE

EPILOGUE

Happily, ever after, what a joke! I knew it didn't exist. My hands tremble as I read repeatedly a petition for the court to establish paternity of Carter Jethro Thomas. Once paternity is established, Logan will try and take my son away from me. I can't let that happen.

I jump up and run into Carter's room and grab a suitcase. I start packing it full of his clothes and shoes, not taking care to fold them. Jethro will have to understand. I am going as far away from here as possible. Maybe he can come later once we are settled. I haven't worked out the particulars, I just know I have to get away from here.

I run around the room dumping everything I think he might need in his full-size Ninja Turtle suitcase. Then I pull it to the front door. I run into my room and start dumping things I need into my suitcase. I keep reminding myself to only take the essentials. I'm in the closet when I hear little footsteps running towards me.

"Mommy are we going on a field trip?" he asks. I look up and see my son skipping into the closet. I smile at him, and then in walks Jethro. I briefly forgot about the armful of clothes I am holding.

"What's going on?" he asks in a panic.

When I don't respond he looks around the closet staring at my open suitcase.

"Carter go get a snack and a juice box," he said bending down to his level. Carter runs out the room no longer caring about what I am doing.

"What's going on, Daryn?" he asks again. I put the clothes in the suitcase then walk past him to grab the court order. I hand it to him and sit on the bed bouncing my knee.

"So, what are you planning to do; run away?"

"I don't know what else to do," I responded, and a single tear slips from my eye. I wipe it and sniffle.

"You're going to take my son and run?" he asks looking pained.

"Jethro, if I don't run with him, Logan is going to try and take him from me as soon as he knows the truth."

"Where will you go?" he asks calmly.

"London, Ireland, I don't know yet. I must get as far away as possible. Away from here so Logan can't take him from me."

He studies me for a while.

"Daryn we will figure it out, but this is not the answer. You can't just run. What about me?" His eyes bear too much weight in them, so I look away.

"I don't know, Jethro. I haven't figured that part out yet," I said.

He comes over and kneels in front of me.

"Daryn, I agree this is not what we were expecting, but we've gotten through tougher times. I know you committing a crime that could land us both in jail, is not the answer. Carter will surely be taken from us then."

"Then what is the answer?" I shoot back and stand up. He stands also loosening his tie.

"I'm sorry I don't' have the answer, but Daryn, we will figure it out." His Adam's apple bob as he swallows hard.

Jethro still doesn't know how to handle my sometimes-erratic behavior. He knows I will do anything to protect my son, and if I let Logan test Carter, all hell is going to break loose. That will be the beginning of our troubles. The only way I know to prevent this is to run.

Carter runs back in the room. He has the energy of ten bulls. I instantly smile when I see him. I sit on the bed and pull him onto my lap.

"How was your day?" I ask still smiling at him.

"Good, daddy told me we could play baseball when we got home." He said wiggling to get down. I look at Jethro, then back to Carter, wondering how I am going to explain to him that he has another father, and Jethro isn't his real dad. I look away as tears threaten to cloud my vision.

"Carter why don't you go and change and let daddy change." He said as Carter ran out the room again.

Jethro stands up straight, then pulls me into his arms. I wrap my arms around him.

"It's going to be okay baby," he said kissing my forehead.

I want to believe him, but I know Logan. This is bigger than Carter; this is about him and me.

CHAPTER ONE

My life is a haze, my day have all run together these last few weeks.

Carter is bouncing up and down as we leave the appointment for the DNA test. I could have smacked the lady when she asked Carter did he get his big blues eyes and curly hair from his dad. My son said no my daddy's eyes are black.

The old Daryn would have given her the business to let her know, if we are doing a DNA test, why would you ask that stupid ass question, but I was quiet.

I keep quiet now and try not to ruffle anyone's feathers.

"Mommy can I get Mc Donald's," he says, and then my phone rings; it's Jethro. I don't feel like talking to him. I let it go to voicemail. I no longer send the calls to voicemail because I don't want to hurt his feelings.

"Granny said she has plans for the two of you and I don't want you to ruin your appetite." He bounces into the backseat, and I close the door.

The next time I look up, I am at my mom's apartment. I have no idea how I got here, but I thank God, we made it safely. We walk in and he runs to my mom.

"Hey, my grandbaby," she says trying to pick him up.

"You're going to hurt yourself picking him up."

"Ah he's not that heavy," she said smiling. "I got you a present. It's in my room," she said putting him down, so he can run and get it.

"So, what's going on with you?"

"Nothing," I respond. I haven't told anyone about the paternity testing.

"You're saying nothing, but you look a mess. Did you even comb your hair, or put on make-up today?"

"I was in a hurry," I avoid eye contact when I say this to her. The honest to God truth, I didn't remember to comb my hair.

"Hurry for what?" she asks.

Carter ran back in the room with another ninja turtle toy.

"Mom, look!" he exclaims.

Saved by the bell! "That's great Carter. Mom I'm going to go. I have a hair appointment." I slide my purse onto my shoulder signaling I'm leaving.

"Thank God!" she said, and I don't respond. I kiss my son and leave.

Truth be told my hair appointment is not for another hour. I tried to plan enough time to visit with my mom. With her badgering me the way she is, I don't think I will be able to keep from telling her, and I'm not ready to talk about the elephant in the room; especially when I don't have a plan.

When I arrive my sister still has someone in her chair.

"Hey Yvette," I said and head for the back.

"Daryn," she calls.

"Yes," I respond stopping in my tracks.

"I want you to meet someone." I look at her annoyed waiting for her to say something.

"This is our sister China," I stare at her dumbfounded. I've stayed away from my other siblings for good reasons.

"So, you're Daryn," she said, sounding unimpressed.

I didn't say anything. I walk into the back. Today isn't the day for trying me.

I busy myself with the books and bills of the shop as I wait for her to leave.

The only sister I am interested in having a relationship with, I already have one.

Yvette comes in the room.

"Daryn that wasn't very nice of you."

"Neither was her comment," I respond. "Since when did you start doing our siblings hair anyhow?"

"This is the first time I've done China's hair."

"Oh yeah," I said sarcastically as I shut down the computer.

"China is planning a get together for all the sisters," she said, and I just walk past her.

"Daryn," she calls.

"Yeah," I respond annoyingly.

"What do you have against them?"

"They are my father's children," I plop down in the seat for her to start on my hair.

"What does that mean?" she asks.

"It means they all have the same crooked blood running through their veins as that of our no-good dad."

"So, do we Daryn," she said putting the cape around me. She came to stand in front of me. I didn't say anything as I raise my eyes to stare at her.

"Daryn, what will it cost you to go to the get together with all of Daryn Carter's children? You are the only sister they have never met. They admire you so much, for all you've been able to accomplish. They want the opportunity to get to know you."

All I can think of is; of all the fucking days this had to be the day she came at me with this bullshit.

"Just do my hair" I respond without saying anything about what she seems so passionate about.

I'm not interested in meeting them, being friendly with them, or being in a relationship with them. I want to be left alone.

When Yvette is done, my hair is laid, but it feels as if she were rougher than normal.

We didn't speak the entire time she did my hair. I stand up to pay her.

"Daryn, please consider it. It's in two months." I give her the money and leave without responding. I love and respect her, but my half-sister is very gullible. She trusts in the positive intentions of everyone, even when they don't deserve her trust. I wish she wouldn't have blindsided me that way and gave me a heads up about the situation I was walking into.

I get in my car and check my phone.

Jethro has called me ten times and sent six text messages. Jethro doesn't understand the concept of needing a moment to yourself. The only way I know to take a moment to myself is by ignoring him.

I stop by my mom's to pick up Carter.

"What a surprise," she says opening the door.

"Surprise? I came to get Carter." I say walking in.

"Jethro already picked up Carter."

I guess I should have answered the phone, or at least read the text messages.

"Oh," I said.

"Are you going to tell me what's going on?" she asks.

"There's nothing going on."

"Are you and Jethro okay? He said he had been trying to call you, but you weren't picking up." She says with too much emotion.

"Jethro and I are fine."

"Then what is it?" she asks. It feels as if the walls are closing in on me. I no longer know how to function since I became this Daryn. I turn to leave.

"Where are you going?" she asks.

"Home!"

I can't go home. Jethro will have 99 questions, and I am not in the mood to be bothered. I stop by my best friend's Cheyenne's place. She can talk enough for the both of us.

"Hey girl!" she said opening the door.

"Hey Cheyenne," I respond with a genuine smile.

"Come on in."

Since Cheyenne forgave her parents and started making the decision to live a better life, she has been keeping a tidier house. I take a seat on the sofa.

"I just ordered Chinese," she said. "I hope you're hungry." She follows up with. With all that has been going on today I forgot to eat.

"Yes, I am hungry, I haven't eaten all day."

"Well your hair is laid. Yvette really did her thang on that do." Cheyenne said, and I smile.

"So, what's new," I ask and that is all she needs to talk non-stop.

"Your brother-in-law called me. He said he will be in town, in a few weeks for the scrimmage game. I told him good for him. He asked can he see me when he comes. I told him I would see him at your house. Then he asked, could we go out. I told him I wasn't ready. Then that bastard hung up in my face.

"Now that I'm on my own, and my mother see I don't need them she's trying to be friendlier. When I first told her about my courses she didn't believe I would complete them. Now I'm a home health nurse, and she had to eat crow. I did it for myself, but I took pride in proving her ass wrong.

"I met my brother's daughter for the first time. She's beautiful she looks like me of course." She said and we both laugh.

"My brother and I have established a really good relationship. My dad told me he redid his will, and left me part of the family business, and an inheritance. He asks if I would come by and learn the business. I told him I would think about it and let him know." Cheyenne talks nonstop jumping from subject to subject until dinner arrives. Then during dinner, she talks some more. I love that about her, it keeps me distracted and fascinating that she can do all this while seeming not to breathe.

By the time I leave her place it is after nine and I have not talked to Jethro all day.

I haven't gone all day without speaking to Jethro, at least twice a day, since Carter was born.

I pull up to the house and it looks like every single light is on.

I decide it is time to face the music.

I walk in the door and my son ran to me and hugs me like I've been gone forever. That alone makes me smile broadly, and my heart melts.

Jethro walks up behind him.

"Carter go to your room and get ready for bed while mom and I talk," he said staring at me.

"No Carter, that's okay. Why don't you tell me about what you and granny did all day?" I said grabbing Carter's hand and walking with him to his room.

I don't know what good that did because he follows us. I sit on Carter's bed, and Jethro sits in the chair. He watches as I prepare Carter clothes for bed.

"I'm getting ready to head out to the club, but I want to talk first," he said with a calm tone, but the bulging vein at his temple betrays his tone.

"What is there to talk about?" I ask as Carter flips through a book his grandmother gave him.

"For starters why didn't you pick up the phone?"

I look at him smile, and say "Why don't we discuss this later," then I look back down at the book.

Jethro stands dressed in all black and doesn't say anything else as he exits the room. Not long after, I hear the door chime signaling he's left the house.

I let out a slow breath and continue to read with my son.

Jethro doesn't understand space or boundaries. He always wants to talk about it. I'm not in the head space to talk about it yet. Jethro doesn't get that a person sometimes need to try and sort things out in their mind before they can discuss what they are going through or put it words.

I'm not in the talking about it phase yet. I'm in the trying to digest what is going on phase.

When I'm ready to talk I'll talk, but he doesn't get that. He wants to know everything right away.

I've told him what is necessary, but for now he'll have to wait, until I decide to share with him what I'm going through emotionally.

It's not even five minutes before he's already calling. I throw my head back on the sofa, then decide to answer the phone.

"Hello."

"I'm just reminding you I will be late tonight because we have the club meeting afterwards."

"Okay," I said and there is a long pause.

"Did I do something to you?" he finally asks. He always finds a way to sneak in something to try and make me feel guilty, so I will tell him everything I know. I no longer curse him out, I just shut down completely.

"No," I said after a bit.

"In the future, can you call and let me know you are at least safe?" he asks.

"Yep," I respond.

"Well I can see that you're full of words tonight, so I will see you when I get off."

"Yep," I respond, and he hangs up. I turn my phone off, so I'm not disturbed anymore.

Logan coming at me, my sister coming at me, and now Jethro coming at me; I'm tired and I need to try and sort some things out mentally before I start to discuss anything.

I am lying in bed when I hear Jethro come in. I couldn't sleep. The clock reads 4:30 in the morning. I try to lie as still as possible, so he won't disturb me.

My mind has been running wild trying to figure out Logan's next move. I even tried social media stalking, but it seems he's shut down all his social media accounts under his personal name. I only found information linked to his job. It made me uneasy.

I know he's plotting something, I'm just not sure of the extent. My thoughts jump to my son and what I'm going to tell him.

Some people are so rude. One lady asked me, in front of Carter, if he was adopted. Carter asked what did adopted mean.

Jethro changed the subject and put him around his neck then

walked off with him.

Instead of cursing her out like the old Daryn would have, the new Daryn just walked off as the lady stood looking dumb. I don't know how to explain to him the man he thinks is his dad is not his dad.

The thought alone makes my heart palpitate and keeps me up every night. It brings tears to my eyes.

Jethro gets into bed and wrap his arms around my waist.

"Daryn," he says, and I try to ignore him. "Daryn," he says again in my ear.

"Yes," I say clearing my throat.

"I didn't mean to wake you, but I need to say this. Don't shut me out. We need to stick together, we must be unified. I have as much to lose as you do. So, please don't shut me out. I love you, and I'm here for you," he finishes.

"I love you too, and I know," I say. If making me feel guilty doesn't work, he always launches into a save Daryn speech.

In the time we've been married I've learned Jethro's ways so well. Next, he will resort to being overly nice because he thinks that will get me to open up.

He doesn't do well with me shutting down. He always thinks he need to fix what is wrong with me. He doesn't seem to understand I'm not broken, this is the way I operate. I don't need anyone fixing my problems, and I don't need saving. I just need time to sort this shit out without him breathing in my ear.

I awake to the smell of something sweet in the air. I should call it the four stages of Jethro. His next and final stage after his overly kindness doesn't work will be to explode.

Not much longer he walks in with a tray of food, and my son in tow. I sit up and smile.

"Mommy we made you breakfast," Carter says bouncing up on the bed. It's way too much food, I think as he places the smorgasbord in front of me. I grab the banana. It will be the easiest thing for me to swallow.

"Mommy can I have a pancake," I give him one and look up. Jethro is staring at me, with a peculiar look. I don't know what to say.

"What?"

"Nothing, the game starts at two today. I want to leave around twelve-thirty." Thanks to Jethro my little cousin Robert was accepted into the football program at University of South Florida. He's doing well. We go to all home games, and travel to a few of his away games.

"I'm not going," immediately I see a shift in his demeanor.

"Why? What's wrong? Are you feeling okay?" he asks moving to sit next to me on the bed.

I want to roll my eyes, but I refrain. Nice Daryn don't do those things anymore. Being agreeable with Jethro was the only way I could keep the kraken from escaping and intentionally saying words to hurt his feelings. My blood no longer heats up in my body, and I no longer feel like it controls me.

"Nothing is wrong with me physically Jethro. I just don't feel like going. You and Carter go." I respond.

"Daryn don't shut me out," I put down my banana unable to pretend to eat it anymore.

"Jethro, I'm fine. I'm not shutting you out. Can't I miss one game without it being a problem? I've been to every single home game, and some away. Please don't give me a hard time because I want to miss one game. I'm not shutting you out. I don't want to go. It's just that simple," I said trying not to elevate my voice.

"Okay," he finally settled, but I know Jethro, he's not done.

"Carter, go and get something to wear." He ran out the room and down the hallway.

Dammit was all I thought.

"What are you going to do?" I give him a sarcastic smile. Is he serious?

"I'm a big girl, I'm sure I can think of something to do, or I might not do anything at all." I said trying to stay calm.

"Daryn..."

"Oh my God Jethro I promise nothing is going on. I just don't feel like sitting out in the hot sun. I'm good. I'm not going to do anything without you. You have to trust me, Jethro." Then I take a deep breath. I know Jethro means well but DAMN!

"Okay Daryn, if you need me call me."

"Okay," I said, finally I got him to leave my side.

We exchange kisses and they are out the door. I exhale and leave the house and go to Cheyenne's place. I need to keep my mind occupied.

"Hey gurl!" Cheyenne said opening the door.

"Hey Cheyenne," I said instantly smiling. "You look dressed to leave the house."

"Nah, just returning," she opens the door wider for me enter.

"Oh, where are you coming from?"

"Well if you really want to know, I went to speak to my Pastor. I sort of broke my no sex rule after two years of celibacy."

"Oh," I don't really know how to respond to her confession.

"Girl it was awful," she said walking to the sofa, and I can't help but laugh.

"He should retire his dick right away." That got me to bend over with laughter.

"Cheyenne it couldn't have been that bad." "It was worse because he boasted himself up. This bastard had the nerve to buy magnum size condoms. Not only was it too big, it slipped off him and got stuck inside of me. Instead of magnum he should have bought miniature. Girl, when I tell you it was terrible, it was terrible. It took three days for the condom to come down low enough for me to pull it out. I thought I was going to have to go to the ER. I would have been on How Sex Sent Me to the ER."

Cheyenne makes me laugh out loud, and I love it. Lately, Jethro and I are having a hard time finding something to laugh about.

"Anyhow I know you didn't come over to talk about my transgressions. How is my nephew?" she asks.

"Ah, he's perfect. He has the energy of 10,000 puppies. I just wish I could get him to slow down before he hurts himself." We are both smiling the entire time I speak about Carter.

"Well he's a boy. They have way more energy than girls. I remember my mom telling my brother all the time to get down before he breaks his neck. He climbed everything like they were monkey bars."

"Oh my God Carter too!" I interject.

"He'll calm down as he gets older."

"Thank God!" I said.

"How's Jethro?" She just had to ask.

"Getting on my fucking nerves," I said, and Cheyenne spit her water across the room, she was laughing so hard.

"Yasss hunty, that is the Daryn Carter I remember and love." She said still laughing.

"I shouldn't have said that," Jethro is only trying to help.

"Yes, yes the hell you should have. If that's how you feel say that shit. You remember our motto, no judgment. Besides I don't know how to take this new Daryn that looks like she stepped out of an Urban Outfitters Magazine. I bet you got a sunhat in the damn car!"

It was my turn to spit I was laughing so hard. Not only did this lacy cream dress, and these brown lace up boots come from Urban Outfitters, I have a sunhat in the car that matches.

I wore the hat to keep my hair from blowing in the convertible. Jethro drives my Porsche, and sometimes I take the top down on the Beamer and drive it when I'm alone.

"You do, don't you?" she said and we both laugh.

"What is going on with you?" She asks.

"I don't know. Ever since I met Jethro at a restaurant with a jumper on that had a plunging neckline, I've changed the way I dress. Some guy tried to pick me up while I sat at the bar waiting on him. When he walked up, we were laughing and having a good time; which pissed him off."

"Hold the hell on. You don't think women are trying to talk to

Jethro when he goes out? You don't see him trying to dress conservative with those tight ass shirts he wears to the gym." This made me bend over with laughter. One-day Jethro had on a dry fit shirt so tight I thought I could see his heartbeat.

"You have a point," I respond.

"You damn right I have a point. You are Daryn "fucking" Carter. You slay bitches. I don't know this Daryn Thomas. This delicate Daryn is so hard to read. If you don't stop acting like someone you are not, you are going to explode."

"It's not that I don't agree I just had to make some changes. I'm a wife and a mother," I respond.

"You're a wife and a mother. You ain't fucking dead.

"The next time I see you, I want you to have on some Gucci, or Wiseman, or something that everyday bitches can't afford. I can afford what you have on; that never use to happen. You can't stop being who you are. He is just going to have to face the fact, that he married a fucking dime piece, and get over that shit. Now I'm getting pissed the hell off. Who are you?" She asked seriously, and honestly, I don't know. I've never conformed in my entire life to anyone and I've conformed totally to Jethro. If he says something I make a change.

"That's a good question," I said looking down.

"Oh, hell no! The Daryn I know, would look bitches straight in the eye, and make them turn away. You've never been this docile creature.

"I like Jethro, and I think he's good people, but you still have to be you."

"I'm just trying to keep things peaceful. I appreciate everything he's done for me, and Carter when he didn't have to." I know I conform to Jethro because he could have left me as a single mom, raising a son on my own. Jethro stepped up to the plate knowing my full circumstances."

"Fuck that! I know where you are going with this. Jethro knew your circumstances before he married you."

"I know but," I pause for a moment thinking I need someone

to talk to about this because I'm drowning in my thoughts.

"Carter's father saw him, and he sent a court order for a paternity test." I blurt out feeling tears well up in my eyes, and that is pissing me off.

"Daryn, I'm sorry. I truly am, but you can't let Jethro insecurities become your insecurities. You knew this might happen someday, and it's probably better since Carter is young. If you kept waiting until Carter was a grownup, he might have resented you."

I remember when Cheyenne saw Carter with his blue eyes she said, 'hold the fuck on who baby is this.' Even in the hospital she had me laughing. I had to confess that Jethro wasn't his biological father, but he knew. She's been the only one I've ever admitted that too. I know my mom knows, but we don't talk about it.

"You're probably right," I said.

"I know I'm right. Whose Carter's daddy anyway?" She finally asked the million-dollar question. The only thing I told Cheyenne in the hospital was Jethro knew. We couldn't talk about it much because Jethro walked in.

"You don't know him. It's a guy named Logan." I said almost smiling remembering Logan's smile.

"I thought it was the guy from Vegas," she said, and I stare at her with my mouth open.

"How do you know about the guy from Vegas?"

"Daryn we saw you leave the casino with a white guy after you were dancing on the crap table. Then we heard you in your room later that night sounding like you were having a good time." She said smiling.

"Oh my God!" I said covering my face in embarrassment, "why didn't you say something." I asked blushing.

"Hell, I just assumed what happened in Vegas stayed in Vegas. Mocha pissed on herself, she got so drunk. I hooked up with some random guy in the Caesar hotel bathroom. It was a wild night." She said and we both laugh. That was definitely a wild night. That was the night I committed to Logan to try and have a relationship.

"Yes, that's him, Logan Anderson."

"How did he run into you here?" She asked, and I thought I might as well come clean since the cat was out the bag.

"He's from here. He used to be the branch manager at the same bank Jethro works at."

"Bullshit!" she yells. "Daryn Carter-Thomas I didn't know you were so scandalous. This shit is better than Power." We laugh. I'm glad I can laugh about this now, because all I've felt like doing is crying.

"They don't work together anymore. When Jethro was promoted he left the bank he worked at with Logan. I really don't know what Logan has been up to lately. I tried checking his Facebook, but he hasn't updated it in a while. I tried other social media, but he didn't have an account with any of the sites I searched."

"Why are you stalking him?" she looks at me peculiarly, and I know I must straighten this out. I don't want her thinking I want him back.

"I am trying to see what his next move might be, but nothing. I didn't find any clues."

"You give me seven days, and I bet I can find out for you. I know a dude name Cornbread that will do anything, for a case of beer."

"Cheyenne stop it," I said laughing. It is nice to have a grown-up conversation without worrying about hurting someone feelings.

"I'm sure whatever Logan's up to he will reveal soon. The DNA test should come back any day now."

"What's your plan?"

"I don't have a clue," I respond honestly.

"Well, do you want to keep him away from his son?" I am too ashamed to speak the words, so I nod no.

"It's just that..." I trail off.

"It's just I'm not sure how Jethro is going to take this." Those are my true feelings. I wish to God when I was younger my dad would have taken an interest in me and tried to be a part of my life, but he never did, and I hated him for it. How can I be mad at Logan for trying to be a part of Carter's life?

"Jethro is a big boy, he will get over it. It's not like you're going to refuse Jethro the right to still be Carter's dad. Daryn, right is right, and as your homegirl I'm going to tell you my opinion. I know how guarded you are about your life, but this is some real shit I'm about to tell you only because I love you.

"Your dad not being a part of your life fucked you up emotionally. My dad not believing in me, and eventually exiling me from the family fucked me up emotionally. You were cold and emotionless, and I was promiscuous and cruel to myself. Do you want the same thing for your son?

"Eventually, Carter will notice the differences between Jethro and him, and figure the shit out his damn self. You don't want him to feel about you like you feel about your daddy. He won't think you kept him from his dad to protect him. He's going to think his dad didn't want to be a part of his life.

Then when Logan tells him, it was you that kept them apart he will be furious with you, and you don't want that."

She is right, and a few tears slide down my face as I think about the reality of my son hating me. He has already asked Jethro why he's not dark like him.

"Ah come on, enough already with the tears." Cheyenne said joking and it makes me smile. I blow my nose and straighten up.

The rest of the night we watch old movies; Love and Basketball, Cheyenne favorite movie, and Deep Cover, my favorite movie. I am shocked and relieved I haven't heard from Jethro.

When I return home, I turn on the lights, and no one is home. I am about to call Jethro when I hear the code being put into the door.

He is walking in carrying Carter, and when Carter turns I see a cast on his arm.

"What the hell?" I said walking toward him and snatching Carter out of his arms.

"Mommy," Carter said and starts crying. I have to walk with him to the sofa he is so heavy.

"Daryn it was all my fault," Juicy, who I hadn't even noticed, said.

"Why didn't you call me?" I shout hearing my voice crack with tears.

"I didn't want to upset you unnecessarily." Jethro said.

"Daryn, while taking him to the bathroom he was hoping down each step. He lost his balance and fell. I tried to grab him, but it all happened so fast."

"Jethro, you should have called me, I'm his mother!" I shout angrily, and now Carter is crying because I am crying.

"Well I'm his father, and I made the decision..." "You made the decision...it wasn't your decision to make." I choke out.

"What does that mean? It's a broken arm. He's fine otherwise," he said with his Bronx accent coming out strong. That pisses me off more.

"You don't make any decisions regarding him without me!" I yell at him not caring that Juicy is in the middle of our screaming match.

"What does that mean?" He shouts back.

"You heard me."

"Daryn!" he said louder than he should have.

"You were wrong for not calling me. I am his mother, and you had no right not to include me in what was going on with MY SON!" I yell. He is trying to keep talking and I walk in my room, slam the door, and lock it. He can take it how he wants to.

It has nothing to do with him being the biological father or not. It has to do with common, fucking courtesy. I pick up my duffle bag and shove some clothes in it. I walk out the room and discover Jethro standing there. "Move!" I say angrily. He moves to the side and I walk past him and into Carter's room to shove some of his things in my bag. I throw the bag across my body and go get Carter.

"Daryn, where are you going? You're over reacting," he said following me.

"No Jethro, on the contrary I'm under reacting. The old Daryn would have cursed your ass out, but this new Daryn is choosing to leave before she says something she regrets, now move so I can get my son." I am ready to claw his eyes out if he doesn't let me by. He steps aside, and I grab Carter. Damn he is heavy.

Jethro came up behind me to grab him from my arms.

"I got him," I said.

"Daryn I'm not going to try and stop you. I know he's heavy. I'm just going to carry him for you." I release the grip I have on him and let Jethro tote him.

We walk out the room and Juicy is bent over on the sofa crying. It makes me feel bad for her.

"Juicy, I'm not mad at you. I know Carter is busy. My anger is stemming from the fact that Jethro didn't call me about something so crucial."

"...but it's all my fault! I should have made Carter hold my hand!" She said between a stream of sobs and tears.

"Juicy it's okay," I said frustrated. The last thing I want to do is comfort Juicy. I am a little pissed at her as well.

"Now you're leaving Jethro because of me!" she chokes out.

"We are coming back," I said and walk out.

"Juicy grab your things so I can take you home." Jethro tells her.

Juicy is still crying, but I didn't say anything else to her. Jethro tried to console her, but I am ready to get away from them. Sometimes Juicy does not use her common sense.

We walk outside, and I light up my Porsche to drive. I see the expression change on his face, but he didn't say anything. Let him drive the fucking Honda. He walks to the driver door and starts to open it.

"Daryn please, I'm sorry. We should talk about this. We are not supposed to go to bed angry." There he goes with the guilt trip.

"I'm not angry, I'm pissed the hell off," I said staring him in the eyes. He is about to open the door then he pauses again.

"Daryn please don't leave. I know I fucked up, but please don't leave. We need to talk about this, so we can get back on track."

"We've already talked about it. There is nothing else to say." He looks like he is about to say something else then thinks better about it, and opens the door for me to get in.

He walks around to the other side and put Carter in the backseat.

"I love you Daryn," he said.

"I know Jethro," I reply then start the car.

"If you need me, I will be at the club. I can come where ever you need me to."

"I know Jethro," I respond. I can see him staring at me out the side of my eye. He kisses Carter's forehead then close the door. I drive off and don't look back.

I go to my old condo. We have it contracted for corporate housing. We have a client coming Monday. I hadn't really thought my plan through I just knew I had to get away from Jethro.

All through the night Carter whines, complains about his arm, and asks for his dad. At one point I became so frustrated I start packing our things, until Carter fell asleep. I take this time and try to go to sleep, but I end up tossing and turning because I am worried about him.

Jethro sends me a text that he loves me, and nothing else. I don't respond.

My phone rings, it is my mom. I don't answer just in case Jethro is using her as a ploy to get to me. I get our things together and wait for Carter to wake up.

He is doing better, and I thank God for that.

I check my phone at least six times and no Jethro. I guess he is respecting my wishes, but I'm not sure if I like it.

When we walk in he is in the living room. He stands to greet us. I thought he would be at church. "Dad!" Carter yells running into his arms. You would think we have been gone for years the way Jethro gets on his knees to hug him.

He stands, and stares at me stuffing his hands deep into his shorts. Jethro is a feeler. He needs to touch. I know he has his hands shoved into his pockets to keep from trying to reach out to me.

"Are you okay?" he asks.

I nod yes.

"Daryn, I'm really sorry," he said.

"I know," I respond. I walk past him and into my room where I strip down to my bra and panties. As I am climbing into the bed he walks in staring at me. I let out a big sigh as I settle under my own covers and lay on my own pillow. It never felt so good.

"I need a few minutes to sleep. Carter had a rough night and I'm exhausted."

"Take all the time you need. I'm just glad you came back," he said.

"Jethro, of course I came back, I'm your wife. I just needed a moment to get my thoughts together before I said or did something I regretted."

"I will go and keep Carter entertained while you sleep. I love you!"

"I know," I respond and close my eyes.

When I wake up it is dark outside. I feel rested. I don't know the last time I was able to rest without interruption.

I stretch, then wrap my robe around me. I walk out to find Jethro and Carter with their shirts off playing video games. It always makes me smile at the way Carter imitates Jethro.

"Hey mom," Carter ran up to me, and hugs my leg. I rub his head full of curls. He's not acting like the cast is affecting him anymore.

"Hey son," I couldn't help but smile.

"Dad took me with him to the gym. I met new friends. Can I go

with him tomorrow? Please mom, please, oh please, oh please…"
"CARTER!" I yell. I immediately feeling bad for yelling as I see his face fall, and tears form in his blue eyes.

"I meant of course you can go," I try to smile the best I can. The tears stop forming, and he breaks out into a smile as he hugs me.

He ran back into the den with Jethro, who is staring at me wide eyed.

Jethro walks into the kitchen after me.

"Did you sleep well?" he asks.

"Yep," I respond checking the fridge for something to nibble on.

He is sitting on the barstool, when I turn around with a bowl of fruit.

"I bought these for our anniversary at the end of the month."

"What is it?" I ask looking at the packet in his out stretched hand.

"I wanted to surprise you, so I bought an all-inclusive trip to Ochos Rios, Jamaica for our fifth anniversary." He lays the packet on the bar when I don't take it from him.

"I thought we could do something big, since we've reached a milestone and made it five years."

"When did you purchase this?"

"Awhile back. I wanted to surprise you, but with what we are going through this weekend I wasn't sure if I should spring this on you as a surprise. I decided to let you know what I had planned so you could have time to think about if you wanted to go."

"What about Carter?" I asked.

"I already talked to my parents, they agreed to keep him. We will fly with him to New York Thursday and spend the night. Then fly out to Ochos Rio Friday. On the way back, we will fly out of Jamaica Sunday morning, pick him up in New York, then fly back home Sunday night." He pauses a moment for my reaction. When I don't respond he continues to speak.

"I know things have been tense around us lately, and I thought we could use some time away. Just the two of us."

He may be right. I've been stressed out, waiting, any day, for a letter, or phone call from Logan about meeting Carter.

"Okay," I said. I don't have the energy to argue back and forth with Jethro about why I don't want to go. It will be too long and drawn out. Jethro would never relent and take no for an answer.

"You will," he said before he broke out into a huge grin.

I nod then take my bowl of fruit into my room signaling I'm done with this conversation.

Just because I agreed to go on this trip doesn't mean I've forgiven him.

The next several days it is more of the same. Jethro is walking on eggshells around me. Each day he asks more questions or tries and makes conversation, but every time I look at my son's arm I get pissed all over again.

The only problem Carter loves it; the attention, the signing of his cast, everyone doing things for him. The presents his grandmother has given him and all the "survivor" presents he's received.

"Are you finished packing," Jethro asks as he enters the bedroom.

He's dressed in all black headed out to the club I OWN. I haven't been to the club in so long no one will probably recognize me. They probably think Jethro owns it now. Once Jethro took over running the club, while I was pregnant, I never looked backed. On most days I don't miss it. I guess I'd become bored of seeing all the same faces and watching all the same scenes unfold. Then there are days like today when I wish I had something to do to occupy my time, so Jethro wouldn't affect me so much when he does something stupid. Sometimes I wish I was the one leaving him here to ponder how his decision making is affecting our marriage. There is also that tiny part of me that misses being in the know. When I ran the club, I knew everything and everyone. Now I barely know the latest music out.

There is a singing competition tonight for a recording contract.

The finalist will be announced after the performances.

Jethro is expecting a huge crowd.

"Yes," I respond.

"I don't know what time, I will make it home tonight, but if you need me just call." He said standing next to the bed.

"Okay," I respond. He's staring at me, so I put the book down I'm reading and stare back at him.

"Are you ever going to forgive me, it's been almost a month." He bends in front of me and takes my foot that I have crossed over my leg and kiss it. Not only have we been barely speaking, but we haven't had sex.

"I have forgiven you," I say. I know in my heart I haven't completely. He sits on the edge of the bed next to me.

"Daryn a million times I'm sorry. What can I do to make things right between us again?"

"I don't know what you mean Jethro?"

"I don't feel as though things have been right between us since we saw him."

I know he means Logan.

"Things are fine between us."

"You seem so distant lately, and I want us to get back on track."

"Jethro, I would be lying if I told you I wasn't concerned about 'his' next move. I know he will want to see Carter, but I can assure you that's all I'm concerned about."

He is resting his arm on my leg and still staring at me.

"Hopefully this will be the trip we need to get us back on track." He said.

"We aren't off track. We are fine. We are just having a disagreement, it happens." I try to reassure him, but I know my face is betraying me. Logan and my mother have told me before I'm a horrible liar.

He leans over and plants a kiss on my lips before he hugs me. When he pulls back, he is nose to nose with me.

"Daryn, I love you. You and Carter are my world. I would do anything to make sure my family is protected. Please don't ever forget that." It dawns on me that my actions are having an adverse effect on Jethro.   I was thinking I was teaching him a lesson for not telling me about Carter's broken arm, but apparently, he thinks I'm not speaking to him because of Logan.

"I know that Jethro. I don't doubt your love for me, for a second. Don't worry about that. We will get through it." I know Jethro is a big guy, but he doesn't take it well when I ignore him.

"Okay Daryn, I love you, and let's go and have the time of our lives." He responds and kisses me again. I nod as he stares at me, kisses my nose, then gets up.

He takes one last look at me, like he wants to say something then walks out.

I lay down, with the intent of forgiving Jethro, and enjoying myself as much as possible.

We board the plane with no problems and arrive in New York without delay. His parents, sister, and brother are waiting for us at curbside. You would have thought Jethro hadn't seen them in years the way they hug and carry on with one another. This is our first time visiting his family in New York. They usually come to see us in Tampa.

Carter is in heaven when his grandmother showers him with kisses. It is amazing how much they love Carter. It makes my heart swell with emotion for the deceit I've done. I decide I will tell his mom before I leave the truth, out of respect.

My in-laws are perfect. They take us out to dinner in Harlem and tell old stories of Jethro and his brother. Jethro was always trying to keep his brother out of trouble. I didn't know, sometimes he would take the rap for him.

For instance, when his brother was accused of stealing candy from a store, Jethro said it was him. He said he was afraid what his dad would do to his brother, Abe, and of him being benched for the big homecoming game. His mama claimed she knew all along. At moments we are laughing so hard we are crying.

We agreed to change our flight to the red eye, so we can go to Abe's game when we return. Jethro hadn't told me about his brother's home game. He said he thought I would be too tired.

We are back at his parents' home in Brooklyn. I decide now is as good a time as any. I walk into his mom's bedroom and close the door.

"May I speak to you a moment," I ask.

"Yes Daryn," the way she said my name almost made me chicken out. She said it like she knows I am up to something.

"I want to thank you for everything you've done for us, but before we go I think it would only be fair that I tell you the truth."

"Yessss," she said drawing the word out. My hands are shaking.

"I know we haven't always seen eye to eye on a lot of issues, but I have a great deal of respect for you, and how you have dedicated your life to making sure your family was taken care of. I often wish I'd had what you accomplished in your family as I was growing up. So, I think it's only fair that I am completely honest with you and not try and deceive you." I take a deep breath as she stares at me, like I am on Maury Povich and she is waiting to see what is revealed in the envelope.

"There is something very important I need to tell you, and I'm so sorry I didn't tell you before. It's just I didn't know how to face the reality of what this would mean for our relationship." I put praying hands in front of my face before I continue.

"Jethro is not Carter's biological father." I said it so quickly I wasn't sure if she heard me. She was looking at me like there should be more.

"I know that, a blind man can see Carter's not Jethro's biological son, but Jethro loves and claims him, so he's my grandson, period end of story. He told me about Carter before he was born. I couldn't love him more than if Carter was born flesh of my flesh and blood of my blood. Now go and get my grandson. Your mama has one upped me, and now it's time for me to get her back," she said as she was setting up ninja turtles on her nightstand for Carter. I walk over and hug her.

When I pull away I have tears in my eyes.

"Daryn who are you?" I hunch up my shoulders.

"I didn't particularly like you when I met you. I felt like you were too proud of a woman to ever love my son properly. Then I saw him stand up for you against me. At that point I thought you had to go. I thought nothing good could come from a son going against his mama.

"Then Senior talked to me and told me you were what Jethro needed to balance him out and make him stronger. You have delivered on that 100%. Lately though I don't know who you are. You have conformed too much to Jethro.

"Getting married doesn't mean you give up being you. You must find a balance. Yes, I do admit the old Daryn was a bit wild and very outspoken, but that is what attracted Jethro to you.

You can't give up yourself completely. You must find a way to merge the two. I hardly recognize you anymore.

"Being married doesn't mean you can no longer have an opinion. Being married doesn't mean you have to give up everything. It means you have to find a common ground.

"Conforming to Jethro is not the answer. He is my son, and I do love him, but you can't let him get his way all the time.

"You have to make him still fight to keep you. If you always give the lion his prey, he will stop hunting for food."

I stand staring at her.

"Now go and get my grandson, so I can spoil him senseless. When he returns home he's going to let your mama know who his favorite grandmamma is." I smile through my shimmering eyes.

"Go!" she yells causing me to jump. I turn to leave the room. All the while her words ring in my ears. 'Who are you Daryn?' I no longer know, but I need to find out before I totally lose myself.

CHAPTER TWO

We board the plane, and for the first time since Carter was born I can relax. I don't have to keep checking to make sure Carter is still with Jethro as we walk. I don't have to get him seated with entertainment for the flight. I don't have to make sure he isn't kicking the seat in front of him.

I can sit back and relax. I let out a long deep breath, recline my seat, and close my eyes.

I awake when I feel the wheels of the plane touch the tarmac. I can't believe I slept the entire flight. I stretch life back into my limbs then look out the window at mountains. I smile as wide as a Cheshire cat. For some reason I thought it would look as flat as Nassau.

As soon as we arrive at the resort I put on my bikini. I don't want to waste a minute of my time sitting in the hotel room.

There is a nice breeze, the sun is shining down on me, and I feel at peace. I've been on edge since I saw Logan. I don't know what it will mean to my family, but for the first time in a long time I feel as if everything will be okay. I am no longer fearful of running into him; that has already happened. I'm sure he will want to see Carter, and maybe it won't be so bad.

"What are you thinking about?" Jethro asks as he wraps his arms around my waist resting his chin on my shoulder.

"How beautiful it is here." I lie to prevent from spoiling the moment.

"Yeah, but you're more beautiful." I smile genuinely. He always compliments me, and I never know what to say in return.

"You want to go for a swim?" I ask.

"Confession...I can't swim." I turn to face him.

"Jethro are you serious?"

"I grew up in Brooklyn; there was no need to learn to swim." He said smiling.

"Well come on," I grab his hand and we run into the water.

Jethro wasn't lying when he said he can't swim. He flops around splashing water like a walrus and going nowhere. He thinks he is drowning in three feet of water. I have to tell him to stand up. I laugh so hard, but he doesn't think it is funny.

"Ah come on Jethro," I said still laughing, and wrapping my arms around his midsection.

He picks me up and throws me over his shoulder.

"Jethro put me down!" I yell still laughing.

"Are you sorry for laughing?" he yells playfully.

"Yes, I'm sorry!" I scream still laughing.

I thought he was going to put me on my feet, but he dunks me underwater. I am glad I decided to wear braids. I come up laughing and wiping my face. He sat me on my feet.

"At least I didn't think I was drowning in 3 feet of water," I tease and take off running toward the shore.

Jethro catches me with no effort, then turns me to face him. He stares into my eyes before he kisses me.

"I love you Daryn Thomas."

"I love you too Jethro Thomas," I said smiling at him. This makes him break out into a broad smile. I don't know the last time I told Jethro I love him. I haven't felt like saying it lately. I've been distancing myself from him, so he won't keep questioning me.

I feel a renewed energy with Jethro and me. It is as if we have both silently vowed to make the best of our vacation.

Jethro hoist me into his arms and I wrap my legs around his waist. He walks us back to our island get away. I am kissing him heavily. I want him badly. It feels like forever since we've been intimate. Off came my top, then bottom. I lay shaking with need for him, as he disrobes before me. I hope he takes it easy on me it's been awhile.

He kisses my toe, my knee, then my inner thigh. My back arches off the bed as he takes one simple lick between my thighs. The warmth alone was enough to make me moan and send shivers up my spine. He kisses the opposite thigh then licks my slit again. I didn't realize how much I'd missed intimacy. I'd become accustomed to not having it.

With two fingers he parts my sex, so he can gain better access; licking and swirling his tongue around. He takes those same lips and seal them around my clitoris and starts sliding up and down. I am about to combust when he stops abruptly, then slides himself inside of me where I detonate upon impact. I had my eyes screwed so tight I can see stars when I open them. He moves slowly letting me relish in the moment. Making sure I can get it all out before he starts to really move.

He pulls back to look in my eyes. "I love you Daryn," he said.

"I love you too Jethro," I moan. He closes his eyes and exhales. It is as if he wasn't expecting me to say it in return. It's like he's constantly seeking reassurance.

He dips his head to kiss me and continues to stare in my eyes until the power of his orgasm forces him to close them.

Afterwards, we both lay wrapped in one another arms sedated from our love making.

It was nice and sensual, nothing to intense.

It is our last day in paradise. We wake up early to make a full day of it. A taxi picks us up to tour the island. We hold hands as we walk. I lay my head on his shoulder as we ride, and we kiss like newlyweds in between talking.

We end the evening on the beach skinny dipping after the sun goes down. When we return to the room our meal is prepared, but it is not food that he wants. He's been sampling rum at every stop, and even I sampled a fruity wine that made me tingle all over.

I pick up a strawberry and pop it into my mouth. Jethro comes over kissing me, and when he pulls away he is chewing half of my strawberry.

"We should shower first," I said as he wraps his arms around me, bending so he can lay his head on my shoulder.

"I don't think I can wait until after we shower," he said and peels off my towel dropping it to the floor. I'm completely naked under my towel.

"Jethro," I said smiling as he nibbles on my ear.

"Yes, Daryn" he says and lifts me in his arms

I smile at him, "I'm all sandy."

"I'm going to explode if I'm not inside you soon," he says grabbing me by the waist and kissing me. He lays me on the sofa; then peels off his basketball shorts. I watch as his manhood springs free thick and heavy. It causes my heartbeat to speed up.

He parts my legs with his legs and slides inside of me. I let out a moan, and squirm beneath him. I wasn't ready for such a hard thrust so soon.

Instead of pausing he continues his sweet assault on my sex. I claw at his back, and squirm beneath his weight, as he relentlessly thrust in, and out of me.

I shout his name, "Jethro," I shout for mercy "Jesus," and I babble incoherently, but he doesn't let up.   It is evident he is a man with a mission, to show me, who is the boss. I'm trying to hang in there; I'm on the verge of my second orgasm. I can feel it mounting deep inside of me. I flex my muscle around him involuntarily. He takes this as a cue to go faster, harder, deeper. I cannot form a coherent thought.

"Jethro please," I shout out as he continues. I burst at the seams, digging my nails deep into his back. He is not affected. He is pounding me so hard I'm bouncing back to him with every stroke of my pussy. My orgasm is long over, but still I didn't draw it out of him. He flips me over; pressing on my back so my ass is in the air. He slams into me so hard, I inch forward. He holds on to my waist giving me all of him. The only way to explain the rate he's going is, insanity. I bite the couch cushion to silence my cries. I beg him, "Jethro please!"

There are a few harder solid thrusts when he finally yells out in pleasure. I collapse then straighten out to lie down. He lies half on and half to the side of me.

We both lie catching our breath. He gets up and starts

dancing slinging his penis around in a circle. I start to laugh.

"What are you doing?" I ask still laughing.

"That's the 'I put a baby in you dance.' That's it right there. I can feel it." He said. I still laugh, but I know the truth.

Jethro asked me six months ago about having a baby. I told him yes and threw my birth control pills away. About a week after that I went back to the doctor and got a refill. I'm not ready to have another baby. Carter is so busy, and he's one child, he's so active it feels like I have more than one.

My every emotion, thought, and life revolve around Carter. I am not complaining, but at times it can be overwhelming. I'm not ready to add to that.

Part of me feels guilty, but I don't know how to tell Jethro I'm not ready. He was so excited about it. I know eventually I will have to confess, but today is not that day. I will let him believe he put a baby in me.

"You want something to drink," he asks after he finishes his "baby making" dance.

"Yes please," I said.

He grabs a drink and lay down behind me. For a while we lay watching TV.

"You ready to go home?" he asks with his head resting on the side of mine.

"Yes, and no," I respond truthfully.

"I feel the same way. Facetiming Carter has been nice, but I'm ready to see him in person."

I know, but he doesn't seem to miss us. Your parents have really been spoiling him." We laugh because every time we try and Facetime him he talks to us about 30 seconds then gives the phone back to his grandmother, so he can go play.

"I know, we are going to have a hard time getting him back on schedule."

"I'm glad he still looked like he was having a good time."

"Yeah, me to. My mom asked if we wanted to extend our trip.

I wish we could. Lately we seem miles apart. Just know that I'm here for you and Carter, and I would do anything to make sure my family is protected."

"I know Jethro, I'm sorry if I don't' seem grateful lately. Trust me I am."

"Some days I wonder where I would be if I didn't have you two in my life. I know that I wouldn't have the peace I have if it wasn't for you. You make me so happy." He said and turns my face to kiss. With his kiss came a need for passion again. I wince as he climbs on top of me, and ease inside of me again.

I don't deny him because I know, this is what he needs to not feel rejected. He's gentler and more intimate as he kisses me while we make love.

CHAPTER THREE

I walk through the front door feeling renewed. I remove my sunhat still beaming from our getaway. I open the mail as Jethro and Carter run around the house playing airplane.

I drop everything I have in my hand when the mail I'm reading says Logan is seeking a custody hearing for Carter. Everything goes black as I start to lose conscience.

"Daryn, baby, what's wrong?" Jethro ask as he catches me, pulling me into and embrace. I didn't even realize I was going down. I immediately start shaking. The hearing is this Tuesday. I can't speak. He walks me to the couch to sit; then immediately takes Carter to his room.

When he returns he picks up the pages. I hold my head between my knees and focus on breathing. I knew he was plotting something, but I wasn't ready for the reality of what that something meant. I thought he would try and contact me to set up a time to meet Carter once the paternity test returned.

"Daryn," Jethro says as he sits next to me rubbing my back. I sit up and look his way. He wipes my face then pulls me to him.

"Daryn it will be okay. I'm not going to let him take our son." I let out an agonizing sob as the reality of what Logan is trying to do hits me hard. He not only wants to meet Carter he wants to share custody. I can barely breathe thinking about it.

"Daryn don't cry," he says, but I can't help myself. I don't know what this means. I am not prepared for whatever Logan has in store for me.

It's a dark and gloomy morning. The sky is gray, and I'm going through the motions of getting dressed. I put on a gray suit that reflects my mood. I am going for a polished business look.

"You ready," Jethro says as I finish buttoning my last button.

"Yes," I respond, but emotionally I'm not. I feel as if we are going into the lion's den.

We drop Carter off to my mom's house.

"You want me to take him in?" Jethro asks.

"No, if you do, she will know something is wrong."

"She is already going to know something is wrong. You have on a suit, and you look like you've been crying." He's right. The only time I ever wear a suit is to a funeral, or a business meeting to renegotiate a loan for the club.

I get out the car, grab Carter's hand, and take him into my mom's townhouse.

"Hey Carter," my mom says hugging him like she hasn't seen him in years. He runs in the house and I turn to leave.

"What's wrong with you?" she asks. I can feel the tears swimming in my eyes.

"Nothing," I say and walk toward the stairs.

"Daryn," she says, and I stop.

"You're a horrible liar," she said and closes the door.

When I get in Jethro drives off without questioning me. I feel as if I'm a ticking time bomb just waiting to explode.

We pull up to the court house parking garage. Normally I wait for Jethro to open my door, but this time when he comes to my side I've already exited the truck.

He grabs my hand as we walk up to the courthouse. I can feel my heart in my throat. He kisses the back of my hand, and starts to caress it. My heartbeat starts to slow, but never steadies.

We sit outside the courtroom. I discretely look around for Logan, but he's nowhere in sight. I pray a silent prayer he doesn't show up.

"You okay," he says.

"No," I respond honestly.

"It's going to be okay," he says.

"Will it?" I ask seriously.

"Yes, I'm not going to let anyone come between our family."

"What if we have no choice?"

"We always have a choice."

"What does that mean?" I asked.

"It means that no matter what happens, we have to consider our options, and what we need to do, instead of what we've been told to do." I look at Jethro dumbfound.

I'm not sure if he's telling me we should flee if the verdict isn't in our favor or what?

"What are you saying?" I asked.

"I'm saying by any means necessary, to protect my family, no matter the outcome in there." He pointed toward the courtroom door.

I don't ask him to elaborate, I can only imagine where his mind is taking him. I know this is hard for him too.

We sit in silence watching as person after person enters the courtroom, and then exit. Some come out in tears, and some come out smiling and cheering. One guy came out in a rage yelling at his ex-wife that she would be sorry. He was two seconds away from being arrested. I saw the bailiff reach for his handcuffs, but the guy walked off before the guard detached them from his belt.

Finally, we are being called. I still didn't see Logan. My heart is starting to beat with excitement until I walk in the courtroom, and Logan is standing in front of the judge, with his wife, and another gentleman.

He takes my breath away. He looks good. He cut his hair a little shorter on the top, and is possibly a shade tanner, but he still looks good. He never looks in my direction as we face the judge.

"Your honor my client is seeking full custody of his son Jethro Carter Thomas." HIS CLIENT! I scream inside my head. He's hired an attorney!

"Full custody!" I shout out.

"Order," the judge yells.

I can't believe how badly I underestimated Logan. He came to war in full body armor, and I came with Jethro.   How did I let this happen?

The judge takes the documents from Logan's "attorney" asks me no questions and orders us to mediation.

He bangs his gavel on the desk and it makes me jump.

The bailiff is calling the next case, but my feet are planted in the same spot.

Jethro starts to usher me forward guiding me out the courtroom. I can't move without assistance. Is he really going for full custody?

We walk out the courtroom.

"LOGAN!" Jethro shouts out.

Logan, his wife, and attorney continue to walk.

"LOGAN!" he calls out again practically dragging me he's walking so fast.

We caught up with them as they wait for the elevator.

"You can speak to my attorney," Logan said turning around.

"Fuck your attorney," Jethro yells. "What are you trying to do? You can't take my son away." Jethro yells.

"Your son…" Logan said with a smirk.

"Gentlemen we can handle this in mediation," his attorney said as they step on the elevator. I pull Jethro back as he tries stepping on the elevator with them.

Logan stares at me as the elevator doors close, and if looks could kill I would have fell dead. I can still feel him staring at me when the doors shut.

"Who does he think he is? Full custody, is he serious?" Jethro said holding his hands on his waist.

"Jethro lets go," I said. People are starting to stare, and I didn't want the bailiff to reach for his handcuffs for Jethro.

I am glad to be outside. I suck in a full breath of air. I can't believe what happened. I don't understand the point of mediation, when he has said he's seeking full custody.

I'm afraid of what the outcome will be if the judge learns that I never told Logan he had a son; especially when I knew the truth.

We are walking to the parking lot in our separate worlds. We went into the courthouse united and strong; we came out the courthouse baffled and confused.

I don't know how to feel. On one hand, I wish my dad would have fought to be a part of my life, on the other hand, I'm probably a better person because he didn't.

I pause from walking as Logan and his wife ride by us.

Logan's forehead is creased, but his eyes are unforgiving. I can tell by the scowl on his face, he is up for a fight. It is personal between me and him, it is not just about our son.

"Daryn," Jethro said to get me to break my stare. "Are you okay?" he asked.

In my head I play out telling him how I really feel. 'No Jethro I'm not okay, and that is a dumb question. The man I once loved and thought about having a life with, is out for my blood. He wants to make me hurt. He is exacting revenge on me and putting my son in the middle. How can I blame him? I kept a precious secret from him. Not only did I not tell him I was pregnant, but I had a kid, and pretended it was yours. I know everyone knows, but everyone is too polite to ask. There were several moments when I thought about telling Logan myself, but those moments grew into years. Those years grew into comfort, and before I knew it I believed the lie. As soon as I thought we'd gotten away with it, we ran into Logan. I should have known there was no such thing, as happily ever after.' But I can't tell Jethro that, he would be crushed. So, I respond with something simple.

"I'm just ready to see my son." He puts his arm around me and we walk to the car. I can feel his arm around me, but I don't feel connected to him. Something has shifted inside of me after seeing Logan.

We pull up to my mom's, I hop out the car without giving Jethro the opportunity to go with me. I need a moment to clear my mind, without him questioning me.

I walk slowly to the door. I stand outside a moment and breathe. I need to get myself together before my mom sees me. I can't do that with Jethro constantly asking me how I'm doing. I knock lightly on the door.

"Hey mommy, my son says running around my mother to hug me.

"Hey Carter!" I say hugging him tightly. It's the best feeling in the world.

"Is everything okay," My mom says as I release him.

"Um hum," I respond and take Carter by the hand, so we can leave.

"Aren't you coming in?"

"No, Jethro has to go to work."

"Jethro's with you!" Dammitt! I think to myself. I shouldn't have told her that part.

"Daryn what's going on?" She wasn't asking, she was demanding.

"I'll call you," but I know I am saying this, so she will stop questioning me. I have no intention of calling her.

I don't know whose worse, her or Jethro, I think as I pull Carter by the hand.

"Hey buddy," Jethro says when we get in the car.

"Hey dad," he says, and they do an exploding fist bump.

That used to make me smile, now all I wonder is how long it will be before Carter knows the truth, and the first part of his innocence is taken away.

We pull up to the house, and to my surprise Jethro is getting out.

"I thought you had to go to work." Honestly, I was hoping to get a moment away from him.

"I need to make a few calls. I know this attorney that handles family law. I want to see if he will take our case."

"What do you mean?"

"We have to be smart. We must fight fire with fire. He's a real pit bull. We played ball in college together. Trust me, he's the kind of guy we want in a situation like this." Jethro said as we head to the house.

Everything seems to be going too fast. I feel as if I don't have a say in my own life.

Jethro immediately starts making calls.

He comes running out the bedroom telling me the attorney is willing to skip lunch to see us.

"What about Carter?" I asked.

"Can't your mom watch him?"

"We just picked him up from her. She will become too suspicious and ask too many questions."

"We can bring him with us," he said.

"Can't we go another time? I don't want to involve Carter unnecessarily."

"This is the only time he has before our first mediation."

"Let me text Juicy," I tell him.

She responds right away with full on emojis and the word absolutely.

We drop him to my grandmother's and head to the attorney's office.

When we get there; he's an Italian guy who looks like he eats people for breakfast he's so ripped. We shake hands and start immediately. He holds back no punches asking every intimate detail about Logan and me. Some questions make me choke, and some questions I want to ask Jethro to leave the room. He is so in tune to all my responses.

- How long were we together?
- Did I know Logan was married?
- When did we meet?
- How did we meet?
- How many times did we have sex?
- Did we live together?
- Were we ever anything besides dating?
- When was the last time we had sex?
- Did I meet any of his family?
- Did he meet any of my family?

- Did I ever try to contact him and let him know about Carter?
- What am I willing to compromise with Carter?
- How many men were I sleeping with when I was sleeping with Logan?
- Why didn't I tell Logan?
- Did I think Logan had a right to see his son?
- Did I love Logan?
- Do I still love Logan?

I stutter on the last question, and Jethro whips his head around to stare at me.

Needless to say, the ride home will be long.

The attorney informs us he will not be able to make it to the first mediation, but he will be to the rest of them. He is going to send representation to start the negotiations. He states nothing is ever accomplished in the first mediation, and I will be fine.

We drive to pick up Carter and I almost flip out when I walk in the house, and my crack head Uncle Buck is playing with my son.

"Come here Carter!" I said in a panic.

"Hey Daryn?" Uncle Buck said with a devilish grin.

"What are you doing here?"

"I don't have to have a reason to come to my mother's house. That's a nice son you got there. We have been playing."

Juicy came bouncing down the stairs.

"Oh, hey Daryn."

Oh, hey Daryn, was what I thought.

"Why weren't you watching him?" I asked.

"I ran upstairs to get Mercy a clean shirt." She responds with her little sister trailing behind her.

"Where is granny?" I asked.

"She went to the social security office."

"Juicy can I see you outside," I said walking outside without giving her a chance to respond. Sometimes I wonder when God was handing out common sense where was Juicy. I try to compose myself, and be responsible before I start, but she pissed me off.

"Juicy, why would you leave Carter with Uncle Buck?"

"I was only gone a few minutes, and part of his probation is to get tested for drugs. So, I know he can't be on drugs with all the testing he has to do."

"Juicy has it ever occurred to you that even though he's not on drugs currently, he's still unfit, or his brain is so fried from the drugs, that it's not a good idea to leave him alone with my son?" I am trying to be patient, but I can feel the patience leaving me.

"Daryn it was only for a second while I ran upstairs to change Mercy. She wasted juice on herself, and I only left him for a minute, at the most."

"You only left him a minute with Uncle Buck, and you only looked away for a minute when Carter broke his arm. Juicy you got more excuses than a man going to jail, and I'm sick of your excuses. You need to stop operating with your head in the clouds and start using your common sense. I swear, Juicy if your head wasn't attached to your body, it would probably float away. You..."

"Daryn..." I hear from behind, and I already know it is Jethro. I look at him with annoyance. I'm sick of him being up my ass.

"Juicy it's cool we're leaving. You can go back inside." There are tears swimming in her eyes, but I don't' care. Jethro holds the door for Juicy to walk through. I walk over to the car and get in without saying anything. I am steaming, and I know if I speak right now it won't be good.

When we pull up to the house I jump out the truck and get in the Porsche.

"Where are you going?"

"Off," I respond.

"We need to talk," Jethro pleads.

"No, the hell we don't. It seems like you got it all figured out. What the hell you need me for?" I zoom out the driveway and head to

Cheyenne's place.

Cheyenne is getting out of her car when I pull up. She is a home health care nurse, and she makes her own schedule. She always keeps her workload light on Tuesday.

"Fancy seeing you here," Cheyenne said smiling, when I got out of the car.

"I was in the neighborhood," I didn't want to break down telling her everything, as soon as I get here.

"Then it's a good thing I purchased enough Chinese food for two people."

She said, and we walk into her townhouse.

"Excuse the mess, I haven't had a day off in ten days," she said picking up clothes off the furniture.

"No judgment," I said as I plop on the sofa.

She fixes us a plate then turns to a judge show.

"I'm glad you stopped by. I haven't had a conversation with someone my age in a while. All my clients are over seventy. So, what's going on D?" She asked smiling at me.

"I'm not really sure I'm ready to talk about it yet," I sat my plate down on the coffee table.

"Then I guess I will talk about my favorite subject...me!" We giggle as that breaks the ice.

"I joined the praise dancers at church. Maybe you can come and see my debut in two weeks." Cheyenne smiles. "I'll try, that is the weekend Jethro's parents and siblings are coming."

"Oh, how is Abe?" Cheyenne and I have never discussed the night I caught her and Jethro's brother on the couch with her in a very compromising position. I've made several unsuccessful attempts to get the image of them out my head.

"Abe's good, they will have a bi-week and he's choosing to spend that weekend here."

"Oh well that's good. I received a letter from my uncle," she said changing the subject abruptly.

"Your uncle?" I said as a question because the only uncle I know she has, is the one that molested her.

"Yes, apparently he wants me to forgive him. Of course, he's found God in prison, and he's seen the error of his ways. Now he would like to see me, so he can confess his sins, and beg for forgiveness."

"You're not going, are you?"

"Don't know," she responds hunching her shoulders.

"Why should you? You're the victim." I am getting angry. They almost destroyed my friend. Now he's seeking her assistance, so he can be "forgiven."

"Vengeance is mine said the Lord. He's the one suffering in prison. I've learned to go on with my life. It takes too much to carry around a grudge."

"Yes, you recently have, but what about all the years you suffered because of what he did to you. I say make him suffer, as long as he made you suffer."

"No matter how much I make him suffer, or how long I wait, I can't get the years back."

"Cheyenne, he took away your youth, your dignity, and for a while your soul. He doesn't deserve you going to the prison so that he can 'beg' you for forgiveness. You can forgive him out here and let his ass rot in prison."

"Yeah, what he did to me, took so much away from me, for so long, but I had to learn it doesn't define me. I am stronger today because of it."

"That's bullshit. You would have been strong without going through what you went through. I hate when people say shit like that. Well, think about all you could have been, or all you could have done had he not done that to you. You shouldn't have had to be a strong 9-year-old. You should have been able to be a kid. He forced your hand and made you grow up before it was time. He stole your innocence and ruined your relationship with your parent's."

"He did, but I won't let him take from me anymore. I am not a scared little 9-year-old girl anymore. I am a grown woman, and I no longer fear him or hold any animosity against him. I don't need anger to be powerful over him. The power was in forgiving him and giving it to God. I've done that, and if I go to the prison it will be because I want to, not because I must. There is nothing hanging over my head anymore Daryn. I am free!" She said and smiles broadly while I sit looking like I just ate something sour.

"Part of forgiveness is letting go, so it no longer has any power over you. Your mom, my uncle, and the countless abusers in the world no longer have dominion over us. We must break the chains that bind us to the sin and break free. We are free Daryn, we are free!" It is like she is trying to get it through my head. I know I have forgiven my mother, but sometimes old demons resurface. "We are better than our uncle's, and mother's we have broken the cycle."

She is right, but I still wouldn't go to the prison. He doesn't deserve it.

"Before we start singing Kumbaya and shit, or Jethro calls and you have to go running home, lets watch a movie." This is Cheyenne's favorite pastime watching movies.

"I turned my phone off," I respond.

"Okay, what's going on?" she asked searching through her Netflix.

"Today we had to go to court over Carter, and I found out Logan is seeking full custody." I've never learned how to sugar coat a situation. I always believed in ripping the band aid off and dealing with the aftermath sooner than later.

"Full custody?" she said like a question.

"Yeah, I was just as shocked. Jethro confronted Logan in the hallway afterwards, and then hired an attorney without consulting with me. He started taking over without getting my opinion on anything, and that pissed me off. I am not a damsel in distress. I don't need a knight in shining armor. I need a partner in this."

"What makes him think he has the right to full custody?" she asked.

"I believe he is pissed and trying to get back at me."

"Probably true," she agreed. "What is your plan?"

"According to Jethro we now have a pit-bull of an attorney. He asked me all sorts of intimate questions in front of Jethro that I didn't want to answer. To make matters worse I stuttered when he asked if I still love Logan."

"Do you?"

"Of course not, I don't love Logan; I just couldn't believe the intimacy of the questions he was asking."

"You sure you don't?" she asked.

"I'm positive I don't. Logan and I were, well into the past until I saw him a few months ago. I hadn't thought about Logan. My only connection to him is our son."

"You mean to tell me, every time you looked into your baby boy's blue eyes, you didn't think about Logan."

"In the beginning I did, but I guess I'd convinced myself we'd won so I stopped thinking about him. Jethro would forever be Carter's father. I didn't have to think about him anymore. Since we saw him that day in Hyde Park I've thought about him every day. I've thought about when we would hear from him. I originally thought he would try and see him, and maybe try to have some visitation rights. Never in a million years did I think he would be this drastic."

I said as she put on a movie.

"You never know what is going on in a person head until they are ready to reveal it. You underestimated Logan; maybe Jethro is trying to make sure you are prepared next time.

"Since it involves my godson, I am glad you have a pit-bull for an attorney. Hopefully he will fight like one in the courtroom." Cheyenne said.

"I hope so too. I am tired of Jethro thinking that he needs to do everything for me lately, like I don't know how to function without him."

"Daryn, that's your fault. You took a backseat to your own

life. I see how you just go with the flow now." She said.

"I know, but I guess today it really got to me. He made me feel like I was incapable of doing anything, without him making the first move." I start stretching out on the sofa.

"Maybe you should discuss this with him. I'm sure he will understand."

"Are you taking up for Jethro?" I asked, and she laughs.

"No, not at all. He's still a cornball to me. I know the old Daryn versus the new Daryn, and the new Daryn lets her husband make the first move."

I thought about it. As much as those words piss me off, she is right. Over the last few years that is how I could keep the peace and avoid arguments. I've let Jethro take the lead on everything. No wonder he decided to hire the attorney without seeking any advice or guidance from me. I've been letting him set the tone for everything.

I watch half a movie with her, then decide it is time to go home and face the music. Jethro and I need to talk no matter how unpleasant it may be.

I pull up to the house and stare at it. I am not in the mood to deal with Jethro, but I know there is no time like the present. When I walk in the house, Carter comes running and jumps into my arms. I swing him around, and sit him down.

"Hey," Jethro is looking as if he is afraid to approach me.

"Hey," I responded and pause.

"Carter would you mind going to your room, so your mom and I can talk a minute?"

"Okay," Carter said and bounces away. I sit my purse on the chair then plop on the sofa.

"Where did you go?" he asked sitting next to me.

"Cheyenne's place," I answer, and didn't say anything else.

"Daryn what is going on? Why are you so upset?"

"You really don't know?" I am squinting at him in disbelief.

"No, I figured it must have something to do with me, but I

can't figure out what I've done."

I turn to face him on the couch and pick up his hand, "Jethro I appreciate you, but I'm not a damsel in distress. I don't always need you to rescue me or take the lead in solving the problem. I was going to sort some things out, give myself time to think about what to do next, and then locate an attorney. Just because I'm not doing anything right away, doesn't mean I'm not going to do anything at all. I don't like making hasty decisions. You may be thinking I'm not going to do anything, but I'm just working out my next move. I would have hired an attorney, but I wanted to take a day or two to process everything that has happened, then determine what to do next."

"I am not trying to solve your problems. This is our situation. I am trying to contribute as your partner, as your companion, but most of all as your husband. I'm not trying to take control away from you, or the situation. Anything I do for us, is done out of the love for my family, pure and simple." I look at him without blinking. I know he means well. Jethro has only tried to help, but sometimes his help can be overwhelming. We handle things differently, we operate differently, and we are almost polar opposites. I guess that's why he does not understand or know what he is doing is upsetting me.

"Jethro, before you go full power, and jump in to resolving the situation, please try giving me a moment to digest everything."

"It's not that I can't give you a moment to digest everything Daryn. Whenever something major is going on, you shut down and shut me out. When we left the courtroom today, it felt like Logan was already light years ahead of us. We were trying to play nice and fair, but he came in with a plan and ready to destroy. I saw the look in your eyes, and I felt your pain when you shouted, 'full custody.' I knew we needed to act fast before he sprung something else on us. I would have talked to you about it, but when you are going through something you don't like to talk about it. I don't operate that way.

"Once I get over the initial shock of what is happening to me I start planning what options I will take. I'm always trying to move forward to resolution." He took my hand in his. "Daryn, if you stop shutting me out, and talk to me, you have my word as your husband, that I will discuss things with you before I do anything. I only ask that you be willing to discuss things with me as a unit."

"Okay," I replied, and he kisses me on the forehead. In the back of my mind I think I will try, but my subconscious knows I'm only trying to end this conversation.

CHAPTER FOUR

I agreed to go with Cheyenne to see her uncle. We are standing outside the prison, staring at it. I see her chest rise and fall, it seems her breathing has become more difficult. I know the signs of a panic attack.   I've started suffering from panic attacks since I started suppressing the Kraken. I grab her hand for support.

"You can do this. You are no longer that scared little girl."

"I know that in theory, but reality seems to be hitting me hard and strong. Those memories have been haunting me since I agreed to visit him. They are getting stronger with every step I take."

"You are in control here. If you want to leave, we can leave. Just say the words. I am with you, no matter what you decide. This does not make you any braver than you already are. You deciding to go in, or leave, does not prove anything."

"I know, but we've driven so far. I can do this, just give me another minute." We've driven two hours to see her uncle. I hold her trembling hand.

We stand a few more minutes and she start trying to calm herself by breathing in through her nose, and out through her mouth. She whispers, "help me Jesus."

"Okay, I'm ready," she finally says, and we walk to the prison doors. We didn't bring anything that must be searched. I leave the remote to my car with the guards, and we go into a room, sit and wait for her uncle.

He sits in front of us and folds his hands. Cheyenne sits straight up in her chair.

"Hello Cheyenne, Daryn, thank ya'll for coming." He said and pauses as Cheyenne nods her head. We are both trying to see what he has to say.

"In Matthew Chapter 6 versus 14 through 15 it states, For if you forgive men when they sin against you, your heavenly Father will also forgive you. But if you do not forgive men their sins, your Father will not forgive your sins." When he pauses I notice that Cheyenne is still frozen.

"Wait a minute, are those your words?" It is sounding like he is trying to lecture Cheyenne, and I'm not going for it.

"No, as I stated, it is from the book of Matthew in the bible."

"I thought we were here for you to ask her for forgiveness, not for you to lecture her on forgiveness."

"I am getting there Daryn, but I wanted to make sure she understood that forgiveness is for her benefit."

"She understands that!" I said with my temperament starting to change and become more agitated as I sit across from this son of a bitch. I don't understand why he thinks he needs to lecture my friend, when he is the one that acted unlawful.

"I am going to get to that part, but as a child of God..."

"You think because you are in prison with nothing else to do, but read the bible, you are now a child of God? You are a rapist, a child molester, and a child predator. You molested my friend for years! You can say whatever the hell you want to say, but your soul will burn in hell for what you stole from her." I am mad as hell, and this crap he is spilling isn't cutting it. It is my mother and I all over again, but the difference is she is my mother, I have to deal with her. This is just her uncle, and she can cut his ass off.

"Daryn don't you think I know that? I know the sins I have committed, and I have asked my Lord and Savior for forgiveness. I am letting her know that I am concerned about her soul and salvation." I am pissed to the highest level of pisstivity. I want to leap across this table and choke the shit out of him.

"What you are doing is trying to exhibit control over her again with this mind game. You are trying to manifest your apology into some kind of Jedi mind trick and turn it on Cheyenne. Well that ain't about to happen in my presence. Fuck you, and your non-apologizing ass. She has forgiven you, and her life is going well, walking around outside as a free woman while you rot your sorry pussy ass in here where you deserve. I hope some big ass man make you his bitch, bitch!"

"Let's go Cheyenne," I said standing. I am so mad I can barely control myself.

Cheyenne slams her fist on the table, and I sit back down as I see my friend gain her confidence. She goes from looking like a scared little girl to a brave woman. I want to applaud.

"You. No. longer. Have. Power. Over. Me!" Her voice is strong as she rises above her attacker and confronts him with confidence.

He went to speak, and Cheyenne cut him off. "Shut-UP!" Her voice cracks and the guards look our way, but she continues. "I came here out of the goodness of my heart, to let you know, that you no longer have dominion over me. I don't need a lecture on forgiveness, I did that a long time ago, but since you want to give me a history lesson on forgiveness why don't I give you a little history lesson on what you did to me.

"You tried to take my innocence, my dignity, and my respect for myself. You almost won. I used my body, my soul, and my integrity until I was almost used up. I hated you for what you did to me.

"It was 1 John 4:20 that got me to forgive you. If anyone says, "I love God," and hates his brother, he is a liar; for he who does not love his brother whom he has seen cannot love God whom he has not seen.

"That is why I forgave you. So, you can cut the bull-shit about me needing to forgive you for molesting me, I've already done it. Also, there is no need to write me, email me, or find me on social media. I'm good. I have forgiven you, but we don't have to stay in close contact." Cheyenne said standing, and I stood beside her. "You no longer have any hold on me. My life is fine, and it is going on. I'm free from you, and I couldn't be better."

"For what it's worth Cheyenne, I'm sorry," he finally apologizes.

"Apology accepted," Cheyenne said and turns on her heels. I follow behind her leaving him sitting at the table with his hands folded looking stupid.

We walk outside, and the fresh air hit us like a nice summer breeze on a hot day at the beach. Cheyenne bends over and grabs her knees taking in deep breaths.

"Cheyenne are you okay," I asked, and she turns her head to look up at me.

"Girl, I am more than okay. Daryn, what you did for me back there, no one has ever done for me. My mother didn't, my father didn't, and my brother didn't. No one has ever stood up for me and defended my honor." She said, and a tear fell. "I walked in the prison thinking I was the baddest bitch, until he sat in front of me. I felt myself reverting back to the 9-year-old girl he use to molest and abuse. I wanted to run and hide. The tears started to materialize.

"I remembered how he once told me, I wore my clothes tight to turn him on. He was playing his same mind tricks, turning it around to make me believe it was me, and not him. Then you spoke up for me, and put him in his place. That gave me POWER! That made me feel like I was worth something, and somebody actually cared. You helped me stand up to my bully and take back what he stole from me...My Self Worth!" She stands up straight and hugs me. "Thank you Daryn, for being my friend, and defending me." She sniffled. "You're welcome, but why are you crying." I said, and she pulled away.

"These are tears of joy! I can walk the walk, and talk the talk now, I am free. He can't hurt me anymore. I am free, to do what I want, any old time!" She sung and we both laughed. "Now let's go and get something to eat. I have been too nervous to eat the past 24 hours." We walk away, both of us stronger now than when we walked in.

We walk in a brunch restaurant and order several things off the menu.

"You still okay," I ask.

"I remember my uncle Nathan being my favorite uncle when I was growing up. When he would come over, I would run and jump into his arms and he would spin me around until I was dizzy. He would give me something every time he saw me, and my mother would say 'Between you and her father, I don't know who is spoiling her the most.'" This made Cheyenne smile. Her smile quickly fades. "Then one day he came over, and I could tell something changed. This particular day he squeezed me a little tighter, and the kiss on my forehead lingered a little longer. My spirit told me to run when he put me down, but instead I stood and stared at him. He smiled at me and gave me a dollar. Later, that night he asked me for a kiss on the lips. That memory had not haunted me until today, when I saw him. I tried to forget every God-awful moment of the things he had done to me. I was only nine when he asked me for the kiss."

"I'm sorry," was all I knew to say, and she smiled at me.

"Girl don't be sorry, I feel like I could run a marathon, and win, I am so happy now. I am on a whole other level. Trust me I'm good! He ruined me in so many ways in the past, and I refuse to let him do it to my future. I know I gave up good relationships because I thought they were too nice to protect me and keep me secure, from somebody like my uncle. I thought I had to be with a thug, or a criminal to be protected. Now I know, I deserve better. I don't need protection from him anymore. Not only did he get 10 years, but if he came my way, today I would bust him in the head to the white meat." She said and we both laugh. "He better be glad the guards were there to protect him, because when I stood up I really wanted to punch him in the face, but I thought to myself he wasn't worth it." She was still smiling.

"I'm glad you didn't because I would hate to go to prison, to visit someone, then end up an inmate," We both laugh.

"How about you? How are you doing?" she asks.

I pause for a minute, and then think, I really don't want to steal her joy. "I don't want to ruin the moment." I said.

"Nothing can ruin my moment." I smile at her. "Listen you are my friend. I know you go to mediation tomorrow, are you ready?"

"As ready as I will ever be," I respond really feeling like there is no way to prepare for this.

"Daryn, everything will work out, the way it is intended to work out. In the beginning you may not believe it, or feel it, but it will." She said.

"I hope so," I respond.

"Trust me it will. In the beginning it may feel so difficult you can barely breathe, but trust and believe, he will see you through." This is the Cheyenne from when we were little before she was weakened by her uncle. She used to be so optimistic, it is good to see some of that optimism returning.

"Thanks Cheyenne. I just don't know what to expect. I know he is asking for full custody, but I don't know if he is serious about it. I feel like he is doing this to hurt me, but how far will he go to make sure I feel that hurt?"

"Daryn, some men will go to great lengths to make a woman suffer, especially if she made him suffer. Don't let that be your focus. If all else fails, you can always go to court. There is no way a judge will take Carter away from a stable family like you and Jethro and give him to Logan, because he is angry with you." That made me smile. "Besides we can still hire Cornbread for a case of beer if all else fails." We laugh.

"You're right, I'm just tripping," I pause before I change the subject. "Abe will be here next weekend," She looks at me and smiles slightly.

"I know," she responds.

"Well, I was wondering if you could come over and run interference. The entire family will be here, and I don't want to spend the evening speaking about what is going on with Carter. I know if I have company they will not bring up the subject."

"Oh, so you're using me." She said smiling.

"No, you know you are welcome over anytime, but I really hope you come next weekend."

"Okay, okay you don't have to twist my arm." She said rolling her eyes that made me break out into a huge smile.

"Thanks girl, I don't know what I would do without you."

Our food arrives, and we have subtle conversation while we eat. We speak about nothing to personal and nothing out of the ordinary; just two friends chatting about the current events of the world.

CHAPTER FIVE

Last night Jethro went to the club, and I tossed and turned. When Jethro walked in, I pretended to be sleep. He whispered my name, but I didn't budge, even though my nose was itching. He eventually turned over and went to sleep. I couldn't take talking to Jethro about tomorrow once more. He would get so angry about the subject that I would just go silent and let him battle with himself. When he asked me what I thought about everything, my response was the same as he felt, which was a lie. Logan has a right to be in his son's life, I am just not sure, how much and how many days he deserves.

Everything is going so fast this morning. One moment we are dropping Carter off at my mom's house the next moment we are getting ready to walk into mediation and face my worse fear, speaking to Logan about Carter, in front of Jethro. I know we will have to compromise something, but Jethro and I didn't discuss a compromise. Jethro doesn't want him to have visitation at all. He thinks it will confuse him because he is so young. I think it will be better to do it now, so Carter can get use to him.

We walk in behind the attorney. Logan, his attorney, and his wife are on the opposite side of the table. There is a tall white male with thinning dirty blonde hair sitting at the head of the table. My hands are shaking so badly I put them under the table. I glance Logan's way and he is staring at me. I look away and make a conscience effort not to look back at him. Jethro is working his jaw and looking across the table like he wants to leap across it and choke Logan. I take his hand under the table to calm him down. He looks down at my hand, then up at me, and gives me a lopsided smile. This seems to calm him down a little. We look toward the head of the table when we hear talking.

"I am Julian Moore a Family Law Attorney. I will be conducting the mediation for Carter Jethro Thomas. We are recording the proceedings as well; my secretary will be taking copious notes for the meeting. Please let me know if there are any objections." He states and pauses. "Can I please have the biological father state their name?"

"Logan Miles Anderson," he said, and I look his way when he said Miles. I never knew he had a middle name.

"Can the biological mother of Carter Jethro Thomas please state their name as well," he asks.

"Daryn Monique Carter," I pause looking down at Jethro's thumb as he rubs it back and forth over my hand.

"Before we get started my client is requesting that the proceedings' take place without the presence of the step father due to his hostility toward my client." Logan's attorney states before the mediator asks another question.

"Like hell it will," Jethro blurts out, and I think, wrong response.

"What do you mean hostility toward you Logan?" I ask. I see Logan lean over and whisper something to his attorney.

"My client has stated, he would like for you, Daryn Carter, to direct all questions toward the mediator or his attorney."

"Excuse me," I said to Logan scooting to the edge of my chair.

"What is the reason this is being requested?" My attorney, the attorney Jethro's friend sent, finally spoke up, and I think he is in over his head.

"My client, Logan Miles Anderson, has requested to have the proceedings without Jethro Thomas. Every encounter they have had since he has found out Daryn Carter was pregnant, from my client, has been hostile and combative. Due to these reasons, we have concluded that we cannot have an amicable mediation with him present."

"That's bullshit!" Jethro yells out, and his attorney might as well yell checkmate.

"I need a moment with my clients," our attorney, Carson, states.

He drops down to a low whisper. "This is only part of his tactic. We could contest this, but the only people required to make this mediation successful are Daryn and Logan."

"Are you going to kick her out too?" Jethro whispers about Logan's wife. If I didn't see him say the words I would have thought it was someone else. His Brooklyn accent is in full effect. The dialect he has inherited since living in Tampa has left the building.

"We can suggest it," Carson said. We turn back to the table.

"My client has agreed to leave the meeting with Logan and Daryn if both spouses are left out of the proceedings." Carson says.

"On what grounds," his wife asks.

"The grounds that the influence of both spouses could slow down the proceedings; besides she is not vital to the negotiation of the custody hearing." Okay, maybe he is not out of his league. She looks pissed at Carson's word choice.

They huddle together, and then his wife rises so fast she almost knocks over the chair. She slings the door open and stomps out the courtroom; with a gust of wind she leaves so fast.

"May we have a small recess," Jackson, Logan's attorney asks.

"Will a fifteen-minute recess suffice," The mediator, Julian, states already looking haggard, and we just started.

"Thank you," his attorney states, and Logan follows the same path as his wife.

I stand up behind our attorney, and Jethro stands also. He wraps his arms around me.

"I don't feel comfortable leaving you alone with him," he said pulling away from me.

"I'm not alone, I have Carson." I smile trying to relieve some of the tension. He bends down to kiss me. Then he wraps his arms around me again.

"I guess I will just wait for you outside," he said.

"Or, I could call you when it is over," I smile up at him to try and lighten the mood.

"Not a chance, I don't want you to have to wait." He kisses me again. I kiss him back as passionately as I can with others in the room. I squeeze him tightly when he hugs me to reassure him there is nothing to worry about. He holds my hands, cups my face, and then turns to walk out the door. When I turn around I look into Logan's beet red face. I turn away and sit next to Carson as he sits next to Jackson looking pissed.

"The proceedings are moving right along, seems like we resolved the first conflict," the mediator said smiling and we look stone face as he tries to add a bit of humor.

"I understand you are seeking full custody Logan Anderson, is that correct."

"Yes," he responds, and I shake my head in disbelief.

"Logan, you can't be serious," I said out loud instead of in my head.

"Can you please remind your client to speak directly to the mediator or his attorney," Jackson states, and I want to punch him in the face.

"Why, when your client is sitting next to you, and can clearly hear what I am saying," I know I'm being petty, but I am pissed. How can he think he has the right to full custody of my son?

"We would like to keep these proceedings as amicable as possible," his attorney retorts. Carson leans in to speak with me.

"Don't give them ammunition," Carson whispers to me, and that got me to calm down.

"She has agreed," Carson said when he turns around.

"Great, another resolution," the mediator said and smiles. "Daryn, I see you are seeking full custody and no visitation for Logan Anderson?" Julian states, and there is Logan looking at me with disgust.

"You really think I don't deserve visitation rights for a son you kept from me for four years?" Logan directs toward me.

"Jackson, can you please have your client direct all his questions to me, or the mediator." I think I love this guy. That made me look at him with a smirk, and his face turns so red it is almost purple.

"Yes, that is correct." I said to Julian and answering Logan's questions without directing it at him. I see him rub his hand through his hair as he tries to prevent another outburst.

"The purpose of mediation is to come up with an amiable agreement since both parents are seeking full custody of Carter Jethro Thomas. We will work together to come up with a parenting plan that is suitable for all parties involved.

"I have a series of questions to ask, and we will start with you Logan Miles Anderson."

"Can you call me Logan," there was such agitation in his voice. I love it.

"Yes, of course. Logan, how many children do you have?"

"I have 4 including Carter." He said, and I can feel he is looking at me, but I didn't return his glare.

"How old are these children?"

"Brooke is 20, Hunter is 11, Bristol is 8, and Carter is 4."

"What is your current living situation and who resides in the home with you?"

"My wife and two kids, we live in a five-bedroom house in Hyde Park," he is starting to sound a little calmer as he speaks about his family.

"Where is Brooke?" Julian asks as he writes down notes.

"Brooke is at Florida State University in her senior year of college."

"How old are you currently?"

"I am 40."

"What is your education and work history?"

"I have a Master's in Business and Finance from the University of South Florida and I am a Regional Branch Manager. I have been employed with the bank for fifteen years." He seems too smug when he said this. I know I only have a high school education, but I am well accomplished in my businesses.

"What is your current drug and alcohol history, including any DUI's?" he asks, and I perk up. Logan looks uncomfortable.

"I have a DUI from 2007, and I haven't had a drink since 2014.

I have never done any drugs of any kind including smoking cigarettes." I should have known he had some type of issue with alcohol the way he uses to drink.

"What were the terms of your DUI?" Julian asked.

"I don't see the relevance since it was over ten years ago?" Jackson states.

"The relevance is in establishing a history and background for anyone that would like to be the custodial parent of Carter. We are also trying to reduce any concerns the other parent may have regarding past convictions."

"I had to perform community service hours, pay court cost, and repair a light pole that was damaged." He looked down the entire time he spoke about the DUI, I could tell he was embarrassed about it.

"We will switch gears a little. Daryn Monique Thomas I am going to ask you the same questions. Please respond to the best of your ability. How many children do you have?" "One."

"What is your current living situation and who resides with you in the home?"

"I live in a four-bedroom home with Jethro and Carter." I try to keep my responses as simple as possible.

"How old are you?"

"Thirty-one," the mediator clears his throat, and it may be because of our age difference, but I can't swear by it.

"What is your education, and work history?"

"I am currently a stay at home mom, but I own several properties."

"Can you please elaborate on those properties to establish a source of income," Julian asks.

"I have a high school diploma. I own a night club, a strip mall, and a condo that I rent out." I've never felt my high school diploma wasn't enough until today.

"Do you work at the night club or strip mall?" he asked.

"No, I have employees that manage these businesses for me,"

I saw Logan whisper something to his attorney, but his attorney didn't comment. I want to tell him to speak up.

"What is your current alcohol and drug history including any DUI's?"

"I don't drink, I don't do drugs, and I don't have any DUI's." Again, I see Logan lean over and say something to his attorney. It is starting to piss me off.

"My client has a few questions he would like to ask Mrs. Thomas," Logan's attorney interjects.

"We can get to questions later; right now, I am just trying to establish a background." The mediator responds.

"This is also to help establish some background information." There is a frustrated look on the mediator's face, and I wonder what kind of trickery Logan has up his sleeve. He knows I do not drink or do drugs.

"Okay," the mediator concedes.

"Thank you, Mrs. Thomas can you please state for us what relationship you have with a Lola Ryan?" This bitch is all I think.

"She is my mother," I respond huffing.

"Does Lola Ryan ever keep Carter unsupervised?" He asks.

"Yes," I said hesitantly.

"Can you please let us know the history of Lola Ryan's use of alcohol and drugs?"

Son of a bitch, I start to breathe hard. I pause instead of answering. My hands begin to tremble, so I place them back under the table.

"Objection," my attorney yells.

"We aren't in court," the mediator states.

"My client does not have to answer."

"My client would like a home study performed on all that are left alone with Carter; a background check, and a mental and physical health evaluation of all that are involved in child care for his son."

My attorney closes his folder and says, "We are done here, Daryn we are leaving."

"Before you leave my client would like to see his son this week. It has been four years, and he is desperate to start a relationship with him before he misses any more precious time."

"Didn't you hear? We are done here!" Carson said picking up his messenger bag to stuff his folder in it. He looks more pissed than I am.

"Gentlemen please, today we are only trying to establish a background, history, and timeline. For the sake of the protection of Carter, a case study will be performed on both parties seeking full custody, as well as background checks. There is no need to leave, we can place our focus on doing what is best for the child and proceed to find a common ground." The mediator said taking control of the meeting. I am so glad he did because I am drowning thinking about having to reveal my mother's background.

"I need a moment alone with my client," Carson said, and I look at him dumbstruck.

"We can take a fifteen-minute recess," Julian states and stands. They all leave the room together to give my attorney and me some privacy.

"Daryn, I operate a little different than some attorneys. I operate in the real world and providing the best advice for my client based on what I've seen, and what I believe to be true. I am going to give it to you straight. This may not be resolved in mediation because your child's father has taken the gloves off, and he's ready for a street fight. My advice to you is to let him see his son this week."

"Absolutely not," I interject.

"Let me explain to you why. If I become to direct, let me know, and I will sugarcoat it for you. The facts are you knew Logan was the father of Carter, and you didn't advise him. You knew his where abouts, and made no effort to contact him. You didn't give him the opportunity of visitation. Did you think Carter would be in danger if he knew his father?"

I shake my head no because I am too embarrassed to answer out loud.

"Did you think Logan would cause his son any harm or become violent toward him, or you?" he asks.

Again, I shake my head no.

"The judge will see it as a selfish act, not letting Mr. Anderson know the whereabouts of his son. We need the judge to see that despite the way you started out with Carter, you are willing to set your differences aside, and act in the best interest of the child. Should we have to take this case to trial it will look better to the judge, but you must trust me. We need to bend on this. You need to let him see Carter this week." I could tell he was sincere the way he looks in my eyes the entire time he is speaking, and from the touch on my arm for moral support. I unwillingly shake my head yes. I don't know how to tell Jethro about this.

"When they return I will do all the talking, we will be out of here in less than ten minutes. I can tell his attorney has a bag of tricks up his sleeve. We will need to meet again tomorrow so you can go over the details about Lola Ryan. I need you to be as candid with me as possible, that is if you want me to be the attorney on this case." Despite Jethro wanting us to use his friend, I am going to stick with Carson. I nod my head yes.

They enter the room, and I sit in silence.

"Mrs. Thomas has agreed to a meeting, in a public domain, of our choosing, Friday."

"Tuesday," his attorney states.

"Friday, take it or leave it," Carson states without hesitation. "Here is the location, and the visit will be supervised. Mr. Anderson is not to mention he is the father."

"My client has waited 4 years he will not wait any longer." Jackson states with so much passion you would have thought Carter was his son.

"Take it or leave it," Carson states, and I think to myself hot damn. I didn't realize my attorney had this ruthlessness in him. He looks to calm and mild mannered.

"Daryn, you are being impossible," Logan speaks out, and I

gaze at him.

"Please have your client direct all questions to the mediator or attorneys." Carson interjects. My thoughts are to say payback is a bitch, but no need. The look on Logan's face is all I need to feel vindicated.

"No, deal, and we will not bend on this."

"If you don't bend, it will be longer before Mr. Anderson can see his son." The attorneys were going back and forth like a tennis ball.

"Got dammit Daryn! You had every opportunity to tell me about my son. Now you are going to continue to deny me what is rightfully mine!" Logan yells, and I look at Carson. I knew Logan couldn't abide by his own rules. I whisper to Carson, and he said it is up to me, that my declaration wouldn't do anything to damage my case.

I scoot to the edge of my chair and fold my hands in front of me before I speak. I make sure to use a calm, although a bit shaky, tone.

"Mr. Anderson, I am aware that you are eager to advise Carter that you are his biological father. My in-laws will be in town this weekend, and I would like the courtesy of providing them with what is going on before we explain to Carter who his biological father is." I didn't want the message lost in translation, so I felt it was better to speak on my own behalf. Logan leans over to his attorney to speak. I sit thinking what a mess. I thought I was doing the right thing by keeping Carter's biological father a secret. I thought I was protecting my son. I thought we were charting a new path for my life not to end up like my mom, but all I really did was make a mess of things. I have no idea how to explain to Carter Jethro is not his real father, and this man he has never seen before is his actual father. Lord help me, please.

"My client has agreed."

"Outstanding, Julian states. Thank you for being amicable and completing the first stage of mediation. We will reconvene in two weeks to continue with the custody agreement for Carter Jethro Thomas." Julian states.

We stand, and Logan and his attorney leave the office. My attorney gives me a copy of everything regarding our supervised meeting, and a card with our appointment time on it.

I walk into the restroom and exhale. I stare at myself in the mirror. It looks like I've aged 10 years since I received the paperwork for the paternity test. I wash my hands and turn to leave. As I'm leaving Logan is walking in to turn and go into the men's room when he sees me. I try to continue walking, but he steps in my path. I back away from him, but he steps into my space cornering me against the wall. I feel weak and vulnerable as he stares at me. I see my son staring back at me as I look into his eyes. The resemblance is uncanny.

"Why did you do it Daryn?" I immediately look down. "It's a simple question, and you owe me that much."

"You have your family, and I didn't want to complicate things any further with you and your wife." I clutch my purse to my chest for support.

"Daryn I asked you to let me know if you were pregnant, but you didn't. Why didn't you tell me?" His voice is ire calm, but the shade of red he is turning is betraying the way he really feels.

"I'm so sorry Logan; I really thought I was doing the right thing. I thought it was the best for everyone." I hold my breath he is so close it is making me uncomfortable.

"How could keeping me from my son be doing what is best for me? How did you justify to yourself that this was the right thing for Carter and me? How could you not tell me and let me make the decision? You took all those decisions from me.

"You took every first, every birthday, and every moment for the first four years of his life away from me. Do you have any idea how that makes me feel? Do you have any idea how Carter is going to feel?" His agitation is now coming out in his voice.

"Logan, you know my background. I didn't want my son to grow up the bastard son of a married man. It was best for all of us if you weren't involved. He's happy Logan."

"He's happy! So, tell me something Daryn were you ever going to tell me?"

"When the time was right?" As soon as the words came out of my mouth I saw a shift in his eyes.

"WHEN DID YOU THINK THE TIME WOULD BE RIGHT!?!" He shouts in my face, and that's when the tears start to mount in my eyes like a helpless defenseless puppy.

"Ma'am, is everything okay," some thick white guy said from behind Logan's back.

"Everything is fine," Logan said without turning around.

"I'm fine," I said trying to wipe my eyes.

"We could have been a family! Just know, everything that is about to happen, you brought on yourself," Logan said, and walks off leaving me crying. I rush back into the restroom to pull myself together. The last thing I need is to walk out and let Jethro see my mascara stained face. The tears are because I know what he is saying is true, and I had no right. I don't know when I planned to tell Logan. I guess, when Carter started to ask questions about his differences I would have told him.

I wash my face and touch up my make-up. My eyes are still red, but there is nothing I can do about that.

When I make it downstairs Jethro is drinking a Gatorade.

"Hey," he said walking up to me. "Have you been crying?" I should have known he would know. Jethro is so attuned to everything about me.

"Maybe a little," I respond.

"Why? What happened?" he asks looking like he's trying to control his temper.

"It was just a difficult long process." He looks at me, as if he knows I was leaving something out. He kisses me on the forehead, lace our fingers together, and we start walking outside.

"How did it go?" he asks. I know I would have been asking the same questions, but right now I want to get out of here, and not think about what just transpired in mediation.

"Can we get out of here, and I will explain it to you on the way home?"

"Of course," Jethro said with a lopsided smile. I secretly thank God, we did not run into Logan again.

We ride in silence to my mom's house to pick up Carter. I know he is just buying time before he starts interrogating me with a list of questions. I don't know how to tell him about Logan's upcoming visit with Carter, no matter how many times I play the scenario in my head. It all ends with Jethro becoming irate and blowing his lid. We pull up to my mom's and we both get out.

She opens the door as soon as we walk up as if she is expecting us.

"Hello Daryn, Jethro. Daryn can I speak with you a minute in my room," she says when we walk in. She doesn't wait for me to respond she walks to her bedroom. Jethro picks up Carter and hugs him as I walk to the back with my mom. I've been avoiding this talk for a while; I guess I can't avoid it any longer.

"Daryn what is going on? You keep dropping Carter off and coming over here dressed like you are going to a funeral. I won't take anything but you telling me the truth right now."

I sit on the bed and exhale. Tears sprang to my eyes. My weakness is not knowing how to sugarcoat.

"We saw Logan a few months ago. He ordered a DNA test. Now he is seeking custody of Carter."

"Oh my God," she said as she sat next to me.

"We went to our first mediation today." I sit fidgeting.

"I'm sorry. I knew something was going on the way you were dressing and acting. I love my grandson, and I will keep him whenever you need me to, but don't shut me out Daryn. I've missed enough of your life. I don't want to miss anymore.

"There is no judgment here. I have enough sins to cover a small city. God knows I'm no angel. I know you did what you thought was right. God knows I understand that. We've all been there Daryn."

"It's just that, I guess I didn't really think it through that much. I didn't really think about what the repercussions would be the day we had to tell Logan, or how Logan would feel."

"Daryn no need to think about it now. It's all said and done."

I stand to leave. I know if I don't step out the room soon Jethro will have more questions to ask.

"Do you have to leave so soon? I don't have to be to work until four." She said.

"Yeah, Jethro has to go to work."

She stands, and hugs me. It is nice to have my mother act like my mother. I smile and walk out to leave with Jethro and Carter.

Jethro has a meeting at work, and is only able to drop us off. He needs to make it into work as soon as possible. I know it is killing him to know what happened, but we couldn't discuss it with Carter in the car. I am happy for more time to figure out how to tell Jethro the agreement I made with Logan.

"Carter," I stare at him trying to think of a way to let him know the man he thinks is his father, is not his father. I squat down to his level.

"What is it mom, I was watching Ninja Turtles?" I look at him, and feel the sting of tears. I can't do it. I can't start taking his innocence away so soon. It must be a better way.

"Nothing, you can go back and watch TV, but before you do, can I have a hug?" I ask, and I might have squeezed him a little tighter than necessary.

Carter ran to his room, and then my phone rang.

"Hey," I say to Jethro.

"Hey, my mom just called, she wants to know if it was okay if they come a day early and stay one night with us. The hotel they booked for the weekend, doesn't have any vacancy's for Thursday." They usually stay with us when they come into town, but this time Abe rented a penthouse on the beach, and invited everyone including us. If they are here Thursday, I will have to explain where I am taking Carter.

"Of course," I respond.

"Okay great, well I love you." He said.

"I love you too," I said and hang up.

I know he would like to know what is going on, but this is not the type of conversation we should have over the phone.

I plop on the sofa to watch old movies and try and think of a way to tell Jethro what happened that will not spark an argument for not "sticking to the plan."

CHAPTER SIX

Jethro is later than normal getting home. He had one person out on vacation and another person call in sick. When he got home, Carter runs to hug him. I wonder if Carter will run into his arms when he finds out Jethro is not his biological dad.

"Dad, can we play your PlayStation?" he begs.

"Maybe later, mommy and I have a few things to discuss right now. How was your day?" he asks.

"Good, can I go to my room now?" Jethro sits Carter down and he runs to his room.

"Are you hungry?" I ask.

"Nah, I had something to eat at the office." He starts loosening his tie and takes off his jacket. He unbuttons a few buttons on his shirt, and then sits next to me on the sofa.

"So, how did it go?" he asks.

"There were a lot of questions like the ones I was asked by your friend the attorney, and there was a lot of emotions in the room."

"Questions like what?" he asks.

"There were questions about our backgrounds, and where we live, and how many people are in our home, where I work, and if we have other children." I said.

"Oh, how did he answer?"

"He was almost the model citizen until he had to mention that he had a DUI about ten years ago."

"Humph," Jethro grunts, but didn't remark. "That should help us. Anything else?" I take a deep breath and let it out. It is time to put my big drawls on.

"They asked who my mom is and started asking for a case study on her."

"Who?" Jethro said cutting me off.

"Logan's attorney?"

"What is the relevance of that?" I almost smile at Jethro's legal term.

"He wanted a case study done on anyone that babysits Carter or lives with him, but Carson shut that down."

"Good for Carson," Jethro was now sitting back and looking more relax.

"Um I knew where Logan was going with this. He knew my mom was once on drugs. My attorney was packing up to leave because he thought Jackson, Logan's attorney, was hitting below the belt. Jackson stated he was willing to take it to court, and expose how I kept Carter from him. Then he said…he wanted to see Carter this week to start the bonding process." I rambled.

"What?" Jethro said sitting up. That makes me nervous, and my heart speed up.

"Carson thinks it will be best if I agree to the meeting between Logan and Carter. When we go to court, I can prove we are trying to work things out with Logan, although I didn't tell him about Carter for four years. He agreed not to tell Carter he is his biological father." I said slowly, as I watch the tension in Jethro's jaw; that eternal sign that he's mad or frustrated. He sits still not speaking for a while. I almost said "say something," but I gave him a moment to digest everything I told him.

"Where will this meeting take place?" he asks too calmly.

"We are meeting at a location my attorney specified."

"I want to go," he said. I know I need to choose my words very carefully.

"Jethro, I know you want what is best for Carter and me. You have been the epitome of what a husband, and father should be. When I watch the two of you together I wish I'd had a father that treated me the way you treat Carter. You treat him, as if you were the one that fathered him. I couldn't have asked for a better father for Carter, than you. I wish biologically he was yours. I wish this day had never come, but it has. I wish he would have just let it go, but he didn't. Whether we choose to delay when he meets Carter, or whether we do it Friday, the inevitable is going to happen. There is no judge that would deny him the right to be a part of Carter's life, since he poses no threat." I try my best to get him to see why I should do it. He stands abruptly, and I stand with him.

"I'm going to go and shower," he said holding his head down as he walks past me. I follow him into the closet as he gets undressed.

"I'm sorry Jethro."

"No need to be sorry. You did what you thought was best." He was standing in his boxers. When he tries to go around me I wrap my arms around his neck and kiss him deeply. I figure we have at least twenty minutes before Carter comes knocking on the door.

I've never work so hard in my life in the bedroom. I nearly choked to death trying to take as much of Jethro in my mouth as possible. I throw it back hard as possible as he enters me between my legs and throws my legs up in the air. I yell louder and ride him harder just to prove to him that he has nothing to worry about. I let him pound my pussy and take his dick as he beats me up with it. I am the aggressor, and I am never the aggressor when it comes to sex with Jethro. I'm sure that makes him happy. The scowl on his face has now been replaced by a smile, and I know I've done my job well. Now I will have to keep this up for the rest of the week

"Where are you going?" I ask as he scoots out of bed.

"I need to go and check on our son. He's too quiet." Before he is out the room I am asleep.

Jethro and I meet with the attorney regarding the visit with Logan. I try desperately to go without him, but nothing I say convinces him it isn't a good idea. He takes it better than I thought, even when I tell him I decided to keep Carson as my attorney. Jethro tells me that is a better choice because Carson has a lighter case load, and can dedicate more of his time to my case.

The days seem long as I tip toe around Jethro like I am on eggshells. I have to handle him with kid gloves, and I think he knows it by the amount of sex we are having. When he initiates I comply. I am grateful that his family is coming so he can have someone else to entertain him. I am exhausted and sore.

Jethro and Carter leave to meet his family at the airport. Cheyenne calls to let me know she is on her way up.

"Hello," I said opening the door for Cheyenne. I think uh, oh, as I look at the way Cheyenne is dressed.

"What?" she said smiling. She knows what she is doing.

"Nice outfit," I said staring at her barely their shorts and half top.

"Thank you, just a little something I threw on," we laugh.

"Thank you for coming. I didn't feel like entertaining them the whole time they are here. You know you are so much better than me at small talk."

"Gurl, don't mention it."

"You want something to drink or eat?" I ask.

"Nah," she responds.

Not even five minutes later the door is opening, and Jethro is entering with his family and another female guest. I look at the woman near Abe and shake my head. I wish somebody would have told me Abe was bringing a house guest.

"The fuck," Cheyenne said, and I hope no one heard her. "Who the fuck is this bitch?" Cheyenne says with so much base Abe looks our way. They definitely heard that. She marches over to Abe. "Who is this?" Cheyenne said directly to Abe. I hold my head down and shake it.

"This is Au-gus-tin-ha," Abe said pronouncing every syllable. As Abe says it, the girl puts her hand around Abe's bicep.

"You can't even spell Augustinha," Cheyenne shoots back with rage.

"Um Cheyenne you remember Jethro and Abe parents?" I ask trying to switch gears.

"Oh, where are my manners. Of course, I do. Hello Mr. and Mrs. Thomas." She walks over to hug them.

"Oh Mrs. Thomas, have you lost weight!" Cheyenne is holding

her arms out like she is examining her. Jethro's mom is blushing from here to the moon, and acting as if she didn't hear Cheyenne's profanity.

"Yeah, I've lost thirty pounds," she said beaming back at Cheyenne. Cheyenne always has a way with parents. "Thank you for noticing," she said looking at me.

"I would have noticed eventually," I said, and went over to hug them also.

"Yes, me and senior are getting ready for his retirement!" she said smiling.

"Retirement! pops you didn't tell me you were thinking about retiring," Jethro said as they all start walking towards the den. I send a special thank you to God, because this could have been so much worse.

Cheyenne is still mean mugging Abe, and the girl he brought with him. I have no idea what to say.

"Yeah, your mom and I finally finished paying off the house. I have been driving for the city now for 30 years. I think it is about time your mama and I see the world, and maybe move closer to you guys," Jethro is smiling so hard he might split in half.

"Seriously dad!" Jethro said with excitement.

"Yeah, seriously! After Abe said he was looking for a home here, we said we might do the same thing."

"Yeah, we went by a home before we came here." Abe chimed in, and why did he do that.

"Who the fuck is we," Cheyenne shot back, and that's when I jumped off the couch.

"Anyone want something to drink," I said, and a few people asked.

I asked Cheyenne to help me in the kitchen.

"I'm sorry Cheyenne I didn't know." I didn't want her to believe I was using her or setting her up.

"Oh, it's not your fault, it is that bastards' fault for not telling me. Did you see all that fake shit on her?"

"Cheyenne behave," I said smiling.

"Fake tities, fake ass, and it looks like fake lips," she said imitating her with her hand motions. Abe walks into the kitchen. Why did he do that?

"I didn't know you were going to be here," he said.

"It's cool," Cheyenne said.

"If it's cool, why did you respond that way?" Abe asked.

"You're right, it's not cool. I've talked to you on several occasions, and you never once mentioned you had a girlfriend," Cheyenne said in a loud whisper.

"The subject never came up," he said nonchalantly. "Besides she is only here until Saturday, then she is flying back."

"So, how long ya'll been fucking," Abe laughs, but Cheyenne continues, "And does she know about our late-night conversations?"

"Cheyenne, you wanted to be friends, and besides nothing happened between us."

"I've snap chatted naked photos to you, and you have snap chatted naked photos to me."

"Allegedly," he said. I stand in shocked silence hearing this new revelation about them.

"What the hell you mean allegedly," Cheyenne yells in a loud whisper.

"They were only from the neck down."

"They have your tattoos on them," she shoots back.

"Allegedly," Abe responded.

Cheyenne hit him, and he shivers.

"I knew you couldn't keep your hands off me," Abe said.

"Shut-up, and move," Cheyenne is mad as fire when she walks around Abe. I hope she doesn't do something stupid since she is heading to the living room with glasses of wine. When I walk in the living room Abe's girlfriend is standing with her mouth open and shaking out here hands. Cheyenne spilled a glass of red wine on her all white dress. I shake my head as the woman looks at Cheyenne, she knows she did it on purpose.

She starts speaking in some random language.

"What did your bitch say to me?" Cheyenne yells standing tall in front of Augustina, but the question was addressed to Abe.

"Hell, if I know, I don't speak Portuguese, but it couldn't have been anything good." I can't believe Abe is being an instigator. It is as if he likes it.

"I will mop the floor up with your ass!" Cheyenne is saying, Jethro steps in since Abe decides to be a spectator.

"Ladies, I'm sure it will be okay. We have a restroom down the hall you can change in," Jethro shows her where to go.

The girl storms in the back not taking her eyes off Cheyenne.

"Cheyenne that was foul what you did," Abe said sipping on his Hennessey.

"Foul what I did! How about what you did by bringing her here! How foul was that?"

"How, was what I did foul?"

"Abe, you just asked me two nights ago, when you come here, can you see me."

"Allegedly, I asked to see you."

"You know what Abe, I don't give 2 fucks about you or her!" Cheyenne shouts, and I can tell she is about to lose her shit.

"Then do you give three fucks!" Cheyenne pushes Abe in the chest, and he stands strong un-phased by her touch. He is staring her deep in the eyes as if he is telling her don't keep challenging him.

"I really don't understand how you can be one person one minute, then another person the next minute. You ain't shit Abe, and you know it!"

"Cheyenne don't try and act like this is all on me. You are the one that keeps putting me off. You think I'm supposed to just pause and wait to see if you ever figure it out!"

"Abe just get away from me."

"Son, let's go." Mr. Thomas said as we all saw the look in Abe's eyes. He was following her because he was about to start something. They walk in the back.

"Daryn do you have something I can get this stain out with." Jethro's mom interjects. For one moment I'd forgotten they were here.

"Daryn you have some interesting friends," Jethro's mom chimed in.

"I'm sure she didn't mean it." I pull Cheyenne to the side and whisper, "What happened?"

"I was handing her the glass, and I thought she had it. I let it go, and it slipped through her fingers and wasted all over her dress." Cheyenne is being so nonchalant. It makes me think she isn't remorseful, and it might have been purposeful. I know that wine will never come out of the white dress she had on.

"Cheyenne,"

"I swear on my Uncle Nathan life." I look at her and we both laugh.

"Seriously, your uncle in prison. You hate him."

"I certainly don't hate him, but I don't care for him either. Look Daryn, she had this smirk on her face like she was looking down on me, as if I am the help. That pissed me off, so the glass may have slipped out of my hands to teach her a lesson."

"Cheyenne, really," I was looking at her in shock. I can't believe she just admitted to me she did it on purpose.

"What Daryn, I didn't appreciate how she was looking at me like she was better than me."

"Oh Lord and look how you spoke in front of Abe's mom. She's an elder in her church."

"That part, I'm sorry about, but that bitch I don't give a damn how she feels. I'm just going to go, but before I do, I want to apologize to Mr. and Mrs. Thomas."

We walk towards Abe mom.

"Mrs. Thomas, I am leaving, I want to let you know I am really sorry for the way I behaved, and the way I spoke in front of you, it was rude and disrespectful. What can I say, God is still working on me?"

"It's okay sweetie, he is working on us all. Please don't leave on my account; I'm sure you have learned your lesson."

"No, I don't want to ruin anymore of the night."

"Cheyenne, you are not ruining the night. We haven't had this much fun since Daryn cursed the whole family out," Mrs. Thomas said laughing.

"I thought we agreed to forgive and forget." I chime in.

"We did forgive Daryn, but nowhere in the bible does it say forget. We have to remember just in case you flip out again, we know what is going on."

"It won't happen again Mrs. Thomas, I am better because of your prayers." I chime in.

"Daryn, sarcasm will get you nowhere." I laugh.

"I don't think Abe wants me here." Cheyenne says seriously.

"You can be my guest," Mrs. Thomas says and lace her arm around Cheyenne's and walks her to the sofa.

"My son is not serious about this girl, I've never laid eyes on her until he pulled up at the airport with her. Trust and believe, he brought this girl in hopes of making you jealous, and you fell right in his trap.

"Stay, enjoy yourself, and show him you can be the better person."

"I don't know if I can I am pretty pis... I meant upset with him."

"It's okay to be upset, we aren't perfect honey. Just ignore him. I assure you, he will be more upset about that, than anything. He hates to be ignored." Cheyenne smiles and nods at Mr. Thomas.

"Why didn't I get any of this advice when I was dating your son?" I plop on the chair as Jethro walks from the back, with Carter and his niece.

"Daryn when I met you, you were already married, and besides you got the good one. All you need to do is realize it."

"What are you ladies talking about? Cheyenne you still here?" Jethro said looking confused.

"Yes, she is, she is my guest, and you need to treat her like one."

"Yes ma'am."

"See what I mean, the good one. Abe would have argued with me until I was worn out." Mrs. Thomas said.

"Where's Pop?"

"In the back with Abe," I told Jethro.

"Okay, let me go and see what is going on." As Jethro is walking in the back, Abe and his father come from the back. Cheyenne tried to ignore Abe staring, but he came and sat right next to her.

"I shouldn't have brought her here." He said looking at Cheyenne.

"No, you shouldn't have," Cheyenne said getting up. It causes Abe to smile.

"No, you are sorry?"

"Sorry for what," she said turning around to face him.

"You really don't know?"

"No," Cheyenne responds crossing her arms.

"Forget about it," he said and walks toward the back.

He returns a few moments later with Augustina.

"We are going to find a hotel tonight." Abe announces.

"No, you're only here for the weekend," Jethro said approaching him.

"You don't have to leave, I will," Cheyenne said grabbing her purse and heading toward the door. I follow behind her.

"Cheyenne," I call out as she walks outside.

"It's cool," she says as she turns around, and I can see the tears swimming in her eyes.

"Don't go please," I ask her.

"Daryn, you and I both know, it is in the best interest of all, if I leave." Then out walks Abe.

"Abe go away," Cheyenne said turning around.

"Can I please talk to you a minute."

"No," Cheyenne says with her back to him.

"Cheyenne, I promise you, I didn't know you would be here

tonight. You told me you had to work." Cheyenne swung around, her eyes red from unshed tears.

"So that makes it right!"

"Cheyenne, you told me you didn't want me."

"Abe, you are such a liar. I told you I needed to get my life together before I start a relationship. I had to figure some things out."

"Okay, figure them out, but don't get mad when I move on."

"Fuck you Abe!"

"I wish you would." Abe retorts, then I stand between them. I can see the look of murder in Cheyenne eyes and I know this isn't going to end well.

"Abe," Jethro calls out the door and I yell out a Thank God! Jethro jogs over to interrupt the stare down between Abe and Cheyenne.

"This is bullshit," Abe says.

"Whatever Abe, do whatever you like, I'm done." Cheyenne said and walks off. I think about following Cheyenne, but I know she needs space.

I feel a gust of wind as Abe walks past me following Cheyenne. Jethro jogs to get in front of him.

"Come on Abe let's go back in the house, give her some time, you are only making things worse."

"That's your wife over there, stay out of me and mine." Abe says pointing to me, and I hear the roar of Cheyenne's engine. Jethro is able to stall him enough, so she can leave.

"This is bullshit, I just wanted to talk to her, and straighten things out." Abe said raising his voice to Jethro.

"You really think you were going to do that tonight?" Jethro is looking at him like don't be ridiculous.

"Whatever," Abe said and sucks his teeth. "I was making sure Cheyenne was okay. That's it. Ya'll act like I'm about to do something to her." He finishes and heads toward the house.

"He's definitely going to text her." Jethro said putting his arms around me.

"Where's his girlfriend?"

"She was sitting on the couch when he went out the door. She asked him where he was going, and he didn't answer. When Abe get in this type of mood only he, can get himself out of it."

"Maybe you should have him say the alphabet backwards." Jethro laughs.

"My wife made a funny. He would probably try and fight me if I suggested anything but calling Cheyenne."

"He was leaving, anyway."

"Shit that was a show for that girl. He knew mama would have begged him to stay, then he would have stayed. He gambled on Cheyenne standing her ground and staying but lost that bet."

"Are you serious?"

"Yeah, I know my brother. He doesn't care about that girl. He doesn't care what she thinks or how she feels. If he did he wouldn't have come out here chasing after Cheyenne. He wants Cheyenne and it pisses him off every time he sees her that she won't be with him."

"Your brother got issues."

"Yep," Jethro said and kisses me on the lips.

We walk back inside, and I send Cheyenne a text.

Please let me know you are okay.

Not shortly after

I'm perfectly alright. I'm not going to let Abe steal my joy.

I send her a smiley face then join in the conversation with the rest of the family.

CHAPTER SEVEN

I hope we don't run into any of Jethro's family, I wake Carter as gently as possible without disturbing his cousin. I dress Carter in a white polo, khaki shorts, and Sperry's. I wish his cast could have been removed before we meet with Logan. The last thing I need to do is give him more ammunition to sue me for full custody.

"You ready son," I whispered squatting down to his level.

"Ready for my surprise mommy," he said smiling.

My heart is beating rapidly, and I can't get it to calm down. The moment of truth awaits.

We walk out the room and Jethro is standing by the sink. I fix him a thermos of coffee, and me a cup.

"You sure you don't want me to drive you?" He asks.

"Yes, I'm sure, we will be done before you get off."

"Okay," he said as I hand him the thermos. "I will be at the hotel waiting for you and Carter." He kisses me, hugs Carter, and is out the door.

Carter and I drive to the centralized location; a clubhouse located in Hyde Park and owned by my attorney. We walk in and Logan is already here. He looks at Carter and his face splits into a grin.

"Hello Daryn," he said walking up wearing an outfit almost identical to Carter's.

"Hi Logan," I respond. There is a lady in the room with us; I guess she is here to make sure we behave. She looks too small to resume any kind of order if we get out of line. We are scheduled to be with Logan from 10am to 5pm. That is going to make for a long day, and I'm not sure I'm up for it. The way he's looking at Carter, and the way his face is lighting up, makes me feel a tinge of guilt for keeping him from his son.

"Hey bud," Logan said bending down.

"Mommy who is this again," Carter said.

"I'm your dad," Logan blurts out, and my mouth drops open in horror.

"We're leaving," I bite out. I grab Carter's hand and start dragging him behind me. Logan ran in front of me.

"Daryn I can't pretend anymore. I can't deny him another second. I won't deny him another second. He looks more like me than my son with my wife. Don't run away please." His eyes are bloodshot, and tear filled.

"We made an agreement, you breached that agreement." I shot back at him pissed off at what he did.

"Daryn it has been four years, you took four years from me, and I refuse to let another moment go by without him knowing. I didn't plan to tell him, but when I saw him, and he asked me, I couldn't lie. I can't deny him any further. He's flesh of my flesh, and blood of my blood, he deserves to know, and I deserve to be his father." He said, and tears start flowing from his eyes. He turns around using his full palm to wipe his face. I pause and try to calm down. I am shaking I am so upset. He is right, but he still shouldn't have said it to Carter that way.

"Mom, what does he mean? I already have a dad," Carter said with a puzzled look on his face. I pull him to a table and sit him in a chair. Logan comes and sits down beside us. I don't know what to say. I press my palm against my forehead trying to search for the right words.

When Logan notices how difficult a time I'm having trying to put the words together to explain his comment he starts to explain. "Carter sometimes there are kids in life that are really special, and fortunate enough to have two dads. You are special enough to have more than one dad. You have your dad that lives with you, Jethro, and you have your other dad that you can visit. I am your dad that you can visit."

"But I only want one dad," Carter responds.

"One dad is cool, but two dads are cooler. You know why?"

"Why?" Carter asks looking back at me confused.

"Because you get two of everything; two birthdays, two Christmases, two presents," he is smiling while he is saying it, but my son is still confused. I have no idea what to say.

"I don't understand," he said.

"It is okay to be confused. You will understand more as time goes on," I said.

"Hey, when is your birthday," Logan asks.

"October 3rd," he said.

"Great, that is just a few weeks away. I believe I owe you at least 4 years' worth of presents. Why don't we go to the Disney store and we can pick them out?" Logan said standing.

"Really!!!" Carter shouts excited.

"Logan, you agreed to visit here."

"I agreed to meet you here; I didn't agree to stay here the full time." He says to me sternly. He looks back at Carter and smiles. "Carter, you ready to go and get your presents?" This mother...

"Carter, we can't," I said, and his face fell.

"Aw mom, why not? He said he was going to get me presents. Please mom, please." Now I'm the bad parent.

"Okay," I concede.

"We can take my car," he said walking outside.

"I can drive," I said when I walk next to him.

"Why can't you ride with me?"

"Carter needs his booster seat."

"I got him one, let's go," he said opening his car door. Carter jumps in the backseat and starts buckling the booster seat. It seems I am outnumbered. He opens the front door for me, and against my better judgment I get in.

"Hey Carter, what happened to your arm," he asks, and I give him a sideways glance.

"He fell," I answer for him, and he knows the way I say it to drop the subject.

"I broke my arm too, when I was young, sliding into home plate," he said.

"I play baseball with my dad," Carter said, and that wipes the smile off Logan's face.

He clears his throat then starts asking Carter questions like, what are his favorite superheroes; his favorite color; his hobbies; and anything else he thought he'd missed a part of until we make it to International Mall.

Logan is all smiles, and I am hoping my compliance will make him drop this custody suit.

We walk in to the play area.

"Mom, can I play please," Carter begs.

"Of course, bud," I give him a dirty look.

"Just for a moment," Logan said, and we sit while Carter starts climbing the toys.

There have been several moments of silence between us.

"You know I came back," he said out of the blue.

"Excuse me," I reply crossing my legs and looking his way.

"I came back after that night you put me out. I came back about 4 days later to check on you. I had just pulled up when I saw you coming out the building in a panic. You looked a mess. You jumped in your car and sped off. Later, I found out from Amber your mom had a heart attack. I knew the last thing you needed was the added stress of me trying to pressure you back into a relationship. That's when I decided it was better if I backed off."

"I tried calling you, but you changed your number," I volunteered. Something calms in me knowing he at least tried to check on me.

"Yeah, when I went back home one of the first things she did was insist I change my phone number. We were arguing every single day when I returned. Minor things turned into major arguments. I knew I'd made the wrong decision, and I came to see you, to see if there was a way we could try again. I was miserable when I went home, and I wanted that feeling I felt with you back. I still wasn't ready to give up on us.

"She came home that same night, and told me about her friend Lola Ryan, as if I didn't know her. I knew you were in no condition to discuss us getting back together, so I backed off. Amber and I argued for three full months because I told her I missed you. I missed you so got damn bad. I would have dreams so real about you that I would wake up thinking you were next to me.

"I was drinking worse than ever. I was drinking on the job, on the way home; I was trying to numb the pain of missing you. She asked me one day why I was so miserable, and I yelled at her 'because I miss her.' I've never seen someone cry as agonizingly as she cried when I screamed those words at her.

"I guess we both thought once I came home everything would be okay, but I didn't consider how much I would miss you. I was thinking I would get over you since we were apart, but the distance between us just seemed to intensify how much I wanted you."

"I missed you too, but I knew you going back was for the better. We were ruining more lives than just your wife's. We were also ruining the lives of your kids."

"When I came to your condo after seeing your photo in Jethro's office, I still didn't know if you were pregnant. I thought you probably got married because you were pregnant, and you didn't want to raise a child alone. I'd convinced myself there was no way you could love Jethro that soon. When I hugged you, I didn't feel a baby bump. Your stomach was still flat. I instantly gave up on the fact that you were pregnant.

"When I saw you four years later sitting at the table outside, and I stopped to say high I had no idea a little boy would come running out the ice cream parlor and call you mom. It messed my mind up. I couldn't function. I didn't get a good look at him, but I saw his eyes, and I knew he was mine. I knew it with everything in my soul, even before the paternity test he was 100% mine.

"When I got home that night I wanted a drink so bad. We had gotten rid of all the liquor in the house, except this bottle of brandy my dad had given me. I went to open it, and Amber said if I take one sip she was taking the kids and leaving.

"She begged me to tell her what was going on. Without thinking I said, I just saw my son. She was confused. I sat her down and told her, you were the woman I left her for. I explained to her that we'd discussed the likelihood you were pregnant before I left, but you never contacted me. I said I saw the eyes of the little boy with you, and I knew that was my son, and I had to find him.

"She was extremely heartbroken. Not only did she have to live with the fact that I had an affair, now she must deal with the fact that I had a child as well. She still hasn't forgiven me, but I assured her I have no feelings for you. She told me she couldn't deal with me having another child. I told her I couldn't deny my son with you, any more than I could deny my children with her. She respects it, and the choices I made, but it is still a touchy subject."

"I think it's time we go to the Disney store, so we can make it back to the club house." I'd heard enough, and we are entering dangerous territory. I already feel as if he has shared too much.

"I have him until five today. We still have time." He said standing also.

"I'm not denying you the time to spend with Carter; I just think we need to get on with everything, so we can get back. We have plans today." I still couldn't say 'your son' to Logan. I know beyond a shadow of a doubt he is Carter's dad, but it is too awkward for me to say the title out loud.

"Oh yeah, what kind of plans he asked." I can feel myself becoming uncomfortable with our conversation, and I need to regain some type of control.

"That's irrelevant. Come on Carter," he ran over and grabs my hand, and Logan grabs his other hand. He looks at Logan's hand, but didn't pull away. We are walking in the mall like a family, and the guilt I feel is starting to become too overwhelming. I am glad when we make it to the Disney store, Carter let go of our hands, so he can pick up a toy.

Whatever Carter wants Logan purchases.

"Who's your favorite superhero?" Logan asked.

"Black Panther," He responds.

Logan crosses his arms over his chest and says "Wakanda

forever," Carter opens his mouth and his eyes go wide, while I laugh.

"You know him," Carter said.

"I don't know him, but I've seen the movie. Let's see if we can find you a black panther suit."

"This is the best day ever!" He shouts, and Logan looks like he just hit the lotto he's smiling so hard.

They walk around the store purchasing everything Black Panther, including pajamas. I don't know how I am going to explain all this crap to Jethro.

"Are you hungry bud," Logan asked Carter.

"Yeah!" Carter exclaims.

"You like pizza," Logan asked with a face splitting grin.

"Yeah, it's Michelangelo favorite food!"

"Michelangelo?" Logan asks.

"Yeah, he's my favorite ninja turtle!"

We both laugh.

"We can eat at the California Pizza Kitchen," Logan said.

"Does your wife know what you were planning today?" I am getting a little pissed off at the way I feel. He is bullying me into spending time with him. I know I should approach the situation delicately because I'm hoping when it is all said and done we can both come up with an agreement that doesn't involve him seeking custody.

"She knows I came to visit my son."

"No, does she know that we are at the mall, like a family, while you buy Carter everything he wants and then some."

"No, but I told her I wanted it to be more like a celebration and not like a stuffy meeting."

"Do you think she would be okay with all this?" I ask with thick emotions.

"I honestly haven't thought about it, but she knows she can't come between my son and me. I wanted to have a good time with him, and not have people dictate to me what we could and could not do for our first meeting. I wanted it to be fun." I didn't say anything else as we walk to the restaurant.

While we wait to be seated I look down at my phone and discover I have a message from Jethro.

How's it going?

I send a message back.

Not what I expected, but at least, we are not arguing.

I know if I only say fine I will get too many questions. I try to respond in a way that I don't lie, but also will not have Jethro alarmed by my response.

How is my son doing?

I take a deep breath then text back.

You know Carter, he is easy going.

"Everything okay?" Logan asked.

"Yep," I respond.

"I know I don't have to ask you how Jethro would feel. He made it loud and clear how he feels about the entire process."

"Yeah, well he has been the only father Carter has known. I'm sure you can understand he is protective of his family. When we are done with lunch we should make our way back to the club house."

"Then I guess we better take our time during lunch," Logan said looking my way. His smile has faded, and I am wondering if part of it had to do with him knowing I was texting Jethro.

The table is ready, and before the waiter can walk away I order pizza and drinks for us. We've been gone long enough, and this was not part of the plan in the first place. I don't want him to take my kindness for weakness.

"What do you guys have planned for next week?" Logan asked.

"Carter is getting his cast off," I said, and Carter cheers. "He has piano practice, and Jethro has been trying to get him into t-ball. I still haven't committed."

"Do you think I could see him again?"

"I don't know Logan," I respond truthfully. I am giving up a lot here, but he has not said he is willing to ease up at all.

"It can be on your terms, I mean, I promise not to derail you this time. I just want to establish a relationship with him, and the only way I'm going to be able to do that is if we can see each other regularly." I take a deep breath.

"Can I think about it?"

"Why because of Jethro?" he asked starting to sound upset.

"Partly, but I don't want to do too much too soon with Carter. He's already confused, and I don't want to make it worse. I think we should be gradual in our process with him."

"Fair enough, here is my card with my new number." I take it and put it in my purse. "Can I at least have a number to contact my son," he asked, and I think what is he up to? Once again, against my better judgment, I give him my number.

"Logan, I am not opposed to you seeing him, or building a relationship with him. We just have to make sure we are not throwing too much at him to fast." The waitress came and sat down our food.

"Can I just say what a nice family you have," The waitress said, and that made Logan smile; showing all thirty-two teeth.

"Thank-you," he replies. "See we have a nice family."

"Eat your pizza," I said to Logan, and for the first time he laughs out loud, which got me to smile.

"I've missed your straight forwardness," he said looking too deeply at me. It immediately makes me uncomfortable, and I look away.

We finish our meal and are on our way to the car when we pass the Apple store.

"Mom, can we go in, please!" Carter's favorite store is the Apple store. He has expressed to me, on numerous occasions, that he would like a big kid tablet, like an iPad, not a little kid tablet like his Nabi.

"We have to get going," I shoot back.

"We have time," Logan said walking toward the Apple store. I roll my eyes at him, but he smiles back at me.

I had to drag Carter and Logan out of the store. I put my foot down, when he tried to purchase an iPad for Carter. To prevent him from purchasing the iPad I had to threaten him that we will not see him next weekend.

We pull up to the clubhouse right at five, and I exhale.

"Do you have any pictures of him when he was born, or younger?" He asks as I am about to exit the car.

"I have some on my phone, but I will bring you photos to the next meeting."

"Can I see the pictures you have on your phone?" I pull out my phone and go to the professional pictures that were taken of him when he was born. There are some of him on my chest, and some with Jethro. I scroll to the pictures that I know will not upset him.

"Wow, I am going to bring you one of my baby pictures, so you can see, we look like twins. I had black, thick, curly hair when I was born. He looks more like me than Hunter. Do you have any more pictures?" He has that glossy look in his eyes how can I turn him down? I'd made a digital photo album of him from age one, but they had pictures of Jethro in them. I find some from his birthday party when he turned one. This time I didn't hand him the phone because if he scrolls to the right he will be pissed.

"Wow, he has changed a lot over the years," he is still beaming. His smile makes me smile.

"Yeah, this picture was right before I cut his hair. It had gotten so long, and thick I use to have someone braid it. I took his braids out, so he could get a haircut the next day." I said, and we were both smiling.

"Thank you Daryn."

"For what?" I asked.

"For agreeing to let me spend time with him outside of that stuffy room, and for letting me feel like he is my son today."

"You are welcome," I start getting out the car.

"Will you please consider letting me see him next week? Anywhere you choose, and any day you choose, is fine with me."

"I will let you know," I got out the car before he starts trying to strike up another conversation with me.

He helps me to the car and to load up Carter things.

When we are at the house I call Carter to the couch.

"Hey, I know today was confusing for you, and I promise I will explain everything to you someday. Please don't tell your dad that you have another dad. We will tell him when the time is right." I said feeling horrible about telling my son to lie or hide the truth.

"What do you mean?" he asked.

"I mean if your dad asks who you met today, or you want to explain it just say you made another friend." I said on the verge of tears. I didn't like what I was doing, but I don't want to ruin the weekend. I will have to break this to Jethro another time; when he can process everything without too many people being around.

"Okay mommy," he says.

We arrive at the resort on the beach. When we walk in Carter ran to his dad, and Jethro picks him up and spins him around. You would have thought we'd been away a month the way he is acting.

"Did you have fun?" Jethro asked.

"Yeah, I met my...mom what was he again?" I take a deep breath and blow it out discreetly, grateful that he remembers and changes his story.

"He was a friend," I said.

"Well anyway he bought me lots of toys. Can I go play?"

"Of course, you can, put on your swimming trunks so we can go down to the beach," Jethro said patting him on the head. Carter took off running to change.

"Where is everyone?" I asked.

"They are at the beach. I came up to wait on you and Carter. How did it go?"

"Um, I'm not sure," I said.

"What do you mean?" he asked.

"I tried to be compliant, and amiable hoping he will change his mind about the custody battle," I said putting my purse down.

"What do you mean?" he asked.

"I mean, why don't we talk about this later. I want to change and make it down to the beach also." I want to change the direction of the conversation, but I know Jethro won't let me off the hook that easy.

"Can you give me a quick rundown of what happened?" he asked leaning against the back of the sofa while we wait for Carter.

"He wanted to get Carter some things, so he did."

"What do you mean so he did?"

"Mom," Carter calls, and I silently thank God.

"Let me check on Carter," I said, and Jethro follows me.

He didn't ask any more questions in front of Carter, he lingers around while I help Carter change. I change and we all journey to the beach together.

I really wish Cheyenne was here, but since the run in with Abe's girlfriend we decided it isn't the best idea to have her come to the beach, while Abe's girlfriend is still here.

Today feels normal compared to the days I've been having with Jethro, and everything going on with Carter. The weather is warm for October, but starts to cool down as the sun starts to set. Jethro looks happy, and laughs, and smiles a lot like he used to. Carter and Melody play so well together, I barely have to say anything to them. Jethro wraps Carter's arm in a plastic bag so he can play in the water. Things are perfect and then my phone rang.

"Hello!"

"Hey, did you have a chance to decide?" It is Logan. Shit I think.

"Logan, you can't just call me whenever you feel like it. I will let you know." I whisper.

"It's just that I can't get him out of my mind. Can you please send me a picture of him?"

"I will send you a photo and I will let you know about next week. Please don't call me unannounced." I said and hung up the phone before Jethro came jogging over. Thank God he is distracted with Abe.

I snap a picture of Carter building a sand castle, and quickly send it to Logan. Almost immediately a picture message pops in. It is a school picture of Logan when he was in kindergarten. My mouth hangs open. Logan had thick curly black hair, blue eyes, a cherub face, and pale skin. The only difference in them was the melanin in Carter's skin. I quickly shut off my phone. I didn't need or want any more messages from Logan.

I thought I'd dodged a bullet. I made sure to come to bed early to try and keep from discussing Carter's visit with Logan.   I hear Jethro stumbling in the room. He and Abe had been drinking a beer called Unholy. After just two of them they are slurring and talking so loudly I thought we were going to get kicked out the resort. The beer had the right name because I declare it makes them act as if a demon has possessed their body.

"Daryn," he said in my ear. I can't fake sleep because I wasn't expecting him to be in my ear, it causes me to jump.

"Jethro," he clicks on the side table lamp, and I suck my teeth.

"Do you love me Daryn?"

Oh Lord I think. Jethro is not really a drinker.

"Of course, I love you Jethro," I say, then he slings his leg across my body and it is heavy. He's not trying to support his own weight.

"I love you too Daryn, and I'm afraid of what it means for Logan to come back into your life."

"He has not returned into my life. He would like to be a part of Carter's life." I am trying to make it clear that this isn't about me, but Carter. I don't know why I'm trying to reason with a drunk, nothing I say right now will resonate with him.

"I get so worried that he's going to take my family away from me, and I can't let that happen."

"No one's taking your family from you. I can't be happier being married to you," I don't know if I'm trying to convince Jethro or me. Lately, I'm questioning my judgment on everything.

"How did Carter react to him?"

"He was fine. He wanted to know why you couldn't come with us."

"That's my boy," I can tell Jethro is smiling. He's breathing heavily in my ear, and the heat from his breath is causing condensation to form in my ear. I wiggle to get from under him and sit up. The stench of alcohol is filling my nostrils and I can't take it anymore. I sit up in bed since he isn't going to let me sleep. He is still lying beside me looking up at me. I giggle at him as his eyes are trying to focus on me.

"Why do you drink that beer?" I am still smiling at him.

"Abe dared me. He said I would be drunk before him. He won," Jethro said giggling. I laugh at him too.

"Cheyenne is coming over tomorrow," I am hoping if I change the subject he will forget all about asking me questions about Logan.

"Oh yeah, I hope she behaves herself."

"Abe's girlfriend will be gone," Jethro started laughing. "What's so funny?" I ask.

"That is definitely not my brother's girlfriend. He confirmed he brought her here to try and get at Cheyenne. I told him he was wrong for that shit, but it's backfiring on him. Cheyenne won't answer his text or calls. He's scared he has messed things up with her."

"I'm sure she will forgive him, but he shouldn't have tried my friend."

"I don't want to talk about Abe and Cheyenne anymore."

Jethro says as he throws his arms intimately around me. I know at this moment I am going to have to comply. This isn't the time to deny him. He will probably go back to asking me questions about Logan if I do.

"We have to be quiet because of my parents," he says as he is pulling up my camisole. I help him remove it. While he undresses I take off my shorts. He returns to the bed then nudges me, so I can flip over on all four. He presses on my back, so I lay my head down, but keep my ass in the air. I put an arch in my back and brace myself. I know Jethro will not be gentle. He inserts a wet finger inside of me priming me for entry. I rock back and forth on him willing myself to get as wet as possible before he inserts his manhood inside. I whimper as he removes his finger. He holds onto my waist then smashes into me causing my body to move up on the bed. I dig my face into the pillow and cry out. He didn't wait for me to straighten or feel comfortable as he starts a relentless pounding. I try hard to keep to a low moan, out of respect for his parents in the house. It last only until I feel that low hum in my core signaling an explosion is imminent.

"Jethro please," I shout, but it is almost as if he is possessed, the way he intensely bangs my sex repeatedly.

The hum is now a raging, maddening, sensation that has surfaced in full throttle. I can no longer restrain my cries as Jethro pounds me from behind, liquefying the innermost part of me. I start to sag as he's rung me out completely and is still going.

"Jethro," I call out of breath.

"Almost, Daryn, almost," he said, my breath is now coming out in low pants.

"Daryn, I love you," he finally shouts in a loud groan while he shoots his semen inside of me. I laid down flat, and he laid half of his body on top of me while still inserted.

"I'm sorry," he slurs. I might have to take some Tylenol after that little escapade I think to myself.

"It's okay," I respond as he rolls us on our sides.

"You just do something to me, when I'm inside of you; I tried to control myself, but damn baby." I giggled.

"I'm not made of glass Jethro, I can handle it. I tried to be quiet for the sake of your parents," I said shyly.

"I'm a Thomas, my dad knows how I get down," he said giggling too. "I love you Daryn, sometimes I think our family is too good to be true. I still think sometimes you might leave me." I wasn't expecting him to say that. I didn't know after all this time Jethro is still insecure about our marriage. It tugs at my heart.

"I love you too Jethro and you don't have to worry about me leaving you. I'm right where I want to be." I guess he has a right to be insecure since Logan showed up with all his demands. "Now let's go to sleep." I didn't want him to get back on the subject of Logan again.

"Instead of sleep I will do you one better," he said and starts moving inside of me. When Jethro drinks it is like liquid Viagra. I knew I should have gone to the bathroom and hid until he fell asleep.

He lifts my leg to gain better access. He holds my thigh above his shoulder as he pumps in and out of me from the side. This position made our love making more intense. With my head to the side I had no pillow to moan in, and nothing to muffle my sounds. I try biting my bottom lip, but how deeply he is penetrating me, it is making it an impossibility. My body is not use to this position, and with the magnitude of Jethro's manhood, it didn't take long before I am hollering his name, and incoherently babbling. As I continue to climax into an unknown hemisphere Jethro starts to move quicker making me bounce back into him. He bends across my body and kisses me to help hinder the echoes of my cries.

Jethro bit my bottom lip and starts to move faster. This is a tell tell sign that Jethro is about to cum with me. I focus on flexing my hips back into him harder and faster, matching his pace to pull his orgasm out of him. Finally, it happens, and he releases my leg, and wraps his arm around me.

"Jethro, I need the restroom," I say wiggling, so he will release me.

"Aw don't move," he said. I wiggle again until he lets go. I head to the bathroom and take care of my womanly needs. When I return he is asleep. I ease in the bed careful not to wake him. I will find some other time to tell Jethro about our visit with Logan.

"Hey Abe," I said as I walked into the kitchen to make coffee. No matter what time Jethro goes to bed, he will wake up at 7 in the morning. He told me early on in our relationship, he can function fully on four hours of sleep, and if he gets more than six hours he feels discombobulated.

"What up?"

"You're up early Bro, you about to take your girl to the airport?" Jethro said walking in heading to the fridge.

"She ain't my girl, that's why I'm about to schedule her ass an Uber, right now."

"Man, you can't send that girl to the airport in an Uber."

"The hell I can't. That bih..." Abe looks my way. "I mean the young lady is getting on my last nerve. She better be glad I didn't put her ass out last night."

"Abe, she may be getting on your nerves, but you can't just send her packing in an Uber. That's disrespectful."

"J, that ain't me. You know I don't give a shit how she gets home, but I figure the least I can do is get her ass to the airport. I don't have to take her, she grown."

"Bro, you brought her here, now you want to let some stranger pick her up and drop her at the airport."

"Hell yeah! If I was back home I wouldn't even call Uber. It would be up to her how she got home, but since we are somewhere she never been I feel this is the least I can do"

"Bro be for real."

"I'm as real as a fucking heart attack. I slept in the chair in the room last night because I didn't want to be bothered with her. I didn't want to be in the same room with her, but Ruth was on the couch. If I have to ride with her to the airport with her I might open the door and push her ass out."

I laugh, but Jethro doesn't think it is funny.

"You mean to tell me, this girl has gotten on your nerves that much in the last two days?"

"Yes! I am glad Cheyenne waste a drink on her. I almost threw my drink in her face last night. She told me to take a shower before I got in bed. Like what the fuck, you a guest here, act like one. She gotta go. I can't stand the sight of her. I'm thinking about getting one of my hood home girls to beat her ass when she gets back."

"Abe," Jethro tries to interject, but Abe cuts him off.

"Jet mind yourn! Daryn over there, let me handle this. I knew I shouldn't have brought her here."

"Hey sons!" Their dad walks in the kitchen grabbing the coffee pot.

"Your son is about to put his girl in an Uber," Jethro song. Abe looks at Jethro like he just might punch him in the mouth.

"She ain't my girl!" Abe said still fumbling with his phone.

"What's an Uber?" His dad says.

"Dad seriously? It's like a taxi, but cheaper, and the people drive their own cars."

"Oh,   is   something   wrong   with   you?" "Nah, I just don't want to be bothered."

"Well you can't just put her in a cab and send her on her way because you don't want to be bothered son. We Thomas' are gentlemen. You have to do the right thing son."

"But I got twenty-dollars off the first ride," Abe said seriously as I spit my coffee out from laughing.

"What time does her flight take off?" Their dad said.

"Hell, if I know. I don't care if it takes off at midnight, it is time for her to get the hell on."

"Take her to the airport son. You'll be glad you did."

Abe left for the bedroom after he popped Jethro in the back of the head.

"Did you see that dad?"

"If you not dying or bleeding you're good." His dad said and walks in the back with his coffee.

"That was my dad answer for everything when Abe and I got in an argument or fight. When he was off from work, he didn't want to be disturbed. I remember one time telling on Abe because he snuck a girl in the house. My dad made me clean the garage. We both learned early on, not to tell on one another. My Pops didn't play that."

"He wasn't mad Abe snuck a girl in the house?"

"No, he was mad that I interrupted his napping in his lazy boy." Jethro said laughing.

"Why did you tell on him?"

"Because the previous week I got caught by moms sneaking a girl in the house." We laughed. "Yeah, dad doesn't really care what we do, but moms...totally different story. My dad wanted me and my brother to have the bond he didn't have with his brother. His tactics worked."

As we were talking Abe walks past us, Augustina walked behind him dragging her luggage. He didn't even hold the door for her.

I knew she and Abe weren't in a real relationship. This chic didn't try to bond with us or talk to us. She spent most of her time taking selfies and posting them on Instagram. She tried to do a few Snapchat videos, but Abe told her to get the phone out his face. When she tried again he told her to get the phone out his fucking face and gave her a death glare. I saw the part of Abe that Jethro warned me about. He didn't care that his parents were nearby, or who was listening. Jethro had to take him for a walk. She didn't try again. She avoided him until we went inside. She seemed to sense not to bother him. He didn't speak to her anymore and she didn't speak to him.

I text Cheyenne and go to take a shower. I beg her to come to the resort. I hope she doesn't try and renege.

Cheyenne text me back, asking if I was sure it was safe to come over. I respond that it is and she responds that she is on her way. It is still early. I start straightening up the room when Jethro walks in looking serious.

"What's wrong?" I stop straightening and sit on the bed.

"Why did I have to hear from our son, about your shopping spree, with "his friend"?" I knew it would come to me telling him sooner or later.

"I was going to tell you."

"When Daryn?"

"When we went home, I didn't want to ruin our getaway discussing the visit."

"I asked you how it went," he is now walking toward me. I stand. I've never liked how Jethro towers me when we are having a conversation. It leaves me to vulnerable.

"I told you it went fine," I respond walking away from him.

"Daryn, you failed to tell me important parts of what happened. Carter just told me he couldn't wait to go home and play with his new toys. I asked him what toys. He said his friend bought him toys from the Disney store because he missed all his birthdays." I pause for a moment trying to choose my words carefully.

"Yes, he bought Carter some things. He said he'd missed all the holidays with him, and he wanted to make up for them. I promise to tell you everything, but can we please wait until we get home, so you won't be upset while we are on our mini vacation?" I am now trying to put my arms around him, but he rejects me. "Jethro," I said assertively.

"Daryn, I want to know everything that happened right now," He said sitting on the bed as if he is telling me he has all the time in the world. I walk over and sit next to him. I knew sex or a diversion would not work this time.

"Jethro, with all due respect, I know you want to know what happened, but what good will it do?" I don't know why I'm still trying to reason with an unreasonable Jethro at this point.

"Daryn, everything this man does matters. I worked with him for years. I know how he operates. He does not stop until he gets what he wants; now please Daryn just tell me what happened."

"He wanted to get Carter some presents, so I agreed to go to International Mall. Carter picked out some toys at the Disney Store. We went to eat pizza, and afterwards, I let him play in the Apple store for a little while, then we came home."

"Carter said you rode in his car."

Dammitt Carter, "Yes, we did. He said he didn't want to spend any time away from him. So, I agreed." Jethro stands abruptly.

"Please don't be mad. I'm trying to be as amicable as possible."

"Amicable! Daryn he's not trying to be amicable, he's trying to manipulate you, by using our son to get what he wants."

"Jethro the attorney told me I need to be cooperative, so I can show that although I didn't tell Lo...him, he was the father I am now trying to make it right by being agreeable."   I dare not use Logan's name. That would set him off more. I try to walk toward him, but he moves away rejecting me again.

"Daryn don't be blind to what he is really doing. This is not about Carter this is about you. He is using Carter to control you and get you to play right into his hands."

"Jethro I'm not being played. I just want to do what is right." It is taking a toll on me being in the middle of Jethro and Logan pissing match.

"What do you think is right Daryn?"

I really didn't know how to answer that question. I stare at him. "I want everyone to be happy." It is the only thing I can think of that sounds neutral.

"That's impossible. He won't stop until he has his way. He will not be satisfied with just taking Carter away from me; he will not stop until he has you too." Now it is my time to be pissed.

"Is that how little you think of me? You think because Logan comes back with demands, I will do what he says, and go running back to him?" This time I didn't give a damn if his feelings are hurt for saying Logan's name. He's making me sound like a thot.

"That's not what I meant."

"You think I'm stupid?"

"No Daryn, of course I don't."

"That's basically what you said. Let's be clear, if I wanted to be with Logan, I could have been with him long time ago. I have already told you what the attorney said. In the end, the judge is going to look at the big picture, and not your feelings.

"Fact, I had a son from Logan, and I knew he was the father, but I made no attempt to contact him. Fact, I raised Carter for four years, and in that timeframe, I still did not try and reach out to him. Fact, if I wouldn't have seen Logan that day God only knows when he would have found out. Fact, Carter was going to start asking questions sooner or later. He is already asking why he's not dark like you. Fact, I was wrong for not telling him about Carter.

"My main concern right now, is not having my son stripped away from me period point blank. So, to hell with your feelings Jethro I have to deal with something a hell of a lot more important." When I am done, I march out the room. He calls my name, but I keep walking. It's a shame I have to step down on him to get him to calm down. While I am trying to be nice and sweet to him he has been giving me his ass to kiss. As soon as I flip the script on him he wants to call my name all lovingly. Jethro and Logan can both kiss my ass. I'm tired of being between the two of them. I have tunnel vision, and don't see anyone, but Carter.

"From lovers last night, to fighting this morning; you are definitely married to a Thomas man." I turn around and it is Jethro's mom, who I still don't know what to call her, after being married to Jethro for five years.

"I'm sorry, I didn't see you there."

"It's okay, those Thomas men can get you so angry. Is everything okay?" We walk into the kitchen, so I can get Carter something to eat.

"Yes, it will be."

"I overheard some of your conversation. He is worried Logan will take custody of Carter from him, and it has been upsetting for all of us. It is a lot to deal with. Just give him time Daryn he will come around."

"I know it is a lot for him to deal with. I know he is getting the shitty part of the deal, but he is not the only one that stands to lose here. I stand to lose my son as well. It has been very difficult to try and appease them both." I'd almost forgotten who I was speaking to, I'm glad her eyebrows went up when I said shitty.

"I've already fed the kids. I didn't think you and Jethro would be up so early this morning, after last night." That made me blush and look down. "Honey it's okay. I would be worried if you weren't hollering his name."

"Oh my God," I said stretching my eyes and laughing. I am so glad she made me laugh.

"Laughter is the best medicine. You look so much prettier when you are smiling. God is going to work it out, just pray about it. I know it is hard for Jethro I've never seen him so into anyone. He loves you and Carter very much, and the thought of losing you two has him a little paranoid."

"He needs to trust me," I said feeling my love grow for her even more. She's not taking sides, and I need that.

"He does Daryn, and I stand behind you, you are still the best thing for him, and sometimes you have to be stern with Jethro. Don't give up on him Daryn he will come around."

"I'm not," I said and hug her.

"I'm trying to get use to this hugging Daryn," she said and I laugh again. It makes the mood lighter when Jethro comes out the bedroom with his puppy dog eyes.

He came up to me, hugs, and kisses me.

"I'm sorry Daryn," he whispers in my ear.

"If you two are going to be at it again, I am going to have Senior take me to the mall because I don't need him getting any ideas." We start to laugh as I hide my face in shame.

"Hey, hey, hey, hey," Cheyenne said walking in the kitchen.

"Hi Mrs. Thomas," Cheyenne said hugging her.

"Why can Cheyenne hug you, without you being suspicious, but I can't?" I ask pulling away from Jethro.

"Because Daryn, I can tell that hugging is natural for Cheyenne. When it comes to you, I know you are not a hugger."

"That is true Daryn, you know I've always been more personable than you." I suck my teeth. "Daryn you never liked people touching you, you know you suffer from OCD" Cheyenne states. That is funny to me. When you are used to being dirty, and you can finally clean yourself up, the last thing you want to do, is let someone get dirt on you.

Cheyenne and I walk to the living room, while Jethro went to make sure the kids were ready for the beach.

"You look cute," I said to her. She is sporting a fishnet tunic cover-up over an itty bitty white bikini.

"Thanks, you know I have to let Abe know what he is missing."

"Seriously," I said.

"Yes, where is he by the way?"

"He should be on the way back. He had to take Augustina to the airport."

"Speak of the devil," Cheyenne said, as Abe enters right after my comment. He looks at Cheyenne and smiles.

"I knew you couldn't stay away from me gurl," he said coming toward her.

"Shut-up," Cheyenne responds and curls her lip at him.

"Girl stop frontin," Abe said to her.

"I am here because Daryn invited me, and your little thot has left." Abe sucks his teeth and came and plops on the sofa between Cheyenne and me. We both move over.

"Um, excuse me. Grown folks are talking."

"Ya'll weren't talking about nothin'" Abe said throwing his arm around Cheyenne.

"You just had another girl in your bed last night, and now you have your arm around me; MOVE," Cheyenne said throwing his hand from around her.

"That girl didn't mean anything, you know you the one I want gurl," Abe said smiling, but he looks more serious.

"Why don't I leave you two alone," I said getting up. "How about not! Abe just spent the last couple days wooing this thot. He will not treat me like sloppy seconds."

"How about sloppy first?" Abe said growling at her, and that got him a punch in the arm. "Ouch gurl," he said laughing.

"That's what you get for being stupid."

"For real though Cheyenne, you won't even let me take you out or nothin when I come. Then the minute you see me with someone else, you pour a drink on her."

"I did not pour the drink on her. It was an accident."

"Accident my ass!" Abe said.

"Watch your mouth!" His mom said walking through to her bedroom.

"Sorry mom!" he shouts as she closes her door. "She always catches me slippin."

Jethro and his sister are coming through with the kids, on their way to the beach.

"You coming?" he asked me.

"Yeah, I will be down a little later," I said.

"Okay," he said and stares at me before they all walk out the door.

"Man, what did you do to my brother now?" Abe said.

"Nothing," I respond.

"Then why he gave you that stare, like something is wrong?"

"Nothing is wrong Abe, geez," I said getting off the couch.

"Let me find out you did something to him," he said as I roll my eyes. "Now back to you pretty lady. When are you going let me take you out?" he asks and Cheyenne rolls her eyes.

"I have church tomorrow."

"What about after church?" he asks.

"How about you come to church with me, and then I will go out with you afterwards." Cheyenne smiles looking like she'd won, because there is no way he is going to say yes to spending his Sunday in church. He sat there for a while looking like he was trying to think up a good excuse to get out of going.

"Okay," he responds, and got up. "I don't want to hear no excuses, and no problems. Right after church, you and me. Don't try that double dating shit either. I mean I love my brother, and Daryn you a'ight, but just you and me," he said then walks off before

Cheyenne or I can respond.

"I don't know what I got myself into," she said looking panicked.

"I don't know what you got yourself into either. Let me go change then we can go to the beach."

"What do ya'll have to eat up in this joint?" Cheyenne asks getting up as I'm going into the bedroom.

"There is plenty of food in the fridge. Make yourself at home." I said and disappear.

When I return from putting on my bathing suit and a cover-up Cheyenne Is sitting in the living room snacking.

"You ready," I ask.

"Not really, the fam just went down to the beach. Take a load off. We can head down in about half a hour." I plop down on the couch next to her and flip on the television.

"So, what's been up buttercup," she said, and I smile.

"Too much," I respond.

"You want to talk about it?"

"I probably should, but I would rather hear about your date with Abe," I said, and she smiles.

"Chile, he is something else. I knew he would say no to church, and I would be home free."

"Yeah, he played you." I said laughing.

"The funny thing is, all this time I have been telling him no, the instant I saw him with someone else I was angry. I felt like he wasn't supposed to ask anyone else out. I was thinking deep down he was waiting for me. I was ready to tell him yes the next time he asked me out."

"It's been over five years," I said stretching my eyes like I am saying how long is he supposed to wait.

"Yeah, I know, but my life has been in shambles since I was fourteen, so five years is really nothing." We both pause for a moment.

"Cheyenne, it doesn't mean you don't deserve someone to treat you nice."

"It's not that. I just need to make sure I am in the right space before I start dating again. I feel pretty good with the space I am in right now. I am not perfect, but I'm on my way to being pretty excellent."

"You are already pretty excellent, Cheyenne," I said and squeeze her hand.

"Yeah well until you believe it yourself, other people saying it doesn't matter."

"Touché," is my response. I can totally identify with where she is coming from. No matter how many people tell you how smart you are, how pretty you are, or that you deserve better, if you don't believe it, then it is a moot point.

"We better go downstairs before we start singing Kumbaya," she said and we both laugh. I want to tell her about the visit with Logan, but I refrain. We both stand, adjust our bathing suits, and head downstairs.

It is a day filled with fun in the sun. Only in Florida can you spend a warm day at the beach in September. I try to help Jethro learn to swim again, but I have given up. He jumps up anytime he thinks he is drowning even though we are in knee deep water. Cheyenne and Abe seem to be getting closer until I see Cheyenne punch him in the arm and stomp off. We all laugh including their parents. After a long day at the beach, Jethro and Abe try to start a fire so we can make smores. After several failed attempts Abe decides to buy a hibachi grill and we make smores and roast hotdogs. It is the perfect ending to a great day.

We are running late as we check out the resort. By the time we make it to church to see Cheyenne, praise and worship is in full swing. Some people are pointing and snapping photos with their phone of Abe, but he pretends not to notice.

"Hey bro can I have your autograph?" Jethro teases Abe handing him the church program. Abe punches him in the arm.

"The two of you behave!" Their mom says in an angry whisper.

That got them to straighten up. It is now Cheyenne's turn to dance with the praise team. She has on a black leotard, and a grey flowing skirt. I give her an encouraging smile, but she appears to be in her zone. They dance to, No Way, by Tye Tribbett.

After church we wait outside for Cheyenne. The preacher comes up to shake Abe's hand.

"Number 28, Mr. Abraham Thomas, it is a pleasure to have you visit our church!"

"Thank you for having me. It was a great service." He said, smiling as he saw Cheyenne walking up.

"Are you responsible for bringing Mr. Thomas," the preacher said hugging Cheyenne.

"He wanted to come on his own," she responds smiling.

"Thank you for bringing more Saints to the church. We love our visitors. You folks have a good evening, and Mr. Thomas please don't hurt us to bad on that football field." he said with his baritone voice walking away as we laugh.

"What did ya'll think?" Cheyenne asks.

"From stripper pole to praise dancer, I would say that is impressive," Abe said, and Cheyenne punches him in the arm as we all try not to laugh. "I mean one of those times it became a little suspect. I thought you were about to put your hands on your knees and start twerking. I was like, this is the kind of church, I can get used to." Abe said, and Cheyenne, punches him in the arm again.

"Shut-up!" she said to him. "You think that's funny Daryn," she said barely able to keep from laughing.

"Noooo," I said trying to keep a straight face, but failing. Even their parents couldn't hide their laughter.

"That's okay girl I liked it," Abe said, and we are still laughing.

"It was a very nice service, and you did an amazing job Cheyenne," Their mom said as she tries to straighten up.

"Thank you, Mrs. Thomas," Cheyenne responds. I can't believe everyone knows what to call her but me. I feel like Mrs. Thomas is too formal, and I wouldn't dare call her by her first name. "Just call me mom," she said smiling at Cheyenne. It's crazy after this weekend it seems like Cheyenne and Jethro's mom have a better relationship than we do. I guess it is because Cheyenne is always the same no matter what. She doesn't care who you are she is always herself. She does not alter her personality for her audience. That is why I have such a hard time with Jethro's mom. I don't feel I can talk to her like normal.

"You ready to go gurl," Abe chimes in interrupting my thoughts.

"I thought we were going later," she said.

"I told you after church. My parents and sister are going to the airport. I changed my flight for tomorrow morning." Cheyenne couldn't stop the smile from creeping across her face. He holds out his arm for her to hold, but instead she laces her fingers with his, and they walk off. We all stand smiling at them.

"She is definitely better than that twit he brought with him, who paid more attention to her phone, trying to snapdragon, and facegram," We all howl with laughter, and she stands staring at us. "What did I say so funny?" she asks.

"Mom, it's snapchat and facebook," Ruth said, and we continue to laugh.

We drive his family to the airport, and then make our way home. Things are going well, until Jethro see the amount of presents Logan purchased Carter. He didn't blow a gasket he just walks out the room, and I decide to respect his privacy.

I am on the couch in the living room, watching television when Jethro walks in to tell me Abe is on his way, and he is bringing Cheyenne with him. We haven't spoken since he saw all the toys in Carter's room. I get up to change into something more suitable for company. As soon as I change I hear the door open. I walk out the room to greet them.

"I wasn't expecting you," I said to Cheyenne.

"Yeah, well neither one of us was ready to go home. I didn't trust myself taking him to my house," she said in my ear as she hugs me.

"It's okay we weren't doing anything," I said as I pull away.

"Auntie Cheyenne," Carter said running her way and hugging her.

"There's my favorite nephew," she has a face splitting smile as she responds.

"Do you want to see my new toys?" I see out the corner of my eyes as Jethro stops speaking to Abe and looks in our direction. I pretend not to notice.

"Yeah, sure," she follows him in the room.

"You want a drink?" Jethro ask Abe.

"Shit yeah," he responds and follows him into the kitchen.

I wait until I see Cheyenne come back toward the living room before we step in the kitchen.

"Boy Christmas certainly came early for someone. Would ya'll adopt me too?" she is laughing.

"You would have to ask his other dad to adopt you," Jethro said in an angry tone.

"You mad or nah," Cheyenne said teasing, but I know Jethro is upset.

"Now is not the time Cheyenne," he responds pouring them both drinks.

"So, you don't think that his "other dad," as you put it, should buy him anything?" I could tell where she is going with this, and this isn't a good night to bring it up.

"No, we should wait until everything is settled through the courts before he starts buying things for Carter. This will only confuse him."

"Are you serious? Jethro listen to yourself. That shit makes absolutely no sense."

"Cheyenne, you need to watch your mouth, my son is in the other room."

"He's in the other room, not right here. If he was in THIS room, I would watch what I say and how I say it. If he was in THIS room, there is no way I would even discuss this. That is bullshit and you know it!"

"Cheyenne your mouth, you just left church today."

"Yeah, I just left church, and God is still working on me. I never claimed to be perfect, I only claimed to be better. Now here is twenty dollars for the curse jar, because I got a lot of shit to say," Cheyenne said slamming a twenty-dollar bill on the counter. "First of all, if one of the hood rats you used to deal with, came to you right now, and said Jethro you have a four-year-old son would you try to see him?"

"Cheyenne this is none of your business." Jethro said now taking a drink of dark liquor and I think oh Lord.

"Oh, now it is none of my business, Jethro that is some bullshit. You know yourself, if one of your hoochies called today, and said they had your little demon seed, you would be on a plane tomorrow to see him. You cannot blame this man for wanting to be a part of Carter's life. You should have been worried, if he saw Carter and didn't reach out to see him. Right is right, and fair is fair. He has every right to try and get to know his son." "Is that how you feel too Daryn?" How did this become about me, I want to crawl under a rock.

"How did I get in this?" is my response. I don't believe Jethro can handle the truth.

"Look Jet, at the end of the day, Carter knows you are his dad, and none of that other shit matters. If I found out I had a son out there, I would want to see my son too, but no one is telling you, that you don't have the right to be upset. Now can I enjoy this Hen in peace? Shit I go back to practicing tomorrow and drinking will be off limits." I am so grateful for Abe, I could kiss him for changing the subject.

What he said definitely lightened the mood, and Abe broke out some playing cards.

"Me and my pot-na are ready. We need our rematch!" Abe said, and we laugh.

"No doubt," Jethro responds and even he has to smile. We sit down to the table for a fierce game of spades.

"Where did ya'll go?" Jethro said slapping a two of diamond on my two of spades. I roll my eyes at him, and he laughs.

"We went to Flemings, the mall," then Cheyenne snickers, "and Top Golf."

"Bro you golf?"

"Hell no," Cheyenne said laughing.

"I beat you," Abe said looking at Cheyenne.

"We played five games, you beat me once. The only reason you beat me the last game was because I was hitting left handed."

Jethro starts laughing. "Bro seriously!"

"Jet you know, ya boy don't golf," Abe said pressing his hands against his chest as if to seem shocked we don't already know this.

"Have ya'll ever been to Topgolf?"

"I haven't, but Jethro has." I respond.

"Okay, there are three floors at Topgolf. Each section is considered a bay. You have comfortable couches, and a table to sit at and enjoy food, drinks, or the ambiance as you golf. There are huge golf holes that you hit your ball in, to gain points. Since it was night the golf holes were lit up different colors and you can see as you hit your balls off the edge of your bay. There is a grass mat that you stand on and hit the ball." After she explains Cheyenne stands up to go get the broom then comes back to demonstrate what happened with Abe. "This is your brother. He got in his golf stance, he had nice form. Then he turned his mid-section back as far as it would go with the golf club high in the air." The whole time Cheyenne is demonstrating. "He paused a second, never looking down at the ball, swings as hard as he can, like he was trying to hit a homerun, and missed the damn ball." Jethro burses out laughing so hard he can barely breathe. "Oh, wait that ain't it. He let go of the damn club. We were on the 3rd floor, the club went flying out on the course." Jethro got up and fell on the floor he is laughing so hard.

"Guys that is not it." Cheyenne said seriously.

"Oh my God there's more, I can't." Jethro said trying to catch his breath.

"Our waitress comes over, I know the bitch was watching Abe as soon as we came in, but anyway, she was all like 'I knew you were going to be trouble when you walked in.' I didn't know if Abe was smiling because he was embarrassed, or because the trick was all up in his grill, but they both almost got cursed out. Abe apologizes. She smiles and walks off.

"Then some random guy is walking by, and he recognizes Abe. Some Big Pun looking dude in a wife beater comes over, introduces himself, and shakes Abe hand like he knows him. Then he asks for a pic. I can see in Abe's face he ain't wit it. So rather than the dude sneak a pic of Abe and post something foul about him on whatever social media outlet. I take the phone from the dude and tell him I will take the photo of him and Abe. Dude shows mad appreciation and then leaves.

"We go back to playing golf. Mind you he has not hit the ball. This time he decides he would do better if he gets a running start. This fool backs over by the couches, takes off running, then tries to stop on a dime and swing at the ball. Only he does not stop on a dime he slides on the mat and almost to the edge scaring the shit out of me, as another golf club goes overboard. I run toward him for God only knows what reason, because all I can see is his mother telling me I killed her son by taking him to Topgolf. I am so freakin scared. I just knew he was going overboard, but he was able to stop himself."

"OH LORD I GOTTA PEE" Jethro shouts with laughter. "This can't be true," he said still laughing.

"Oh, it's true, and there is more." Cheyenne says with a

straight face. "You can laugh right now, but when your brother almost fell three stories because he decided to run to hit the ball like he was playing tennis you wouldn't have been laughing."

"Please Cheyenne stop I can't anymore." Jethro said sitting on the sofa laughing so hard he was shaking.

"Mind you he has lost two golf clubs and he still hasn't hit the damn ball. The waitress comes over again. She says 'You again, I know it probably seemed like a good idea, but you can't do a run and start to hit the ball. You must stay on the mat and swing the club. We wouldn't want anything to happen to you, now would we?' At this point I feel like she is openly flirting with him. She has this Elementary school teacher tone as she is speaking to him. I let her know I got it, and to get the hell on." We can't stop laughing especially with how animated Cheyenne is being.

"So, I say, why don't you let me go first, so I can teach you. He tells me he got it. He reaches way back again and hit the ball. It goes straight up in the air in front of us, and drops down barely over the side. He lets out a stream of curse words and start beating the mat with the golf club." Jethro runs in the back he is laughing so hard. Even I can't believe he is doing so poorly. I am no longer trying to tone down how funny this is, I burst out laughing, and tears start streaming down my cheeks.

"Daryn, I am so embarrassed by now." Cheyenne said dramatically holding her head down with her hand on her forehead like she is ashamed.

"Look shorty, I was just trying to have some fun. I knew I couldn't come to your city, and beat you at your game," Abe said sipping on his drink.

"The next time Abe actually hit the ball, and it went pretty far. It made it into the big hole in front of us. The people around us start clapping and cheering." We laugh so hard, Cheyenne joins in with us.

"I'm dead," Jethro says rolling around on the couch.

"Jethro if I'm lying I'm flying. I was so embarrassed to know they had been watching us the whole time. I am sure there is a

YouTube video floating around out there, with your brother, titled what not to do at Topgolf."

"Lies," Abe yells laughing.

"So, he keeps hitting the ball. He hits ten in a row, and gets three points."

"Cheyenne, please stop," Jethro says still unable to control himself. Cheyenne takes a pause.

"It is finally my turn, to hit the ball."

"Cheyenne how many points did you have?" Jethro ask between his fits of laughter.

"I had forty-two after my first ten balls." Cheyenne said polishing her nails on the shoulder of her shirt.

"Cheyenne is over exaggerating some of this shit." Abe couldn't even say it with a straight face.

"Am I lying Abe," Cheyenne asks looking serious.

"Nobody said you were lying, I just said you are over exaggerating." He said laughing too at the absurdity of what he was saying.

"I only wish I was over exaggerating. Daryn the crazy part is that when I suggested Topgolf he was all pumped like 'Yeah, we can do that,' flexing and shit. I thought he knew how to play. It was only after the first game, when he finished with his lil measly three points, that he confessed he's never been golfing before and demands a rematch."

"I'm like okay whatever let's go. He decides its' the club he's using and opts for a smaller lighter club."

"No way Cheyenne, please don't tell me he lost another club, I can't take it." Jethro is breathing hard trying to catch his breath while wiping the tears from his eyes.

"Worse," Cheyenne says, pursing her lips together and folding her arms.

"He steps up to the ball and take it off the tee. I guess he thought since the people next door weren't using the tee he wouldn't either. Once again, he brings the club as far back as possible, or should I say bat, because he's treating it like it's a bat, and he swings with all his might. This time the club flies out of his hands and behind us where another family is golfing. Luckily it doesn't hit anyone."

Jethro no longer looks like he is breathing. He almost passes out he is laughing so hard.

"Man, my hands were wet, from my drink," Abe says laughing at himself.

"The lady comes back over, this time with a pair of golf gloves. Abe puts on the gloves and it is safe to say he doesn't lose any more clubs the rest of the night.

"Periodically they send a guy around in the little golf cart gathering up the golf balls. Abe decides instead of hitting the golf balls in the hole for points, he's going to hit the dude in the cart with his golf balls."

"Listen it was worth it when I hit the golf cart with my ball and the dummy ducked, like he wasn't protected." Abe says laughing.

"Abe if a ball is coming at you at ninety miles per hour you will duck too. Abe hits the ball like he is Venus, or Serena Williams hitting a tennis ball. He ends up with three points again, because he used all his balls, trying to hit the guy picking up the balls." I don't know how Cheyenne continued to tell the story with a straight face. Jethro and I are dying laughing.

"Every game after that he improved. The last game I took pity on him and decided to hit lefty to give him a chance to win. He only beat me by five points."

"I didn't take it seriously; we were out to have a good time."

"Abe when have you ever, not taken anything seriously? You are probably the most competitive man I know, next to me." Jethro said trying to straighten up.

"Man, ain't nobody paying me for this. If it would have been some coins involved I would have taken it more seriously."

"Besides, watching Cheyenne hit a golf ball is some of the sexiest shit I've ever seen."

"Abe please," Cheyenne said sitting back down at the table

where we left the hand of Spades.

"Seriously," Abe said picking up the broom to demonstrate. "Cheyenne walks up to the golf ball, spreads her legs apart, bounces her ass a few times, then shimmies down into position before twisting her perfectly form tities my way to hit the ball." Jethro keeps laughing, I laugh, and Cheyenne punches him in the arm.

"That's why I hit the balls so quick, so she can get back up to the tee."

We all sit back at the Spades table trying to finish our game, but no one remembers who played the last card, and we aren't into it anymore. We opt to go to the couch and watch Abe's favorite movie Deep Cover.   He explained to us it was the first rated R movie his dad let him watch.

I watch Abe and Cheyenne snuggle on the couch. Cheyenne laying her head on Abe's shoulder, and I start to feel panic. My heart starts to palpitate. What if something becomes of this? Cheyenne knows a lot about me, I wouldn't want Jethro to know. What if Cheyenne tells Abe, and he repeats it to Jethro. This could be Jason's Lyric all over again. Lyric interferes with her brother's business by telling Jason his brother is going to rob a bank with her brother, and Lyric ends up shot in the arm. Oh Lord I don't know how I feel about this. I tell myself to calm down and enjoy the evening. They've only had one date and he leave tomorrow.

CHAPTER EIGHT

I must be stuck on stupid. I can't believe I agreed to meet Logan for a second time. I didn't tell Carson, our attorney, or Jethro because I know this is a bad idea. When Jethro leaves the house, I rush and get Carter dressed.

"Where are we going mommy?" Carter asks.

"You remember the friend you met last week?"

"Um hum" he responds.

"He would like to see you again. Is that okay?"

"Uh huh, will I get more presents?" Carter still doesn't get it, and I don't know how, to make a four-year-old get, that he has two dads.

"I don't know, he just wanted to spend more time with you."

"Why, because he's my other dad?" I pause for a moment.

"Yeah, because he's your other dad."

"When can I tell my real dad?" he asks, and that makes me feel like shit. What kind of mother encourages her kid to lie?

"Soon, okay," I say, and he shakes his head. We rush out the house. Jethro usually calls me around his lunch time. We must be back, or at least away from Logan by then.

We pull up to Curtis Hixon Park. He meets us as we are walking up.

"Hey buddy! Can I have a hug," Logan asks squatting down. Carter looks up at me and I shake my head yes. He releases my hand, so he can hug Logan. "I brought a baseball for us to toss around while we are out here."

"All right!" he yells.

"Thank you for doing this," he said, then he did something I wasn't expecting. He hugs me. It was awkward, but I hug him back.

"You're welcome," I said as I pull away from him. "Here you go," I said handing him some pictures.

"What are these?"

"Those are yearly pictures of him starting with his first pic." He stops in his tracks and starts going through them. His face is turning red as if he is going to cry, but he quickly straightens himself.

"Thank you," he said clearing his throat of unshed tears.

"You're welcome," I respond as I rub my hands through Carter's hair.

"I can't believe how much he looks like me. It's uncanny how his features mirror mine at these ages, I am going to have my mom ship some of my baby pictures, so you can see them."

"Besides the obvious of you both having blue eyes, I can definitely tell the resemblance between you two."

"Resemblance," he laughs "he's a mini me." "Can you hold these for me while we play a little baseball?"

"Yes, of course." I said smiling.

Carter has the energy of ten bulls, but Logan keeps up. They first play catch, then they start hitting the ball. When they are done with baseball we walk to Starbucks to get drinks. When we return they run around the open field taking turns being "it."

"I hate to bust up the party, but we need to get going," I said.

"Aw mom," he responds.

"Carter, we have to go home." I said.

"Can we have five more minutes," he said with those puppy dog eyes.

"Yeah mom, please five more minutes," Logan chimes in with laughter.

"I'm sorry, maybe some other time, but right now we have to get going."

"So, there will be another time?" he asks.

"Carter, can you throw the ball around a few times, and let me speak to Logan." He is more than happy to run along and start to play again.

"Thanks again for doing this for me. He can keep all the equipment for next time."

"He already has all these things at home. Maybe you can keep them for another time. I don't have a problem with you trying to see Carter. I'm sure we can work something out to see him again during mediation." I explain.

"So, I can't see him again before then?"

"Mediation is next week; hopefully we can work out something that we can both agree on." I left it at that. "Carter time to go," I give Logan the pictures.

"Thanks again, this has been an unbelievable day. One of the best I've had in a long time." He smiles at me, as if he wants to say something else, then walks off.

We are driving home when Carter starts speaking. "Can I tell dad about my other dad now?"

"We will soon baby," I said looking at him in the mirror.

"Okay," he responds and goes back to playing on his Nabi.

I know I need to explain to Jethro, but I can't right now. I don't know how to explain this to him.

We stop by Chic Fil A to get Carter something to eat. By the time we make it home, my phone is ringing with Jethro's number. I let it go to voicemail. When we walk in the house the phone is ringing. I know it is him; I make it just in time before it goes to voicemail.

"Hello," I said.

"Hey you," he responds. "What are you doing?"

"Carter's eating, and I'm not really doing anything."

"I got Ro to watch the club tonight I thought we could go out to dinner."

"That sounds good," I respond.

"Okay, can I speak to my little man," he asks, and I know that isn't a good idea. As soon as Jethro ask him what he has been up to he will spill the beans.

"He's eating right now, we can call you back, so you can speak to him."

"Nah, that's okay. Just tell him daddy loves him."

"Daddy said he loves you Carter,"

"Which one?" he said out loud. Oh my God, I hope Jethro didn't hear him.

"What did he say? It sounded like he said which one," he said, and I had to think quick on my feet.

"He said okay dad."

"Oh, I thought he said something else. My heart just dropped, but I picked it up again." he said and laughs.

"Nah," is my response.

We chat a little while longer then hang up. I need to help Carter with what he doesn't need to tell Jethro today.

CHAPTER NINE

The time has passed so quickly, and we are back in our second mediation. Not once has Logan looked at me. That is concerning me. I am hoping that since I've been cooperating with him and allowing him time with Carter he will stop seeking full custody.

"I do understand that Logan Anderson is seeking full custody, and Daryn Carter would like to retain the rights of custodial parent. Today we are going to discuss a timeline for everything to take place. For starters we will have a case study performed on both homes. We will have court ordered personnel visit each home to determine the current living situations and report back. My assistant will provide you with the card of the person so the two of you can schedule a home visit. During that time, you will have to show Carter's living space.

"I have several questions I need to ask regarding Carter Thomas wellbeing. We will start with you Mr. Anderson. If you are awarded custody, where would Carter attend school?"

"Carter would attend the same school my children and I attended Christ the King."

"What is your plan to get him to and from school? Also, will he need to attend any aftercare program?"

"My wife does not work. She will be responsible for picking him up and dropping him off." Logan stated fumbling with his tie.

"What will be his religious upbringing?"

"We are Catholic. He would be a member of the Catholic faith."

"Are there any plans to relocate or move out of the city in the next five years?" Logan pauses for a minute, and that is the first time he looks at me.

"I have been offered a position in Connecticut that I turned down, but if the position comes around again in the next five years, I may consider it." He said, and that causes my heart to palpitate. Not only is he trying to take my son, he is trying to take him out of state. He will have to kill me dead first.

"How is Daryn's parenting?" He asked.

"I don't know outside of our meeting. I haven't had the privilege of seeing her handle him as he was growing up. He has a broken arm right now?" He just hit below the belt.

"It was an accident," I interject.

"Mrs. Thomas, we will provide you with the opportunity to explain," the moderator states.

I fold my arms over my chest and sit back in the chair. I wish at this moment I would have told him no to everything he requested. I can't believe I was so gullible to think that just because I cooperated with him, he would drop this custody suit.

"Mr. Anderson, if you are granted full custody how do you plan to communicate with Mrs. Thomas, and do you plan to allow her access to her son?"

"Access," I blurt out. Is he serious?

"Please Mrs. Thomas you will have your turn." After I am scolded again by Julian, my attorney leans over and let me know it isn't a good idea to appear combative.

"The mother can have all my contact information. If we don't have anything planned, or he's not in school, we can agree on dates and times to meet."

"Does Carter have any ongoing medical issues?"

"I wouldn't know since he has been kept from me for almost five years. I only know of his broken arm," that bastard brought it up again.

"Do you have any concerns with Daryn Thomas being the custodial parent?"

"My concern is her lack of judgment. She thought it was beneficial to keep my son away from me, and not give me the option to get to know him. Her husband does not care for me, and I wouldn't want him to take it out on my son." I leap out the chair.

"Logan, you have gone too far!" I blurt out.

"Can you please calm your client," Julian said.

"May we have a recess please," Carson turns to Julian and

said.

"Yes, how about a ten-minute recess. Then we can finish up when we return."

Logan walks out the room, and I charge after him, but my attorney grabs my arm. I look at his hand, and he let me go. The mediator and his assistant walk out the room to give us privacy.

"Daryn, I know this is upsetting, but you have to calm down. He is using all sorts of trigger statements to show your temper in front of the mediator. That will not go over well with the mediator, or the judge. If we cannot come to an amicable agreement the mediator will report all his findings back to the judge including any anger or aggression on your part. Please let me do my job, so you can keep custody of your son."

I nod my head in agreement. I want to kill Logan with my bare hands.

Everyone returns to the room, so we can reconvene.

"Mrs. Thomas what school will Carter attend?"

"He attends a preschool at my church for half a day right now; The Church of Holiness."

"What religion has your son been brought up in?"

"We are nondenominational." As soon as I said that Logan snorts, and it causes me to give him a wicked look.

"Please Mr. Anderson you had your chance," Julian is scolding him now.

"How does he get to and from school?"

"I am a stay at home parent. Currently his dad drops him off, and I pick him up." I know calling Jethro his dad will piss Logan off.

"Are you referring to your husband?" Julian clarifies.

"Yes," is my only response.

"Are there any plans to relocate?"

"No, I am a Tampa native, and there are no plans to leave."

"What is Logan's parenting style?"

"I am not sure, but I know when his oldest daughter was 16 he and his wife were arguing about getting her breast augmentation."

Now it is his time to give me a dirty look.

"That never took place," Logan blurts out.

"I didn't say it took place, I said you were arguing about it. It goes to show the lack of judgment on his wife's part, for considering giving a growing girl a breast job."

"Mr. Anderson, we will give you a chance to respond in the end." Julian said.

"Do you have any concerns with Logan as the custodial parent?"

"Yes, I know Logan has had issues with alcohol in the past, and I am afraid he will relapse. He has relapsed in the past. I also know his wife is not fond of me because of the affair I had with Logan, and I am not sure she will be able to put those differences aside for the sake of my son." I almost mirror his exact words. I want him to know two can play that game.

"Here is the rundown that will need to happen between the two of you by the next meeting. A home inspection will need to be done for the case study. A sample of a parenting plan will need to be presented. In the parenting plan I need to know how you intend to co-parent. Meaning if one of you were granted full custody how will the visitation look for the other parent. Mr. Anderson, I will need you to include if you moved out of the area how would you co-parent.

"The point of mediation is not to dictate who will do what, but to come up with an agreement, that will work for all. To figure this out we will need cooperation. You both can't be the custodial parent, but you both can come up with an agreement that will work. The two of you must be willing to work together.

"We will not reconvene until the beginning of next year. I know there are holidays in between. How will you work out those dates?" Julian said a mouth full, and I really didn't know what to say.

"Julian, Carter has a birthday coming up, and my client would like to be a part of that. Also, Logan's family will be celebrating the week of Thanksgiving in the Cayman Islands and he would like his son to come and celebrate with them." Logan attorney states.

WHAT? I want to shout, but I remember before when I had my outburst how it didn't go over well.

"Lastly, we understand that Carter is spending quite a bit of time alone with Daryn's mother Lola Ryan, we would like a case study performed on her as well and a background check." I want to slap Logan and his attorney.

That bastard, "Excuse me," I blurt out.

"Carter has only spent the day with him, he is not ready to go away from the only family he knows, and spend time away for an entire week," Carson counters.

"Mrs. Thomas trusted my client enough to spend the day with their son shopping and eating. She also trusted him enough to meet up with him twice so Carter could spend time with him." I am horrified that my kindness became my weakness.

My attorney turns to look at me. He leans in and whisper, "Daryn, is this true?"

I nod. "Daryn, we discussed this before your visit. You were supposed to stick to the plan." Maybe it is the way he gritted his teeth that let me know he is pissed.

"He's never spent time with Mr. Anderson alone. We have to keep in mind the best interest of the child."

"The best interest of the child is to bond with his father, as soon as possible. My client has been deprived of almost five years of his child's life. He would like to have the chance to have a first birthday, Thanksgiving, and Christmas since your client decided he was not worthy of those things the first years of his life." I am now mean mugging Logan not believing that he would throw me under the bus the way he has.

"Carter needs the opportunity to get to know his father. We have already agreed on that by being considerate enough to meet with him when it wasn't mandatory."

"Considerate, considerate, are you kidding me. What would have been considerate is your client notifying my client that he is a father. What would have been considerate is taking the time to let my client be a father to his son. What would have been considerate is telling Logan the day she saw him in the streets that he had a son." The mediator is sitting back, and letting the attorneys hash it out. He needs to step in and control the situation before it gets out of hand. I look over at him, but he won't look in my direction.

"Gentlemen can we settle down please," Julian finally decided to speak.

"Daryn, is it possible, to agree on an acceptable timeframe, on Carter's birthday, that Logan can spend time with him?" I didn't respond.

My attorney leans over to speak to me. "Do you have plans for Carter on his birthday?"

"Yes, we are having a party for him at Chuckie Cheese," I whisper to him.

"The family already has plans for him on his birthday, maybe the day after or day before," Carson counters. Logan's attorney leans over to speak with him.

"That is unacceptable he has already missed four birthday's he will not miss another one."

"Take it or leave it," Carson replies.

Logan's attorney leans over and speaks to him.

"Then I want it unsupervised," Logan said out loud to me.

"No," I reply instead of using Carson. He wants to be nasty I can be nasty. He leans into his attorney again.

"We will take the day before, but at a place that Logan chooses," he responds.

"Where?" Carson is right in sync with me. That is the exact question I am thinking.

"My client would like it at his home, so Carter can meet his other siblings."

That is giving me anxiety.

"No," I said out loud.

"My client will not budge on this one. We will see you in court if we cannot agree on this!" Jackson threatens slamming his billfold close.

Carson leans into me. "Daryn, you are going to have to compromise something? If it comes to it, we want the judge to see how you tried to be agreeable and include Logan in Carter's life despite the way everything started out."

"I prefer a neutral location."

"Do you have one in mind?" I shake my head no. "Do you think he would be in any danger?" I shake my head no again. "Then I say we concede on this one." I shake my head yes.

"Okay, we will meet the day before at Logan's residence with Daryn present. She has agreed to be there from ten to two."

"There is also the matter of Thanksgiving and Christmas, we are willing to not disturb Christmas if he is able to spend the Thanksgiving holiday with them in the Cayman Islands."

"My client is not prepared to let her son..."

"He's my son too," Logan interrupts loudly.

"We do understand he is your son as well, but we need to consider the best interest of the child." Carson rebuttals.

"Mrs. Thomas is there any way you could possibly meet him in the Cayman Islands with Carter maybe not for the full week?" Julian intervenes.

"I have plans," I respond.

"Daryn, why do you continue to deny me?" Logan said so loudly he was almost shouting.

"I am not denying you. It is inconceivable that you think we can just pick up and go for a week. We have traditions that we have started, and before those traditions are over we would like to have one more Thanksgiving together. We spend time with his parents and my parent."

"Yes, there is the matter of your mother Lola Ryan. We would like it on record that Carter is not to spend time with her alone until a case study is done." Jackson states switching gears.

"Lola Ryan is his grandmother and she has a right to be a part of Carter's life."

"If your number one priority is the safety of Carter, then it should be your concern in every aspect of his life. We have records from Mrs. Ryan's past that indicate she would be unfit to watch Carter unsupervised." Jackson is reaching into his briefcase and pulling out a stack of documents. My mother has been arrested for prostitution, drugs, theft, and God only knows what other crimes. I cannot let Julian see the documents Jackson has in his hands.

"You win," I yell out in a panic. He stops pulling the documents out, and everyone looks my way. "You win Logan, we will spend Thanksgiving with you, but Jethro gets to come too."

"Daryn," Carson said turning my way. I turn to Carson and whisper to him.

"Trust me Carson the documents he has in his hands will destroy my mother's reputation. She has been through enough. If it will stop him from releasing what he has in his hands, we will go. I have no choice."

"My client has agreed, and we are done here." Carson looks angrier than I am. He stands and starts packing up his messenger bag.

"We will reconvene next year January 4th. We will have the case study back, and what our findings are, and how we can try and settle a shared custody agreement of one Carter Jethro Thomas." The mediator is looking like we took ten years off him during this mediation. I don't think I realized before how thin the front of his hair is.

"I want him to have my last name," Logan said. I walk out the room as if I didn't hear him. I am walking so fast I am almost running to the car. I didn't want to chance running into Logan and his attorney. I rush down the stairs and I am about to pass the elevator when the doors open and Logan steps out. He grabs me by the arm and walks me in an empty room behind us.

"I want my son to have my last name," he said standing in front of the door like he was baring me from leaving

"I don't care what you want. I have been more than generous in letting you see Carter, and this is how you repay me."

"You have been generous? Daryn, he's my son, there is no generosity involved. I want more time with him, and I want his last name changed." He is aiming for calm, but I know Logan, and he is one step from blowing up, and probably two steps from drinking.

"Then stop pursuing custody, and I will work with you on visitation."

"Daryn, you are the one that should consider being more amicable. My attorney has assured me I am in an excellent position for seeking custody of Carter. With your mother's history, and the way you purposely kept the paternity of my son away from me, any judge would sympathize with me."

I didn't know if he was right or not, but the reality of everything is making me feel as if I am having a panic attack.

"How could you bring my mother into this? She has never done anything to you." I said feeling my breathing becoming heavier and more difficult.

"She brought herself into it, she didn't tell me the truth when I saw her. She aided you in hiding my son from me."

"She was only protecting Carter," I remark.

"From what Daryn, you and I both know, I would never hurt Carter."

"I don't know what you are capable of," I know in my heart that isn't true. I know Logan won't hurt Carter, but after the stunts he just pulled in mediation, I will never tell him that. There is no way I will give him any more leverage.

"You pretend you don't know me Daryn, but you know me. I may be a little greyer, but I am the same Logan you fell in love with. I am the same Logan you let come live with you, and I am the same Logan that made love to you and gave us a son."

"Move out of my way," I said walking up to Logan with my fist balled at my sides. I can't take it anymore; I need to get out of this room with him. The walls feel as though they are closing in on me, and I am having difficulty breathing.

"You can make this easy, or you can keep trying to make this hard, but I will win," Logan said, and steps aside. I step out the office and my attorney see Logan step out behind me. He comes toward me in full stride, Logan turns and goes in the other direction.

My hands are shaking at my sides; I must lean against the wall. I am sweating profusely. I need to try and gain control, and focus, but it is too much. I walk back in the room and fall in the seat. I unbutton my jacket and take it off, so I can get some air.

"Daryn, are you okay," Carson said kneeling in front of me.

"No," I said as it starts to become harder and harder to breathe.

"Should I call a medic," he said, and I shake my head no. I bend over trying to put my head between my knees. I tell myself to calm down. I try to focus solely on my breathing and getting it under control. Carson is asking me questions, but I ignore him. I can't focus on him and trying to breathe.

There are people rushing into the room. When I sit up, I did it too fast, and spots are threatening my vision. A mask is placed on my face, and as soon as I breathe in the cool crisp air my lungs feel as if they are opening again. The spots are disappearing, and I can breathe again. Tears start to trickle down my cheek as I suck in massive amounts of air. The pain that I feel in my head is going away. I can breathe without feeling like I am not getting enough oxygen.

"Daryn, are you okay," Carson said, and I shake my head yes. I am too afraid to speak. It seems as if I have replaced the kraken with panic attacks.

I don't stand, I sit and try and continue to gain control.

"Your oxygen levels are going back up," the medic says. I look at the light on the tip of my finger. I didn't realize it was placed there.

"Do you feel like you are going to pass out?" I am asked louder than necessary.

I shake my head no. The words no longer echo in my head. Had he been a few seconds later I would have been on the floor.

"Would you like for us to call an ambulance," he is annunciating every single syllable as if I am hard of hearing.

I shake my head no because all my faculties have return. I know I only need a few more moments of breathing oxygen and I will return to normal.

A few moments pass, and my oxygen level is back to one hundred percent. He checks my vitals, and then gives me the thumbs up.

Carson stands beside me rubbing his hands through his sandy blond hair.

"Now that you have scared the shit out of me, maybe you can explain what you are so afraid of regarding Lola Ryan." Carson looks too nervous to sit.

"Can we do this another time?" We have until next year to get everything straightened out. I need a chance to clear my mind. Mediation takes such a toll on me, I don't know if I can survive another one.

"Daryn, we don't have much time. It is already October, and if you are going to keep custody of your son you must do everything I tell you. Tell me everything don't leave out anything. What are you so afraid of regarding Lola Ryan?" He isn't going to let this go, and I need to cooperate, so we can make sure Carter stays with me. I will die if he takes my son from me.

"My mother, Lola Ryan, who is now an exceptional grandmother, was once on crack cocaine. She has been arrested numerous times for prostitution, drug possession, theft, and maybe other reasons. Those are just the ones I know about. I am quite sure the paperwork he was pulling out his briefcase was my mother's arrest record. She sometimes keeps my son. She has been clean for six years." I am ashamed to tell my mother's story. I keep my head down the entire time I speak about her.

"We've all made mistakes in our past we aren't proud of. Some people are fortunate enough to get away with crimes without ever being caught. The good news is she's clean now. During the case study we can have her drug tested. We can have pastors, employers, friends, and family members write letters on her behalf, how she is now the model citizen. We can combat these things, but only if I know about them. Yes, you want to be cooperative. You don't have to let him bully you into doing things you don't want to do, like going to the Cayman Island for the entire week. I can only imagine you breaking this news to your husband."

I have no idea, how I will break this news to Jethro. He will be livid, and I will definitely have to go to the extreme of having a baby now.

"What did he say to you that had you about to pass out?"

"He pretty much said it is a slam dunk case, and he has been assured by his attorney he will win custody."

"That's bullshit! Don't you believe that! He will not win custody. Just don't let him sweet talk you into doing anything without your attorney. You see how he used it against you."

"I promise not to keep anything else from you, and to do as you tell me," I said weakly, but I know he is right.

"Okay, well I will let you go. You need to get some rest. We will need to go over what you need to say, and do, for Carter's birthday, the case study, and for your week-long vacation in the Cayman Islands. It could be a lot worse than going to the nice white sandy beach with aqua water as far as the eye can see. Have you ever been there before?" Once again, I was looking down as I get a flashback of the time I spent with Logan at his place.

"Yes, when Logan and I were together he was having the place renovated. I met him at his home to spend time with him. His wife didn't know." I didn't realize how embarrassing my affair with Logan would feel when I had to talk about it. At the time we were together I could only think about that moment, and how perfectly he fit into my life. Now I see how selfish I was being.

"Once again we've all done things we are not proud of. We should learn from our mistakes. You think you are the only person that has been involved in an extra marital affair? I can assure you, you are not.

"Go home, get some rest, take care of yourself. I will have my secretary call you to set up a meeting to discuss our game plan." He smiles, and I stand. I am glad I stuck with Carson. His caseload is not as heavy, and he assured me he would be able to give my case more personal attention than his boss could.

I know the sooner I explain to Jethro what happened at mediation, the better, but it has my stomach in knots. I decide to put on something sexy, so we can go to dinner. I put on a satiny metallic slip dress with my back out, and some strappy sling backs before he comes home. I check myself in the mirror and hope he goes for the distraction. I figure if I tell him in a public place he will be less likely to flip out.

"Daddy," I hear Carter yell.

"Hey, you look nice," Jethro said placing the mail on the table. He seems to quiet. He is paying more attention to the mail than me.

"I thought we could go out to dinner," I said after a brief pause.

"Hmm," is his response.

"Is everything okay?" I ask walking toward him.

"Long day, just give me a moment to change out of my work clothes, and we can leave." He walks away without kissing me. I wonder what is bothering him.

The only noise in the car, on the way to dropping Carter to my mom's house, is Carter's tablet. It is annoyingly quiet. I have no idea what is wrong with Jethro, and my mind is telling me to chicken out. I know his silence cannot mean anything good. This time I let him take Carter in to my mom. I'm not in the mood to face her. She will see my face and know something is wrong.

While he's taking Carter in I decide to put on Solange's CD to surround us with some type of noise. When he gets in the car he looks at me suspiciously.

"You look really pretty Daryn," he says as he's putting on his seatbelt.

"Thanks," I smile at his compliment. "Are you sure you are okay," I ask.

"Yep," I know the way he says it, there is something behind it, but I don't pry.

We pull up to the valet, and he opens my door. Jethro still walks around to assist me out the car.

We are seated within fifteen minutes of arriving at Eddie V's. I still haven't found out what is wrong with him.

When we are seated Jethro order's a Cognac, and I order a glass of Riesling.

"A pretty dress, ordering wine, dropping Carter off, and expensive restaurant, you must have a hell of a story about mediation." Jethro says after the waiter walks off with our drink orders.

"You're right, but we can wait until after dinner, I want to hear about your day," I said folding my hands in front of me and smiling. I want our night to be as positive as possible before we discuss our Thanksgiving plans. I'm starting to perspire under my arms just thinking about it.

"My day was shit!" he blurted out. Our waiter is back sitting down our drinks. I take a big sip trying to summon some courage.

The waiter goes over the menu, and specials. Jethro orders the Point Judith Calamari.

"I'm sorry about your day," I said looking at him empathetically.

"Yeah, well it happens. I just keep sitting here thinking it is about to get even shittier because of what you are about to tell me."

"Can we just be two adults, out on a date, having a good time Jethro," I am more so pleading.

"I can play along," he said draining the rest of his glass.

"Do you want to talk about why you are upset?" I am hoping we can salvage the evening.

"I have a new boss. New bosses mean new processes. I've heard folks call him the Terminator because of the number of people he has fired. He will be here all next week for an "audit." He is going to do a mock audit to make sure we are up to par. I was questioned on policies and procedures we have been implementing since I took over. He is trying to infringe on our processes that have worked because he wants all branches to follow the same procedures. The thing is, it is impossible. Some branches may be in an urban neighborhood and the volume they have on loans won't be quite the same as say, some branches in the suburbs. So, with that being said, trying to operate every single branch exactly the same, will not work, and would cause all types of conflicts."

"Can you tell him that?" I asked. The waiter came over to serve his food and take our dinner order. I order the Chilean Sea Bass and he orders the Bone in Ribeye. Our waiter declares they are excellent choices and take away Jethro's drink for a refill. I take another long sip feeling the slightest buzz. Since I had Carter I drink wine on occasion, but I am such a light weight.

He scoffs down his Calamari, and then drinks half of his drink.

"I can't take it anymore, you have to tell me what happened," he demands. He has exhausted his patience, and he deserves the truth. Tonight, I decide I am going to tell him everything, and not leave anything out. As soon as he said it our food is being placed in front of us. I take one bite out of my seabass, and as dreamy as it tastes, I can barely get it down I am so nervous. I put down my utensils and look at Jethro.

"During mediation there were several things brought up," my hands are trembling, so I sit on them. I decide to bring up the smallest of the issues. "We must have a case study done on our home. They want to see how we live. I'm sure that will be fine." I take another sip of my wine and continue when he didn't say anything. "He would like to spend Carter's birthday with him. I turned him down, but then Carson reminded me that we need to be amicable. We need to show the judge that even though I didn't tell Logan about Carter in the beginning, I am trying to work with him. I am trying to right my wrong. So, he is going to spend the day before his birthday with

Carter." Jethro put his knife and fork down and shoves his food away.

"What else?" he said finishing his drink and signaling for another. I eye him and want to tell him another drink is not a good idea.

"He also would like to spend Thanksgiving with Carter," by now his other drink is in front of him. He takes a big gulp and is half finish.

"What did you tell him?" I look at him finish the rest of his new drink.

"I told him no, then his attorney asked me who was Lola Ryan. I had to let them know, she is my mother. His attorney said he didn't want Carter to stay with her alone until a case study is done on her. Then they were pulling out a file on my mom… so I had to agree to the Thanksgiving arrangements."

Jethro pounds his fist on the table so hard it makes me jump and the dishes rattle.

"Maybe you shouldn't order any more drinks," I said as a few folks look over at our table.

"It's either drinks, or go over Logan's house and punch the shit out of him. As bad as this is for us, I know you Daryn, and I know there is more than this as to why you are all dressed up, and brought me to this fancy ass restaurant." Oh God the Brooklyn is coming out. That is not a good sign. Maybe being in a public place isn't such a good idea.

"You're right Jethro," my heart is beating so fast I think it might leap out my chest. "His family is spending their time in a home they own in the Cayman Islands, the week of Thanksgiving. I told him we would all go."

He didn't speak. He signals for the waiter.

"Please bring us the check," he said pulling out his wallet.

"Can I box up the food for you," the waiter asked.

"No, just the check, and hurry please," Jethro said handing him his card.

"Was there something wrong with the food? We can have our

chef prepare something else for you."

"The food is perfect, we just have an emergency."

"Right away sir," the waiter responds scurrying away.

Shit I think. He isn't saying anything, but the vein is alive and thriving on the side of his temple. He is sitting with his hands folded on the table. The waiter came over, he signs the check and stand signaling it is time to go.

I stand, and he put his hand on the small of my back not as a romantic gesture, but to hurry me alone. The valet pulls up and he is walking to the driver side.

"What are you doing? I will drive," I said walking to the driver side after him.

"I am fine Daryn, I can drive," he said opening his door to get in.

"Jethro, you just downed three drinks in less than an hour. I'm driving."

"I'm fine," he states still getting in the car.

"Fine, you drive, I'll walk," I said and start walking toward the main highway. The valet is looking at us uncomfortably as he holds open the passenger door for me. My feet are already starting to throb, and the chill in the air has me crossing my arms.

"Daryn," Jethro said grabbing me by the arm. I snatch my arm away from him and keep walking.

"Daryn stop please," Jethro said walking behind me. "You can drive," he finally said. I turn around to face him.

"That is why I always debate if I should or shouldn't tell you everything that happens in mediation, or when we have a visit with Logan. You can't handle it, and you go off the deep end."

"I know Daryn, I will try to do better. Now can you get in the car, please, I'm sorry." He said, and I walk toward him. This time when he put his hand on the small of my back as we walk toward the car it is more affectionate.

We pick up a sleeping Carter and make it home. I am in the room changing when Jethro walks in wanting to finish our conversation.

"Daryn, what is the deal you made with him regarding Thanksgiving," he said as I am putting on my camisole. I walk out the closet into the bedroom. He follows me.

"His family is celebrating Thanksgiving in the Cayman Islands, and I agreed to join him. I told him we would all come."

"I have to work the day after Thanksgiving and that Saturday, Chip, the assistant bank manager will be out on vacation." He said running his hands over his mouth.

"Can't you come the beginning of the week?" I asked.

"Then leave my family there the rest of the time? I'm supposed to spend Thanksgiving alone?"

"No, maybe you can fly back home on Thanksgiving or early Friday morning. We haven't checked any flights yet."

"We?" he asked like a question.

"I, he has not given me all the details. I just know it is the week of Thanksgiving, and that's all."

"I wish you would have called me before you made a commitment," he said sitting on the edge of the bed. I walk in front of him, but he doesn't try and reach out to touch me.

"He didn't leave me any choice," I said.

"You always have choices," he responds looking me in the eyes.

"You're right, we do. What do you think would have happened if they would have given that file to the mediator, and then turned it over to the judge? My mother was a drug addicted felon," I said with thick emotion in my voice.

"She is an ex-felon, an ex- drug addict."

"You think the courts care about that? All I could see was him handing the file to Julian, and them taking Carter away for leaving him with my mother. I could see them telling me I am unfit to be his mother."

"Daryn, that's not true. We can prove she is a productive member of society. We can have letters written by her employer, church, and show how she has improved her life. He is just holding that over your head, and you fell for Logan's bullshit. You played yourself, and he played you."

"Wait a damn minute," the emotions in my voice are gone, my tears are no longer threatening to fall, and the deep dark monster that lives inside of me is trying to emerge. The kraken is ready to make a comeback. I can feel my blood start to boil in my veins, and that impulse to let him have it. I haven't felt this type of rage since I had Carter.

"Daryn,"

"Don't Daryn me! I didn't get played at all. If you think any judge is going to keep Logan away from Carter, then you are playing yourself. If you think that Carter wouldn't hate us for putting up roadblocks when he's older then you are playing yourself. If you think for one damn minute Logan would just go away and let you win, then you are playing yourself!" By the time I am done I am huffing, puffing, and trying to calm myself down.

That's when he stands up, and all my senses go on high alert to defend myself.

"Logan is just using Carter to get you to be his puppet, and you are falling for it. If you think this is about Carter, then you got a lot to learn. This is about you, and him wanting to be next to you. Don't be so simple minded." I unleash the beast I call the kraken that lives deep inside of me, on him so quickly I didn't know what was going on.

"FUCK YOU JETHRO! I can take care of myself and Carter. I don't need your permission for a damn thing. For the record if I was fucking around with Logan you would never know it." I said and walk in the closet to get my shoes. He is right on my heels, but I don't care. I have to get away from him before this argument gets any worse.

"What does that mean Daryn?" I put on my shoes and exit the closet as I ignore him. "Where are you going?" he asks.

"Away from you!" I grab my purse and head for the door.

"It's like that," he said, and I don't dignify it with a response, I walk out the front door slamming it behind me. I am so pissed I cannot see straight.

He has me so pissed, I pick up my phone and type in Logan's name. The only reason I don't press the call button is because I think about the likelihood of his wife picking up his phone. Besides he will probably use it against me in court.

I decide to head to Cheyenne's place. Before I can hit the corner, my phone is ringing. I send him to voicemail. Then in pops a text message.

Where are you going, to meet him?

I smile at the message then quickly type one back

Wouldn't you like to know?

I hit send, then turn my phone off.

I feel some guilt for what I said to Jethro, but him calling me simple minded made me want to punch him in the throat. I should take some pity on Jethro because I know he's been drinking. Part of what Jethro is saying, has to do with the dark liquor he consumed.

I drive to Cheyenne's and pound on the door.

"Where's the fire?" she said opening the door as I rush past her.

"Your sister-n-law is here, and from the looks of it your brother has really pissed her off."

Dammitt she is on the phone with Abe, and he's going to tell Jethro where I am. I grab the phone from Cheyenne.

"Don't call him telling him where I am," I huff.

"I am not getting in between you and Jet, but if he calls me, I'm not lying to my brother. What did you do to my brother anyway?"

"Nothing, your brother needs to learn how to hold his liquor, or don't drink at all." I was still whirling from the argument with Jethro.

"Bet," he responds, and I give the phone back to Cheyenne. She giggles at something Abe said, then hang up. I am in her living room pacing back and forth.

"What the hell is going on with you and Jethro?" Cheyenne said sitting on the sofa.

"He's just being an asshole, and I don't want to deal with him, because I might kill him."

"Let me guess, Logan!" I stop pacing and look at her.

"Why would you guess that?"

"You went to mediation," she responds sitting on the sofa and kicking her legs behind her. I start pacing again. "You want to tell me about it?"

"The condensed version, I agreed for Logan to have Carter the day before his birthday, for us to spend Thanksgiving holiday with Logan's family, and I just sprung it on him." I pause my pacing to see what she has to say.

"Daryn, I can see how he would be upset, you just have to give him time I'm sure he will come around. This is a lot for him to deal with, and he's probably feeling a little insecure right now."

"Let me get this straight, you are defending Jethro?" I ask folding my arms.

"No, I'm not taking his side. You must admit he's been good to you and Carter. While I agree Logan should know he has a son, and be allowed to see him, I do understand why Jethro is upset. You are shutting him out. You tell him everything after the fact." I sigh and sit next to Cheyenne on the couch.

"When did you become the mature one?" I ask and she giggles.

"God has been working on me. While I know I am a work in progress, and I still curse way more than I should, I no longer do over half the things I use to do before I was baptized. I didn't even sleep with Abe, and for me that is progress." I had to smile at her joy through my anger.

"You're right I can definitely see a change in you," I smile at her genuinely.

"It has been the most amazing journey. I've gotten more joy out of my life now than when I was drinking, whoring around, and partying nonstop. Life for me is amazing."

"So, what were you and Abe talking about?"

"A little bit of this, and a little bit of that. He likes to talk just as much as I do, but mostly joking around. He makes me laugh uncontrollably, but most of all he is respecting my wishes. I explained to him where my life was compared to where my life is. He has been very supportive. He asked me to come to New York for one of his games."

"That's cool, but be careful," I said remembering the brunette Abe brought down here.

"Trust me, I ain't no fool, but I am considering going to see him." She smiles the entire time she speaks about Abe. Then Cheyenne's phone rang. "It's Jethro," she said. "You should probably talk to him."

"No, I shouldn't. He has been drinking and we will probably both say something we regret. Just let him go to voicemail," I plead with her, and she put the phone down.

"You are welcomed to spend the night," she says.

"I know, but I am going home in a couple of hours. I just need time to clear my head, and deal with everything. It is not easy trying to please everyone."

"That Daryn, is damn near impossible. You will not be able to please everyone especially when you have two souls in as much conflict as Logan and Jethro. You have to do what you think is right and pray to God you are making the right decision." She is right.

"It is hard for me not to consider Jethro's feelings when he has done and sacrificed so much for Carter and me."

"I agree he has, and I agree he did something that perhaps a lot of men wouldn't have done, but he knew what he was getting into. At the end of the day he understood that biologically, this is not his son, and at any moment his biological father could return."

"I guess understanding and being placed in the moment are two different things. We had gotten so comfortable that we no longer considered running into Logan. We started to feel safe. It caught us off guard. It was almost like I'd started to believe Jethro was his dad, and we would live happily ever after," I respond looking down thinking how ridiculous I must sound.

"We never believed in happily ever after, but when I started seeing the interaction you were having with Jethro I started to believe in the possibility that maybe it does exist." Cheyenne says, and I smile at her thinking we have both changed significantly.

We talk several more hours. Around two in the morning I reluctantly decide, it is time for me to head home.

When I open the door, Jethro is sitting on the sofa watching television.

"Hey," he said sounding sober.

"Hey," I respond. He stands and walk my way. I walk around him toward the bedroom. I hear the television click off, and I know it will only be moments before he follows me.

I am getting under the cover when he comes in the room and get under the cover also. I face the wall, and he comes up behind me and flattens his front to my back.

"I'm sorry," he said.

"I've heard that already," is my response.

"I know you have, and I will do better. I know you are only trying to protect Carter, and if you had any choice, you wouldn't have agreed to his demands." I turn to face him.

"Why couldn't you say that earlier? Why does talking about Logan always have to turn into an argument?"

"Truthfully?" he said like a question.

"Is there any other way?" is my response.

"I know how Logan operates. He can manipulate and keep going until he gets what he wants. It angers me, when I think about how he is trying to take advantage of you. He has taken someone as precious as Carter and used him as a weapon, to get at you. It infuriates me, and when I lash out at you, it is only because I can't lash out at him."

"Jethro, you have to trust me. Carter is my number one priority in all this, but you are my number two. I know we will have to go to trial. My attorney is working on a way to make it, so he won't get more than every other weekend; to which I am fine with. You must trust and believe that we are doing everything possible to make that happen.

"In the meantime, I may have to agree to some things that we don't want to just in case we have to prove to the judge that we are cooperating." He kisses me, and I didn't turn my head.

"I got it Daryn, in the future instead of getting upset, I will work on being more supportive." I smile at him and turn back over to go to sleep. He is once again behind me resting his hand on my hip.

CHAPTER TEN

We make it to the beautiful, warm Cayman Islands. We'd just had a cold front back home, so I am looking forward to tropical beaches and sunshine. There is sun on my face, wind blowing in my hair, and a boat waiting to take us to Logan's place. When I walk up I am shocked at who I see.

"Ms. Daryn, it is a pleasure to see you!"

"Hi Henry! It is nice to see you too!" I said smiling. Henry took me sightseeing around the island when I came to spend time with Logan as he remodeled his vacation home. When Logan couldn't get in touch with me he tried to fire Henry, until I stepped in and told him if he fired him I was leaving.

"Henry, this is my husband Jethro, and our son Carter," I said, and Henry looks confused.

"Nice to meet you Mr. Jethro," he said quickly recovering and shaking Jethro's hand. Jethro looks at me out the corner of his eyes but didn't say anything. I guess I will have some explaining to do later.

We enter the boat, and Henry cruises to the island pointing out iguanas to Carter, and the beaches and eateries for Jethro and me. He promises Jethro, he will take him to get some of the best conch in town. By the time we make it to the house Henry has Jethro smiling and laughing.

The smell of island food is in the air. I smell the curry, as we walk up to the door; it makes my mouth water.

Henry and Jethro walk through the door toting our bags.

Carter ran inside and hugs his brother Hunter then Logan.

This is the first time Jethro has seen the interaction between Logan and Carter. It seems almost magical how close they have become in such a short amount of time.

"You guys can come in," Logan stands and said after he hugs Carter. I lace my fingers with Jethro's which make him smile, and then we follow Logan.

"You will be staying in here," he shows us our room, and nothing in this house looks like I remember it. It was a work in progress when I came, and the finished product is tremendous. I don't know how someone can have a house this extravagant, and only visit it a couple of times a year.

"I know this room is at the front of the house, but the entire place is yours to explore. This is the only other bedroom with an in-suite bathroom. There is a pool out back, feel free to take a swim.

"We have a cook that will prepare dinner daily. The fridge is stocked with fresh food, seafood, and vegetables for those meals in between. The cook is preparing dinner now, but you can feel free to raid the fridge. If you need anything, please don't hesitate to ask. I really appreciate you doing this for me, and I want to make you feel as comfortable as possible."

"Logan, this is a very nice place you have here," Jethro said looking his way.

"Thanks, it was my father's place. He left it to me when he passed. It took me years to finally restore it the way I wanted too." I smile at the way they are trying to make an effort.

"I didn't know your father passed, I'm sorry to hear it." Jethro responds.

"It was a long time ago. I don't talk about it, because I was raised by my stepfather, and he did an amazing job. Well I will let the two of you have some privacy." He said walking toward the door, and Jethro stuck his hand out to shake his. Logan smiles and shakes his hand, then walks out the door.

"Thank you, Jethro. I won't pretend to know how hard this is for you, but I appreciate the effort you are making for Carter and me."

"You are welcome Mrs. Thomas," Jethro said and kisses me. "I'm going to ignore the fact that Henry already knows you, and you have probably been here before." He said and kisses me again. I didn't deny it or confirm it. I didn't want our first day of vacation to begin with an argument.

I shower and change then we join the family in the family

room.

"Hello Daryn and Jethro, we are so glad you could make it." Logan's wife said approaching me for a hug. I dig deep to plant a phony smile on my face.

"This is, Brooke my daughter who is home from college. I know you two haven't met," she said, and we both waive at each other.

"Dinner is ready, you must be starving," she said, and we follow her to the table. I wasn't expecting the family size table. Carter sat next to me, and Bristol, their youngest child, sat next to Carter.

There is a feast the length of the table. Jethro smiles, as he notices the conk fritters, and starts rubbing his hands together.

"How was your flight?" Logan's wife asked, just as I am putting peas and rice in my mouth. I hold my hand to my mouth.

"Nice, and quick. We had a smooth flight." I respond.

"We came up with an itinerary. There are sights. Have you been to the Cayman Islands before?"

"No, we haven't been before," Jethro chimes in. I am grateful he addresses her. I didn't know what to say. Judging from her question, I don't believe she is asking because of her "itinerary." I wonder if she is asking because she has a suspicion I have been here with Logan before. Logan didn't look our way, but he paused while he was loading his plate, and didn't start back again until Jethro answered. Judging from his reaction, I'm pretty sure he has not told her. How do you tell your wife that you brought your mistress to your family home before you brought your family?

"I see you like the conk fritters." she said smiling at Jethro.

"Yeah, one of my employees is from the Bahamas, she brings them in for us from time to time, but they aren't as fresh as these."

"Yeah, well that conk was caught this morning," Logan said smiling with pride.

"Yeah, I can tell," Jethro said munching. He has a plate full of conk fritters and nothing else. "I need to kiss the cook," he said and we all laugh.

"I will make sure she introduces herself," Logan interjects.

"Daryn, the kids seem to be getting along quite well." She is sitting with her hands intertwined and poised under her chin, while an empty plate sits in front of her. Why isn't this bitch eating?

"Yes, they hit it off right away." I respond and smile. Then I put a piece of fish in my mouth trying to signal I am eating, and stop talking to me.

The cook brings out another plate of conk fritters, and Jethro might get up and dance he is so happy. He stands up and hugs, her and she laughs at his excitement.

"Eat up, there is plenty more where those came from," she said with a heavy island accent.

"You don't have to tell me twice. What is your name?" he asks, and she looks shocked Jethro asked.

"My name is Rosa," she responds.

"I am Jethro, and these are the best conk fritters I've ever eaten."

"Try something else. You may be surprised at how good that is too," she said smiling.

"Yes ma'am," he responds, and puts some of the fish, and pigeon peas and rice on his plate. She picks up some of the dishes, and Jethro stands to help her.

"Jethro please sit, she can get it," Mrs. Anderson said. "No, I don't mind. After you Ms. Rosa" he said and she almost split open she is so happy to have assistance. Rosa looks as old as my grandmother, I know Jethro isn't going to sit back down and not assist her. He's a gentleman in all aspects of life.

He returns with a salad full of bright colors. "What is that?" I ask.

"Conk salad, made just for me," he said smiling broadly and sitting. I am happy he is making the best of such an unstable situation. This is only day one, but I am glad we got off on the right foot.

"Daryn, maybe we can have a girl's night, and let the gentleman have a night together." Why is she trying me?

"With all due respect Mrs. Anderson, I only have my wife for three days before I leave to go back home. You will have to postpone girl's night until I leave. Henry told us about this place, we can listen to some authentic island music. We have plans to go there tonight." Jethro was still popping fritters in his mouth as he spoke. Note to self, kiss Jethro later. If he keeps this up, I might have to go to a fertility clinic, um nah, I'll just buy him a present.

"Maybe another night," she said.

"So, you will be leaving Carter with us," Logan asked smiling.

"Yes, if you don't mind," Jethro said looking in Logan's direction. For the first time since we sat down he is not chewing. This is more progress than I thought I would ever see.

"It would be my pleasure," he is still smiling as if he is in disbelief.

"Dad," Carter calls.

"Yes," they both answer in unison.

"Not other dad, my dad, dad," Carter said, and not only did Jethro smile wider but he looks like he stuck his chest out a little bit.

"Yeah son," he said.

"Can we go play, I ate all my rice. I didn't like the fish."

"Yeah, son if it is okay with Logan for Bristol to go."

"Yeah sure," Logan said losing some of his smile.

"Tomorrow we would like to have a day at the beach if it's okay with the both of you." Logan said as we were nearing the end of dinner.

"That sounds like fun," I respond, and then place my napkin on my plate to signal I'm done. Jethro is too busy popping conk fritters in his mouth and humming to notice. I'm ready to get up from this table before they continue with the questions, and the planning.

"Man, that was good," Jethro now has his right arm thrown across the back of my chair, rubbing his belly, and of course smiling. I look at him and smile. He leans over and kisses me. When I look up Logan's wife is smiling at us. I guess that makes her feel safe, and not like I am coming to get between her and her husband. I didn't look in

Logan's direction.

Rosa clears the table, and Jethro assists her.

"Oh no, I can do it," Rosa said smiling at Jethro.

"It's no bother," he responds. I stand to go to my room.

Logan stands also. I look in his direction.

"Feel free to roam all over the house. I know the boys are probably in the family room. There are all sorts of rooms in this house, and you are welcome to use any of them. Please make yourself at home. Amber and I will be on the deck, by the pool, if you'd like to join us."

"Thank you, but right now I am going to rest for a bit before Jethro and I go out tonight." I smile at him and leave the dining room before his wife has a chance to chime in. To say it is a bit awkward sitting at the table with them, like we were one big happy family, would be an understatement. I breathe a sigh of relief as I enter our room, closing the door behind me. I sit in a chair in the room and put my feet up on the ottoman.

Jethro walks in moments later.

"Did you check on Carter?"

"Yeah, he's good. He's playing with Bristol," he is removing his shoes and came and sat on the chair next to me. I knew this was not going to be a good conversation. "Why did Logan invite you out here?"

"He wanted time with Carter," I feign innocents.

"Before," he says.

"Before what," I am stalling for time. I wasn't expecting to have this conversation.

"Daryn, I know you have been here before. Henry spoke to you like he knew you. Logan almost shit himself when Amber asked us if you'd been here before. So, why did he ask you out here before?" I pause for a moment searching for the right words to say.

"It's water under the bridge." I respond.

"How can it be water under the bridge, when I didn't know the bridge existed."

"Jethro, let's not have this conversation. It was long before I dated you that I came out here with Logan. I'm not going to ask you about your past relationships, and all the things you did. Please don't question me about mine, every time you learn some new information about me. Can we bury what happened with Logan and me once and for all?" I plead with him.

"I guess the reason it is so hard to bury it, is because Logan is still a part of our life. None of my exes are a part of our life. So, when I come to this island trying to have an open mind, and trying to play fair, and the driver knows you, it raised several questions. Then Logan's wife asked if you've been to the Cayman Island, and I saw your expression, I knew this was a secret that the two of you shared, and you didn't think either of us would ever find out. So, when I ask you questions about your past with Logan it is only because he is still a part of our life, and I'm trying to get it. I'm trying to get where you were in that moment of your life. We need to get over and through all of this. So, I'm sure this is frustrating for you, and I will try my best to be sensitive of that, but I still have questions."

"What Logan and I shared was toxic. I never intended to be hooked up with Logan for life. The affair we had, had no choice but to end badly. I was comfortable with being the side chic because I thought it worked. Little did I know I would end up attached to him forever. Before I knew it, the conveyance of being with a married man became the inconvenience of being in a relationship. Don't get hung up on Logan because there aren't any feelings there. You are the one I chose, and the one I love. So, what do you want to know, because I want to lay that relationship to rest once and for all?" I am tired of questions about Logan resurfacing.

He clears his throat then leans in closer to me.

"Are there any other secrets you think I should know about?"

"Yes, I once met Logan at Curtis Hixon Park, so he could play catch with Carter." He looked like he had a follow up question but was battling if he should ask me.

"Are you sure that's all?"

"I'm positive that is all I can think of. I don't have anything I am purposely keeping from you. I wasn't trying to keep the fact that I've been here from you. I can't think of anything that happened between us that you would need to know."

"Okay," he said then he leans over to kiss me.

"I'm going to the beach with Carter. He asked if I would help him pick up seashells. Then we can go out, say around eightish?"

"Okay," is my response. Since they were going to the beach I decided to take a nap to try and sleep off this food.

We leave Carter for the first time with Logan's family. I have reservations about it, but I didn't think he would be unsafe. I make sure my phone is on and has a signal when we arrive to our destination.

I dressed in True Religion jeans, a velvet cameo, and black over the knee boots, I got from Neiman Marcus. There is the sweet sound of island steel drums playing as we approach the club. They have me in the mood to leave everything outside the club and have a great time.

When I walk in I like the atmosphere. It puts me in the mindset of a beach hut with a few tables and chairs around the perimeter of the dance floor. The singer is cooing the right melody. We are seated near the band.

"You look mighty sexy, Mrs. Thomas," Jethro said, and that makes me smile. Logan stopped in his tracks when I walked out the room. It made his mouth pop open a bit.

"Thank you, Mr. Thomas," he rewards me with a kiss. I smile at him, as he picked up a menu. "You can't possibly be hungry again." I know Jethro has an extremely high metabolism, but this is ridiculous.

"I'm looking for a drink. You want a glass of wine?"

"I will have one," I respond which made him smile wider.

"Good because I hate to drink alone." He calls over the waiter and orders us a drink, him an appetizer, and of course conk fritters. I roll my eyes when he orders them.

We have a great time dancing exotically on one another. I love dancing with Jethro he has been the only man I've ever dated that can keep up with me. We kiss like newlyweds, and keep touching one another like we are the only ones in the entire place.

We leave still kissing and hugging as Henry skips across the sea on the way to the vacation house.

We are letting our body language do the talking. We kiss, we hug, and we are entangled with one another. I am unbuckling his pants while he is simultaneously unbuckling mine. I am so anxious to be with him that as soon as I unbuckle his pants I shove my hands in them, and grab hold of him making him gasp. He laid his head on my shoulder as I massage him he lets out an audible swallow. "You like that," I whisper, and his head motion yes.

He unzips my pants, and ease his hand inside my panties, using his fingers to skillfully stimulate my clit. It is now my time to gasp. I start to falter, some on massaging him, as he works me vigorously. I spread my legs wider, to give him better access, and he takes this as an invite to insert one digit inside of me, and my knees almost buckle. I stop completely from handling his manhood. I bite my lip as an attempt to silence my moans. I am ready, and I don't want to wait anymore.

"Please Jethro, now," I beg. He removes his finger, picks me up, and carries me to the bed. He lays me down gently, then works off my boots followed by my jeans, and underwear. I lay panting and waiting for him to finish undressing, so he can be inside of me. He slowly crawls up the bed, and eases between my thighs taking time to lay light kisses on my body as he travels north. Leave it to Jethro to be smiling as he comes nose to nose with me. His sex is rubbing against mine, and I am throbbing with the need for him to be inside of me. He starts his slow insertion. I let out an exhale as I feel the pressure of him easing inside of me. He is barely inserted before he starts pulling out, and easing back in again, trying to give me a chance to get use to him. He bends down to kiss me. My body immediately tenses feeling like this is it, he is driving completely inside of me penetrating deeply to my core. I lift my head off the bed because that is the only thing I can move under the weight of him.

He looks deeply in my eyes and says his signature statement "You ready!" I take a deep breath and shake my head yes. I know what that means. I know he is done being gentle. He is done easing in and out of me. He is ready for heavy and hard, and so am I.

I claw at his back as he penetrates me deeply. I bite into his shoulder to calm my cries. The antics I use to slow him down, only edge him on. I can feel my body mounting for the big release.   It is coming on hard, and strong. My moans are already muffled by biting down on Jethro's shoulder. I don't know how much more I can take. He takes my right leg and places it over his shoulder for deeper thrusting. I can no longer muffle my cries.

It is becoming unbearable to restrain my moans as Jethro flexes his hip just enough to start the sensual torment of climaxing.

"It's okay Daryn, let lose," Jethro whispers to me. I let lose thrashing around and shouting out Jethro's name. The intensity of the stimulation, from Jethro's movements, has me in a sexual trance. I can't think about anything but the feeling of euphoria as the orgasm has taken over my entire body as it powers through me. Finally, it starts to slow down, my body starts to cooperate, and my cries start to mellow out. My body relaxes as the overwhelming sensation starts to leave my body.

Jethro lets my leg down, and I wrap it back around his body as he lays his head on the side of my body steadily moving. My muscles clench around him, and I squeeze hard begging him to release his sexual peak as well. The muscles in his back flex as he speeds up. A moan escapes from his lips and I know it is time.

I grab hold of him wrapping my arms tightly around him as he continues with his unyielding thrusting. I keep my sounds down as Jethro freed himself of all his passion inside of me. His body stiffens in the end, and then he drops his head to my shoulder catching his breath. Soon after he is rolling off me but taking me with him. I lay my head on his chest, ad he wraps his arms around me.

Jethro is the first to speak after several moments of silence. "Shit you were looking to sexy when you put those heels on and stood in front of the mirror admiring your fit. Homeboy stood at full attention. That's why I had to go to the bathroom to splash cold water on my face, and calm down." I laugh at his comment.

"I had no idea I had that kind of effect on you," I said resting my chin on his chest.

"Shiiiit, you have an unbelievable power over me Daryn. Sometimes just your scent gets me excited. You do this thing where you lotion your leg, then extend it out, and I guess check to make sure you hit every spot. It gets me every time."   I never knew he was paying attention to what I was doing.

"I have to get all the ash," I let out and he laughs.

"I got the sexiest wife out there. I just wish we could extend our legacy."

"Yeah, I'm sorry that we can't." I know how much Jethro wants biological children, so he can see a reflection of himself when he looks at his child. He will just have to see a reflection of himself in the way he raises Carter. There is nothing inside of me that has the desire to have another kid. I won't ever tell him this, but I feel this is a blessing that we can't conceive.

"I've been thinking about our options, and I believe if it is God's will he will make it happen." I straddle Jethro. I lay my head on his chest and pull the covers up over my shoulders. I want to be skin to skin with him. I know how badly he wants a daughter, but sometimes things just aren't meant to be, and we never understand why.

"Yes, I agree." I respond and close my eyes. The last thing I remember is him caressing my back before I fall asleep.

CHAPTER ELEVEN

I try to wake Jethro to get him to run with me, but he won't budge. If I break routine and don't run this week it will be hell to start again. I went to get a bottle of water out the fridge. When I close door, I yelp. It is Logan looking angry.

"I understand Jethro is your husband, and you will have sex with him. My only request is that you keep it down so the entire house doesn't hear you." He is trying to walk off, but the way he came at me pisses me off.

"What happened to my house is your house? If you are going to scold me every time I do something you don't agree with then what's the point of that statement?"

"You are on the other side of the damn house. I didn't expect to hear you on the way to the kitchen. I'm not ready to hear you with another man."

"That other man you are referring to is my husband, and instead of listening to us, why don't you focus on making your wife scream!" I said and walked off leaving him speechless. I don't have time for Logan and his bullshit.

After going back and forth with Logan I needed that run. When I returned his wife is in the kitchen cooking breakfast. She didn't look like much of a cook, with her fluffy kitten heals, and satin robe.

"Hi Daryn, did you and Jethro have a good time," I tried to sneak past her, but no luck. I didn't know if she was being sarcastic, or genuine.

"Yes, the spot Henry took us to was very nice."

"Feel free to go out again. We enjoyed spending time with Carter. He kept us on our toes, but we loved every minute of it," she said laughing. Once again, I'm not sure if it is sarcasm or genuineness.

"Thanks, I am going to shower," I know we need to be civil to one another, but this is too weird for me. There is no way I would spend my vacation with a woman that had an affair with my husband

and showed up four years later with his kid. I am the other woman and it bothers me to be in the house with his wife.

"Of course," she said flipping something that resembles a pancake.

"Mommy," Carter ran to me as I walk in the room.

"Hello son," I said sitting and pulling him on my lap. "Did you have a good time?"

"Yes, my other dad made popcorn and we watched Ninja Turtles, and he let me drink Sprite." I smile at him. Jethro walks out the bathroom fully dressed.

"I thought you would still be asleep." I smile at him.

"Nah, you know I can't sleep in. Come on buddy!"

"Where are you going?"

"We are going to eat breakfast," Jethro said. I didn't want to burst his bubble about who is cooking breakfast, so I just smile at him. He kisses me and walks out the room.

I shower then lay across the bed. Jethro came back about an hour later and said he was heading to the beach with Carter, to pick up seashells. I nod and go back to sleep.

When I wake-up I am famished. I change into my bikini, put a sarong around me, and walk to the kitchen. Logan's daughter is in there.

"Hello Brooke," I said. She walks toward me, arms crossed, and a unit on her face. I prepare myself for attack mode. I feel the kraken bubbling under my skin, but I will it to stay back.

"How can you come here with MY mom and dad, and waltz into our kitchen, like you haven't done anything wrong?"

"I beg your pardon?" I respond. I read her body language; she isn't happy with my presence, but I wasn't expecting her to attack me.

"I told my mom she was crazy for letting you come to our family home. I told my dad he was crazy for inviting you. Haven't you done enough?" I know she is young, and I know she is hurting so I try and take that into consideration when I respond.

"I am not intentionally doing anything to your parents. I am only here so there can be a smooth transition for my son."

"You could have just sent him. Why did YOU have to come?"

"Look Brooke..." she cuts me off.

"My dad maybe okay with having his whore here, but I'm not. I will never accept you, or what you did to my family."

Lord please help me, I shout in my head because civility is not the first thing that is coming to mind. "You don't have to like me! We don't have to be friends, but you will not speak to me that way." I said straightening up to let her know I am not one of her little college friends. If she keeps it up I will forget she is Carter's sister and drag her all up and through this house.

"How dare you talk to me like that? You are not my mother."

"I wouldn't be your mother if you paid me all the tea in China. What happened between your dad and me was a long time ago, and we are both over it. We have both moved on."

"Is that what you think? If that is what you think you are more pathetic than I thought. My parents haven't moved on! My dad running into you only resurfaced all the emotions, and problems they were going through while he was fucking you and making my bastard brother!" It is to late the kraken showed up and showed out. My hand is across her cheek before I can register in my mind that isn't a good idea. She grabs her cheek. If she doesn't get out my face in the next few seconds I will not be able to refrain from jumping on her ass. I was barely able to only slap her.

"What I did with your father is none of your got damn business. And if you ever say anything else negative about my son I will do more than slap the shit out of you, I will beat the shit out of you!"

"None of my business. It was our business. Do you think your having an affair with my dad didn't affect us? Well that goes to show how much you know. It was because of you that my mother had more surgeries and became addicted to pain pills. It was because of you my dad started drinking so much he almost lost his job. It was because of you my parents were about to get a divorce. Of course, what you did affected us because it was me who had to take care of my siblings, because she was too high to do it. Of course, it affected us, because when my dad started his drinking rants and rages I had to tend to my siblings until he calmed down. I delayed going to college until I felt my parents were stable enough to be parents. So, I know you thought you were living in a perfect bubble with my dad, but it was at the expense of popping ours. WAS IT WORTH IT!" She shouts with her eyes turning red and starting to gloss over. The kraken, that I tried to control, wouldn't let me feel sorry for her.

"If you are looking for an apology you are not going to get one. I didn't pursue your dad, or try to break up your home, your dad pursued me. It wasn't my fault Logan had an affair on your mom. I am not to blame for your shattered childhood dreams, or what your parents put you through. I'm not here to argue with you or to take your dad away; I am only here so he can get to know Carter! You will have to grow up and realize this isn't about you. Your dad wanted to spend time with Carter, I am not imposing."

"Ha imposing, you have imposed on our entire life since the day he met you. I wish you would go back into hiding and never return." She was trying to walk away. I grab her by the arm. She tries to jerk away, but I don't let go.

"My son is your brother, your dad is my son's dad, and your siblings are my son's siblings. If you have a problem with that, it is too damn bad! All I know, if you try me again, I will not be able to contain myself." I stare into her eyes, and she looks afraid. I want her to know she can't try me like she tries her mother. I am not the one.

"Daryn," Logan calls and I let her go. She ran out the room, probably into her room to cry. I look at Logan.

"What is going on?" He asks.

"Your daughter is what is going on! You should have warned me about the feelings she has toward me, so I would have been better prepared when she confronted me."

"She confronted you?"

"It doesn't matter," I said walking toward the door. He

follows me.

"Of course, it matters. I'm sorry; I thought she'd gotten past this. She made up excuses for not coming, but I thought if she got to know you and Carter she would change her opinion."

"She has clearly not gotten over it, and she called my son a bastard."

"What? Are you certain?"

"Do you think I'm lying?" I shot back.

"No, not at all. I'm just shocked. I can't believe she would say that. She took it the hardest when we told the kids. She cried worse than I'd ever seen her cry, and accused me of being a liar and a fraud. I never thought she would confront you. She used to be such a sweet child."

"Well, that sweet child has definitely changed. She gave me the business." I said, and he hung his head down.

"You think when things are going on you are protecting your kids, but you don't realize that the things you think you are hiding from them is impacting them. She knew before we told her that I was having an affair. She knew, before we told them I had another child. She overheard her mom and me arguing one night. She hasn't been the same since." He's not mine to comfort, I had to say in my head. This scene looks all too familiar from the days when we were together.

"I'm sure she will forgive you. She needs time, and patience, to get over the heartbreak that you caused her."

"I hope that's soon, because I miss how sweet my daughter use to be."

"Give her time," I respond then walk out towards the beach.

I am too late Jethro and Carter are walking back to the house with wet shorts and sandy feet. He looks at me and smiles. I try to smile in return, but it comes out weak and crooked.

"Hey, you," Jethro said and hugs me. I squeeze him hard.

"Mommy look!" Carter is excited to show me one of his seashells.

"That's awesome!" I respond.

"It's a conk shell!"

"It's beautiful!"

"You okay," Jethro ask lacing his fingers with mine, as we walk back toward the house. As we approach the house Logan, Brooke, and Amber are engaged in an argument. Brooke has several bags on her shoulder. There is a taxi waiting out front.

"Mommy what is wrong with my sister?" She is visibly upset and crying.

"I'm not sure," I respond, and Carter let go of my hand and starts running.

"Brooke, Brooke," he is shouting.

"Carter," I shout running behind him. He makes it to Brooke and she bends down to hug him.

"What's wrong Brooke?" he asks.

"Carter, let's give her some privacy," I said.

"No!" she yells back at me. "He's my brother, and I might not see him for a while. Why don't you give us some privacy?" She snaps at me.

"Daryn," Jethro said pulling me to the side.

"I'm sorry," Logan said to me.

"For what?" Jethro asks.

"For the commotion," he responds.

"No need to apologize, it's just a little family drama. We've all had it."

I turn around to see what is going on with Brooke and Carter. I don't trust her. She is smiling through her tears and looking at his conk shell. She hugs him once more and stands up.

"Daryn you and Jethro seem like good people, despite the affair you had with my dad. If I were you, I wouldn't let my parents fuck up any more kids. I'd take my son and get as far away from them as possible." She said and got in the cab leaving us all with our mouths hanging open. Her mom ran in the house crying. I pull Carter away, so they can drive off. He waves at her then starts to cry.

"Why can't Brooke stay?"

Jethro picks him up. "She had to go back to school. We will see her again," he said and walks in the house, He left me outside with Logan.

"I don't know what to do to get my daughter back."

"You can't force her; you have to give her the time she needs."

"Time, we've given her time. It's going to take more than time. I'm afraid one day she is going to leave and never come back. She has been so disconnected from all of us, way before she left for college."

"It took me until I had Carter, to fully forgive my mom, for all she put me through as a kid. I had to grow up before I was ready. I missed my entire childhood because I was too busy trying to raise myself. I never went to prom, homecoming, grad night, or anything to solidify my life as a young adult. I went from child to adult. You, I meant we, robbed her of her childhood, because while we were off having an affair and worrying about our secrets, she was busy being an adult and taking care of her siblings. So, the least we can do is give her time. She will forgive you, but you can't force her."

"Thanks, I'd better go inside and see about my wife."

"Yes, you should." I said, and he walks inside. I follow but turn into our room. Jethro is drying off Carter and helping him get dressed.

"This is some Thanksgiving vacation," I said and plop on the chair.

"I wonder what that was all about," I'm not sure he's asking because he doesn't know, or if he's asking for confirmation.

"I am sure I can guess," is my response.

"Oh yeah, what happened?"

"She told me how unpleased she was with me and her dad. I might have slapped her for the statements she made. I came to find you, then when we returned she was leaving."

"You slapped her," he was trying to whisper, but failing.

"I shouldn't have, but she called Carter a B-AS-T-A-R-D," I spell out so Carter wouldn't repeat it or ask what it meant.

"Well then, she brought it on herself," Jethro said, and I laugh, but I know I shouldn't have.

"I still should have showed restraint."

"I'm glad all you did was slap her. She better be glad you have changed some."

"I didn't think you noticed."

"Yeah, I have definitely noticed how you've changed. You make me more and more proud of you every day." I smile at him. "I'm going to shower," Jethro said walking back in the bathroom.

"Can I go and play with Hunter and Bristol?" Carter asks.

"Aren't you hungry? You've been gone all day. Why don't we get you a sandwich first?" Carter will forgo food to play.

We walk in the kitchen, and Hunter is in there. He only wears black, and he barely speaks to me, but him and Carter get along great. I wonder if he feels the same way about me Brooke does.

"Hey Hunter," Carter said.

"Hey buddy," he said and walks out the kitchen.

I never felt like the other woman when I was having an affair with Logan, but now that I'm not having an affair with Logan I'm being treated like the other woman. I know I wouldn't have cared when I was Daryn Carter, but now that I'm Daryn Thomas wife and mother I care more than I want to admit.

"Carter, I have a surprise for you," I said and gave him his tablet.

"Oh boy!" he yells, and immediately starts filming video. He ran to the back of the house no doubt to show Bristol.

"Hey baby!" Jethro said kissing me on the cheek. "I was thinking," he pauses. This is not good is my first thought. "I've been thinking since Mrs. Anderson looks so upset maybe you could do something with her, and Logan and me can do something with the kids."

"Ah Jethro, no, I don't want to." I whine, and he smiles at me.

"You are cute when you whine." He responds.

"Why don't we all just do something together? I'm not ready to be alone with her."

"If the kids see us getting along maybe they will be okay with the transition. Besides you should face your demons. She's good people Daryn," Jethro tries to convince me.

"I'm sure she is, but I'm not the one she would want to entertain her right now. If the shoe were on the other foot, I wouldn't want anything to do with her."

"Daryn we are better than that. I'm going to recommend to Logan that we go and hang out while you two hang out. While I don't think you will solve her life problems, I think you humbling yourself, and showing a little support might be just what she needs right now. If not for her do it for me." He is always pulling out the big guns.

"Hello Mr. Jethro," Rosa said interrupting me trying to think of an excuse to get out of hanging out with Logan's wife.

"Rosa," Jethro said rolling the R. He got up to help her with the groceries she was bringing in.

"Hello Mrs. Jethro," she said to me with her rosy cheeks. I never told her my name, and at this point I don't think it is any point in telling her.

"Hi Rosa," I smile waving at her.

I stay up at the bar listening to Rosa chop and dice food as the various aromas waft in the air. She made Jethro a special batch of conk fritters while she prepares dinner. He is humming and eating. I watch as Bristol and Carter run around playing and making videos.

Logan and his wife finally emerge from the bedroom.

"Hey guys," Jethro said enthusiastically.

"Hey," Logan said, and his wife just smiles the best she can.

"I had a great idea! Since Carter is so into ninja turtles, I thought we, the fellas, could go to the turtle farm while the women hang out." He is of course smiling and rubbing his hands together.

"That sounds like a great idea, if it's okay with the 'ladies'," Logan said laughing.

"Yes, I'm okay with it if Amber is okay with it."

"Yes, of course!" She finally speaks, and gives a genuine smile.

"Everybody put your shoes on, so we can go," Logan said. Now everyone seems to be smiling but me. I am the only one skeptical of this idea. I have no idea what to say to her for an entire evening.

"What about Hunter?" Jethro asks Logan.

"I doubt he will want to come" Logan looks solemn when he responds.

"Nonsense, it's the guys night out. I'll get him." Jethro walks into the back. A reluctant Hunter comes out and Jethro is following behind him. I would have loved to have heard that conversation.

"Let's load up!" Jethro came over to kiss me. When Carter came over I had to pry his iPad out of his hands. There is no way I am letting him take this around water.

When they leave Amber came to sit next to me on the bar stool.

"So, what would you like to do?" I ask.

"I'm not sure, something that doesn't require much. I'm exhausted. I'm exhausted all the time," she said with shimmering eyes.

"I'm sorry," for lack of a better word that is what comes to mind. "I didn't think about the repercussions of my actions, and for that I'm sorry." It came from nowhere. I never intended to apologize, but here I am apologizing for my affair with Logan.

She shakes her head in a yes motion, and a few tears fall before she straightens up. "You know Daryn ya'll made a beautiful son, and please don't take this the wrong way. I can't, I can't do it all over again. It's not that I don't love him, because I do. He's apart of Logan, whom I've loved since high school.

I go along with everything he wants, but I can't go along with this. I can't take care of another child. Brooke hates me, Hunter barely speaks to me, and I am engulfed in Bristol's extracurricular activities. Not to mention volunteer hours at their school and trying to stay healthy. I can't take on another responsibility. I just can't." She said weeping.

"Why won't you tell him?"

"He thinks this is his chance at redemption for not being present in our other kid's lives while he was building his career. When we went to court I thought it was for partial custody, it wasn't until we were in court that I found out, it was for full custody. We only discussed having rights to spend time with Carter. We never discussed full custody." She is wiping tears from her face, and I am trying to think of a way to get her to get Logan to back off.

"Why don't we go out where there are no kids, and we don't have to be afraid to let our hair down," I said, and she smiles. This vacation must get better at some point.

"Hey Rosa," I shout over her music.

"Yes," she responds.

"Can you give us a spot to go to so we can have some fun." I said and Amber giggles.

Rosa is all too happy to tell us where we can go, and not only have a great time, but great drinks, and who to ask for when we get there. We call a taxi. We are ready and out the house within 20 minutes.

As soon as we let the waitress know we are friends of Rosa we are treated like celebrities.   The waitress came over with complimentary shots of rum.

"Um, that's okay I don't drink hard liquor."

"Ah come on it's girls' night out, which is something I never get to do." She is already picking up her shot for us to clink glasses.

"What the hell! When in Rome," I pick up my glass, toast her, and down the shot.

"Woooo!" We said in unison then giggle. I have a small buzz from that one shot. Before we have that shot down good there is another on the table.

"I think we should eat something," I said afraid of where this night is heading.

"I think you're right." Amber responds.

We are at the table like two old friends. After a while I'd forgotten my plot to get her to tell Logan she didn't want to raise Carter, and I started having fun. Shot glasses are stacked on our table. We played limbo, and every time we make it under the bar we are given a shot of rum. The MC would pour as much as you can hold in your mouth when you make it under the bar. I get down to the last two in limbo and fall on my back. I am laughing so hard Amber must come get me, and escort me back to the table.

"You know I don't hate you," she slurs after we get back to the table. I look at her still grinning but thinking to myself I need to try and look serious. "I basically pushed Logan into your arms. Before we went on the cruise I told him, I didn't love him anymore. I told him he'd sucked all the life out of me."

"I think you are too drunk to know what you are telling me, so I am going to stop you before you wake up tomorrow full of regret." This conversation is somehow making me come down off my high.

"I am tipsy, but I can handle my liquor. I know exactly what I'm saying.

"He was taking so much out of me because he wanted to get promoted at his job. He had a ten-year plan, and that involved me doing everything. I was exhausted. They were all in several extracurricular activities. I told Brooke she had to pick two. She was in soccer, volleyball, cheering, violin, and the church choir. When I told her, she told her dad, and he had it out with me right in front of Brooke. You should have seen the smug look she gave me at 12. You would have thought she was a grown woman the way she looked at me like she'd won, and I was nothing. That was the beginning of me resenting him. He wouldn't back me with the kids. I'd had it. I told him I didn't love him anymore. He told me I owed it to him to try, and he came up with the idea of the cruise.

"From the moment we got on the ship, I made excuses, so I did not have to spend time with him. I scheduled Brooke and me a spa day the first day on the ship. Brooke met new friends and wanted to hang with them, so I was on my own. I did everything to stay away from Logan. When we got home he seemed different. He wasn't hounding me about staying together or having sex. I felt free.

"One day that freeness wore off, and I started wondering why he wasn't hounding me about sex, or trying to reconcile anymore. Then the arguing started again, because I started picking fights. I had another surgery, and it was botched. I had an infection that almost killed me, and I became addicted to painkillers. The painkillers numbed my physical and mental pain.

"I was finally feeling better, and I decided to try and seduce him, but he wouldn't respond. It was like I had no effect on him at all. I kept trying and he told me to stop. He said he'd met someone, and he didn't know how, but he'd fallen in love. I let him leave thinking it was for the best.

"Well the joke was on me because I'd never been as stressed out as I was when he left. The kids were blaming me for him leaving. Hunter started skipping school and hanging with kids much older than him. He was kicked out of private school, and I had to put him in public school. My life that seemed perfect to everyone else, was now flipped on its axis. That's when I started calling him, begging him to come back. He'd warned me that I would miss him if he left. He warned me that if I thought it was hard with him it would really be hard without him, but I didn't believe him. I was more upset about him being right than him being with another woman. So, Daryn Thomas, I don't blame you, I don't blame you at all. I pushed him into your arms because deep down inside I knew the reason Logan was giving up was because he was with someone else. I never thought he would fall in love with that someone else and have a baby from her." This night is turning into a sad party, because now I feel compelled to say something on my behalf.

"I used to be a selfish person. I didn't think about the consequences of my actions, and I didn't know anything about his home life. I wouldn't let him tell me. I thought if I limited my time with him, and limited our conversation I could stay in control of the entire situation. Little did I know the things he was sneaking in were making me…" I cleared my throat ashamed of my own admission. "love him. I tried fighting him at every turn, but my resistance wore down as he continued to work on me. I started to let him in more than I wanted to. Loving him was never in the cards for me, but it happened.

"I don't think Logan meant to hurt either one of us, but it is something about his swagger that you can't help but falling for. He treated me kind, he gave me respect, and he fulfilled a need. That's all it was ever meant to be. I felt like one day I looked up and it was out of hand. We should have been more respectful of you and resisted temptation even if you were pushing him away."

I don't know why, but she looks at me with admiration for giving her some insight into the short timeframe that Logan and I tried to become a couple.

"Can I ask you a question?" I didn't like the look in her eyes. I know what she is about to ask is going to be something deeper than I want to discuss.

"Yeah, but just be prepared for what you are about to hear. It is sometimes better not knowing, because once you hear something, you can't unhear it. So, be sure before you ask the question, do you really want to hear the answer." I am dead serious, and I look her in her eyes the entire time, so she understands.

"I understand once I ask you I can't undo what I hear. I once asked Logan to tell me everything about his affair. The things he told me, I wasn't expecting. I thought it was going to be an infatuation. I thought there was no way, he could possibly love you, but when he described you, and your routine, I could tell by the look in his eyes he did love you. So, Daryn I am fully aware of the question I am about to ask and the consequences of my asking." She took a deep breath, then proceeds. "Did you love Logan more than you love Jethro?"

"There is no comparison. I loved Logan differently than I love Jethro. What I had with Logan was toxic. I didn't think I would deal with him long as I did. I usually get tired of people, but I didn't get tired of him I'm sure it's because we weren't exclusive. Majority of the time I was with him I found myself trying to guard my heart, so I didn't fall in love with him, because I knew inside he was not mine to love.

"When it comes to Jethro I can just love him, because he is mine to love. We are exclusive. We don't have any barriers, I am not limited to time with him, and I don't have to worry about one day it all being gone."

"Do you still love Logan?"

"I don't love him in the sense that you think. I love him as a friend or a person, but not as a lover. I no longer have a desire for him like I once had."

"Why did you decide to put him out?" I don't want to play this game of twenty questions, and I feel like this conversation is unhealthy for the both of us. Her demeanor has changed.

"I know you think knowing the answers to these questions will make you feel better about your decision to stay, but they won't. I respect your wanting to know, but there is nothing I can say to you to get you to understand. I will only say this to your question. It never felt completely right. What we shared was unhealthy. We had no place to go no matter how much we pretended when we were in our bubble. We both made the decision to end it and it was the right thing to do.

"Now, enough of this sad shit, let's get another round," I said and signal for the waitress to bring us a few more shots.

We can barely walk to the taxi. We can't get it together. We are laughing at everything. We see two iguanas mating, and Amber yells at least somebody is getting some, as she hung half out the van window. I laugh until I'm crying. When we get back to the house the men had to come and get us out the car.

Jethro half drags me out the van, leaving Logan to try and get Amber. She keeps telling Logan to get his hands off her. That made me crack up laughing. I have no idea why, but I'm going to go out on a limb and say it is because I'm drunk. When Jethro got me in the house I plop on the sofa laughing. He stands staring at me and shaking his head.

"Daryn, this wasn't what I meant by spending time with Amber," he said looking confused, and disappointed.

"You told me to spend time with her, now you are complaining. Jethro this is what she wanted to do, so I did what my home girl wanted." I whine the entire phrase.

"Your home girl?" he said shaking his head.

"Yeah, my home girl. She's not that bad."

Amber and Logan walk in. She plops on the sofa next to me, and starts hugging me. "Thank you for the night out, since Logan wouldn't take me." I cut my eyes at Logan, and he looks surprised by her comment.

"Amber maybe we should go to bed," Logan said.

"Why, will you promise to do rude things to me?" she said trying to unzip his zipper. I start clapping and laughing. Logan backs away from her looking embarrassed. "I told you he doesn't touch me," she said.

"Okay, let's go to bed," Logan said helping her up. She laid one fat, wet, kiss on him, and I yell out "OHHHH!" He didn't look like he enjoyed it, but he got her to go with him to the bedroom.

"Daryn wait right here while I go and move Carter, okay," "Aye aye captain," I said and salute.

Logan walks out, and I stand stumbling. He laughs at me, and I start laughing to.

"What's so funny?" I slur.

"You, I can't believe you are drinking. You being drunk is kind of cute," he said still smiling at me. He drops his eyes to my feet, and slowly brings them up to my mouth, then my lips. He licks his lips.

"You should go, and make love to your wife," I said feeling uncomfortable.

"You're right, but she's passed out right now." He responds with his eyes dropping to my lips.

"Then wake her up," I said.

"This reminds me of the time we were in Vegas. Do you remember that?" he asked smiling. Jethro walks in the room, and I sigh with relief.

"Is Amber okay?" He asked.

"Yeah, I was just getting her some water," he said and walks away. Jethro walks me to the room, and helps undress me, and get me into bed.

"Daryn," I hear in a distance, as I am closing my eyes.

"Hmm," I respond.

"Promise me you won't drink when I leave."

"Why?" I asked.

"I don't like how Logan has been looking at you, like he still wants something from you, besides Carter. Now promise me you won't drink when I leave," he said with an assertive tone.

"I promise," I respond, and he gets in the bed behind me, and put his arm around me.

"I trust you Daryn, but as a man, I know the look in his eyes when he sees you. I can tell he still wants you. I love you Daryn," I turn around to face him.

"Don't worry Jethro, those feelings are not mutual. I married my MCM, and I love you too!" I said, and he bent to kiss me. It wasn't ten seconds before I'd fallen to sleep.

CHAPTER TWELVE

Yesterday is a blur. I experienced my first hangover. Logan brought me a hangover potion that I threw up as soon as it went down. He laughed, but Jethro didn't find it funny. It seems Logan thinks everything I do is funny which causes Jethro to scowl even more. Jethro is annoyed, because Logan, as Jethro put it, is more concerned about me than his damn wife.

Jethro received a call Tuesday; his assistant bank manager has the flu and will be out Wednesday. So, instead of him flying home Thursday after our meal he is returning Wednesday morning, so he can work for his assistant. He thinks I should come home with him, so he can take care of me, and we can spend Thanksgiving together. I want to take him up on the offer, but my plan is to befriend Amber and get her to concede. I need her to agree to tell Logan that he should stop the custody battle. I can't do that if I go home. This is my only chance.

I am up still feeling a little sick, but not as bad as yesterday. I have on a pair of boxers, and a camisole. I can feel him staring at me. I know he is disappointed that I won't agree to come home with him. He has on his navy-blue suit, a light blue shirt, and a navy-blue tie; his standard banking outfit. He's standing with his hands deep inside his pockets.

"When I arrive, I have to go straight to work, I will call you when I land. know I will be extremely busy throughout the day since we are closed tomorrow and short staffed. Of course, if you need anything you can call me. If I can't pick up, I will call you back as soon as I'm available. If it is anything important call back to back or text me. I will call you right away." He's rambling as if he is trying not to forget anything.

"Okay," I respond.   Sometimes I can't deal with the many expressions of Jethro. He wears his emotions on his sleeves, and it makes me feel guilty when I have to deny him what he wants. I often wonder if I will feel guilty about telling him no forever, because he married me knowing my circumstances.

"Are you sure you will be okay," he said walking toward me. I stop doing little things trying to distract myself and look his way.

"I'm sure. We can facetime when you get home, and when we have our Thanksgiving meal." He wraps his arms around me. I tiptoe to put my head on his shoulder and wrap my arms around his neck. He takes a big whiff in the crease of my neck.

"Jethro, we will be fine. Be sure to call me when you land."

He pulls away and we put our foreheads together. His alarm on his watch beeps signaling it is time for him to go. He kisses me long, but closed mouth, then pulls away.

"I feel like I'm leaving my family, in the hands of my enemy." He says in a low voice, but still looking at me.

"You aren't handing me over to the enemy. I'm still your wife, and Carter is still your son."

"You believe that Daryn," this got me to look into his sad solemn eyes.

"It doesn't matter what I believe, do you know it?"

"I know it Daryn. This is not the ideal situation for me to leave my other half with her ex. This is all coming to fast, and I am doing my best to be okay."

"Jethro, you are doing an amazing job. If the shoe were on the other foot, I am not sure how I would feel. I am not discounting your feelings. If I felt there was another way out of this mess, without using Amber, we would be packing up to leave with you. Just know that I love you, I chose you, and I want to be with you." I stand on tiptoes and kiss Jethro on the lips. We lace our hands together and walk out to the kitchen. I am shocked to find Rosa cleaning the sink.

"Mr. Jethro, I cooked these for you!" She said picking up a package and giving it to Jethro.

"Don't tell me these are what I think they are!" Jethro said with a face splitting smile.

"Yes Mr. Jethro, they are!" She is beaming back at him. She made me smile. I can't believe her generosity. I can't believe she made a special trip to come at five in the morning to make conk fritters. I hug her also. I know this will make his morning, and hopefully take some of the edge from him going back home.

"This was the best present Rosa, thank you so much. You made my day."

"You're welcome Mr. Jethro," she said and walks off.

"Wow, that was very kind of her," I am still smiling about her kind gesture.

"Yeah, I'm stunned. I'd better go; I know Henry is waiting to take me to the airport." I reach up and hug him again and give him another kiss. He hugs me so tight I can't breathe. He kisses me on the top of the head then pulls away.

I go in the room, curl up in bed before Carter wakes and wants breakfast, all the time wondering if I'm doing the right thing.

Carter and I were dressed for the beach by ten thirty in the morning. We are walking through the powdered sand when Logan comes jogging up behind us.

"Carter," he said and swung him around as he laughs.

"Hey, other dad," he responds all smiles. "My dad had to go," Carter said as Logan put him down.

"Yeah, I know buddy," he said. Then he looks at me, cheesing. I wonder if this sudden happiness is because Jethro is gone.

"Can we go back to the turtle farm?" Carter asks.

"Yeah, this time maybe your mom will come with us," Logan said looking at me.

"No, no I brought him out here to look for seashells; you can take him to look at sea turtles." I said and we both laugh.

"I'm going to go and change out of these sweaty clothes, do you mind if I come back and join you to look for seashells?" he asked, and my gut told me to say no. Jethro warned me to be careful that Logan was looking at me like he still loves me.

"Yeah, that will be okay." I said and Carter shouts for joy.

"Okay, I will be right back," he said smiling and jogging off.

He returns alone. I tell myself not to read too much into it. We are walking down the beach looking for seashells. When Carter finds a conk shell he thought he hit the jackpot the way he is hollering. He is so excited, it makes us both laugh. We both hold the conk shell to Carter's ear, so he can hear the ocean. As we hold the shell to his ear, Logan's hand is on top of mine. I try not to recognize the electric current running from his hand to mine. I feel the energy from him, transferring to me, and I'm ashamed of the warmth that came over me. I snatch my hand away, and Logan looks at me as if he knows why. He felt it too. It is like his energy is draining from him into me. He looks at me, and smiles, but I don't smile back.

"Maybe we should head back to the house. Carter is probably ready for lunch, and Jethro will be calling me soon." I must remind him I am married. I must remind him and myself that we are no longer lovers, and we both have responsibilities.

"Do you think we could come back later?"

"Yeah, mom, can we please?" Carter begs.

"Maybe everyone will want to come later," I don't trust myself with just Logan and me. I don't feel like I still love him anymore, but I definitely felt something radiating from him, when his hand was on top of mine. I'm just not sure what it was I felt, and I don't want to find out.

"I doubt it, I'm not sure what kind of drinking you were doing, but Amber still doesn't feel quite right. I can see if Bristol and Hunter want to come."

We start walking back to the house in silence.

"I know I told you this before, but I really thank you for allowing me to spend Thanksgiving week with my son. You have no idea how much this means to me."

"You're welcome," is my only response.

"He's a great kid. Contrary to everything going on you've

done a really good job of raising him."

"Thanks," I respond.

"Don't take this the wrong way. I know you aren't lacking for anything, but if there is anything that he needs or wants just let me know, and I can get it for him. I know you can afford it, but please let me know, I would like to help in taking care of him. He's my son, and he is my responsibility too."

"He's my responsibility," my tone is not pleasant when I respond.

"Daryn," he says touching my arm, so I will stop walking. "That is not what I meant. I know he has been your responsibility for the first four years of his life, but now I know I have a son we should share that responsibility. Please don't continue to take that away from me. I don't want you to depend on me. I want to help raise him. He's my son and believe it or not, I love him, just as much as you do." He clears his throat and pauses.

"The minute I saw him I knew he was mine before I took a test, but I knew you wouldn't let me see him without the results. You were so independent when we were lovers, and I knew you wouldn't want my support.

"I remember you telling me about your childhood, and that you were abandoned by your dad. I swore I would never do that to you if you were pregnant with our child. Everything I'm doing is because I want to be a part of his life.

"I'm his real dad, and I want to help raise him. Don't take that away from me. Let me have the luxury of co-parenting with you and helping raise him. He's my son, and I love him too." I look, at him, and continue walking after he spoke. Sometimes his speeches are too deep. I believe that I need to chill.

"I think I felt a raindrop. We better hurry," I said walking faster.

"Nah, it rarely rains in November. This is considered the dry season. It was probably the wind blowing the ocean." As soon as he finishes his statement, the clouds open, and start pouring on us. He scoops Carter and slangs him around his neck. We ran the rest of the way to the house, laughing as we walk in.

"I'll get us towels," Logan said walking away.

He returns as I am stripping Carter's shirt and shoes off.

"Thanks," I said grabbing the towel from him. He is staring at us when I look up.

"What?" I ask. He takes his index finger, traces it across my forehead, and push wet hair behind my ear.

"I've enjoyed seeing your interaction with our son. I didn't understand how much this would mean to me at the time I asked you to come for Thanksgiving. It matters more than you could ever know or understand." I see something in the distance move, it is Amber. I'm not sure what part of our conversation she heard, or if she saw the intimate gesture of Logan pushing my hair behind my ear.

"Hi Amber, are you feeling better." I ask. She snaps out of her stare and walks toward the sofa.

"I'm no longer vomiting." Amber believes she is suffering from alcohol poisoning. She hasn't recovered. This is the first night I've seen her since our night out.

I take Carter by the hand, to walk him to the room.

"You don't have to leave," she says.

"I have to change Carter. He's wet from being rained on. I don't want him to get sick." I keep walking before she responds. I see the way she is looking at me, and it isn't pleasant.

"Mom, can I go play with Bristol," Carter asked while I am dressing him.

"After you eat," is my response.

I don't know what Rosa is cooking but my mouth is watering. "Hey Rosa," I said, and Carter bounces in behind me.

"There's my little man," Rosa is smiling at Carter, and she hands him a plate with chicken nuggets.

"Thanks Rosa, you didn't have to do that."

"No worries," she is still smiling at Carter. I sit at the breakfast nook while he eats his nuggets.

"Something smells wonderful," I said.

"I'm cooking curry chicken for dinner, and I've seasoned a jerk turkey for Thanksgiving. Mr. Anderson told me you only eat seafood. I have a nice grouper for you." My phone rings and I excuse myself.

"Hey," I answer Jethro's call.

"Why didn't you answer your phone?"

"I don't know; when did you call?" I ask.

"About a half hour ago," he sounds upset.

"Probably because Carter and I were running in the rain trying to get back to the house," the last thing I want to do is argue with Jethro.

He audibly sighs. "How is your day going?" I try distraction.

"It's been a shitty day. I've been running since I got here. I will be glad when this day is over. What are you doing?"

"Carter and I just got back from the beach, he is eating chicken nuggets." I dare not tell him about Logan being with us. I know that wouldn't have gone over well especially since I didn't answer my phone.

"I miss you," he sounds sad.

"I miss you too. I wish you didn't have to leave." Jethro is a feeler. I have to help him feel like we miss him too, and not like we are having the time of our lives.

"I wish you would have come back with me." I wasn't prepared for this response, but I didn't want to make him anymore upset than he already was.

"I'm sorry, this is the first Thanksgiving we will be apart. I will make sure we are together for future holidays." There is a long pause. "Rosa is cooking a jerk turkey," I try to make the conversation more upbeat.

"Be sure to bring me some. I have just about polished off those conk fritters she sent with me." He finally sounds as if he might be smiling.

"I will let her know."

"I'd better get back to work. I'm supposed to be at lunch, but we are so busy I don't have time for much of anything. I love you!"

"I love you too Jethro. Call me when you get off," I say, he agrees and hangs up.

When I walk back toward the kitchen Carter is finishing his food. Logan walks in looking like he'd just taken a shower. "Hey other dad," Carter said and jumps in his arms. He swings Carter around in a big circle making him squeal.

Logan's hair is still wet and mused. He has on a pair of jeans and no shirt. I get a flashback of us in the shower; me against the wall with my legs wrapped around his waist as he...

"A penny for your thoughts," he says taking me out of my revere. He caught me staring. I can sense he has an idea of what I might be thinking.

I smile before I speak, "Oh nothing."

"I'm almost ready to go to the turtle farm. Are you coming with us?" he is smiling at me, and I am not sure why.

"Is Amber coming?" I am trying to remind him that we both belong to other people.

"No, she is still not one hundred percent, but Bristol is coming with us."

"Ah, come on mom."

"Yeah, come on mom," Logan said whining like Carter as he put him down, so he could run to me.

"I guess so," I said and they both smile at me. I send Carter to get his shoes.

"Would you like something to eat?" Rosa asks me.

"No thank you, I'm not really hungry."

"You don't eat much huh?" she asked.

"Not really," I respond.

"How is Mr. Jethro?" I feel she is baiting me for something or trying to make sure I don't forget who I am married to.

"He's good, he has almost polished off the conk fritters you sent him, and he wants me to bring him a plate of the Thanksgiving meal." She smiles broadly.

"I will be sure to make him a plate, and some fresh fritters." She still has the smile in her voice when she responds.

"He will like that."

"You have a very nice family. I've been cooking for the Andersons for almost forty years now. I knew Logan's biological father. He was a great man. He was not like your average person. He was different, and very smart, freakishly smart.

"Logan is a lot like him with his intelligence, and in the way, that he collects things. Just be careful that you don't become a part of his collection." I knew exactly what Rosa was hinting at. I could tell she'd figured out I had an affair with Logan and Carter is Logan's son. I need to make sure I keep my wits about me. I can sense she is speaking from experience, and not assuming. I don't try to deny it, I heed her warning, and nod my head in agreement.

I am nervous about meeting Logan's extended family. We hear them outside about to make a grand entrance. My nerves are getting the best of me. I don't know what they will think of me. I don't know how much they know about me. They are coming into the house from the back door. Carter and I stand waiting for Logan to lead his family inside. His mom, stepdad, brother, brother's wife, and their kids come in smiling, hugging, and kissing Amber and their kids. We stand off to the side watching.

I assume the older woman is his mother. She walks toward us with tear filled eyes. She bends down to speak to Carter.

"I'm your grandmother," she says. "Can I please have a hug sweet boy," Carter hugs her. She stands and looks at me. "You must be Daryn," she said holding out her hand to shake.

"Yes," I said smiling at her and shaking her hand. The rest of the family descends on us hugging him and shaking my hand.

"He looks so much like Logan's biological father," his mom said tearing up. "It's almost like it's him reincarnated," she said folding me into a hug.

"Dinner's ready," Logan said leading us to the dining room table. It is only one in the afternoon and we are about to eat dinner.

Dinner is in full swing with light conversation.

"Daryn, I hope we can spend time with our grandson. When do you return to the states?" she asked.

"We leave tomorrow," I said. Out the corner of my eyes I see the stun look on Logan's face. I changed my ticket to leave Friday, so we could get home to Jethro, and reality.

"I was hoping we could spend a little time together," his mom said. His stepfather is still eating like we don't exist.

"Yeah, we were staying until Sunday, but my husband was called back home early for work. So, I thought we'd surprise him, since he has to spend Thanksgiving alone." I feel Logan looking at me, but I don't look his way.

"When were you going to inform me?" I can tell Logan is trying to keep his composure, but I hear the shaking in his tone, and I know he is upset by my announcement.

"I had to see if we could change our flight first. We won't be leaving until 3 in the evening, so you will have all morning with him, and part of the afternoon."

"I think Jethro will be very happy with your decision," Amber said smiling. I haven't seen her smile since our night out drinking.

"Then I guess I'd better get in all the kisses I can now," his mom said kissing Carter.

Once dinner is over, we head to the beach, so the kids can play, and the grownups can socialize. His step-dad came over to introduce himself.

"It's nice to meet you," I said shaking his hand.

"You can call me Frank, it's nice to finally meet you." His voice is raspy, and he doesn't give off the feeling it's nice to meet me. I give him a tight smile. "Daryn, can I be honest with you?" He asked, and I cross my arms thinking here we go.

"Sure," I said no longer feeling like I need to fake smile.

"My wife doesn't know the extent of what your relationship was before Carter was conceived, but I do. I had to talk Logan off the cliff many times and get him to return to his wife.

"Logan is a great man, and I'm sure you are a great woman or else he wouldn't have chosen you. He was willing to give everything up in his life to be with you.

"You're a very beautiful person, and I appreciate you brining our grandson here to spend your vacation with us. You are right in leaving to go home to your husband. I do hope that when we visit, you will let us see him, and spend time with him."

"Of course," is my response after I figure out it isn't a rhetorical question.

"Good, I can tell you are more level headed than Logan. He's been confused since he saw you, and his son at the ice cream parlor, but he will get over the confusion. You just have to make sure you don't give off any signals that can be misread."

"I'm not giving off any signals, and I don't want any relationship with him that doesn't involve his son. So, thanks for the talk, but you don't have to worry about me."

"I knew I could count on you," he said and walks off. It makes me wonder what Logan has been telling his stepdad.

I am packing our things looking forward to getting home, and back to reality. There is a soft tap on the door. Amber enters after I shout come in. She closes the door, and leans against it as I stare at her wondering what is this about.

"May I speak with you woman to woman," she asks.

"Sure," I respond still folding and putting clothes in our suitcase.

"I'm not feeling my best, I'm still a little weak from all the vomiting I've been doing since our night out. I haven't drunk that much since college. I thought I could handle it, but you definitely handled yourself better than me. I'm sorry I have to be so direct, but I have no choice, do you still love Logan?" She is serious, I can tell from how she looks at me as she sits on the dresser.

"No," I respond.

"I've seen how he stares at you, and I've seen how you smile back at him. I'm not so sure you don't still love him."

"When you catch me smiling at him, or staring at him, my look is not for the love of him. My look is for the admiration and love of his relationship he has established with his son.

"I always wondered how he would be with him, and now that I see their relationship, I love seeing them together. I have no other interest in Logan." That is the truth. I've come to the realization that Logan and I function better apart. We were never meant to be together.

"I can't go through what we went through again. You don't know the Logan I know. The one that I had to put back together once you put him out. The Logan that I had drunken arguments, with because he wasn't happy with me, and he wanted you back. The Logan that I've had to pick up in the middle of the night because he was too drunk to drive home. The Logan that used to curse me out in front of the children and then act like nothing happened the next day.

"You have no idea what the real Logan is like. I refuse to put him back together again, if you are planning on getting back with him. This time you will probably destroy him, and us completely. So, maybe I should rephrase the question. What are your plans for Logan?" I want to put myself in her shoes, but the way she is looking at me, my niceness is about to wear off. I know I am the one that had the affair with her husband, and had a kid from him, so I understand I need to be reasonable, but she already asked me this question.

"Amber I get it. In your eyes I'm still the other woman. In your eyes, I'm still the woman that used to fuck your husband. I get that you need reassurance that I no longer want to fuck your husband. I get it, Logan is good looking, a great lover, and the father of my son. I get it that no matter what I say to you, you will always be skeptical of it. I do have unexplainable feelings for him, because he is the father of my son, and I see so much of him in Carter. If I didn't have feelings for

Logan I wouldn't be able to love those characteristics in my son that resemble his father, but that is where my feelings for him end. I told you my relationship with Logan was extremely toxic. That is the only way I can describe it. I cannot go back to that.

"You are right, I have no idea what the real Logan is like, I spent one night a week with him. We lived in a fantasy world, that only included us. The minute we tried to blur the lines between fantasy and reality it fell apart. I don't ever want to experience that again.

"I am with Jethro, whom I love so much. He is the man that I am meant to be with. Jethro keeps me grounded and level headed. He does not try and fix me or my problems. I have a balance with Jethro I could never have with Logan. He's with who he should be with, and I'm with who I should be with." I tell her more than I want to tell her, but she was asking for it. She shouldn't have closed the door, and made me feel like I was backed in a corner.

"I have a confession to make. I had an ulterior motive when we went out for girl's night. I wanted to get you to understand you must win this custody battle without my testimony, because not only can I not do it all over again, I can't raise a son you made with my husband.

"When he told me he saw his son, there was no doubt in his mind Carter was his. I told him let's wait until the test come back. He insisted he didn't need a test. He didn't sign the birth certificate, so the attorney told him we had to have a paternity test. I prayed to God several times a day that the test would come back negative. The test came back 99% positive, but still I was hopeful that we still had a one percent chance that he was not his. Then he came over for his birthday, and the moment I laid eyes on him I knew it was true. I wouldn't accept it, until I saw him myself. He looks more like Logan, than our son. I wondered how you could have a son that looked exactly like Logan, and you'd only been with him for a short amount of time compared to the years I've been with him.

"Seeing him made me angry all over again. I wondered, how

could he? How could you? You knew he was married yet you didn't care." She was now wiping tears from her eyes. I gave her a moment to compose herself and continue. "My entire world almost collapsed when you two decided to become a couple. When he returned, he was upset with the entire world. He blamed me for you two not working, and he yelled at the kids for anything they did wrong. When we saw you that day we were in a good place. We'd had a good year, and then we run into you, and Carter, and it was almost like that year was obliterated.

"Carter is a sweet kid, and you are right, so much of Logan is in him even though they haven't been around each other. I have even caught them holding their head the same way, and there is this face Logan makes when he's thinking or trying to figure something out, and Carter makes that same face. I wonder how that is possible?" She is smiling when she said this.

"It's bloodline," I interject. "My grandmother said, the blood of parents and grandparents run so deep inside a human being that all kind of traits come out if they raise the person or not. I've noticed some of the same things, and that is why you sometimes catch me staring. I also can't believe it. I'm in awe of how alike they are. I wasn't raised by my parents, and I didn't get a chance to see how their bloodline affected me, so seeing him with his actual dad, has me mesmerized." I'm still trying to convince her that there is nothing between Logan and me. There was a moment when he put my hair behind my ear that felt extremely intimate, but I shook it off. We both understand our predicament, and we both know we can no longer be selfish and inconsiderate by being together.

"You have done a phenomenal job with Carter. He's so full of love, respect, and manners. I am fortunate enough to have him as a step son, but there are moments when I know how he came about, and it hurts like hell. I want Logan to have a relationship with Carter. I want Logan to co-parent with you, but I don't want to take him from you. He's yours, and he belongs with you. I can't go on record saying these things it would put us against each other again, but you must find a way without going to trial. I know things were nice and friendly here in paradise, but rest assured he is still seeking full custody when we return. It is personal for him." I should have known Logan wouldn't give up, but I was hopeful, and I was stupid.

"Okay, well if you have any suggestions, I'm all ears. You know my mom's situation, and he's going to bring that up."

"Yeah, but he has situations too, if your attorney does a deep dive he will find out about them." She said looking at me to make sure I understood what she was saying. I nodded my head to let her know I understand.

"Well, nice talking with you Daryn, and sharing a home with you. The only thing I ask is once you win custody, please let him have visitation. He deserves it. He's a good father when he's not drinking." She said and exited the room. I finish packing our bags, and call Carter in the room to go to bed. The sooner we go to sleep the sooner I can be home, and back to normalcy.

CHAPTER THIRTEEN

When we arrive in Tampa I call for an Uber, because I want to surprise Jethro. It takes a while for the driver to come, because of all the traffic surrounding the airport. I try to entertain Carter, we are both anxious to get home.

We pull up to the house and walk inside.

"Dad, daddy," Carter is yelling as he runs around the house.

"Carter, Jethro is not here. He hasn't made it home from work yet."

"Then can I play on my iPad?" He asks.

I hand him the iPad out of my purse, he takes it and runs off to his room. I drag my luggage to the bedroom to unpack.

It's after seven when I finally hear the door chime. He's walking into the bedroom stripping off his jacket when he spots me by the bed. I smile at him, and he stares back at me like I'm a mirage.

"Hi," I say breaking the silence. He makes it to me in two steps placing his hands on both sides of my face. He pulls me in for a deep kiss. Then he starts kissing me all over my face. I giggle.

"Hi," he says when he pulls back then he pulls me into a full embrace and sighs deeply.

"Have you been holding that breath since you left?" I ask still giggling.

"Yes," he responds without laughter. He pulls back and places his forehead to my forehead. "I've missed you so."

"I missed you too."

"How? Why?" I know what he means without asking complete sentences. I pull back from him and look at him.

"We'd stayed long enough. We missed you, and it was time to come home. I never should have let you leave without us."

"What about the custody hearing?"

I pull away from him and sit on the bed. "I've been very compliant with him, even when I didn't have to be. If he holds leaving early against me, it is not because we left early, but because he never really saw what I did as a courtesy, or as a compromise. His wife said something to me right before we left. She said we may have had a great week together, but Logan will still be seeking full custody. So, none of what I do really matters in his eyes."

"I don't care, I'm just glad you're home. I'm glad you're both home." He says and reaches over to hug me again. He pulls out his phone.

"What are you doing?"

"I'm calling Ro to let her know I won't be in tonight."

"You do know, we will be here when you get back?"

"You have no idea how lonely I've been without the two of you...Ro," he says, and laughs at something she says. I roll my eyes because I know it can't be that funny. "Yeah, I know it's Black Friday, and last Friday all in one, but do you think you could run the show for me if I didn't come in." Jethro laughs again. "I knew I could count on you. I purchased some extra liquor just in case we needed it for the black Friday specials we are running. I'm going to text BJ, so he can come and pick up the key to the storage cabinet. Call or text me if you need anything." He pauses a moment. "Okay, I will." He hangs up and starts texting. "Ro said hello," he says after he's done, I assume sending a message to BJ.

He sits back on the bed then lies on his side. He pulls me down so I'm facing him. I bring my legs up to my chest. He puts his hand on my hip as he faces me. He rises on one elbow.

"Do you know how much I've missed you?" He asked and kisses me.

"No," I respond smiling at him.

"I've never been so lonely, on a holiday, in all my life. Besides going to Boston Market, I stayed in the house all day watching football and wishing you were here. I was miserable. You don't know how much it means to me that you shortened your trip and came home." He puts his hand on the side of my face and bends to kiss me.

"I was ready to come home. I missed you too. Things seemed awkward without you there. If I could do it all over again, I would have come home with you." He smiles at me as if I'd just told him he'd won the lottery. He swoops down kissing me harder this time and a little longer.

"How did things get weird? Did something happen? Did Logan try you?" He rambles off the questions so fast.

"No, he didn't try me. I don't know how to explain it. I felt as if Amber was looking at me weird. His parents arrived, and I didn't feel like I belonged there. It just felt weird. Here I am the other woman, staying in the house with his family, and acting like it was okay. It wasn't okay, and I could tell it was starting to get to Amber. Things started to feel so tense. When you were there I think it buffered some of that feeling, but as soon as you left, I felt as if I was getting the side eye. I felt like the other woman." I really didn't give a damn that it was getting to Amber, but the things she was asking me and the way she was starting to act towards me was making me feel uncomfortable. I'm not sure if she was being strategic, but whatever she was being, it worked, because I left earlier than I was supposed to.

"Whatever your reasoning I'm glad you're home." He slings his leg across me as he kisses me again. This time the kiss is more urgent. It makes my heartbeat speed up.

"Don't you want to see your son?"

"You must have been reading my mind." He smiles devilishly.

"I was reading your mind and going to see your son was definitely not on it." He laughs and gets off the bed then pulls me up. We walk arm in arm to Carter's room.

When we walked in the room I could have sworn I heard Carter speaking to someone.

"Daddy," he said bounding for Jethro. I look around and see his television on. It must have been coming from that.

"What were you doing?" Jethro asked him as he scooped him up in his arms.

"I was just watching Jake and the Netherland Pirates." Jethro carries him out to the living room and I follow.

"Are you glad to be home," he is asking him as they sit on the sofa.

"Yeah, it was fun, but I missed my toys." I laugh.

"Hey what about me?" Jethro protest.

"Oh yeah, I missed you too dad. I didn't have anyone to play football with, and Hunter wouldn't let me play with his video game."

"Ah, well I missed you too. I'm glad you're home."

"Can we play your videogame?"

"It's kind of late, and I was hoping to play with your mama."

"Mom plays videogames too?" He asked, and I cover my face in shame.

"Something like that. I guess we can play one game.

CHAPTER FOURTEEN

When Carter and I walk into the house Jethro is playing a God-awful song on the piano. It sounds like the march of death. He looks like he's had a grave day. I take one look at him and wonder if something serious happened to a family member. I bend over to Carter's height.

"Can you go in your room and play or watch television while I speak to daddy," I smile at him, so he won't feel like something is wrong.

He shakes his head then hugs Jethro on the way to his room.

I go and sit next to Jethro on the piano bench.

"Is everything okay," I ask to get him to stop playing the song. Now instead of playing with both hands he is pecking at the keys with one. The same song only with less dramatics and the sound of doom is not so eminent.

"Nope," is his response, then he takes a sip of the brown liquor he has resting on the piano.

"Is it your mom or dad?" I feel my heart starting to palpitate.

"Nope," is his response again with another swig of his drink. I lay my hand on his, so he will stop playing all together.

"Do you want to talk about it?"

"I really thought that by now you would have been pregnant. I mean I know we aren't as active as we use to be, but we are still active enough that by now you should be pregnant."

Now my heart is really palpitating. I am ready to go on the defense for taking birth control pills. I try to pretend like I am not affected by what he is saying. What if he has found my pills?

"We've been at it now for almost nine months and no baby. My mom told me after she had me, it was easier to conceive the next time. Since you can clearly get pregnant, I started to think maybe I should have some test ran. I went to my regular doctor and had a physical. I told him we'd been trying for a while to have a baby, but nothing so far. He started telling me how sometimes these things take time, and if you'd been on the pill awhile it may take time for us to have a baby. It put my mind at ease, but I still insisted on the testing.

"After all my test were complete, he told me I was healthy and there shouldn't be a reason why, we aren't pregnant by now."

Shit, shit, shit is all I keep repeating in my head. I need to stay calm. My throat feels dry, and I want to bolt out of the room. This is why he is so upset, he knows I've been deceiving him. I can't tell him I don't want to have another baby, it will destroy him. I keep thinking the feeling will go away, but it hasn't. I don't think it ever will. Honestly, I think the feeling has intensified since I realized I don't want another child.

"The doctor sent me to a fertility specialist. If everything went well he wanted to bring you in for testing. He reassured me everything was fine, and if anything, you might have to take a few pills to increase your chances of fertility.

"I went to the fertility specialist, had a full work up, and today I was called and told the reason why we are not pregnant is because of me. My sperm has a motility problem." I breathe out a sigh of relief. Thank you God I am safe. I want to jump up and shout HALLELUJAH!

I didn't know how to tell him I don't want any more children, and now I don't have to tell him. I hug him to console him, but really, I am comforting myself. I should have known with an anaconda size penis like Jethro's, something was wrong with it.

"Jethro, it is okay." I whisper to him.

"No, it's not. As a man do you have any idea how this makes me feel? Do you understand we may never have children together? They gave me a packet with information on fertility drugs and IVF, but I couldn't hear them. I was devastated by what I was told.

"I dreamed about us having a little girl with your looks, but it does not look like it will happen." He pauses, and I know, I am supposed to say something profound at this moment, like I will try anything or we can keep trying, or we can pray about it or, I will go with him for treatment ideas; but that isn't my mood. I am elated. I feel as if God did hear my un-prayed prayer and saved me. I feel blessed. God did not put more on me than I can bear.

"Jethro, it is okay, we have Carter, and each other. We will just have to be comfortable with the idea that it may only be us."

"Do I really have ya'll Daryn?" he looks at me with such sadness. I want to help him through his problem, but not if it means doing something that will cause me to get pregnant. "Yes, Jethro you do. Logan's wife said she doesn't want Carter full time. She said she can't do it anymore. Now we just must figure out a way to get her to say it, so it is not hearsay."

"When did she say that?"

"When we were in the Cayman Islands, but she said she couldn't tell Logan. You just must trust me. It will all work out in the long run. You have nothing to worry about. I love you, Carter loves you, and as far as we are concerned you are his real dad." I said and kiss him. That is all I have, and I hope it is good enough.

"Let me check on Carter. I can't believe he hasn't run in here for water, or juice, or a snack. He must be up to something." I said and stand. He pulls me between his legs and wraps his arms around my midsection. I rest my arms on his shoulders. He releases me, and I walk away. As I am walking toward Carter's room, he sounds as if he is having a full fledge conversation.

When I walk in the room he has the cover over his head, but I can see the glow from his iPad. I pull the cover from over his head. "Who are you talking to?" I ask.

"Uh, oh," is his response. I snatch the tablet from him, and there is Logan all smiles staring back at me.

"What are you doing?" I ask him.

"I'm talking to my son, you look lovely," he said, and I disconnect the Facetime.

"Carter, how long have you been doing this?" I asked.

He hunches his shoulders. "Carter, how long have you been

Facetimeing Logan?" I ask more forcefully.

"Since my birthday, when he gave me the iPad," Carter responds.

"Why didn't you tell me?" I was trying to be calm but failing.

"My other dad told me not to," was his response.

"You don't keep secrets from me," I said forcefully.

"We keep them from dad when I see my other dad." I immediately feel guilty. What the hell am I doing? I am teaching my son to be a liar. I sit down on the bed next to him.

"Carter, it is not okay to keep secrets from your father or me. I'm sorry I ever told you to keep anything from him. It can be dangerous to keep secrets. What were you talking about?"

"We were talking about baseball. He told me to make sure I practice keeping my elbow up, and he asked me when my first game was. I told him I would find out and tell him."

"What else have ya'll talked about?" I asked.

"We talked about me spending the night at his house with him and Hunter. Do you think I could go to their sleep over?" He is so enthusiastic.

"We will talk about that later. Do you understand it is important not to keep secrets from me?" He shakes his head.

"I want to hear you say it," is my response.

"Yes mommy, I won't keep secrets." He responds pouting. "Now, I am going to keep this for a little while. If you want to speak with your other dad you must ask. You can't sneak around and do it." I stand with his iPad in hand and, feeling hypercritical.

"We aren't keeping anymore secrets, not even from dad." I will deal with the consequences of being honest and truthful with Jethro all the time. I walk back into the living room. Jethro is no longer there, I went into our room, and he is just sitting on the bed. I walk over to him, sit on his thigh, then put my arms around his neck.

"Everything happens for a reason. We might not know the reason right now, but everything will work out for the better." He leans his head on my shoulder and I caress the waves in his hair.

After our sexcapade I get up and wrap my robe around me. Jethro is fast asleep, and I don't want to wake him. He may want to go for another round. I pulled out all the stops to help him feel better, and I am too exhausted to go for another round. I grab Carter's iPad and head out the room. I close the door behind me. The house is so quiet. I sit on the sofa and start going through his iPad.   There are several videos from the Cayman Islands. I click on a video and smile as I watch Carter and Bristol act like they are making a youtube video. I click on another one and he's just running around the house with it recording. He's not filming anything in particular. I'm about to click off the video when I hear my voice telling him to give me the iPad.

"Ah mom," he says on the video. When I take the iPad from him I must not have realized he was recording because it is still playing. I hear my voice, and then I hear Amber's voice. She is explaining to me how she can't do it again. I keep listening to the video. After I listen to the video I hug it to myself as tears stream down my face. The entire conversation is recorded of her saying she does not want to take Carter away from me. I take a moment to thank God. I gather the tablet then walk into the room.

"Jethro, wake up," I say shaking him as I sit next to him on the bed.

"What?" He says his voice thick with sleep. "What's wrong?" he asks in a panic as he takes one look at my tear stained face.

"Listen,"   I   say   and   play   the   video   for   him. "Is that Amber," he asks. I shake my head, as I smile at him. "Did she say she can't do it again?" He asked, and I shake my head. He sits up and hugs me. "We have to get this to the attorney!" he says with the same excitement I'm feeling.

"I'm already ahead of you. I plan to notify him Monday."

"This will be huge when you play this in mediation."

"I know," I say with tears falling anew. He hugs and kisses me.

"Oh my God! This is a huge stress reliever. You just don't know how much this has weighed on me day after day, thinking he is out to destroy my family by taking Carter from us." I could hear the emotion in his voice. I hug him again.

"I told you he couldn't take our family away."

"Yes, you did," he whispers in my ear.

CHAPTER FIFTEEN

We decided to let Carter spend Christmas Eve with Logan's family, since he won't see him on Christmas Day. I know, I don't have too, but I feel guilty for all the Christmases he's already missed with Carter. We are walking up to the front door and my heart is fluttering. I haven't seen him since Thanksgiving, and the secret I'm holding regarding his wife is weighing on me. I want it to be over. My attorney assured me we have a smoking gun as he downloaded it on his computer. I asked if we could move up the mediation, but he informed me the courts were already booked. We have our appointment right after the new year.

I ring the doorbell and we wait for Logan to come to the door.

"Don't forget to call me, if you get ready to come home before we pick you up tonight." When it was Carter's birthday I stayed with him. This time we decided to drop him off to stay until seven tonight.

Logan opens the door, smiling at me before he looks at Carter. "What's up bud?" he says high fiving Carter.

"Nothing, other dad," he is still holding my hand.

"Are you ready to celebrate Christmas?" He asks Carter. I bend down and hug him.

"Have a great time."

"I will mommy," he responds then bounds inside.

"I know I've told you this before, but I really appreciate you letting him come celebrate Christmas Eve with us. I didn't realize how much I would miss him. Spending a week with him made me want to spend more time with him. When I got home his laughter and energy wasn't with us to fill the room. I found myself trying to figure out how I was going to see him again. He's a wonderful kid."

"Thanks," is my only response.

"I know you've taken his iPad, do you think he could have it back with your supervision?" He pauses for me to say something, but I didn't respond. "Please, I just want to be able to tell him good-night." I now understand how bad my decision was to take Logan's rights away to be or not to be a parent, but I also remember what Amber told me. She told me he would not stop pursuing custody of his son.

I know I have a smoking gun with the recording of Amber, but I am still nervous about everything. What if it doesn't go down like I think it will?

"I will think about it." I say.

"Thinking is better than saying no. Is there something I could say or do to make you say yes?"

"Stop pursuing custody," I say, and he laughs. He takes a moment to order his words before he speaks.

"I am not pursuing custody because of all the years I can't get back, I'm pursuing custody for protection."

"Protection against what?" I shouldn't continue this conversation, but we may not have another chance to talk about custody before the last mediation.

"Against you running off with him, against my rights as his dad, against any kind of say so in my son's life." "Why can't we have an agreement between us? Why does it have to include the courts?" He shakes his head and looks away like he didn't want to have this discussion right now. Like he doesn't want to blow his chance of me leaving with Carter. "Just say what you are thinking. I promise I will still leave him with you."

"You had your chance. You had four years to do the right thing with him and you blew it. I never thought you would keep something this important from me, but you did. I hoped you were pregnant, so you would take me back. As days grew into weeks and weeks grew into months, I realized, if you were pregnant you got rid of our child. It angered me beyond anything I could have ever imagined. I lashed out at those closest to me, as I thought about the likely hood of you getting an abortion instead of having my child. I didn't feel closure, but in about the last year before you saw me, I started to accept what it was and move forward. I decided to make the best of my own happiness.

"Then I saw you with my son, and the anger I felt then, was nothing compared to the anger I felt when I thought you aborted my son. Every single emotion I'd felt since you put me out came sailing back through my mind in slow motion. Everything was so vivid, like I was watching it on a big screen. To know that you would keep something this critical from me, let me know I didn't know you as well as I thought. I wasn't prepared for that moment. So, when you say to me why can't we work something out…my answer is had you came to me before that day I would have been willing to do whatever you said, because I would have appreciated that you did not abort my son. I loved you so much that I wanted us to share something as intimate as a child, but you betrayed me. You led me to believe all this time, your love for me was an illusion I'd created.

"After everything played out in my mind, and the way you left me so quick and, in a hurry, I realized you never intended to tell me I had a son. You never intended for me to be a part of his life. You never intended for me to know him. So, you had your chance, and what you did with your chance I can't get out of my mind. No, we can't come to an agreement. You had your chance." There is such seriousness in his eyes as he looks at me. I wanted to see where his mind was, and now I know. I wanted to give it one last chance before final mediation. I wanted to come up with something together, but now I know.

"Thank you for your honesty. If the shoe were on the other foot I might do the same thing. I know you are telling me we can't come to an agreement, but you have until mediation."

"Or what?" he asked.

"Or nothing, I no longer believe Carter is better without you in his life. As you can see I am being cooperative. I am not trying to keep you away from him."

"You're cooperating now; you are not trying to keep him away now."

"What does that mean?" I am still holding my cool, but I can tell Logan is losing his.

"You ran as soon as you saw me. It means you're cooperating because you are scared if you don't, the courts may not have leniency on you. You are cooperating now, because you know you were wrong for what you did, and you think this will atone. You are cooperating now because you know he's my son and I deserve to be in his life."

"Well, I can see it is no longer worth discussing."

"You're damn right it's no longer worth discussing. We are well past discussing."

"How long do you plan on being angry with me?"

"How about four years?" He said turning a flash of red. I turn to walk away.

"That's it walk away like you normally do. We are finally having a real conversation and you are walking away from it." I pause at the bottom step. He comes down the stairs behind me, and I turn around.

"I'm not walking away, I am choosing not to continue with this pointless conversation."

"What makes it pointless? The fact that you think it's pointless?"

"No, what makes it pointless, is the fact that neither one of us is budging. We have our stance on it and we are at complete opposite ends of the spectrum. You want Carter fully and so do I, case closed." He huffs a moment then runs his hand through his hair.

"I wish I could trust you, but everything tells me if I do, I will be holding the short end of the stick.

"As you know my biological father died when I was young, and although my stepfather stepped in and did a wonderful job helping my mother, I still wish to God my biological father would have lived and raised me into a man. My son won't have to wish he was raised by his father because he will be."

"That's your position," I say understanding him more than I really want to.

"Yes, that's it."

"I am sorry I brought it up."

"That's the first time I actually believe you are sorry about anything we are going through."

"I'm sorry you missed the first four years. I'm sorry for keeping him from you."

"If we weren't in a custody battle, I would probably believe you. You are telling me sorry after the fact makes me wonder if you are only saying it because you feel right now, it's the right thing to do."
"You know me, I don't apologize."

"Correction, I thought I knew you. I don't know what you would do now that you know I'm after something you are afraid of losing."

"Fair enough," I say, and we stare at one another for a moment. Him with his hands on his hips, me with my hands in my jacket pockets. "Well I'd better be going, I have things to do, and I know you want to spend as much time with Carter as you can before I pick him up later." He stares at me hard for a moment then nods his head and walks off.

I get in the car, drive off, and head to the store. I figure if I bring home some groceries I won't be questioned about why I took so long. The entire time the conversation with Logan plays out in my head. I wish I'd gotten from him what he thinks would be reasonable visitation. I wish I hadn't said anything to him. The conversation did nothing but confuse me more about what we should do.

I walk through the front door with bags in my hand, hoping this will distract Jethro.

"Hey, I thought we were going to the store later." Jethro said grabbing the grocery bags from me.

"Yeah, well I was already out so I stopped by Publix."

"Cool, Cheyenne is here. She is in the backyard. She brought over some football decorations."

"I'll go help her."

"Did everything go well?" I know what this question means, but the less he knows about my conversation with Logan the better.

"Yes, things went fine. Carter seemed really excited to see his siblings."

"Oh," is his response. I know he is only responding this way because that isn't the response he is looking for. He wants a blow by blow account of my conversation with Logan. I know Jethro won't understand so I turn and walk toward the patio.

"Hey, hey, hey, hey," Cheyenne says when I step out.

"Hey Cheyenne. I thought you were coming over later." She lets out a deep sigh and gives me a look like I'm being ridiculous. Then she smiles before she responds.

"I can't come over later because I will be waiting on a call from Abe."

"What do you mean?"

"I spoke to Abe last night, and he told me he was going to call me after he was done with all his football shenanigans. He said it would be in the afternoon. When I told him, I would be at your house helping to prepare for the tailgate tomorrow, he said he wanted to speak to me alone. He asked if I could come over to your house earlier."

"Why do you have to talk to him alone?" I asked helping put up a banner up.

"I'm sure it's so he can be perverted." I laugh as she rolls her eyes.

"We have other rooms in the house, you can go talk dirty to Abe. I promise not to listen."

"I know you are an old married couple, but he likes for me to put on a show. I get dressed up, and..."

"Okay, enough, enough!" I say raising my hands to stop her before she goes into too much detail. She laughs at my reaction.

"You wanted to know."

"Correction, I didn't want to know, I was just letting you know, you could use one of our rooms."

"When do you think you will be able to go visit him?" We are decorating the tables with football tablecloths.

"I am actually going to New York for New Years. He has a New Year's Eve game I am going to, and then we are going to hang out on New Year's Day. I got someone to cover my patients so I don't have to be back for almost a week." She is smiling the entire time she is speaking.

"That sounds great. I wish we could join you."

"You can," She said.

"No, we have mediation on the 2nd. We have to prepare for that."

"How is that going?"

I pause then sit down hard on the patio sofa.

"That bad," she said sitting opposite me on the chair.

"Actually, not that bad, we had an amazing break through. I have Amber on audio stating she doesn't want custody of Carter."

"That's great," she said, but I look down. "Isn't it?" she asked.

"It should be," I said looking up.

"Well, what's the problem?"

"I am conflicted with what I should do."

"Use the damn recording," she said strongly. "That's a no brainer!"

"I'm not conflicted about using the recording. I know I must use it. He has told me he is not backing down from going after full custody. I am conflicted about what to do after I use the recording."

"I guess I am confused. What do you mean?"

"I mean I don't want to keep Logan away from Carter." "You shouldn't keep Logan away from Carter." "Cheyenne, I know you will be honest with me, and tell me the truth no matter what. How do I do that without offending my husband?" Cheyenne chuckles before she responds.

"Jethro is a grown ass man, and he's going to have to act like one. You can't keep a son from his father because his step father feelings might get hurt. I can't believe you are tripping about what to do."

"If it were up to Jethro we would lock him out altogether, and go about our lives, but I am not willing to do that."

"That would be fucked up, if you did that."

"I know, I'm not going to do that. I tried to get Logan to talk to me about an agreement. That turned out to be a disaster. What do you suppose I do?" I am so conflicted, I don't know what to do.

"This may not be what you want to hear, but it needs to be said. I know you thought you were doing the right thing, but you were wrong. You never gave Logan a chance. You did the choosing for him when you decided not to tell him. The fucked-up thing about it, you were never going to tell him. If I were Logan, I would want to make you hurt and suffer, like you made me hurt and suffer. So of course, he doesn't want to come up with an agreement now. You had four years to come up with one."

"That's what he said."

"Truth be told, you lucky he's willing to even speak to you. You're lucky he hasn't tried to do anything more than he has, like keep you from leaving town with Carter. At this point, I know you have the upper hand. You are going to have to do what you believe in your heart is right, when it comes to Logan and Carter. Whatever you decide Jethro will forgive. He always does. Besides if the shoe were on the other foot, you would think lesser of Jethro as a man if he gave up so easily on being a part of his son's life."

I let out a gigantic sigh because I know in my heart of hearts Cheyenne is right.

"I would definitely think less of him if he had a kid out there, and he wasn't involved in his life. I just don't want him to feel unappreciated. I want him to know, no matter what, I don't regret my decision to marry him, and him being a father to Carter." Cheyenne sat next to me.

"You don't owe Jethro a damn thing. What Jethro did was out of the goodness of his heart, and if he did it to gain something more than a wife, and son, shame on him. You can't keep living in the shadow of Jethro. You don't owe him anything. He didn't marry you, so he could hang it over your head like you are some charity case. He married you because he loves you, and you gotta let that feeling of entitlement go. He will love you regardless and despite your decision with Carter."

"Thanks Cheyenne, I needed that talk."

"Do you know what you are going to do?" She asked.

"No, I have no idea what I'm going to do, I just know that whatever I decide, I have to make sure it is a decision I can live with."

We finish decorating the patio for the game day party, we decided to have on Christmas day. His parents will be at the game, but we decided to have a party at the house and invite some of our friends over to watch. In all honesty I'm not in the mood to entertain, but I know I don't have a way to get out of it.

Cheyenne stayed around until late afternoon. I received a facetime from Carter and Logan, that had me smiling as he showed me a craft he'd worked on with his dad.

"It's your Christmas present mommy, do you like it?" I giggle.

"It's great, but I thought I wasn't supposed to see it until tomorrow." I said still giggling.

"That's what I told him, but he said he wanted to make sure you liked it before he spent time wrapping it. Isn't our son brilliant? I wish I'd thought about making sure people liked their presents before I spent time wrapping them."

"I love it Carter, you did a very good job."

"Thanks mom, I can wrap it now."

"You better make it quick, I'm getting ready to come get you."

"Aw mom, but we are about to make hot chocolate with marshmallows."

"Yeah mom," Logan said smiling extra hard. "How about I just bring him home when we are finish."

"How about, I give you one more hour, and then I'm on my way."

"Aw only one-hour mom?"

"Carter, that's sixty minutes." His eyes light up. Carter has no concept of time. I knew if I changed it from one hour, to sixty minutes he would think it was a lot of time.

"Okay mom."

"Clever," Logan said as Carter jumps down out his lap to go and play.

"Yeah, I learned a while ago, he has no concept of time. If you say the bigger number he thinks it's a lot. Although he is figuring out 60 seconds is not a long time." Logan laughs.

"Thanks again, we are having a great time. You better bring your SUV, if you still have it; I kind of went overboard with his first Christmas."

"Logan, what did you do," he looked sheepish. "You might as well spill the beans."

"I sort of bought him an indoor fort, a big kid bike, some clothes, shoes, and possibly a power wheel!" I hung my head, and he laughs.

"I don't have a U-Haul truck, I only have an Escalade."

"That's another reason why I volunteered to bring him home. I have a pick-up truck."

"You have a pick-up truck."

"Yes, and I can bring all his things home."

"Um, nah, I will come get him, and whatever we can fit, we can, and whatever we can't fit we leave."

"I really don't mind."

"I know you don't, but it's okay."

"We've had a great time. I keep learning so many things about him. He's really bright for his age." I was smiling until I looked up and saw Jethro has been watching me have a conversation with Logan. My entire demeanor changes, like the fact I didn't realize I was touching my chest in an intimate way. I drop my hand to my side, and clear my throat.

"Well you better get to making that hot chocolate I will be there soon." I say with no emotion. I can tell he gets what has happened because his body language changes as well. He's no longer smiling, and his posture has straightened.

"Okay, see you in an hour," he says and disconnects.

"Don't stop on my account," is Jethro's response when I hang up.

"I didn't," I say and go to walk away. I'm not in the mood for Jethro's emotions.

"What were you smiling about?"

"Does it matter?"

"I asked you a question," he demands.

"You're not asking me a question because you are interested in what I have to say. You are asking me a question to see if your judging me is justified."

"Forget it Daryn," he says.

"Already forgotten Jethro," I said and head to the room to get my purse.

"I thought you were going to get him in an hour," he says, but I don't respond.

"I asked you a question Daryn," he follows up with when I keep walking.

"No, you made a statement," is my response when I pivot around to face him.

"Why are you leaving so soon?"

"I am leaving so soon because I don't want to continue with this conversation. I know if I stay you will have something else to say."

"Why don't you want to continue with this conversation? What are you hiding?"

"Absolutely nothing, but I know how you get when I talk to Logan. I'm not in the mood to argue."

"You're the one arguing."

"You're the one who started questioning me as soon as I got off the phone."

"I was just wondering why my wife, is on the phone with her ex, touching herself, and smiling like she's enjoying her conversation with him. Why do you have to be so friendly with him?" This time I laugh.

"Are you serious?" Is my response.

"The attorney has assured us, we have slam dunk case, and he will have to agree to our terms with the recording. I don't understand why you are still kissing up to him."

"He is still Carter's father, and we still must have a relationship for our son's sake. Yes, I have the recording, but that doesn't mean I am going to start being an asshole, because we know something he doesn't. You have to get over yourself Jethro and realize this is not about you. This is not about me, this is about making sure we are doing right by Carter. If you can't do that then we will never get past this point."

"Daryn you don't see that he's manipulating you still, and you are his puppet."

"His puppet!" I yell! "Fuck you Jethro," I head toward the door.

"I'm coming with you," he says.

"I don't need a chaperone," I shout back and slam the door behind me.

Sometimes I swear Jethro is too much to deal with. I hurry to the car thinking, he might try and follow me. I zoom out the driveway in the Honda. I know I told Logan I would drive the truck, but if I drive the truck I have to go back inside and get the key, and I be damn if I'm going back in that house.

I pull up to Logan's house looking like a bum. I put on shades to hide my eyes since I have no mascara on them. I will look like an idiot getting out of the car with sunglasses and it's night time. I throw the glasses down, smooth back my ponytail and decide to get out the car.

When I ring the doorbell, Amber opens the door.

"Hi Daryn," she says a little to chipper.

"Hi Amber, is Carter ready?" I know he's ready, but I didn't know what else to say.

"Yeah, come in. I hope you brought a U-Haul for all the presents we bought him," she said giggling. I stood by the door.

"We are in the living room, come on back," I follow her reluctantly.

"Hey mom," Carter says jumping out of Brooke's lap, and running to hug me. I hug him, like I haven't seen him in years.

"It's been a hour already," Logan says in the middle of what I hope are not all Carter presents.

I take an exaggerated look around.

"Please tell me, these are not all his presents."
"These are not all his presents." I let out a deep breath. "This one is yours, now the rest are Carter's presents." He says, and my eyes go back wide again.

"I can't believe you bought all of this."

"I had to make up for lost time," he said, but I didn't respond.

"Isn't it great mom?"

"Yes," I say not really thinking it's great.

"I guess we better start loading up, but we are going to have to leave some things.   I forgot to bring the truck."
"Please tell me you didn't bring the Porsche."

"No, I brought the Honda, but that power wheel is definitely not going to fit. Neither is the bike. By the way he already has a bike."

"Yeah, I figured I'd buy him one for when he's here. Sometimes we all go bike riding on Bayshore."

"Oh," I say and don't say anything else.

We load up the car, and get Carter buckled in.

"Are you okay?" He asks after I close Carter's door.

"Yeah, I'm good."

"You sure?"

"Yeah why?" I ask fidgeting with the keys in my hand.

"I don't know, you seem distracted or something."
"Maybe a little, but I will get over it," I say. "It was nice to see Brooke today." A vision of our last encounter flashes through my mind as I think about me slapping her.

"Yeah, I was trying to give her 'space,' but then I realized she was slipping through my fingers. That space was starting to feel like a void. So, I took a chance and called her. She didn't answer. I called her again the next day, and she answered. We started talking and when I asked her about coming home for Christmas she accepted."

"I'm glad she has forgiven you," I responded smiling.

"Forgiven, might be a bit of a stretch, but we are working on it." He said and we both giggled.

"I feel partly responsible, so it was good to see her. It looks like her and Carter are getting along well."

"That's the amazing part. Although there were moments when I could feel the hate radiating off Brooke when she spoke to me, the moment she met Carter she bonded with him. He brings a certain...innocence that you can't blame him."

"I'm glad, I could tell he had a certain connection with her during the time in the Cayman Island."

"Daryn, thank you for today, you have no idea how important today was to me. When I called, I expected you to give me every reason why Carter couldn't come over for Christmas Eve, but you didn't. You not only let him come over, but you let him stay all day. For that I am grateful, and I really want to thank you. It was the highlight of the last couple years of my life."

"You're welcome." I say and head to the car.

"You know the next time we see each other, it will be on opposing sides." He says, and I stop in front of the car and face him.

"Yeah, I know." Is my only response.

"You could always concede," he says smiling.

"And so, could you," I say smiling back at him.

"I find myself sad and missing him whenever he's not around. I want him around all the time."

"He has that effect on people."

"I'm not just people I'm his dad."

"Yes, yes you are, and I'm not trying to keep that from you. I'm merely stating a fact, Carter has that effect on everyone he meets.

Nothing more," I said letting out a sigh.

He pauses, but stares at me.

"I had all these scenarios, of you telling me you're pregnant. Sometimes it ends well and us living happily ever after. Sometimes I find out you're pregnant, and it is too late, it ends with you deciding not to have him. Every day, what ifs ran through my mind like wildflowers, and I couldn't control them.

If you'd only told me, I know our outcome would have been different. I know we could have all been happier."

"Logan, do you really think that is how God works? You really think he meant for you to marry your wife, have three kids from her, only to leave her for your mistress? You think there was ever going to be a chance for us, the way we snuck around, had a secret love affair, and had a son outside of your marriage?

"Come on Logan, there was nothing for us but doom."

"You never gave us a chance, for what we could have potentially become," he retorts.

"There was no potential in our situation. You were married. We both made the right decision."

"Except I'm the one that was screwed in the decision."

"A thousand times, I'm sorry Logan, but I can't change the past."

"Did you ever consider being with me?"

"I let you move in," I respond.

"Yeah, you did, but I wonder how much of that was real."

"All of it was real to me. Giving you up was the most selfless act I've ever done in my life. With the life I had, and all the circumstances I'd been through, I never cared about anything that didn't benefit me until you. I truly loved you, and I still believe we made the right decision whether you believe it or not."

"I want to believe you Daryn, but I trusted you before and look how it ended."

"Okay," I respond rolling my eyes and getting ready to walk away.

"Don't walk away in the middle of our conversation as if it means nothing to you."

I turn around angrier than I want to be. "I am sick of beating a dead horse. This argument is like the song that never ends. Every time it is the same old argument. Why didn't you tell me, I no longer trust you, what about you and me, why did you leave me, the list goes on and on, and I'm sick of it. So yes, I'm leaving in the middle of our discussion because there is nothing left to discuss!" By now, I am panting, and I hate myself for not being in better control.

"Mommy," Carter says, when I turn around he's standing outside the car. "Are you okay?" He asks looking afraid.

"Yes, we were just having a discussion. We are leaving now." Logan walks past me to Carter, and I follow.

"Hey buddy, we were discussing you, and when you can come back" Logan said kneeling beside him.

"You look like you were arguing." Carter said sadly. This night just keeps getting better.

"No, we weren't arguing. It is just sometimes when we discuss you we feel really passionate about it and we get a little animated."

"Animated," Carter repeated.

"Yeah, sometimes we use our hands and voices to act out how we are feeling. Sort of like, show me how you look when you are happy?" He asked Carter, and Carter smiles.

"Show me how you look when you are mad?" Logan said, and Carter scrunches up his face, wrinkles his brow, and ball up his fist.

"Now show me a silly face, "Carter made a face that made us both laugh. He stuck out his tongue to the side and crossed his eyes. "You see you were just being animated with your facial expressions. That's all your mom and dad were doing. We weren't arguing, and everything is okay." Carter looks my way.

"Yes son, everything is okay." I say to him, and he smiles.

"Then you have to hug," he says, and we both look at one another. "When Mercy and me argue, you make us hug, now hug."

We look at one another, and then we hug each other. I exhale. "I'm sorry," I whisper to him.

"I'm sorry too," he says. Then we pull apart and smile at one another.

"Was that good enough," I say to him.

"Yes, and can we go now, I want to show my dad my toys." Carter asks, and I saw Logan's smile shorten, as if he were hurt that Carter is still calling Jethro dad.

"Yes, we are done here." I say looking in Logan eyes.

"Can I get another hug? I won't see you again until next year?" Logan says then breaks our stare. They hug.

"Come on mommy," Carter says.

"Have a Happy New Year Daryn," he remarks after he pulls away from Carter.

"You too Logan," I say and walk to get in the car. Logan helps Carter into his car seat. We drive off leaving Logan watching us.

We both walk in with an armful of toys. Jethro is fully dressed in all black looking like he is about to leave.

"Where are you going?" I ask as I put down the toys on the couch.

"To the club," he says.

"I thought you took tonight off."

"I did, but apparently there is more traffic than Ro can handle. She has called me several times, about several problems. The last time she called I told her I would come in."

"Problems like what?" I ask.

"Low on liquor, I didn't leave her a key to the overstock. With the renovations, everyone will have their own code to the liquor closet. Based off last year's numbers I thought I left enough. I didn't consider Christmas Eve was on a Friday this year, and last year it was on a Thursday. The VIP sections are sold out and we don't have enough servers for each section. We are short a couple of bartenders. If I go in I can manage, and Ro can bartend. We are looking like we will hit capacity tonight, and I didn't predict we would come anywhere near it."

"Dad, I wanted us to play with my toys," Carter said walking up to Jethro. Jethro squats.

"I will try and come back as soon as possible, or as soon as you get up tomorrow, we will play with your toys." Carter hugs him.

"I wish you didn't have to go," Carter said pulling back from him.

"I wish I didn't have to go either. Did you have a good time?" Jethro asked smiling.

"Yeah, I did.   Got lots of presents, we had to leave my car, but I brought home my bike."

"Bike, you already have a bike."

"Yeah, but he bought me a big kid bike."

"Is that right," Jethro responds.

"Yeah, we also had hot chocolate with little bitty marshmallows. Do you think we can make that again on Christmas?" He asked Jethro, and Jethro smiles at him.

"Of course, we can. What else happened while you were visiting with your other dad?"

"My mom and other dad started arguing, but it's okay now because I made them hug." I cringe at his words but try not to let Jethro see.

"Is that right," Jethro said standing, and looking at me.

"I better get running Carter. Maybe if I work hard when I get there, I can make it home before you fall asleep."

"If you want, I can get Cheyenne to watch Carter, and I can come and help out."

Jethro stares at me for a long moment, as if he were considering what I was saying to him.

"Nah, I don't need a babysitter," he finally said and strolls past me and out the door.

I have no idea what time Jethro finally made it home. I told Carter he could watch tv in our room, since he was waiting on Jethro to get back. Carter moves so much in the bed I took a sleeping pill to help me fall asleep. I did not want to be disturbed by Carter's movement. When I finally open my eyes, my body is sore, and I feel groggy. I look over and Jethro is hugging the side of the bed, while Carter has his leg throwed on top of him. I ease out the bed. I don't want to wake either one of them. When I go in the livingroom I discover it is nearly six in the morning. I start brewing a pot of coffee. I am going through my phone when I feel something move. I look up and Jethro is standing there. I should have known this moment of peace and quiet was too good to be true. I look back down at my phone.

"Good morning," he says.

"Morning," I respond, still not bothering to look at him.

"You made enough coffee for me?"

"It should be enough," is my response.

"I remember on Christmas morning I was always the first one up. I couldn't wait to see what I got." I think Jethro must be bipolar. I can't turn off my anger as quickly as he can.

"Oh yeah, well Christmas wasn't filled with presents for me." I respond.

"Oh yeah, then what was it filled with." He says and comes to sit by me.

"Nothing nice, I was mostly on my own. Christmas didn't carry the same meaning for me, as it carried for you. It was just another day of being let down. There was no Christmas tree, no stockings hanging by the chimney, no presents, but most of all, no mother. I can't think of one single Christmas I spent with my mother. I mean, I would see her on some Christmas's, but we didn't 'spend' Christmas together like you think. Once I started making my own money, I would buy my own presents, wrap them, and put them under the tree.

"One year I was so excited because I hustled so hard and purchased my first Louie bag at seventeen. When I came back to school all the kids were jealous. I don't know what good that did. My mother ended up stealing it and selling if for probably, no doubt $5.

Those are the standard crackhead rates."

"Wow, I still can't believe your sweet mother was strung out like that. I really can't picture it."

"She was never a bad person. Yeah, she was caught up in the streets and addicted to drugs, but when she wasn't, she was amazing. I had to come to grips with the fact that although she sucked at parenting, she wasn't a sucky person. You see how she is with Carter."

"Yeah, I see her with Carter, and that is one of the reasons why the stories you tell me about her are hard to believe. You know she still apologizes to me, for the things she did to you. She will say to me 'Jethro don't give up on Daryn, she has turned out mighty fine for raising herself. Just give her time she will come around.' Sometimes, I forget that, and I must be reminded. I'm sorry for the way I left last night."

"It's okay," sometimes I don't know what to say to Jethro. I feel as if I'm walking on eggshells around him.

"I'm going to make cup of coffee; do you want anything?"

"Nah, I'm good."

He walks away then return with a Tiffany Blue Box and his cup of coffee.

"What's this?" I ask.

"Just open it," he says.

After opening the present, I stare down at the humungous clear diamond in the box.

"What is this?"

"I upgraded you baby, I hope you like it." I smile down at the box and my eyes shimmer with tears.

"I finally saved enough money to get you a Daryn, noteworthy ring." He takes the box and gets down on one knee. He removes the old ring.

"Daryn, I know we had a rough year, but I am still the happiest man on this planet. I love you so much, and pray with this ring you will always be mine."

"I am yours forever," I say to him and kiss him. We hug. He places the new ring on my finger. It is so big it takes up the entire section of my finger.

"I hope you like it" he says beaming back at me.

"Who wouldn't like a diamond ring from Tiffany's." He sits next to me.

"You better, because nobody does returns or layaways at Tiffany's. You should have seen the lady face when I told her the diamond I wanted, and paid cash. I think she locked her register and quit her job." I laugh at Jethro. Only Jethro can turn a second proposal into a joke.

"Since we are exchanging gifts, I got you something too." I get his present from under the tree and give it to him. He tears the paper off the box in true Jethro fashion, of course smiling. He pulls the papers out the box.

"What's this?" he asks.

"Read it," I say smiling.

"Wow, I can't accept this."

"Yes, you can, and you will. You've earned a partnership with me and the club."

"Daryn,   it's   yours,   I   can't   do   that   to   you." "Jethro, you aren't doing anything to me. You have single handily ran the club without me, for over five years. Your vision, and the heights you have taken the club are beyond my wildest dreams. I'm grateful that God sent someone like you to help me get better, in every avenue of my life." He stares at me as if he can't believe what I am telling him.

"Just say thank you," I say smiling at him.

"Thank you Daryn, for everything." He says and kisses me.

"Yuck," we hear behind us. There is Carter, ruffled hair and looking like he still needs more sleep.

"Hello son," Jethro says walking to him and picking him up.

"At some point you are going to have to stop picking him up." I say.

"I know, but not right now. You ready to open your presents lil man?" Jethro says, and that one phrase knocked all the sleep out of his eyes.

"Can we please!"

"Let's ask mom!"

"Mom can we oh, please can we?" he begs. I motion for him to go ahead.

Carter opens his presents, and has a lot of repeat gifts. We tell him he can donate some of the repeat gifts to Metropolitan Ministries. A few we let him take back, get a refund, and keep the cash. He likes that idea the most. We get dressed and prepare the house for our guest.

When my mom comes I hug her extra hard.

"What is wrong now?' she asks, and I giggle at her.

"Nothing, I'm just glad we can start over with new traditions."

"Me too, sweetie!" She says smiling until her eyes catch the new diamond on my finger.

"Daaaaammmmmn! Jethro must have gotten a good bonus at the bank." She says laughing.

"I don't know." I said laughing at her comment.

"Oh my God, I've never seen a ring so big, and so gorgeous. You deserve it baby." She said and hugs me again.

"You really think so mom," I said looking down at it.

"Hell yeah, he better thank God he married Daryn Carter. There is no woman greater." I smile at her and lace my arm with hers as we walk toward the backyard.

"Hey mom," Jethro says hugging her.

"Hey Jethro, that is a mighty nice Christmas present you got Daryn."

I got you one too," he says, and my mom eyes go wide. "A Christmas present," he says for clarity, and we laugh.

We watch the game, play a few games of cards, listen to music, and try not to think about, or talk about anything that will spoil the mood. We have a good time with good food, fellowship, and being with one another.

CHAPTER SIXTEEN

There is an accident in the path of Logan and the courthouse. He is already half an hour late. He's called his attorney twice. He insists he doesn't want to re-schedule the mediation. I am ready to get it over with. I didn't sleep last night. I'm exhausted, and I know if we continue to prolong this hearing, the sleepless nights will continue.

The door opens, and it's him. He looks flustered, but he still looks good. I straighten in my chair so I look more confident. He sits, and whispers something to his attorney.

"Glad you could make it, Mr. Anderson. If no one objects, we can start with the proceedings for the custody hearing concerning Carter Jethro Thomas."

Logan just nods his confirmation, and the mediator continues.

"When we left for the holidays, Carter Jethro Thomas was able to spend the holidays with his biological father, Logan Anderson. During the break time, and your time with Carter, have you had a change of heart about seeking full custody?" The mediator looks just as exhausted as I do.

"My client is still seeking full custody of Carter," Logan's attorney answers.

"Daryn Thomas has anything changed regarding your custody of Carter Jethro Thomas."

I am not up for the shenanigans, and I don't want to draw this day out. I am drained, and I have hit a pinnacle moment. I can see things as they should have been from the beginning. I reach for my purse and pull out the iPad Logan purchased for Carter, and I give it to the attorney. He queues up the video and gets it ready to watch.

"There has been a new development in our case regarding custody of Carter Jethro Thomas, for his wellbeing and safety." Logan perks up, and so does his attorney. They both lean forward.

"What new development are you speaking of?" The mediator states.

"We have a recording of one Allison Anderson, Logan's wife,

stating she does not want custody of Carter.

"That's a lie!" Logan shouts, and his attorney speaks to him and attempts to silence him.

"We are prepared to play the recording," my attorney states.

"Can we hear the recording," the mediator states, and my attorney presses play. He sits the iPad down on the table for all to watch and hear.

In the beginning Carter is running around, and recording everyone, Logan smiles. Then he hears his wife's voice. When he hears her say she can't do it anymore, he closes his eyes, and pinch the bridge of his nose. He knows we have him by the balls. My attorney presses pause and then speaks.

"We are willing to take this before the judge if we must, but we can put an end to all this. Logan can start spending time with his son immediately if he agrees to the custody agreement we have drawn up."

"This is ludicrous! We need to have the recording authenticated," Logan's attorney states.

"My client doesn't have a problem getting the recording authenticated, but that will delay everything that much further. At least your client can hear the agreement."

He leans over to whisper something to Logan, and I see Logan nod.

"We will hear the agreement, but we are not agreeing to sign anything before the tape has been authenticated."

"Fair enough," my attorney states and pulls the custody agreement out of his messenger bag. I intercept the agreement and start to read over it silently. The agreement Jethro and I came up with is not an agreement at all. I look at Logan thinking he does not deserve this.

"Contrary to what you believe I don't want to keep your son from you. I thought I was doing what was in the best interest of everyone. You had a family and I had a son I thought I needed to protect.

"Contrary to what you believe I still love you, and if things were different, I know we would still be together, but...that's not what life dealt us. You have Amber, and I have Jethro, and that's the hand we must play. If I could turn back the hands of time, I would make a lot of changes. Starting with telling you I was pregnant, and I was keeping your baby. I have learned from my mistakes and I pray to God I don't duplicate them." I tear up the bogus agreement I wrote with the attorney and Jethro. It just wasn't right or fair. I decide to provide the agreement that is in my heart.

"I am amending the agreement, and I believe you will find it very considerate in the terms I've come up with."

"And if I don't agree," he interjects.

"Then too damn bad, we will go to court, and you won't see Carter until then." He sits back in his chair, face beet red, and anger so thick I can feel it.

"It will be agreed upon, that I will remain the custodial parent of Carter and he will live with me. You can pick him up from school every other Friday and I will pick him up on Monday from school. Carter will spend Easter and the week of Thanksgiving with you. He will spend even years for New Year's Eve with me and odd years with you. All other holidays will be given to you if it falls on the weekend you have him. Carter's name will be hyphenated to include your last name. If you agree his name going forward will be Carter Jethro Anderson-Thomas. Do we have an agreement?" I ask as I stare at him. I try not to, but the corners of my mouth have an unintentional smirk as I think to myself, got him. This nightmare is finally over. I exhale.

"Do I have a choice?" he asks.

"Not if you want to see your son before he turns 18."

"Is that a threat?"

"Hell yeah," I say. He is trying to come for my son. I had to take the gloves off.

"What about his birthday, and Father's Day?"

"You can have him on odd years for his birthday, and the years that it is your weekend you can have him for Father's Day."

"What about this Father's Day?"

"That can be arranged," I say and pause.

His attorney says something to him, and we all pause and wait.

Logan nods his head.

"Gentleman, I think we have reached an agreement. Is that so?" The mediator asks the attorneys.

"Yes," Logan's attorney says.

"Yes," my attorney says.

"If I can have you both sign that an agreement has been reached..." he starts reciting what the agreement is, and I start zoning out. I don't have the energy to focus.

We sign the agreement, and Logan and his attorney leave. As they exit the room tears of joy start streaming down my cheeks. My attorney sits next to me.

"Are you upset about the agreement?" he asks me.

"These are tears of joy. I'm happy. For the first time in my life, I took into consideration someone else's feelings and not just my own. I am happy with the decision, the outcome, and that it is over." I said giggling through tears.

"I must say you were very generous in your agreement. I have seen a lot of cases, and he was ready to fight you to the death. If it wasn't for the recording, I know he would have gone all the way. Do you think he would have been so generous with you if he won custody?"

I wiped the rest of my tears, and smiled. "I would like to think so, but knowing what I know about Logan, he would have made me suffer as I made him suffer."

"Then why did you do it?" he asked.

"I finally realized this wasn't about me. I had to put someone else's needs before my own. I sacrificed my feelings, and all my misgivings for my son." My attorney looked shocked, I guess he thought I was going to say Logan.

"Well, whatever the reason you made the right decision, now let's get out of here and celebrate."

CHAPTER SEVENTEEN

I arrive home, and the front of the house is empty. Jethro called while I was out celebrating with the attorney, and I told him Logan signed the agreement, I just failed to tell him I altered it.

"Babe is that you?" Jethro yells out.

"Yeah," I say, and Carter bounds out of the back and jumps into my arms.

"Hey Carter, I missed you today." I say and give him a fat kiss on the cheek.

"Hey pretty lady," Jethro says, and bends to kiss me.

"Well how'd it go?" he ask sitting next to me.

"It went," I said. "Carter can you give daddy and mommy a moment?" I ask, thinking there is no time like the present. I'm ready for us to put all this behind us.

"Okay mommy, can I get a juice box?"

"Yeah of course," I say, and watch him as he gets a juice box and runs into his room.

"I thought we would be celebrating a win today, but why do I feel like we aren't going to be celebrating."

"It's still a celebration. I'm just not sure you will see the win after I give you the details."

"Try me," is his response.

After I gave him all the details of the custody hearing, and why I did what I did he sits with his hands steeped in front of his face.

Say something, I hear in my head, but I am too afraid to speak the words out loud.

Finally, he stands towering me. He looks down with disappointment. I didn't look away because I know what I did was right, and I'm proud of myself for having the courage to do the right thing.

"We had a plan."

"I know, but it didn't seem like the right thing to do."

"Once again, you did whatever you wanted to do without including me. Tell me, did you ever intend on doing the agreement we made, or were you just playing me until you saw Logan?" Wow I can't believe he just asked me that, but okay I can understand he's upset.

"He was late showing up to mediation because he was stuck in traffic. The longer I sat there the more I thought about the agreement we made. I wanted to right what I'd done to him by depriving him of a relationship with Carter. I didn't know exactly what I was going to do until it was time to discuss our arrangement."

"I guess it doesn't matter right? It is what it is. Once again, you went off halfcocked and did whatever you wanted to do whether I liked it or not." He goes to walk away, and I stand abruptly.

"If you found out you had a child from Jessica, you would have moved heaven and earth to be in his life. You would have done what it took to see him as much as possible, but you're mad because Logan wants to be a father to his son."

"Well we both know that won't happen," he said in a low voice.

"Wait, is this why you are so upset because you can't have kids? This entire situation boils down to your bruised ego because you can't have children? All this time this is what your attitude and reluctance has been about?" I look at him waiting for a response, but his silence answers the missing puzzle piece. For the life of me I couldn't understand why he was so mad at Logan being involved in Carter's life. He didn't want Logan to have a relationship with Carter.

Now I get it. It's still fucked up, but I get it.

"I have to get to the club," he finally says and walks toward the bedroom. I stand grounded where I am before I snap out of it.

"Jethro," he pauses, but he doesn't turn to face me. I walk up behind him.

"I won't try and downplay the fact that we haven't been able to have children. I have no idea how that's making you feel as a man, but I couldn't in good conscience, deny Logan his rights as his biological father.

"Jethro, you are good to Carter, and he knows you are his dad. That hasn't changed. He still loves you the same. He still sees you as his dad. We just have to share him with another family a couple weekends a month.

"I get why you feel the way you feel, but everything will work out."

Instead of responding, like I thought he would, he walks into the bedroom. Five minutes later he walks pass me and out the door without saying a word.

"Damn," I say and sit down.

A few hours later I am calling Cheyenne asking if she will keep Carter, so I can try and repair things with Jethro.

"Hey, hey, hey, hey," Cheyenne answers.

"Hey girl," I respond trying to sound upbeat.

"What's going on D?" she asks.

"Not a whole lot. What were you up too?"

"Watching reruns on TV One."

"Oh, did you have any plans for tonight?" I ask hopeful of her saying no.

"No, why? What's up?"

"I was wondering if you can do a solid for me?" I don't know why I'm being so hesitant with Cheyenne.

"Sure, what's up?"

"I need for you to watch Carter for a few hours while I go to the club?"

"Yeah, of course, we can watch Teenage Mutant Ninja Turtles 2. When are you coming?"

"In a few," I say.

"Okay see you soon," she responds and disconnects.

I run around getting Carter, and myself dressed. I put on a pair of white high waist pants and a white off the shoulder midriff. I strap on crystal Louboutin's and take one look at myself before I apply a dark red lipstick. My eyes are smoky and cat like. I grab Carter, with his arsenal of toys, and head to Cheyenne's.

When I arrive, Cheyenne gives Carter a big hug then gives me a once over.

"Wow, you look hot! What's the special occasion?"

"Nothing, I just thought I'd surprise him."

"Uh oh, what'd you do?" Cheyenne asks.

I let out a big sigh. "I sort of changed the terms of the custody agreement without telling Jethro."

"Why did you do that?"

"Because the agreement Jethro and I came up with was shit. I believe when we discussed it, we came up with something spiteful rather than something good for all parties."

"Well, you had to make sure you made a decision you could live with."

"Initially Jethro and I decided Logan could have Carter one Saturday a month. We would drop him off at a neutral location and pick him up at the same location later that day.

"We would revisit his visitation rights in five years. When I looked across the table and thought how I've already robbed him of the first four years of Carter's life...I couldn't in good conscience do it. So, in a spur of the moment, I changed it to what I felt in my heart was right.

"Which was," Cheyenne prompted.

"Every other weekend, with Logan, picking him up from school on Friday, and taking him to school on Monday. He will have the week of Thanksgiving, and for some other holidays he will have Carter on odd years, and we will have him on even years."

"That's a good ass agreement," Cheyenne said smiling like she was proud of me.

"Yeah, but Jethro and Logan are both pissed at me."

"Logan don't have a right to be pissed. That's better than what most women in your position would have given him. He's probably more pissed at his wife for what she said."
"Yeah, I thought that might be the case too."
"Give him time to heal, he'll come around."
"Who, Jethro, or Logan?" I ask.
"Both, Jethro is being a big ass baby right now. Once you give him some special attention he'll be fine." Cheyenne starts moving her hips like she is twerking. We both laugh.
"I better get going."
"Cheer up D, I'm sure everything will go well."
I hug Carter and leave wondering how I ended up in this predicament because I did what is right.
I bypass the line at the club, and make it to the front. One of the twins is working the door. I can never get their names right. They should be called Big and Bigger. They both have muscles everywhere.
"Hello Mrs. Thomas," he says moving the chain, so I can walk through.
"Hello, how are you?"
"I'm good, will you be needing an escort?"
"No thanks, I'm just here to see Jethro."
"He is by the south bar."
"Okay," I said walking in thinking what is the south bar? As soon as I cross the threshold the music assaults all my senses. My clothing feels as if it is vibrating from the base of the music. I immediately realize I don't miss this at all. Jethro is constantly changing things around to make the club look more modern. The section that once had sofas and chairs has been replaced by high top tables that women are leaning against to rest their feet. There are three small bars in a row instead of one major one. I walk toward the bar in the middle. People are heading up stairs. When did he start granting access for people to go upstairs? I stop dead in my tracks several feet away from what looks like Jethro side profile. He's sitting on a stool, leaning to the side, partially on the bar, with his legs open.

There is some random chic standing between his legs, with her hands resting comfortably on his thighs. He looks up and spots me. He half knocks the girl out the way trying to stand. I turn to run and hit a brick wall. I look up and it's BJ.

"Hey D, what's going on?" he's smiling.

"I try and go around him."

"It ain't nothing D!" He saw what I saw. "Jethro is here every night, and I've never so much as seen him sitting down, let alone him posted up with a woman. I know it's nothing."

One of the twins call BJ, and when he turns his head I duck around him. I weave through the throng of people and out the club running as fast as I can to my car. When I reverse I see Jethro in the rearview mirror waving his arms, but I speed off.

I know I don't have long before Jethro gets home. I pace around the living room breathing erratically. I feel the sting of tears, but I'll be damn if I'm going to shed a tear over Jethro cheating ass. I can't believe I've been played. I'm smarter than this. I squeeze my eyes shut, and try to stop them, but I still feel the burning behind my eyelids. The last thing I need is for Jethro to think he has me so gone, I'm crying over him. I know what will stop the threat of tears. I pull out my phone, search through contacts, and select Logan. There is nothing sweeter than revenge on a mother fucker that thinks he got you.

I stare at his name to send a message, and think fuck it

Can you meet me somewhere? (send)

I immediately see the three bubbles like he's responding.

Why? (receive)

I think we should talk (send)

Is this some sort of joke? (receive)

No, please (send)

Daryn never says please (receive)

You said yourself you don't know me anymore.   How

about tomorrow night? (send)
Give me one good reason (receive)

I tap the screen a few times, then say the first thing that comes to mind.

Curiosity (send)
I stare at the phone, and there aren't any bubbles to signal he's typing. I hear a car door slam, and I know Jethro's home.
Humor me (Receive)

I smile at his message, maybe he doesn't hate me after all.

I send one last message
I'll text you the location tomorrow (Send)
I hear a key in the door and put my cellphone away.
I look up as he's walking through the door, looking a hot mess. He's facing me.
"Daryn…" I don't feel like hearing it. I immediately cut him off.
"Jethro, it is what it is. You would think by now with all I've gone through nothing would surprise me. Even though I had a crack head mother that taught me not to have faith in humanity, you taught me that I could. Even though I've never met my father, and he took no initiative to meet me, still I thought you taught me it was okay to let down my guard and trust a man.
"Well take a bow Jethro because after 30 years you've been the only person to make a fool of me and prove what I already knew. Don't trust anybody, but your damn self. Congratulations Jethro, you are the real MVP." It is taking everything in me not to break down in tears. I can't believe how badly this hurt.
"Daryn," he says stepping toward me.
"Don't Daryn me, and don't touch me. The sad part is that if I wouldn't have seen it with my own eyes, I don't think I would have believed it. That's how bad you had me snowed."

"Daryn, it wasn't what it seemed," he said swaying.

"It seemed like you had a girl between your legs, and not a very pretty one at that."

"That's what it looked like, but that's not what it was. When I got to the club tonight I was furious. I was out of my mind. I couldn't hear the voice of reason you were trying to get me to hear because all I heard was rage. It felt like Logan won."

"My son is not some part of a contest. The sad part is, you don't realize all that has been going on with the custody battle is not about you, me, or Logan. It's about Carter and taking care of him."

"You don't understand what this means to me."

"Jethro, if we had tried to keep Carter away from Logan, or limit him to one visit a month, Carter would have started to ask questions as he got older. It would have made us look like we were trying to keep him from bonding with his dad."

"I understand what you are saying Daryn, but I can't comprehend it."

"Jethro that makes absolutely no sense," I say taking my defensive stand, folding my arms in front of me.

"As a man it is hard to explain to you how emasculating it is not being able to do what I feel should be my duty. I can never give you what Logan has given you, and that shit hurts more than you will ever realize."

What he did was wrong, but I still want to comfort him. I try to refrain, but a few tears fall, and I try to wipe them quickly.

"Jethro, you are right I don't know how you feel as a man, but I know you being reckless with our marriage will worsen our situation. You will be childless and wifeless.

"I had complete and total trust in you, and you destroyed that in one night with one gesture. I am sympathetic to what is going on with you, but to a certain extent. You put our marriage in jeopardy for what?"

"Daryn I was so lit, I didn't even realize that girl was standing between my legs. I stand up the entire night roaming around and making sure things are running like they should. BJ noticed I'd been drinking, and sat me down at the south bar where Roe was working so she could keep an eye on me. Roe said to me, 'get that girl away from here.' I said to Roe 'what girl.' She said 'the one standing between your legs.' I turned around to tell her she had to go, and I saw you out the corner of my eye. I thought my mind was playing tricks on me you turned so fast.

"I ran after you, because I know how it must have looked, but I swear to you on my life, that has never happened before. I won't lie, I can tell some women are trying to come at me, but I'm never in one location more than five minutes. Everybody in there knows you are my wife. There is absolutely no woman that can compare to you.

"Besides think about it Daryn, do you honestly think BJ would allow me to play around with various women in the club you own?"

"I don't know, men seem to stick together."

"BJ is a different kind of loyal, and you know it. He would never tolerate me coming in and playing around with different women….I gotta sit down." He stumbles over to the couch and plops down, leaning his head on the back of the couch. I still have my arms wrapped around myself. I know what he is saying is true. BJ wouldn't let him come in night after night and cheat openly on me.

"I have to go and get Carter," I say picking up my keys.

"Please don't leave me Daryn," he says picking his head up off the couch.

"I'm not leaving, I'm just going to get my son."

"I'm sorry Daryn, I honestly didn't realize she was there. If you noticed I was having a conversation with someone to the side of me. She had to come up sometime while I was talking."

"Who is she?"

"Her first name is Dena, I don't know her last name. She comes almost every night we are open. I knew she felt some type of way about me, but I didn't think she would try me, like she did tonight. Then again, I've never had more than a ten second conversation with her. She told me she sings, and she would like to be given the chance to perform. I told her to talk to BJ, and that was it. You can ask BJ." He said pleading.

"I shouldn't have to ask BJ." I stated.

"You're right, and once again, I'm sorry for putting you, us, in this predicament. It won't happen again."

I didn't respond. I stared at him hoping if he vomits, he makes it to the restroom. He looks terrible.

I walk toward the door.

"Please tell me you are coming back home."

"I'm coming back home."

"Please tell me you forgive me," his eyes are bloodshot red. I wasn't sure if it was due to the drinking, or because his eyes look a little glossed over.

"I'm still mad at you, forgiving you is not even on my mind." I respond.

"Fair enough, but that will never happen again."

"It should never have happened in the first place," I respond playing with the keys in my hand.

"You're right," he responds, and I walk out the door.

When I walk outside there is a tall dark shadow coming towards me. I stay still, literally holding my breath, thinking I don't have my gun with me. Then I recognize it's BJ. I relax and start breathing again, until I start thinking something happened. I am panicking again. Why is BJ here?

"Yo D!" he says in his baritone voice as he approaches me.

"Hey BJ, what are you doing here, is everything okay? Did something happen at the club?" The last thing I need is a shooting at the club to shut the place down, especially when I've been considering selling it.

"Relax!" he says holding his palms out toward me like he's telling me to calm down. "Nothing has happened. I was trying to make sure Jet made it home safely."

"Yeah, he's here."

"Cool, I've never seen him drinking before at work. Even when we did a champagne toast for the renovations he did the toast, but didn't drink it. Is his family good?"

"Everyone's okay, thanks for checking on him."

"Ah man, don't let what you saw tonight trick you into thinking it was something it wasn't. He's a good dude. You know I would have handled him for you long time ago if he was fucking up."

"Did Jethro put you up to this," I am in full blown skeptic mode.

"Fuck no, D you've known me for over 10 years. You know where my loyalties lie. If that nig....I meant if he was fuckin up you know I would have shut that shit down long time ago. I ain't no snitch, but I would have beat his ass." I know BJ is telling the truth, but still Jethro was wrong.

"BJ this really doesn't concern you."

"You are correct, and D if it had been that lame ass nig...I meant dude, you use to mess with, it would have been whatever it took to get rid of his ass, but I know how Jethro hustles daily to keep the place running smoothly, and for your marriage.

"I feel partly to blame."

"That's ridiculous, did you put that woman between Jethro legs?"

"Hell naw, but I saw he was off, and should have told him he could go home, and me and Roe had the place."

"Every night before we open Jethro does this walk through with an actual check list. It never fails, but tonight he had me do it. Then he stands at the door for at least thirty minutes greeting people as they come in shaking hands and kissing babies like a politician. Then he starts strolling around. He is never in the same place long. After I did the check I came back upstairs and discovered him drinking. He wanted to come downstairs, but he could barely walk, so I sat him at the bar for Roe to watch while I roamed the club. I should have sent him home or left him upstairs."

"Don't worry about it BJ." I know he's trying to take up for his boy, but right now I don't really want to hear it. "I have to go and get my son."

"A'ight D, but don't sweat that shit, none of those hoes got nothing on you, and Jet know it. He wouldn't have jeopardized your marriage for that chipmunk looking ass hoe anyway." With that we parted ways.

Before I enter Cheyenne's house I shoot Logan a quick text to meet me at Ciro's Speakeasy and I tell him the password is handcuffs. Almost as soon as I send the message he responds.

I guess you're serious.

Yeah, see you tomorrow (send)

I head to pick up Carter.

Cheyenne opens the door.

"That was quick, I thought I'd be keeping him all night."

"Yeah, well plans changed." I said walking in looking for my son.

"Jethro still mad at you? He'll come around, he always does."

"On the contrary, Jethro had a woman between his legs when I showed up."

"The fuck?"

"No, not like that. He was sitting at the bar and a woman was standing between his legs like she wanted more than to talk."

"Jethro?" Cheyenne asked looking confused.

"Yes," I respond.

"The cornball?" she asked, and I snickered despite how I feel right now.

"Yes, when I walked to the bar he was sitting down talking to Roe, and there was a woman between his legs. BJ tried to cover for him, saying he'd been drinking..." Cheyenne cuts me off.

"Say no more," she said waving her hands animatedly in front of her.

"What do you mean?"

"We both know it takes only two beers, and Jethro is drunk. You know Jethro can't handle his liquor. Ain't no way in hell, Jethro is fucking around. Who was the bitch?"

"I don't know, some girl named Dena." I said.

"Bucktooth ass Dena, she sings?"

"Yeah," I said.

"Oh, hell no," she said and walks in the back and return with tennis shoes.

"That bitch stay in Seminole Heights, I'mma fuck her up!"

"Cheyenne, the leader of the praise dance team, cannot be going to bitches house to fuck em up." We both look at each other and laugh uncontrollably.

"Listen D, that shit probably looked fucked up, but trust, Jethro ain't messing around because if I thought for one minute he was I would fuck him up." I laugh at her again. I can't believe just a few minutes ago I was on the verge of tears, and now I'm crying laughing with Cheyenne. Everybody needs this kind of friend.

"You want to stay here," as soon as she said that my phone starts ringing. Of course, it's Jethro, I send him to voicemail.

"Nah, I'm good. I got a plan." I say thinking about Logan.

"Oh yeah what's that plan?" I debate on telling her, then think better of it, especially since she's been dating my brother-n-law.

"Nothing to serious, just something to have him wondering. What about you? What's going on with you and Abe?"

"We are still good. He is more willing to agree to my terms especially since he thought I was going to cut him off when he brought that Argentina bitch."

"Well I better get going. Thanks for the laugh."

"Yeah, but all seriousness Jethro is the real deal. He ain't cheating, and definitely not with that bitch. He wouldn't do anything that would jeopardize you leaving him. He's too into you D." She walks off and returns with Carter. We head home to face Jethro.

In the hour and a half, I was gone Jethro called me eight times. Every time I let him go to voicemail. He would always follow up with a text message:

I love you Daryn
Don't leave me Daryn
I'm sorry Daryn
It won't ever happen again Daryn
I was wrong Daryn
Please forgive me Daryn

I was getting so frustrated with the fact that he wouldn't just let me be for a while. We walk in the house, and he raises his head off the back of the sofa. He's on the couch in boxers. I don't say anything to him. I walk Carter in his room and get him situated. When I turn around he's at the door watching us. I walk past him and too the room. He's right on my heels. I start taking off my jewelry.

"You want me to sleep on the couch, or in the other room."

"Suit yourself Jethro."

"What would suit me is sleeping in my own bed, but I understand if you don't want me too."

"Jethro that's up to you." I walk in the bathroom and start removing my make-up.

"Daryn, I'm sorry," he says again.

"I've heard that already Jethro."

"I know, but..."

"But what,"

"I'm just scared Daryn that's all. I know how things must have looked and I shouldn't have been in that predicament, no matter how upset I was."

We don't say anything else to one another. I change my clothes, get in the bed, and scoot as far away from him as possible. I fall asleep excited about seeing Logan tomorrow.

CHAPTER EIGHTEEN

I am bouncing my knee vigorously waiting for Logan to show. Everything in me is telling me I made the wrong decision. I shouldn't have told him to meet me despite Jethro. I know this is a dangerous game I'm playing, but I'm committed now.

I check my phone; he's fifteen minutes late, and he was never late when we were dealing. When the waiter pulls back the curtain to our private area I order a glass of cranberry juice. I need to keep a clear head. If he's not here by the time I finish I'm leaving.

Logan was so pissed after the custody hearing that I didn't try and contact him. He looked at me with hatred in his eyes, and I wanted to forget that feeling, and that moment. I would like to think that despite what we've been through these last few months, we can still be friends. Friends "yeah right," I say under my breath. The likely hood of us being friends after all this is slim to none. I start to wonder if maybe he told me he would meet me, so he could stand me up; then he is shown in by one of the hostesses. I smile at him, but he doesn't smile back—he hates me.

The waitress sits down the cranberry juice, and I take a sip.

"Hello, have you been here before," the waitress says and we both shake our head no.

"We have several options on the menu that are delish, but we are famous for our prohibition drinks. Can I interest you in an appetizer? She asked a little to bubbly for me. We both shake our head no.

"Please take a moment to peruse the menus and I will be back to take your orders." She says and walks off.

"Hi Logan."

"What do you want Daryn, did you want to meet so you could gloat?" His eyes are cold steel, his demeanor is sovereign, and his mouth set in a hard line. Even with all this going on he is still handsome, not a thick string of hair out of place.

"I want us to be friends..." before I can get the rest of my sentence out he is laughing; a big gigantic belly gut laugh. I sit looking stun.

"What's so funny?" I am now the one getting pissed.

"You want to let bygones be bygones! You could have texted me that you wanted to be friends. It has been over a month since I've seen you. Daryn, does Jethro know you are here with me, in this intimate setting, planning our friendship?" I look away and start fidgeting with my fingers.

"No, he doesn't," I respond.

"I'm asking again, what do you want...friend!" I'm not use to this Logan; the blunt and directness.

"Honestly," I respond.

"Please, the main thing we always shared was honesty, well at least I thought we did." Now he is looking at me skeptically, instead of menacingly. I feel butterflies fluttering in the pit of my stomach.

"I wanted to see you." The waitress came by to take our order. I let out a sigh of relief. I didn't think he would want to get straight to the point. I was hoping we had a little playful banner first.

"A beer please," I look at him, but I don't say a word. "Can you also bring the lady a glass of red wine," I look at him, but he gave me a look, so I wouldn't try him.

"What kind, we have Cabernet, Pinot Noir, Port..."

"She likes semi-sweet," he responds.

"Oh, we have a red shiraz she would absolutely love, it's very light very smooth," the waitress stated.

"Excellent," Logan said, and she scurries off. "I believe we will both need an alcoholic beverage, or two, to make it through the night."

"Do you hate me that much?" I can't believe I am asking him, and I can't believe I care.

"I don't hate you at all. I can sense your hesitation, and I've found, from previous experiences, that if you drink a glass of wine or two, you loosen up."

I look down at the menu and close it when I figure out what

I'm ordering. I look up at Logan, who is staring at me.

"Why did you want to see me?" he asked.

"I wanted to make sure there are no hard feelings between us," that is part of the reason, but if I'd never gotten angry with Jethro, I know I wouldn't have requested this meeting with him.

"Daryn, I don't know how I feel, and that is the God's honest truth. I am at your mercy when it comes to our son, and I don't like that. You could take him away at any moment, and I wouldn't have a say."

"We signed an agreement," I said cutting him off.

"Daryn, you and I both know, at any moment you could take it back. If you showed the courts the video of my wife breaking down about not wanting Carter, they would take away everything we agreed upon."

"Why would I do that?"

"I don't know Daryn, the same reason why you kept him from me for four years." I close my eyes and take a deep breath. I don't know why I thought somehow, I would be the hero, after being so generous with him in mediation.

"Please forgive me. I was wrong. I'm sorry Logan, I shouldn't have kept him from you, and if I could turn back time I would do it differently."

"Do you mean, you would have let me stay, and not kicked me out?"

"No, I don't mean that." I take a deep steadying breath; this conversation is not going like I pictured it in my head. I pictured him sitting down, smiling, and being ecstatic that I wanted to see him.

"I don't believe we made the wrong decisions by choosing, who we chose. I do wish however, once I had Carter, I'd made a better decision and contacted you. It's just that it never seemed like the right time."

"Why didn't you think you should have contacted me when you were pregnant?" he asked.

"I wasn't in the right frame of mind when I was pregnant. I was hostile and volatile and full of rage. It wasn't until I had Carter that I was able to let everything go. I was very angry while I was pregnant.

"I broke down and called you a few days later, but you changed your number." Why am I so emotional right now? It's almost as if I'm trying to convince him to believe me. I feel as though I've given control to Logan.

The waitress came over brought our drinks. He took a long pull of his beer, and I took a long sip of my wine.

He closes his eyes, as if he'd just reunited with his best friend.

"Now what," at least he is no longer looking like he wants to choke me.

"That's a good question," I didn't have a response. I am normally a planner, but I couldn't think straight since I wanted to get back at Jethro.

"Did you and Jethro get in an argument," he is now done with his beer. I drain the rest of my wine glass, now I have a small buzz.

"Something like that," I don't feel the need to fake it. I don't really have anything to lose with Logan, he already hates me.

"Daryn, as much as I am enjoying this game of twenty questions, I am really in no mood to play games. Since we returned from the Cayman Islands I have been walking on egg shells in my own home. Instead of proving there is nothing between you and I, she seems to think the trip solidified what she has been thinking. She thinks I've been looking at you a particular way or smiling at you when you weren't looking. She is convinced now, more than ever I will eventually leave her for you.

"So, I ask you again, why I am here?"

As he asked the question, the waitress returned with our meals, and asked if she could replenish our drinks. We both agreed that she could.

"Logan, I guess this was a mistake, I didn't think your meeting me would cause you to become so upset. Just forget I ever called you," I was about to get up, and leave everything.

"Oh no you don't, you got me here, now you are going to tell me why. When you first texted, me I thought it was to renege on some of the promises you made at mediation. The moment I slid in the booth, the way you are dressed, your dress hanging off one shoulder, and your hair resting on that naked shoulder, I knew that wasn't the case.

"Then I started thinking maybe just maybe you had some good news for me to make this partially shitty day go away. Hunter has gotten in trouble yet again at school. We have been informed if he causes trouble one more time, he will be expelled. My oldest daughter Brooke, is still not speaking to me, yet she is still taking money I send to pay her tuition, and meal plan. Bristol has been asking when Carter is coming to live with us. I haven't had the heart to tell her he's not coming to live with us.

"So, at this point, you choosing to leave, and waste the last little bit of energy I have, is not an option. We aren't leaving until I feel you are being completely honest with me." The waitress placed fresh drinks on the table. He drank half his beer, and I look at my wine, and think I'd better slow it down before I must call an uber. I opt to go with the truth. I take a deep breath and blow it out before I start speaking.

"When we came back from the Cayman Island I wasn't sure what would happen with Carter. After Amber told me she couldn't be responsible for raising another kid, I tried my best to get her to convince you of this. I went out with her, and drank rum which I hated, to try and get her to tell you, then she ended up with alcohol poisoning. So, my plan to continue to work on her fell through.

"When we came back home Jethro and I started trying to come up with the worst-case scenarios. When you said jump, I said how high. I found the video of Amber a few days before we were to go to our final mediation. I thought about how you treated me, like you never gave a damn about me in mediation and was going for blood. When you took out the case file on my mother, I knew it was by any means necessary. Jethro told me we had you, and we celebrated, but believe it or not Jethro was the voice of reason. He said he had time to think about what my friend Cheyenne told him, and what if he had a child out there. He would want to start spending time with that child right away, and wouldn't stop at anything to make that happen. So, we sat down together, and discussed what we both thought was reasonable. It was Jethro that suggested we give you as much time as we did.

"We both got over ourselves, and agreed to do what was best for Carter, and shutting you out was not the best answer. I know you mean him no harm. I know you love him as much as you love your other kids. I watched you with him, and him with you, I could not tell by the way ya'll were together you weren't in his life since birth. I see how much he loves you, and you love him." I might have embellished the truth some, but I need him to see Jethro in a different light.

"I must admit I was surprised at how generous you were when you told me the agreement. I was upset at how everything went down. To be honest I've been harboring ill feelings toward you and Amber since we returned. My attorney said with a video you had, the way your attorney could have spent it, you could have guaranteed I had nothing but supervised visits, and for Amber never to come around."

"I know I had you by the balls," I said, and he actually laughed. "I knew in my heart that wasn't the right thing to do, even if you were about to drag my mom's name through the mud."

He was half way done with his meal, and mine was still sitting in front of me untouched.

"I was pissed with you, your mom, and Jethro," he said eating his bloody steak.

"Why my mother?"

"I saw your mom at the restaurant we use to go to, and I specifically asked her did she notice anything different about you. She told me no. She should have known you were pregnant, and she chose not to disclose that information to me purposely, so I blamed her too."

"My mother didn't know you were the father of my child. She was suspicious of you questioning her, but she didn't know until afterwards, when she called me, and my silence pretty much confirmed why you were questioning her."

"Hmm," was his response as he looked off in the distance. He starts back on his food, looking like he is in deep thought.

"A penny for your thoughts," I said, and he rewards me with that bright white smile of his.

"Honestly," he stated, putting down his knife and fork, and taking a sip of his beer.

"Always, we both agreed honesty was all we had."

"Did you only want to tell me about your feelings regarding Carter?"

"I wanted a truce between us."

"A truce? What kind of truce?"

"I don't know, maybe we can be friends. Maybe have dinner every now and then?" I smile at him, but he looks like he is on to me and what I am trying to do

"How will your husband feel about this?" He is regarding me carefully surveying my every mood.

"I'm not sure I haven't told him." Logan gave me a sardonic smile.

"I don't think you have what it takes to keep our 'relationship' away from Jethro. Do you think you can handle secrets and lies about our meeting up with one another?   What exactly would we be meeting to do?" He is not taking his eyes off me.

"I don't know, whatever?" My heart is now beating wildly and out of control. My mind asked me what I am doing, but I feel like I am too far in to stop. He gives me one long look as he takes a moment to ponder exactly what I said, and he is giving thought to what I mean by my words.

"Daryn, when we broke up, for lack of a better word, it consumed me with thoughts of how to get you back. I went home, angry, and bitter. I couldn't understand how everything went bad so fast, and I thought if I gave you enough time, you would come around, and return to me. That never happened, and up until now I wondered what it would have been like if we stayed together. I desperately wanted to stay together. I believe we would have made a great couple.

"I'm sitting here looking at you, and how beautiful you are. I remember how good you use to make me feel. I still remember how soft your skin felt, how your body conformed to mine, and how sweet you tasted.

"A few months ago, I would have paid, whatever you asked, to have one night with you. That is how much I missed you.

"I believe you are offering yourself to me. I want to say yes so badly, but I know I can't. I can't go back to being your Wednesday night lover, or boyfriend, or whatever we were. We have surpassed that. We have a son together, and history so deep I still dream about you. So, if you are asking me to sneak around with you, I can't." He pauses.

"I understand," is my only response.

"No, I don't think you do. I would leave my life in a heartbeat if you left yours, but I cannot, and will not reduce myself to being just your lover. I want all or nothing. Are you willing to give up everything for me, and be committed to me, because I'm ready for you Daryn?"

I cleared my throat. I don't know what I was thinking. He is right we are miles past being lovers.

"You are right. We are past being Wednesday night lovers, and I should have never brought this up. It was good seeing you." I am about to leave, again.

"Please stay, we can talk a little longer. You know, just long enough to make him wonder, but short enough that you couldn't have done anything to serious." He is smiling, and I smile back at him. He understands what is going on, even though I hadn't told him. He knows my being here had something to do with me being upset with Jethro.

I pause and put my purse down.

"Aren't you going to eat?" he questions.

"My nerves got the best of me," I said honestly, and he smiles.

"It's not the lying, it's not the cheating, it is the guilt that would eat you up. You're not cut out for the guilt you would feel by betraying your spouse."

"You are probably right," I take another sip of wine.

"Besides you are a terrible liar, and Jethro would never give up. You would crack under pressure. Amber and I were at a time in our marriage where she didn't question me, because she didn't really care.

"I saw how Jethro is with you, and I know as much as he loves you he would be devastated. As much as it pains me to admit this, you married a good guy. I worked with Jethro for over a year, and he was consistent. He smiled all the damn time," we both laugh when he said that because it is true. "The patrons loved him, baked cookies for him, knitted blankets for him, and asked for him by name. He was always nice, even to the worst customers. If it weren't genuine, he wouldn't have been able to keep it up for that long. The guilt of you destroying the man that he is, would eat you up.

"So, trust me, you couldn't do it, but...I would like it very much if we can be friends." He is now smiling at me, and he reached for his beer, but decided not to pick it up. I guess he figured he'd had enough.

"I would like that too." I smile back at him.

"Daryn, some of the best times in my life I spent with you. I still think about when I came to see you in Vegas, and you were dancing on the table." He is laughing.

"Those were the good ole days. I'm not that interesting anymore," I am smiling at the memory.

"Why aren't you that interesting anymore?"

"I'm a mom, and a married woman. I try to be a little more conservative."

"Even moms, and married women need to have fun. Take it from me. The minute you stop the fun, the minute you stop the spontaneity, you will go looking for it somewhere else. Keep your marriage thriving, keep it fun, and keep it entertaining." His words were heartfelt, and I appreciated Logan giving me words of advice.

We talk for about another hour, and he announces it is time for us to go home and face the reality we chose. We hug probably a second too long for what is acceptable, but just under enough time so it isn't awkward. We vow to be friends, but we both understand what that means. No more meetings without spouses or kids, and to be amicable to one another. I start my car, and ride home in silence with a large grin on my face.

I walk in my house filled with panic, and chaos. "Why didn't you answer your phone?" Jethro approaches me as I walk into the house.

"I had it on silent." I respond.

"Juicy has been calling you!" He bit out grabbing his keys.

"Is it my mother?" I said now panicking.

"No, something is wrong with your Uncle Buck, and she said she needs us to come over." I turn around and follow him and Carter out the house.

We are speeding toward the highway when I turn to him, "what exactly did Juicy say that has you driving so fast?" As soon as I said it my seatbelt hitched up around my neck as he turned onto the interstate without using breaks.

"She was crying, and she sounded panicked."

I tried calling her, but Juicy's phone is going straight to voicemail, and my grandma's phone is ringing busy.

"Did she say if Buck is terrorizing them again?"

"No, she just said come quick it's Uncle Buck. She said she had been trying to call you, but you weren't picking up, then the call disconnected.

"I understand if you are upset with me, but you should always answer your phone in case of an emergency." I left my phone in the car, so I wouldn't be disturbed. I felt a little guilty about not answering Juicy's call when she needed me, but I wasn't commenting on Jethro's remark just yet. This was not the right time.

"Why didn't you answer your phone?"

"We can discuss it after I find out what is going on with my family," with our current situation he better be glad I came home. If it weren't for Logan pulling me back to reality, I would have still been with him, possibly in a rather compromising position.

We pull up to the house and everyone, including my grandmother, is standing on the porch. I wonder what exactly my Uncle Buck is in the house tearing up. With Jethro rushing me I didn't think to bring my gun. Jethro carries Carter to the house, as I walk up to my grandmother who is crying.

"What's going on?" I asked kneeling in front of her. She put her head in her hands and cried harder, as Juicy comforts her by rubbing small circles on her back.

"What's up Juicy?" I look at her.

"It's Uncle Buck, he's dead," my grandmother started crying harder when she said that.

"Where is he?"

"He's in the house, on the floor,"

"Wait a minute, no one called 9-1-1?"

"No, granny was afraid of how they would treat him because they know he was on drugs." I stand to walk in the house.

"I will come with you," Jethro said, and sat Carter down for Juicy to watch.

"What? Where is he?"

"He's in the living room." As soon as we walk in the house, he is on the ground in a fetal position clutching his chest. He looks like he had a stroke the way his fist is balled up.

"You okay," Jethro said rubbing my back. For a moment I'd forgotten he was in the house. I stare at Buck. I didn't know what to think or feel.

"Yeah, I'm fine." We walk outside, and I call Cheyenne to come and pick up Carter. I'm not sure how long we are going to be.

"How long has he been like this?" Jethro asked as I dial 9-1-1.

"He's been complaining about his chest all week. He had a bad cold, but that didn't stop him from begging me for money. I'd gone to bed around eight, because I wasn't feeling well. When Juicy came home she came running upstairs. She asked me when the last time I saw him. I told her around eight. She said, 'granny I think Uncle Buck is dead!' I ran downstairs as fast I could and he was on the floor. I don't know how long he'd been there. Oh Lord, I should have never left him." She is back to crying again.

Cheyenne came to get Carter.

Since it is a non-emergency, they said they would be here as soon as possible.

"Juicy whose car?" There is a white Honda Civic parked in the driveway. She smiles.

"That's mine, my dad helped me buy it," she is beaming with delight.

"Oh," I remark.

"You want to see it?" We walk toward her car, as Jethro stands with my grandmother. I want to get her mind off the situation at hand.

"My dad is helping me move into my own place. I'm going to take Mercy with me, but the rest of them will have to stay with Granny. I can't afford to take care of all of them." I know Juicy needs her own life, but these are her siblings. Why should my granny have to take care of them?

"Did Ja'net say she would get the other kids?" Juicy laughs. I guess it is funny. Ja'net has never taken care of any of her kids. She has them and drop them off to my grandmother's house.

"My mom came by several months ago, to inform us she was moving to Atlanta with her new boyfriend. He doesn't know she has kids, so she will not be able to take any of us with her, and we should start calling her Aunt Ja'net just in case her boyfriend is ever around.

She also informed granny as soon as she gets 'settled' she will send her some money. We haven't seen anything yet. I tried calling her tonight about Uncle Buck, but her phone has been disconnected, or she has changed the number.

"It doesn't matter anyway. Mercy is scared of her, and my brother's cry when she come around because they want to follow her. She causes more confusion than anything."

"What about your oldest sister," I asked.

"She is still living with her boyfriend, and on baby number two. At least she is trying. She goes to a college online to learn medical billing and coding. She said once she gets certified she can work from home."

Ja'net is so damn sorry. What kind of parent would tell their children to call them auntie.

Three hours pass before they arrive to pick up my uncle. It is after two in the morning before Jethro and I get on the road to head home. I call Cheyenne, and she said Carter is asleep and she will bring him over tomorrow, so we can watch Abe's game together.

"You okay," he asked.

"Honestly," is my response as I stare off into space.

"Of course," he is now rubbing my back with one hand as he drives with the other.

"My uncle has been on crack since I can remember. My mom would at least try to get clean, but not my uncle. I know recently he was "supposedly" clean, but Juicy told me last week, he was over harassing my grandmother for money.

"He stole from me, my grandmother, my little cousins. He didn't care. He would take food out of granny's fridge and sell it. If he thought, he could make $5 from something, he would take it. He terrorized everyone at my grandmother's house. I hated him, I'm glad he's dead." My voice broke on the last part of the sentence as I thought about my grandmother having a better life with him being gone. "My granny will no longer have to hide her valuables, he sold her pearls, her mother gave her for $10. He sold her cellphone, that's why she doesn't have one. It was just a matter of time before he was going to get violent and hurt someone. My grandmother can finally have peace." I mean every word of what I am saying. My reasons for being glad he's dead are not personal or selfish. I know he will be missed, but he's better off dead, and that is the ugly truth. I know Jethro don't know how to deal with my response. He hasn't said one word to my comment, and gratefully he stopped rubbing my back. I don't need comforting I'm not sad.

When we walk into the house, I immediately go to my room to undress and take a shower. I lock the door behind me, so Jethro can't follow.

When I emerge from the bathroom he is sitting on the edge of the bed. He didn't try to come into the bathroom. As I am putting away my jewelry he starts speaking.

"I know I didn't grow up like you did. I do remember my parents arguing maybe once, about him gambling, but he never stole from us. To hear you say you are glad your uncle is dead, seemed morbid. I've been sitting here trying to understand why you would say you are glad he is dead. Your grandmother is mourning him, and Juicy is mourning him, but you are unfazed by the death of your uncle; your mom's brother. He is a human being."

I'm not sure if this conversation is coming from what I said about Buck, or if it will emerge into something else. I sit down in the chair at the desk.

"I know he is a human being, but, Buck has been dead for years. He didn't belong to himself. He belonged to drugs. My mom could become so desperate that she would say some of the vilest shit to me. My uncle was becoming so desperate I feared him getting violent. I never saw my uncle hit or push my grandmother. She used to say he would never hurt her, but I've noticed in the last few years, she no longer says that. Lately she would say she wish he would leave her alone. When he was being court ordered for drug testing she was relieved that he couldn't come by as often.

"What my uncle battled was a fate worse than death. He'd already deteriorated years ago. He wasn't my uncle, he wasn't my mother's brother, and he wasn't my grandmother's son. He no longer belonged to himself." What I said was dark, and harsh, but it was factual.

"What about your grandmother losing a son?"

"She lost her son long ago. After the mourning of her son, relief will follow when she no longer must live in constant fear. She will no longer wonder if tonight is the night she will get that phone call about him being dead, in jail, or far worse. She can go on with her life without the burden of her son bringing her down." I meant it, and I have no intention of changing my stance. I know no one else in my family will have the guts to admit it, but it is the truth. He is not only causing harm to himself, he is starting to harm others around him.

"He is still a person, and he was still your uncle. That alone should make you miss him, and wish he was still here. If I'd lost my uncle, I would be devastated."

"You can't compare my uncle, to your uncle, because your uncle has never been a crack addict. I loved my uncle, and I still love him, but I understand how the game works. He is better off dead, so he no longer has to struggle with the addiction that had consumed him. He is better off dead, so he can lay those beast and demons that he struggled with to bed. He is better off dead, so he can't cause himself and others around him any more harm. He is better off dead, so he can finally rest in peace."

"I'm trying not to judge you, but your words and actions lately are making me question some things I thought I knew about you."

Here we go, I thought. I knew eventually this would come up, and I would have to explain myself. Although I've been married to Jethro for five years, we've never really been through why I'm the way that I am, and why my emotions are the way they are. My life has made my interior and exterior harder than most people. For some reason I was hoping I could prolong this conversation maybe never have it.

"Love is a new emotion for me Jethro. When you are used to being abandoned, treated like you were unlovable, and neglected, you start to think in life that is all you deserve. Growing up I went back and forth between living with my grandmother, when my mom was doping, and living with her when she was trying to clean up her act. I never had stability.

"There were times when teachers told me they believed I was gifted and have me tested. As soon as I was tested, it never failed I was pulled out of whatever school I was in because I either was going to live with my grandmother, or my mother was trying to make amends with her demons and raise me. She didn't care if I protested or what I had going on in my life she would just uproot me without warning. She would show up to the school withdraw me and enroll me somewhere else.

"When I became emancipated by the state I was already living on my own. I was sixteen, and by the age of 18 I owned a duplex I rented the front, and I stayed in the back. I went to school to get my diploma to prove to my mother I was nothing like her. I wanted to prove I was responsible, and even though I was on my own I would still make the right decisions.

"I did all my class work, aced all test, and completed homework I could do before school let out. I knew once I got out of school I had to grind. I hustled from sun up to until I felt accomplished. Some days I hustled until it was time to go to school the next morning. I would be up all night and go to school the next morning.

"I couldn't prepare for prom because I was too busy doing hair for the people that were going to prom. I couldn't go to grad night because every night I had to write papers that I needed people to pay me for. "When I started working in the club I was drawing in a crowd, and the owner started trusting me with ideas he would implement.

One day he approached me and told me he was going to sell the club. I immediately started thinking about the next hustle. He told me I had a great business mind, and if I could come up with the money he would sell it to me. That was the first time I thought about turning my hustle into a business plan. That pushed me to work harder.

"I dated, but I didn't have time for a personal life. The guy I was a little serious about didn't work out because my grind never stopped. He would come to the club, and I would ignore him all night. He became jealous of the men I talked to, and me putting my work before him. So, without hesitation I let him go. I knew happily ever after was just for television in my world, and the empire I was working on building would far outweigh a life tied down with some guy that would eventually leave anyway. He thought I would contact him, and after I didn't he showed up to the club and tried to show out. I had security escort him out and banned him from coming back. I never saw him again because he didn't know where I lived. He tried to call me, and I never answered. It was easy to let him go.

"I sold my duplex for three times what I paid for it and was able to give him a third of what the club was worth. We stayed in partnership until I secured a loan and finished buying him out. Within a year I'd grossed enough to secure a loan for the condo I lived in, and then the strip mall. I'd accomplished all this by the time I was twenty-three.

"Then at twenty-six I met Logan."

"I don't need to hear anymore," Jethro interrupts.

We've never discussed my personal relationship with Logan, but I was making a point about me, love, and why I'm so disconnected from my feelings.

"I know you don't want to hear anymore, and I promise not to be too graphic, but when I'm done, you will understand me better." I pause, and when he didn't say anything I continued. "I met Logan on a cruise. I didn't think I'd see him again once we got off the ship, but I did, and what he offered me helped me to continue to keep my hard exterior and interior. He didn't require more than I could offer him because he already belonged to someone else, and I told myself that was what I deserved. After all I'd accomplished in my life; delivered from a crack head mother, owner of the number one-night club in Ybor City, a millionaire, and still I thought I didn't deserve better than a married man one night a week. After everything I'd been through in life, I knew happily ever after just wasn't in the cards for me.

"Then I met you. You were kind for no reason. You made me smile, laugh, and feel like maybe, there is something better out there for me, and that scared me shitless. I knew the type of life I deserved, and you were not it. I thought I had to get away from you.

"Then I found out I was pregnant, and my world collapsed. It was a reminder that my fate was sealed, and my legacy would be that of my mothers. When I saw you in the hospital you had every right to leave me and tell me you didn't want anything to do with me ever again, but you didn't. You stayed, and showed me so much love, and support that I was skeptical, but you remained consistent. No matter how much I pushed you away, and tested you, you remained consistent. I was not use to the kind of love you showed me. At moments it was overwhelming, but I started to accept it, and started to change for you. I wanted so much to be the wife that you could be proud of and be worthy of the kind of love you were showing me. I changed so much I didn't recognize myself. You made me feel special.

"Then when I walked in the club to surprise you, and you were engaged in what appeared as an affair, I thought I'm really not special at all."

"Daryn, it was nothing at all. It wasn't what it looked." I place my hand on his lips.

"You say it's nothing, but I know what I saw. She is into you, and you knew you were wrong. Your face said it all. You should have never been in such a compromising position with this woman, but you were, and I felt two things, confusion, and relief.

"The confusion came from me not believing what I saw. If anyone else would have told me they saw, you with a woman between your legs I would have denied it. My relief came from knowing you are not perfect.

"When I met up with Logan tonight, I had every intention of getting back at you. I was devastated. I couldn't believe you got me. You got me believing you were better than an affair or being with a woman in a bar while I was at home. The fact that I never would have believed you were capable of anything resembling an affair, made me understand just how much I'd changed, and how much I needed to bring some of the old me back.

"I met up with Logan for all the wrong reasons, and for that I am sorry. It was a mistake, and while I was there Logan and I both knew it. I am still glad I went because it got me to understand that changing myself completely was not only wrong, but impossible. I love you Jethro, and you must let me, be me, without looking at me with such disappointment when I fall off your pedestal.

"The Daryn you are hearing tonight is part of the old me. She still resides in me, and I need to keep her. It is the Daryn I have suppressed, and that is why you are questioning my judgment. That Daryn was the Daryn that you fell in love with. Just take a moment to think about the me you remember, and I guarantee you will not question my heart."

"Daryn, I never asked you to change for me. The fact that you would get back at me for something you thought you saw, lets me know you've been going through the motions. If you want to have another affair with Logan, be my guest. I'm outta here," Jethro said and stood abruptly grabbing his keys to leave, and the old Daryn showed up and showed out. She has no fear.

Oh, hell No! He's the main one always telling me we don't need to go to bed mad, and now he's trying to leave. I jumped in his path and said with such vehemence "If you leave I am assuming you are asking for a divorce and you won't be returning. Where should I send your shit, because you, will not be allowed to come back. I'm telling you some real shit, not for approval but because I don't want any secrets between us anymore. We need to put all our cards on the table." When I see I have his attention, I continue to speak. "I will not apologize for what I saw, and I know what I saw. You were engaged in inappropriate behavior, that is why you jumped up like you did." He stands with his keys in hand, like he is still debating to leave or stay. I am not going to cry or beg Jethro. I'm over walking on eggshells when I'm around him, and trying to live up to his unbelievable expectations. "You are not innocent. I don't care that she was trying to get a singing gig. You were wrong, but you are human and so am I. Logan was where I turned because he was familiar, not because it was right. I knew if I wanted to get you back that was the best way to do it. I was wrong, and I am admitting that. The fact that you are still treating me like I'm the only one wrong, that's where it stops.

"I'm not perfect, and you have to stop treating me like I am. You used to have a fit when I ran, and now you think it is okay for you to run because you have heard some things you didn't want to hear. Well Jethro I've told you everything and if you still want to leave the choice is up to you. Do understand if you leave there is no coming back. If you leave there is no forgiveness and moving forward. We can work this out now, or not at all, but you throwing a temper tantrum and trying to storm out the house will not work for me, and will not work for this marriage. The choice is yours and I will be good either way." I want to take a bow after my declaration, I didn't realize how much I'd missed me.

I stood straight and tall. I braced myself for whatever he chose. If he leaves I won't beg him back, and I won't rescind my speech.

"I never asked you to be any more than you are, I never told you to give up who you are, and I never cheated on you."

"You never asked me to change, but I felt the need to change from the way you treated me. I felt I needed to be a great wife for someone who held me in such high esteem. I changed so I could be the wife I thought you wanted me to be. It was all for you.

"Do you have any idea how big of a fool I felt when I saw you? Yeah, you keep saying you didn't cheat but emotional cheating is just as bad as physical cheating. I saw you engaged in emotional cheating, whether you want to admit it or not."

"Daryn we can't be married if every time you think I'm doing something out of line, you run back to Logan. I knew loving you came with challenges, but Logan continuing to be a problem is where I draw the line. I was all set to run this race together. I knew loving you would not be easy, but I was up for the race. I knew there would be hurdles, but together we could jump them. I knew some of those hurdles we would jump and trip over them. Sometimes even fall, but I knew we would brush ourselves off and get back in the race. I knew we would have some straight aways, and turns around the track. I was geared up to pace myself around the turns and give my all during the straight aways just in case I needed to make up time. We had a great straight away for four years, but since we've seen Logan it's been falling over hurdle after hurdle. It seems no matter how high I jump I still get my foot caught on the hurdle and knock the damn thing down. I can't seem to jump high enough for you or for us.

"When you saw me 'engaging in inappropriate behavior' I didn't see it that way. I saw the look on your face, and imagined how that must have looked from the outside looking in, for that I am sorry. I swear to you I had no idea she was standing between my legs. Maybe I did pick up on she may have felt something more than friendship or business. She would lean in a little longer, she would laugh a little harder at my jokes, but I can assure you my feelings are not mutual. The only person I have eyes for, the only person I love is you. I want you to feel that way too."

"Jethro, you are human, I am human. We have both made mistakes. We won't make it if you continue to have unbelievable expectations of me."

"Where do we go from here?" He is asking me, and I think, hell if I know, you are the one with the parents that have been married 40 years.

"We kiss and make up," I said approaching him.

We decide not to cancel folks from coming over to watch Abe play in his football game Sunday. Hopefully that will cheer everyone up. Quite honestly, it is giving me something to look forward to. Jethro and I are better, but not on the best terms. He's looking at me like I'm human now, and no longer on this superficial pedestal I could never live up to. He has expectations of me even the pope would have a hard time delivering on. At least if he sees me as human he knows I have faults. If he sees me as human, he won't look so devastated when I disappoint him.

"Do you think we went overboard?" he asks. I'm looking at the spread of dips, exotic cheeses, assorted fruits, veggies, wings, empanadas, beers, wines, and punches.

"Nah," I say and we both smile. We definitely went overboard. The doorbell rings signaling our first guest. We are walking to the door, and he pulls me close to him. When I look up at him he kisses me, genuinely kisses me, for the first time since I told him about Logan. It causes me to smile at him.

The party is in full swing, and the game is back from half time. Abe is running the ball, and he does a spin off a defensive player causing him to break free. He's running toward the end zone, and we are all on our feet cheering. He has a few yards to go, and out of nowhere comes a cornerback; wham helmet to helmet. Abe lays facedown not moving. We all stop cheering and stare at the television for any form of movement.

"Get up Abe, get up," Jethro whispers. We are all still standing and staring at the television. There is a team of people running out on the field, then a commercial, and Jethro's phone rings.

"Mom," Jethro says. "I don't know anything yet. I will call you when I know something," Jethro hangs up. Jethro tries to call Abe's agent, but he doesn't answer. I try to comfort him, by rubbing his arm and assuring him that Abe is strong, and he will be okay.

I look at Cheyenne and I can tell she is barely holding it together. The game comes back on and Abe is still lying on the field on his stomach, motionless.

"Juicy can you take Carter to his room."

"What's wrong with Uncle Abe?" he asked as he's being dragged into his room.

"He's okay," Juicy says to him.

Medical personnel are on the field, and a cart is being brought out. He still isn't moving. I try holding on to Jethro's bicep while he folds his arms. That telltale sign that he is stressed is there as he flexes the muscle in his temple. They go to another commercial.

"Why aren't they saying anything?" Cheyenne sits bouncing her knee and still holding onto her pom pom.

"I'm going to call to see about a flight going out," Jethro said walking away from me causing me to drop my arm.

"Include me," Cheyenne yells.

"And me," I chime in as well. I sit by Cheyenne trying to comfort her as Jethro makes phone calls. When they flash back to the game they are carting Abe off on a stretcher and he is still not moving.

"Oh God, please let him be okay! I never told him how I really feel!" Cheyenne said starting to break down.

"You will still get a chance to tell him how you feel." I grab her hand in mine. "Now listen to me, it is not the time to break down. We must pray and believe that he will be fine. We have to be strong for him."

"Cheyenne, I need you to provide your information for the flight," Jethro hands her the phone.

"They only have three open seats; do you think your mom will keep Carter until we get back?" he asked.

"My mom has to work, we could charter a plane," I respond.

"That would take too long, and cost too much. This plane leaves in a little over two hours."

"I can ask Logan and his wife to watch him," I chance saying this to him. This isn't Logan's weekend, but Logan is his father, and he's stayed there before. He is staring at me like he is trying to digest what I am saying.

"Okay," he said, grabs the phone from Cheyenne, and walks

away.

I pick up my cell and dial Logan. He answers on the first ring.

"Is everything okay," I guess he would think something is wrong since I don't call unless Carter is at his house.

"Carter's fine, but Jethro's brother just suffered an injury on the   field."

"Yeah, I'm watching the game. He's still unconscious." He remarks.

"Um, I don't have a lot of time, I was wondering if you would mind watching Carter a few days while we fly out to make sure Abe is okay," I don't know why I'm nervous to ask him this.

"Of course, we would love to. Do you need me to come and pick him up? I don't mind."

"No, we can drop him off on the way to the airport." I let him know we would be there shortly and disconnect.

"Cheyenne, do you need to go home and get clothes? We can pick you up on the way." I told her.

"No, I'm fine. I will just buy stuff when I get there. It will take me to long to go home and try to pack."

"I'm sure I have some things you can take with you." I told her, and we set off to pack. I guess I shouldn't call it packing because I'm not sure what I threw in the suitcase. I try to remember it is cold in New York even though it is not cold in Florida. I take more time at packing Carter's things. Jethro came in the room and told me it was time to go.

"We load up and head out. When we pull up to Logan's house, he is already outside waiting. Jethro hops out the car and escorts Carter. I keep my eyes trained on looking forward.

Cheyenne isn't very talkative, and when I try to ask her something she only gives me one-word responses. After a while I stop asking.

We fly Southwest and because we are last minute there aren't two seats together. Jethro took the very last seat, so he didn't have to fly in a middle seat.

When we arrived, there was a car for us sent by Abe's agent.

Jethro is on the phone with the agent, as the driver loads up the car with our bags. It is freezing, we packed outer wear, but failed to put any on.

At least Jethro is smiling now.

"What did he say?" I ask when Jethro finished praying.

"He said Abe is up, and responding, but they are still checking him out. Thank you, Jesus!" he shouted. I put my hand in his, and in Cheyenne's, to try and comfort them both.

We ride to the hospital in silence praying and hoping Abe will be fine. We are met by his agent he told us they aren't letting Abe have visitors yet.

I walk off to call Logan.

"Hey," he answers right away.

"Hey, how's Carter?" I asked.

"He's fine. He's running around playing. More importantly how's Abe?" I let out a big sigh.

"We haven't seen him yet, but we were informed he's responsive."

"Take all the time you need," he responds.

"Thanks, I'm sorry for the way I packed his things. I did everything in such a hurry."

"No worries, we have things here for him."

"Oh, I wasn't aware of that."

"Well, I can't stop spoiling him. When I'm out, I always seem to end up in his department." I can hear the smile in his voice.

"I'd better be going. Let Carter know I love him, and I will be calling back later this evening. I will try not to call too late."

"No worries, you can call any time. I'm going to take off tomorrow and spend the day with him. I will let him know Abe is doing well since he has been asking about him."

"Thanks Logan," I say.

"No need to thank me, it's my pleasure." With this I pause a moment then hang up, deciding his comment didn't need acknowledgement.

We waited almost two hours before doctors let us visit him. They told us he might be a little groggy, but other than that he is okay.

We walk into his room, and he looks funny sitting up in the hospital bed. He has an IV to hydrate. He looks almost like the bionic man they have so many gadgets hooked up to him.

Jethro wiped his eyes a couple of times, and I squeeze his hand to comfort him.

"Man, you cryin'," Abe asks with a sleepy tone. That causes us all to smile. Cheyenne walks over, kisses him on the lips, holds her forehead to his, then exhales.

"Shiiit if I knew this was going to be the outcome I would have done this months ago." Abe said, and Cheyenne laughs through tears.

"How can you joke about this?" she said still smiling.

"I turn everything into a joke, ask my crybaby brother over there." We are laughing again. Jethro walks over and daps his brother.

"You scared us," Jethro finally admitted.

"Yeah, he scared me to, the way he came outta nowhere and lit my ass up. Shit, I saw stars, moons, stripes, and everything." We are laughing again. Why is it that Abe is the injured one, but he's cheering us up?

"Don't joke about this Abe," Cheyenne said, and starts crying.

"Girl you know I can't leave you before I get you to say yes to you and me," he said seriously.

"Why don't we give you two a minute alone?" I said.

"We just got here," Jethro whines.

"Come on Jethro, we are just going to take a trip to the cafeteria." I have to drag him away from the room. Jethro is pouting like a baby.

During this time, we call to speak with Carter.

"How's Abe?" Logan answers with more of a smile in his voice than concern.

"My brother's good," Jethro said. I had Logan on speaker.

"That's good to hear," he lost the smile I heard.

"How's Carter?" I chime in.

"Carter's good, he was asking about his uncle. Would you like to speak with him?"

"Please," I already miss him.

"Hi Mom," his voice makes me instantly smile.

"Hi son," we said in unison. "What are you doing?" I follow up.

"Hunter and me are playing his game. Then after the game me and my other dad are going to play baseball."

"Okay, be good," Jethro shouts.

"I will dad. Love you," and with that he is gone. He didn't give us the chance to say we love him too.

"Hey, Daryn, take as much time as you need. He's fine." I ignore the fact that he totally disregards Jethro is with me.

"Thanks."

"My pleasure," he said, and we hang up.

"I hate to say it, but Carter sounds like he's having a good time."

"Yeah, he loves the fact that he has other kids to play with. I meant..." Damnit me and my big mouth.

"Nah, it's okay. I know you don't mean any harm. It's cool. I'm coming to grips with it. Well, what you said hit home. I can't blame Logan for wanting to be a part of his son's life, any more than I can blame him for me not being able to have kids. Why wouldn't he want to be in Carter's life, he's a great kid. You were right, if he saw Carter, and never tried to see him I would have thought he was a worthless piece of shit. So, you were right, and it's cool now. You don't have to avoid the conversation with me, or walk on eggshells around me, I've come to grips with it. Besides it just means I get to have more time with my lovely wife, all to myself." I stand on tip toes and he bend his head to kiss me. It makes me feel good knowing he is dealing with everything so well.

Since Abe is okay, and my uncle's funeral is Saturday we decide to fly back home the next day. Abe is in good condition, good spirits, and they are releasing him the next day.

CHAPTER NINETEEN

The person my uncle friends and family spoke about, I didn't know, but I wish I had. As soon as I can remember my uncle was already strung out on drugs. I heard stories about my uncle that I had no idea. There were stories about him that made me proud to be his niece for the first time ever. He was in the army and served in the Gulf War. He was a virtuoso's saxophone player, and there was video of him playing. It filled the sanctuary and for a moment, my grandmother smiled fondly at the memory. I wish I'd known this uncle, but unfortunately because he'd been on drugs my entire life, I didn't know this man. I had no idea this man even existed.

I wanted to call foul for the predicament he'd been placed in. I wanted to cry foul for the legacy he'd be remembered by. Instead of a decorated war veteran he was a mere crack head not worthy of any assistance or help, for the mental anguish he suffered. Most of all I wanted to cry foul because out of all he had gone through he turned to crack to get rid of his memories of war. He should have never had to go out like this.

When the eulogy was performed, by some random preacher, who had to look down at his notes to get my uncle's name right, Eugene Franklin Moss. My uncle wasn't affiliated with any church, so we had the service at the funeral home. The preacher said very little about my uncle, then he said I'm here to speak to the living. Anybody that has ever been to a black funeral knows exactly what that means. It means the preacher doesn't think my uncle's soul will be saved in the afterlife, so he's here to preach to those he thinks can be saved.

He said my uncle's name twice. At the beginning of the sermon, and at the end. The second time he stuttered over his name until he found it in his notes. For $6,200 you would think he would have at least remembered his name.

My uncle had a life insurance policy, but somehow, he figured out how to borrow against it. There was only $500 of it left. My grandmother paid on that policy at least 30 years faithfully $42 a month. I was okay with putting his ass in a pine box. When my grandmother broke down after the news of my uncle siphoning all the money out of his life insurance policy, Jethro spoke up, and said he would pay for it. It hurt all our hearts whenever our grandmother cried. There is no person I know sweeter than her.

After the funeral we try our best to keep everyone away from my grandmother. She is strong, but she looks like she is at her breaking point. Everything is going well until Ja'net shows up, and all hell breaks loose. She came marching toward us at the gravesite as everyone is starting to dissipate from under the green tent, to proceed to the repast. I see on her face she is ready for a fight, and she has another baby bump. Just great.

"How could you keep the death of my brother from me?" she shouts at her mother. My grandmother is holding on to Jethro's arm, so he can support her weight. She looks at my Aunt Ja'net as if she is trying to find the words to say.

"Mom," Juicy interrupts like she is in shock.

"Mom?" a guy behind her questions.

"Shut-up Juicy, I'm not speaking to you! You could have called me too, but you didn't!"

"Ja'net, it's funny how you are the one that left your kids stranded without their mother, now you want to come back and play the victim. You are some kind of loser. You are the one," She cut me off in midsentence.

"Daryn, don't you dare. Your crack head mother always thought she was better than us, because of you. She thought because you made it, she was better than us, but you are cut from the same got damn cloth as the rest of us. We know your dirty little secrets."

"Ja'net, don't do this," Jethro was saying when she cut him off too.

"Jethro, you haven't been in this family long enough to tell me a damn thing. I suggest you stay out of this."

They think because Jethro wears a suit, smiles all the time, and speaks properly, they can speak to him any kind of way, and he will take it. They don't know the Brooklyn Jethro like I've gotten to know. The one that when his accent comes out you better watch out. The not so polite Jethro. Ja'net has no idea who she's speaking to, but she's about to learn today. Jethro is about to lose his shit.

"This is not the time, or the place, for this type of conversation. You will respect Buck, and your mother," he was still trying his best to stay calm. The Brooklyn is starting to come out.

"Ya'll didn't have enough respect for me, to tell me about my brother, so why should I have any respect for you? He was my only brother, and no one bothered to tell me, he was dead. I blame you and Daryn for running him off. If he wouldn't have been scared to come around, maybe he would have survived.

"You didn't call me because you know you were wrong, and I will never forgive you for not including me."

"Mom, it wasn't their fault we tried to contact you, but you'd changed your number."

"You're all liars," she struck Juicy across the cheek as she said this, and that is when Jethro lost.his.shit.

He grabs Ja'net by the arm and drug her off to the side. I follow behind him, and the guy behind her follows.

"Ja'net I have never hit a woman before in my life, but I promise you, if you touch Juicy again, I will not be able to restrain myself. I don't give a damn that you are late to your brother's funeral. I wouldn't give a good got damn, if you missed the whole damn thing. It is your own damn fault. You did this, not Juicy, not my wife, YOU!" He was pointing in her face.

"You are dead ass wrong for blaming everybody, because you chose to leave your five kids, and change your fucking number. Now if you can't calm down, and respect your brother you can get the fuckouttaheah; because the one thing you will not do, is come out yo face blaming everyone for your fucking problems. Now you can decide to stay, or you can decide to go, but whateva decision you make, know that you will not touch Juicy again, you will not insult my wife again, and you will respect your mother! You made your bed hard, so don't get mad when it gets too hard for you to lie in. No one gives a shit about your feelings when you didn't give a shit about your own damn children! Ju heard!" I look at Ja'net with a smirk on my face thinking, welcome to Brooklyn Biotch.

"Can someone tell me what the hell is going on? What five children?" The man with her is shouting. We all look at him speechless.

"It's nothing Reginald," Ja'net is saying as she tries to walk off, but he catches her by the arm.

"Why is she calling you mom?" His face is as stone.

"I had children before I met you," she was nonchalant when she said it.

"Have," Jethro bit out.

"You never told me you have children," he looks baffled and stupid.

"It wasn't important," she responded.

Ja'net is such a cold-hearted bitch.

"You failed to mention you have children?"

"Five, she failed to mention, she has five kids." Jethro chimes in with a scowl on his face.

Reginald let her go, and went to walk away.

"Reginald please don't leave me," she pleads following behind him.

"DON'T FOLLOW ME!" he shouts, and she stops, and starts to break down. We all walk around her, leaving her on the ground clawing at the dirt. No, one cares about Ja'net's predicament. She's getting what she deserves.

"Jethro," I say as we walk back to the car.

"Yes babe," he responds picking up my hand and kissing the back of it. I smile at him.

"I don't have the energy to go to the repast."

"Whatever you wish," he says.

"Let me tell Juicy and we can go and pick up Carter."

"Okay," he says. I approach Juicy as she is strapping her sister in the back seat.

"Hey Juicy, can I speak to you a minute?"

"Yeah, sure," she says standing.

"A couple of things. I'm not going to the repast."

"Aw man, why not?" she asks.

"That's not important. I wanted to come over and let you know how proud of you I am. You are doing an amazing job, taking care of your sister, and granny told me how you still come by and help with your other siblings when you can. You have always been so smart and so responsible. Don't let your mom deter or distract you from the progress you have made. If there is anything we can do for you, name it and it's yours."

"Thanks, Daryn," Juicy says hugging me.

"Can I ask you something," she says when she pulls away.

"Anything," I say.

"What makes a woman, deny her entire family for the sake of love?"

"Honey that ain't love. I have no answer for what your mom is doing, and I don't want to speak ill of your mom, because I know no matter what she does she is still your mother. I would like to believe your mom is sick, or has some type of ailment that makes her keep having kids and dropping them off, but I know you know better. What kept me strong all those years, and helped me make it through, was always having a real outlook on life.

"The only thing that can make a person, male or female, behave as irresponsible as your mom is selfishness. She thinks having a kid from a man will make them stay, and when they leave, she leaves the kid and starts the cycle all over again. She can't comprehend that she has tried that way several times and it didn't work. I suspect when Reginald leaves her she will leave the one she is pregnant with now with granny, if he doesn't take the baby from her."

"Do you think she ever wanted any of us?"

"I think that is irrelevant at this point. What is relevant is how even in the face of adversity, you pulled through. Don't sit around wasting your life on unanswered questions from Ja'net. You will never get the answers. There are questions I still don't know the answer to from my mother, and I had to find a way to be fine with that. You just concentrate on continuing to improve your life, and pray to God he has mercy on your mother's soul. Because there is no vengeance like God's vengeance, and she is going to feel it soon. I love you, and call me if you need me." I hug her and leave hoping Juicy gets it.

CHAPTER TWENTY

It's our sixth wedding anniversary, but I'm exhausted. I don't feel like celebrating, but Jethro was adamant. I want a quiet meal at home, just the two of us.

"You ready," he says smiling as I am fastening my Fendi sandals.

"Yes," I say and stand.

"You look like an angel," and that gets me to smile.

"Thanks!" I think we look like choir singers. We are dress to closely alike. He purchased me this all white strapless poufy dress with sequence at the top. He has on an all-white tuxedo with a black sparkling bowtie.

It is Logan's weekend to have Carter, and I miss him. I think I miss him so much because this weekend Logan, Hunter, and Carter went on a camping trip.

When I talked to him he thought the best part of his trip was peeing on a tree in the woods. His dad sent me a picture of Carter holding his first fish he caught.

I follow Jethro to the Porsche, he holds the door open as I get in.

Although Jethro is making small talk, I'm barely paying attention and I provide him with one-word answers as I gaze out the window.

He squeezes my knee, "I miss him too," he says. I look Jethro's way and let out a sigh.

"I know he's okay, I just wish he was here with me this weekend."

"Yeah, me too. I also wish he would at least act like he misses us. I mean damn." That got me to laugh.

"That part! He is acting like we've never taken him anywhere."

"I guess I'm going to have to buy a fishing pole, and learn how to fish." I give him the side eye.

"Seriously, you already know you are too impatient for fishing. You can't sit for hours and wait for a fish to bite." I know Jethro, he can't sit still. He plays sports that require high intensity like basketball and football. When he plays video games he stands while he's playing them. Jethro is the assistant coach for a little league football team and he runs up and down the side lines the entire game. There is no way on God's green earth he can fish.

We pull up to the club.

"I'll just stay in the car." I tell him.

"Can you come in a moment. We had a meeting, and I just need your opinion on some things."

I let out a sigh and climb out the car. I'm not in the mood. I haven't been back to the club since the incident. We walk in the club, and the lights are low. Jethro turns up the dimmer.

"SURPRISE!!!!!!!!!!" People yell!

"What the hell," is my response. People laugh, as I turn around and see my family and friends. Including a few of my sisters I finally met at a family picnic. I hold my hands around my nose and face in shock.

"Daryn Thomas, this is your prom." I look at Jethro with shimmering eyes.

"I know in high school you said you missed your prom because you were always grinding, so I wanted to recreate your prom." As I look around I see everyone in prom attire. It is amazing. I am so excited. The DJ put on Love by Keyshia Cole.

"Daryn Carter, can I have this dance, I promise not to rub on your booty." I laugh as Jethro escorts me to the dance floor. As we are dancing others join in and Cheyenne and Abe come up beside us.

"Daryn you look so beautiful!"

"So, do you Cheyenne, I hope Abe is treating you right."

"Better than right," Cheyenne says and flashes me a tennis bracelet sparkling with diamonds. I smile at them both as they dance off.

"This is probably one of the nicest things anyone has ever

done for me. All that time I spent grinding I never allowed myself to think about what I was missing. It feels like a real prom."

"It should. I had Cheyenne help with the theme and music. She said your high school theme for prom was Las Vegas, and this was your favorite song."

I hadn't really notice, but as I look around there are tables set for roulette, black jack, and a few other
games.

"Wow, you really put a lot of effort into this. It's perfect."

"Yes, and it took even more work, trying to keep you from finding out."

"I have another surprise for you," he said taking me by the hand to lead me upstairs.

"Jethro, we have guest," I giggle, but I'm down for it.

"No, not what you're thinking, unless you want to." He says, and I giggle shyly.

We walk into the office and BJ, Ro, and the attorney are sitting on either side of the desk.

"Jethro, what's up?" I ask feeling ambushed.

"Ro and BJ have both proven themselves to be effective at running and managing the club. So, with your permission, I would like to turn the duties over to them. I will come in on Thursdays for stock and miscellaneous operations, but the day to day operations will belong to them. I have the contracts drawn up, all we have to do is sign, and it will officially make Ro the Operations Manager and BJ the Floor Manager. That means I will be home every night with my family."

I hug Jethro tightly, I didn't even realize I wanted this, or that it was a possibility.

"Where do I sign," I said. BJ pulls out a chair for me to sit. The attorney, Mitch, explains all the documents, including their new raises, then gave me a pen to sign.

After signing the documents, I stand Ro and BJ both hug me.

"It means a lot to us that you would trust us with managing

the club, and we won't let you down." Ro said. I look at Jethro.

"I really didn't think this was possible without selling the club. I'd talked to Mitch about legalities of selling the club, but I couldn't quite go through with it. This is my baby, and it felt as if I was giving it up for adoption every time I considered an offer someone gave me. This is amazing."

"Jethro and I talked, and we both knew this place was a piece of you. Jethro made it all possible," Mitch states.

"I leap into Jethro arms, and kiss him inappropriately in front of guest. I smile at him as he lifts me in his arms and twirl me around."

"You sure you good with this," he says and sit me down on my feet.

"I'm more than good. I am elated." I say laughing which makes him smile too.

"I thought you liked this too much to give it up."

"Hell no, I've been working on turning the club management over for a while. Ro got her final degree in management a little over six months ago, and BJ has proven himself worthy time and time again. I honestly don't know if things would have gone so smoothly without him. He even completed a few management courses regarding communication, emotional responses, and critical thinking."

"BJ?," I say raising an eyebrow, which causes Jethro to let out a belly gut of laughter.

"Yes, BJ. Once I dangled the carrot in front of him, and we went over a business plan of what I was looking for, he took the initiative to complete everything on the list. I told him we just had to make sure you agreed."

"What if I'd gotten in here and said hell no!" He laughs.

"Then it would have been a no. I work for you, but I had Mitch here just in case, so he could be a bipartisan person to explain the benefits to you."

"Thank you for the best anniversary present EVER!" "You're welcome my Queen."

THE END

EPILOGUE (5 YEARS LATER)

"Just breathe out through your nose and in through your mouth like they taught us in Lamaze. We're doing great. If it's anything like the last two babies, the baby won't be here for another five to six hours. We still have time."

"I don't know Daryn, these came on a lot stronger than the other two," Cheyenne says through quick breaths.

"Abe is on a plane as we speak on his way here. I'm sure the baby will wait."

"I'm not so sure, oh GOD, there's another one. That was only ten minutes, we'd better get to the hospital."

"Yeah, it was ten minutes, but they aren't consistent. We can go to the hospital if you want."

"Yes, I want, I need drugs, lots and lots of drugs. I hope they can slow him from coming. It's our first boy."

"Okay, well let me get your bag."

"Okay, hurry Daryn please before another one hits me. I really don't want Abe to miss our son being born," she says, and a tear slides down her cheek.

"I'm sure he won't." I try to comfort her then I get up. I go out back where Carter and his dad are. Carter is standing as tall as me, and he's extra lanky.   They are throwing the football back and forth. My son's voice is starting to change, and he is looking more mature every day.

"I am going to take Cheyenne to the hospital."

"It's time?" Jethro asks.

"I'm not sure, but she believes if she gets the epidural when she gets to the hospital it may slow down the labor.

"Okay, we can come too," he says.

"Nah, I think it's too early. Besides, Carter has practice

tonight, maybe you can come afterwards."

"Okay," he said.

"Bye mom," Carter yells and I blow him a kiss.

Jethro finally got use to the fact that it will only be the three of us after he got a second opinion. However, I did decide to get a white German Sheppard. We named him Ghost. Carter stopped asking for a sibling once we got him a puppy.

"You ready, I got your bag," I said to Cheyenne. She came over to stay with us just in case she went into labor. The kids are up the road at Jethro's parents' house. Cheyenne and Abe have been married for four years. She was six months pregnant when they got married.

"Yes, I only had one contraction while you were gone, and it wasn't as bad."

"Okay great, let's get moving."

She waddles to the car. This is the biggest Cheyenne has ever been.

Thankfully she didn't have another contraction in the car. As soon as we get to the hospital she is whisked into the back and measured. She's only four centimeters when they give her the epidural. Her nose looks like Rudolf's she's been crying so much because she feels as if Abe is going to miss the birth of their son.

"I told him not to go," she says as I watch a contraction go off the screen it is so powerful.

"I'm sure he'll make it."

"I'm not so sure."

"I'm sure everything will work out."

"I'm sure it won't," she said with tears she was no longer bothering to wipe.

"Hey, since when did you become such a Negative Nancy?"

She smiled threw tears. "Since I've been carrying a boy, I haven't liked Abe very much. His breathing gets on my nerves." She said and we both laugh.

"I know the feeling," I had a flashback when Jethro was at the table eating cereal, and humming. I wanted to punch him in the face for always smiling.

"Knock, knock," the doctor said walking through the door.

"I need to check your progress."

"Okay," Cheyenne says without putting up a fight.

When she was finish she stands and looks at Cheyenne solemnly.

"You want the good news, or the bad news first." The doctor asked as she remove her glove.

"It doesn't matter," Cheyenne says without looking.

The doctor clears her throat. "The good news, your baby has a head full of hair. The bad news you're already ten centimeters, and I can already touch his head. He's ready to come out, we have to start pushing."

Cheyenne burst into tears.

"I'm sorry hun. I know how much you were hoping the epidural would slow down the birth, but when babies are ready, no amount of medicine will stop them."

"He's going to miss it, and I'm not naming my baby after him." Cheyenne is being so dramatic. I want to laugh, but I know she is serious.

By the time they are through setting up, and Cheyenne starts pushing, I take a chance and facetime Abe. He picks up right away.

"I'm on my way, but the traffic is horrible. I could probably run faster than we are traveling."

"He's almost here," I say.

"Damn," he says.

"Here's Cheyenne," I turn the phone to face her while she's in the middle of pushing. He waits, and she lays back down.

"I'm sorry baby," he says.

"I hate you, and I'm..." Cheyenne starts screaming, and crying again as she pushes.

"One or two more pushes and he should be out." The doctor says. "Alright Cheyenne give me a huge push."

Cheyenne starts pushing, and I hear suction, then a whale of a cry. When she holds the baby up I point the phone in the baby's direction. He is huge. He comes out looking like a linebacker.

After they cut the cord the nurse immediately walks over and lays little Abe on Cheyenne's chest.

"Hey, you," she says to him and kiss him on the forehead.

"Hey son," Abe says. "It's your Pops, I'm almost there."

"I'm sorry, Abe I don't hate you. I love you, and I wish you were here." Cheyenne has return to her senses.

"Don't worry about it baby," he says as I continue to point the phone toward Cheyenne and the baby. Then the door opens, and in walks a haggard looking Abe. I don't think he showered after the game. I hang up as he walks over and wraps his arms around them both.

"I'm sorry, I shouldn't have gone to the game."

"I'm sorry, I shouldn't have said I hate you. I love you baby."

"I love you too," Abe says.

I take this opportunity to back out, and report to the family. Everyone stands as I enter the waiting room."

"It's a boy 10 pounds!"

They cheer and hug.

"I knew that baby would be as big as Abe was, let's just pray he doesn't have his temper." Mama Thomas says.

"Do you think I can go back to see her," Cheyenne's mom asks.

Cheyenne has "forgiven" her mother, but she feeds her with a long hand spoon.

It kills Cheyenne the way her mother loves telling her friends her daughter's husband is a NFL star, yet she was to embarrass of Cheyenne to claim her when she was coming up because she thought she was promiscuous.

Cheyenne broke down to me one day about it, but Cheyenne got the last laugh. One of her mother's friends said in front of everyone 'I never knew you had a daughter.' The look of embarrassment on her mom's face was judication enough. Cheyenne won't leave the kids with her, and she must call before she comes over.

"Abe just got here, so maybe we should give them a little privacy."

"Okay," she says, and nods her head. I can tell she's pissed, but I don't care she shouldn't have treated my friend like she did. I guess I'll let her go back in about 20 or 30 minutes.

"Hey wifey!" Jethro says, and hugs me.

"Hey hubby!"

"How's she doing?" he asks.

"A lot better since the baby's here, and Abe made it."

"God knew to only give us one since we have to keep running to the hospital for all Abe kids."

"Yeah it looks like they are working on their own football team." I say, He smiles down at me.

"Ma, my other dad is outside," Carter says.

"Okay, Jethro, I'll be right back." I escort him outside to meet with his other dad.

"Hey," he says, and kisses me on the cheek. He hugs Carter, and I kiss Carter before he gets in the car.

"He's taller than you," Logan says laughing.

"No, he's not!" He holds up his hands to surrender still able to give that thousand-kilowatt smile.

"What are your plans for the weekend," he asks still smiling.

"Probably hang out with Cheyenne at the hospital. She had a boy."

"Tell her congrats," he says.

"I'm sorry we didn't think to bring his clothes. If you want I can bring his bag when I leave here." I lean against the car as if I have nowhere to be. I'm grateful that conversation with him has become easy again.

"No need, he has an entire wardrobe at my house. Do you think you will make his baseball game tomorrow?"
"I don't know. Jethro and I have our nieces this weekend. They are a

handful." I say with an exaggerated look.

"Oh, how's Jethro?"

"He's good, you're about to be a grandfather how is that going?" That is the only question, that seems to have taken the smile off his face. I laugh.

"Every time I see my son-n-law I tell him I hate him for knocking up my baby girl. Brooke and Amber are out doing some last-minute shopping for the nursery."

"How are Hunter and Bristol?"

"Bristol has promised me to never get married, and love only me," we both laugh.

"Hunter's doing well, he's working on turning his cartoon characters into an actual comic book. He will be home this weekend. We are going to have a boy's night."

"That sounds...interesting."

"It's good seeing you Daryn. I know we have the arrangements where I pick him up from school, but it doesn't give me the opportunity to see you unless you make it to a baseball or football game."

"It's nice seeing you too. Well I better get back in the hospital."

"Have a good weekend," I say. He starts walking back to the car.

"Daryn, you know I only ask about Jethro to see if you're still married." He says smiling at me.

"Logan, I know." We both laugh, and I walk back inside. I walk over to Jethro.

"How's Logan, and Amber." I laugh because I know Jethro is only asking me to make sure Logan and Amber are still married, and Logan won't be coming after me.

"They are fine."

"What's funny," he says wrapping me in his arms.

"Nothing," I say and we kiss.

"Did you hear from Mom's?"

"Yeah, her and Dennis made it to Aruba safely. I'm not sure how I feel about her having a husband."

"He's a good dude. I ran a background check on him. He has an 803 credit score, no priors, he's an upstanding citizen. Besides he adores your mom."

"Yeah, yeah, I'm just glad she has truly found happiness and a nice guy after some of the men she's dated."

"Me too, Mom's deserves it. She has paid her debt to society."

"You're right," I say.

"Wait a minute, what was that? Did you say I was right." "Yes, Jethro you are right. You were right about everything including us. Thank you for sticking it out with me and staying the course. I love you Mr. Thomas."

"I love you too Mrs. Thomas!" he says and swoops down to kiss me!

"Get a room," Abe yells!